APOCALYPSE RECON
OUTBREAK

PAUL MANNERING
BILL BALL

A PERMUTED PRESS BOOK

ISBN: 978-1-61868-644-2

APOCALYPSE RECON
© 2016 by Paul Mannering and Bill Ball
All Rights Reserved

Cover art by Christian Bentulan

PERMUTED
PRESS

Permuted Press, LLC
275 Madison Avenue, 14th Floor
New York, NY 10016
permutedpress.com

CHAPTER 1

"*South American leaders continue to call for calm as civil unrest
continues to break out across Mexico, Bolivia, Colombia, and Brazil.
While observers are suggesting that the cause for the uprising is the influence of
communist guerilla factions, Preside—*"

Robby "Minty" MacInnes jabbed the off switch on the car radio.
The news irritated him and he needed to be supremely chill for a job
like this.

The Crown Victoria sedan he drove wasn't as nimble or as cool
as the Harleys, but it made less noise even when it rode low on the
suspension with all 350 pounds of Tim "Fish" Muller pressed into
the front passenger seat. Less heavy, yet no less hairy, Richie "Rim"
Neidman and Larry "Chops" Ericksen rode in the back. They all wore
the leather vests and oil-stained jeans that made up the uniform of the
Locusts Motorcycle Club.

Like his biker brothers, Minty did what Jethro "Jesus" Williams
ordered. Jethro ruled the Locusts, and Minty had followed and feared
the man, whom he once saw beat a shit-heel narc to death in a Seattle
bus station restroom, for over twenty years.

The car rolled through the inner-city slum. Most of the houses
here stood empty and rotting. The rest now housed crazies, squatters,
and crack whores. Bone-thin dogs scavenged through overturned
garbage cans, snarling and snapping at each other over scraps of decaying

hamburger. A dog burst out of the darkness and careened along the street, a long bone from what might have once been a junkie dragging in its jaws.

Minty killed the lights and parked the car. In the back seat, Rim and Chops readied their 9mm semiautomatics. Fish rocked to his feet outside the car before leaning back in and pulling a nail-studded baseball bat out from under the seat.

"Goddamn thing kept poking me in the ass," he said.

The Crown Victoria's engine shuddered and died. Minty stepped out and pocketed the keys, keeping the pistol grip, pump-action Mossberg 500 shotgun hanging down by his side as he scanned the area. The streets were dark around here, but there could be sentries watching the streets from behind boarded-up windows or from the piles of trash in the stinking alleyways.

They gathered at the car's trunk. Minty opened it and the prospect sat up, blinking in the evening light.

"Get the fuck outta there, Freak." Fish reached in and lifted the scrawny kid out onto the road. He was skinny, but tough. His name was Francis, but they all called him Freak because he was a maggot prospect, seeking full entrance into the Locusts Motorcycle Club. Until that happened, Freak was lower than dirt and unworthy of a real name. He acted like a stray dog that, no matter how much you kicked it, would always come crawling back and lick your hand.

Freak swept his hair back off his face and grinned like a kid at Christmas.

"Do I get a gun?" he asked, eyeing up the hardware the others carried.

"You ain't old enough to hold your dick, let alone a real weapon," Rim scoffed.

"Yeah, that's what your old lady's for," Freak shot back and Rim was on him in an instant, fists flying at the kid's face. Freak bounced away from the first punch, laughing as he dodged behind Minty, grinning and making faces at the enraged Rim.

Minty slammed the giggling prospect in the mouth with the sharp end of his elbow.

"Back the fuck off. Show some fucking respect," Minty growled. The cliché of being too old for this shit never felt truer than at a time like this. This was no time for these assholes to be pounding on each other. They had a house full of crackheads waiting for that action.

They stood down, leaving Minty scowling at them until he was sure the moment had passed. Chops opened a bag of flashlights and handed them out to everyone. "Don't turn them on; wait 'til you're inside," he warned.

Minty lifted a short crowbar out of the trunk and shoved it into the back of his jeans, feeling the cold metal press against his butt. Leading the group across the street, Minty heard Freak yelp as Rim smacked the prospect in the back of the head with the butt of his pistol.

"Quiet the fuck down," Minty said. Jethro's instructions were simple: get the assholes who had been dealing high-quality cocaine out of this house and making a shit-ton of money. If it all went according to plan, their cash courier would be lying in a gutter somewhere trying to hold his guts in while the Locusts watched him die. The dealers were reportedly sitting on an even bigger bag of cash that Jethro also intended to acquire for himself.

The Locusts swaggered into the overgrown yard of the decaying house. It had two levels, with a couple of rooms up top and the main living area downstairs. The porch out front was collapsing under its own weight and Fish chewed his lip looking at the weather-stained boards.

"You go round the back, Fish, cover the exit," Minty whispered, his eyes travelling over every inch of the building. "Any fucker comes out, you shoot him in the face."

Fish nodded and hitched up his stained jeans as he hurried into the gloom down the side of the house.

Rim and Chops crept up the front steps. They moved carefully, letting the boards take their weight slowly, avoiding the creaks that could alert those inside. The house loomed quiet and dark; no dogs barked, and the neighborhood seemed asleep.

More likely they're stoned out of their gourds, Minty thought.

He waited until Rim and Chops were in position, Freak crouched down behind him. (*Just like a dog,* thought Minty.) The two at the door looked toward Minty. He took a deep breath and nodded, his hands dry and steady on the shotgun.

Rim stepped in front of the door, reared back, and kicked it in. He vanished into the silent house, Chops on his heels. Minty and Freak strode in after them.

The first room of the house was awash in filth and rot. The light of their flashlights showed flies crawling over soiled diapers and reflected off the eyes of the rats burrowing into a broken easy chair in the corner.

"Fuck me," Freak said, covering his mouth and nose against the stench.

"Rim, check the back. Chops, upstairs. Freak, stay here and keep quiet."

They moved without question. Minty had been Jethro's right hand since the beginning. Twenty long years of riding, fucking, fighting, and making money any way they could. They were free though, and Minty wouldn't change that for anything. The Locusts were his family, a loose brotherhood of bikers, whores, and hangers-on. Old horses like Rim and Chops would do anything Minty asked; he was the mouthpiece of Jethro, and Jethro's word was law.

Chops filled the narrow stairway. His broad shoulders, long hair, and beard would scare the shit out of anyone sober enough to walk out of the upstairs bedrooms. Minty joined him at the landing. Chops silently pointed at the nearest door. Minty nodded. Chops kicked the door in, gun leveled and ready.

The smell in the room hit harder than the stink downstairs. Chops backed away from the door, cursing under his breath. Minty lifted his arm and pressed his nose against a sleeve. "Fuck me," Chops echoed Freak.

Stepping forward, Minty clicked his flashlight on revealing a kid's room. A battered crib stood against one wall. Clothes, food wrappers, and more soiled diapers were scattered on the floor and piled in the corner.

"No one in here, man," Minty declared. Something caught his eye. A blanket in the crib moved. *Just a rat.* But he turned the flashlight on it anyway. Stepping around the trash, he peered over the wooden rail of the crib. *Too big for a rat.* Minty reached out to jerk the blanket back.

"Jesus fuck!" he yelled and the flashlight fell to the floor, its beam swinging across the wall as he raised the shotgun. From the crib came a mewling cry. A deep, wet, feverish sound, like a child near death from some terrible, lung-eating disease.

"What the fuck, man?" Chops hissed from the doorway. The crib dweller still made baby moans that didn't have the strength to become full cries.

"Fucking sick kid, fucking assholes," Minty growled. He didn't give a shit about kids. But there was something wrong with this one. The biker picked up his flashlight and peered into the crib again. The kid's warm brown skin had a dull grey sheen to it, like all the life was leeching out of him. He moaned and writhed, pulling himself free of the blanket. Reaching up to the vertical rails, he climbed up to stand against the wooden bars of the cage.

Minty pulled back. The kid had maybe two teeth and he'd been chewing on something. Dried blood and shit smears stained the mattress and bedding. The baby's hands curled around the bars. The thumbs were gone, chewed off along with most of the kid's fingers. Tiny blackened stumps slipped through the bars and reached for the flashlight beam.

"Jesus Christ," Minty swore again.

"Come on, man, we ain't social services." Chops looked around the hallway; the other two doors remained closed.

"That's fucked up," Minty said and backed toward the door. The child whimpered and began to pull itself along the bars of the crib.

They left the room and approached the next door. Someone had padlocked it. Chops grinned and nodded. "This'll be what we're looking for."

Holding the flashlight and shotgun in one arm, Minty pulled the crowbar out of his pants. "You do it," he said to Chops.

Chops shoved the 9mm into his belt and slammed the wedge end of the pry bar into the metal hasp of the lock. Grunting slightly, he pulled on it. The bolts holding the lock to the door squealed and tore free. Something thudded against the door. Minty thought he could hear a muffled moaning coming from inside the room.

"You hear that?"

Chops ignored him and jammed the bar into the edge of the doorframe, levering it out until the door popped and almost opened. The stink coming out of this room made the kid's room smell like a rose garden.

Chops forced his way into the room. Whatever was blocking the door gave way and it swung wide. The windows in the room were boarded up from the outside, blocking most of the dim light from the street. A table where drugs were weighed and packaged had been knocked over. White powder and little plastic bags were scattered everywhere. Footprints smeared on the floor, where someone had been shuffling around, pacing endlessly in the room. Something worse than the smell made Minty hang back. Chops had his gun up and the flashlight held level with it. *Christ, he thinks he's a cop on a raid*, Minty thought.

They came at the two bikers out of the dark. A black man and a woman, their mouths open wide and drooling some kind of frothy pus. Both of them were moaning, making a grown-up version of the wet-lung noise the baby made. Their faces were scarred with bulging grey-white lines, as if their veins were swollen with the powder on the floor.

Chops didn't say a word—he just shot the guy in the face. The compact 9mm boomed in the small room, the flash casting long Halloween shadows up the walls.

The woman was on Chops before he could adjust his aim. She grabbed his arm and sank her teeth into the tattooed flesh of his wrist. Chops howled, dropped the flashlight, and pressed the muzzle of the pistol against the top of her head. He fired and the back of the woman's skull exploded. Hair and skull fragments splattered against the floor, dark blood glowing against the snow-white powder.

Minty pulled Chops out of the way as he gritted his teeth and clutched his wounded arm. "Fucking cunt," Chops spat. "*Fucking cunt!*"

"Do you see the money?" Minty asked as he warily ducked inside the room. The two bodies lay still on the floor. Both of them a stinking mess. They'd been chewing on themselves or each other for a while. Big chunks of flesh were missing from the man's arms. The woman's neck was a ragged mess of bites and open wounds, all fringed with a white mold, like bread gone bad.

Wishing he'd brought duct tape to attach the flashlight to the shotgun, Minty paused in front of a closet door. Hearing nothing, he reached out and twisted the handle.

The door popped open, spilling an avalanche of loose bills onto the floor. Shoe boxes, shopping bags, and a kid's school backpack, all overflowing with creased bundles of cash. Minty crouched and started stuffing the money into the kid's bag. Thousands of dollars, tens of thousands. He packed wads of it into his shirt. *Fuck it. The prospect can bring the rest out to the car.*

Straightening up, Minty looked around. A table in the corner was loaded with large packets of white powder, a pile of smaller Ziploc bags, and a set of kitchen scales. Minty picked up a sealed baggie. This wasn't cheap crack—he was holding at least an ounce of pure cocaine. Jethro would want to try this shit.

Slipping the packet into his pocket, Minty headed out into the hallway. Chops leaned against the opposite door, his face drenched in sickly sweat.

"Let's go, man," Minty said as he hoisted the bulging backpack. Chops nodded, then staggered slightly as he made for the stairs. Putting out his uninjured arm, he leaned against the wall, stumbling down the steps like a drunk.

Downstairs, the prospect was practicing his karate moves, chopping at the air and twisting to block invisible enemies.

"Freak," Minty hissed. "Where's Rim?" Freak jerked to attention. The prospect shrugged. "Uhh, he ain't back yet."

"The fuck? Help me with Chops. We get him in the car and then come back here. I have a job for you."

Freak hurried forward and slipped Chops' injured arm around his shoulder. "Did we get it?" Freak asked as they helped him through the door. Chops leaned heavily against Minty, and he could feel his friend's body burning up with a fever.

"Yeah, now fucking hurry up."

They got Chops into the backseat of the Crown Victoria. "Freak, follow me," Minty ordered as he headed back into the house. "Upstairs, second door on the left. There's a closet full of cash. Get as much as you can and put it in the car. Fucking move!"

He waited until Freak hurried up the stairs, then went through to the back of the house, where Rim had been sent when they arrived.

"Rim?" he hissed, "Where the fuck are you?" Silence. Shotgun ready, Minty opened the door that he hoped led to the kitchen.

The flashlight illuminated a scene of carnage. Four rough figures knelt on the floor. Rim lay stretched out between them, his belly opened up like a gym bag. The blood-smeared ghouls plunged their hands into his quivering gut and tore out chunks of glistening red meat. They stuffed their faces with bits of Rim, snarling like the starving dogs around the trash cans down the street.

The nearest freak rose to its feet. Fresh blood gushed from his mouth as he chewed and shuffled toward Minty, slipping in the thick pool of warm blood spreading across the floor. The biker raised the shotgun and fired from the hip. The close-range blast tore a softball-sized hole through the freak's side, ripping chunks of flesh and organs away and spraying thick blood across the already crimson room. Strands of white waved in the wound, probing the empty space where the crackhead's left kidney had been.

The cannibal opened his mouth wider and howled, lunging at Minty, who worked the slide and fired again. The second shot shredded the freak's arm, ripping it away at the elbow in a cloud of vaporized flesh and bone. The maimed and bloodstained freak did not stop. He kept coming, howling and bringing the others away from the feast of Rim to lurch after Minty.

The biker staggered back through the kitchen door. The crackheads blocked the doorway, pushing and snarling as they tried to come through all at once. Minty pumped the shotgun again. Never did he think he would need more than two shots on a job like this. Not in a million years.

The first freak broke through the press of writhing bodies. He fell against Minty, knocking him back against the wall. Cold fingers tore at the old biker's shirt, shredding it with jagged nails and spilling crumpled handfuls of bills onto the floor. The freak clutched a handful of blood-splattered bills in his fists and then started stuffing them in his mouth, a weird expression of surprise slowly dawning on his face. Minty bolted for the front door.

Running across the yard, he remembered Fish. *Fish, where the fuck was Fish?*

"Fish! Get the fuck outta here!" Minty yelled as he ran through the waist-high grass. The Crown Vic waited on the other side of the empty street—Freak was shoving bags of cash into the backseat where Chops sat slumped against the window.

Minty slid across the hood of the car, rolled off, and landed heavily. Scrambling up, he yanked the keys out of his pocket and snatched the driver's door open.

"Where's Rim?" Freak said as he climbed in the back and slammed the door.

"Rim's dead." Minty slid the keys in and twisted. The Crown Victoria's engine roared.

"What the fuck?" Freak sounded genuinely shocked. "Hey, you fucking niggers! Come here and fuck with us!" Freak leaned on the window button and hurled abuse through the widening gap.

"Freak! Shut the fuck up!" Minty dropped the car into drive and burned a long curve of black rubber as he turned the vehicle around. The flesh-eating crackheads from the house were coming across the yard. Minty heard Chops moan in pain as he was thrown against the car door.

"Fish!" Freak yelled suddenly. "Come on, you fat fuck!" Minty slammed on the brakes, his head nearly cracking on the steering wheel. Fish came waddling out of the darkness at the side of the house. He hitched his jeans up and then swung the spiked baseball bat at the nearest crackhead. The bat connected with a dull *whack*, like the sound of a melon being hit. The freak's head snapped back and the momentum of the swing nearly twisted Fish off his feet.

Hitching up his jeans again, Fish moved on to the next guy. This one he hit overhand, as if he was aiming to ring the bell at a carnival test-your-strength game. The crackhead dropped without a sound, the baseball bat bouncing off his skull as the nail spikes drew blood. Minty leaned on the horn; Freak was laughing and yelling; Fish looked up and waved, grinning.

"Fish! Get in the fucking car!" Minty would have left him, but Fish was a patched Locust and that made him family.

The third crazy swung around, lashing at Fish with clawlike hands. Fish pushed the guy back and did a shuffling dance, which made Freak shriek with laughter.

"Fuck him up, Fish!" Freak yelled through the open window. "Come on now!"

The crackhead came back at Fish, intent on tearing him apart with his bloodstained hands. Fish pulled the bat over his shoulder like some major league star and then let fly. The freak's skull was knocked sideways with a crack worthy of a home run. The bat splintered and the heavy end flew off into the darkness.

Freak managed to get the car door open and dragged himself out.

"Get back in the fucking car!" Minty yelled after him. Freak had Chops' gun. He held it on its side, like some kind of two-bit gangster. Marching toward the final crackhead, Freak grinned with a fixed leer like a carved pumpkin. He pushed the muzzle of the gun up against her eye and pulled the trigger. Nothing happened and Freak, looking puzzled, squeezed again.

"Jesus Christ!" Minty roared. "Safety! You dumb fuck! The safety is on!" The female freak knocked Freak backwards. Falling on top of the prospect, she snarled and gnashed with broken teeth. Fish loomed up behind the crazy and stabbed her through the back with the broken end of the baseball bat. She howled and Fish heaved her away from Freak. The kid scrambled backwards, sliding away on his ass, squeezing the trigger on the locked gun and sobbing like a girl. Fish pulled the gun out of Freak's grip and flicked the safety off. Stepping up to the writhing freak, he aimed and fired twice. The woman's head shattered and Fish came over to the car, pulling Freak off the ground as he passed him.

"What happened?" Fish asked after he squeezed into the Crown Vic's front seat.

"I have no idea," Minty said as he tore out of the neighborhood. A minute later his cell phone buzzed and he flipped it open. "Yo?"

"Minty, we may have a problem," Jethro said down the line, his voice as calm as the Dead Sea.

"No shit?" Minty kept his speed under the limit. No point in attracting attention.

"We collected our bagman. He was freaked out, reckons there's something wrong with this new batch of coke they're selling. Says it's making the customers sick."

"Well, I'm really sorry to hear that a bunch of fucking junkies are getting the shits from smoking Drano." Minty's strained nerves put an edge in his tone.

"It seems that the problem is worse than that. The bad batch is making the customers crazy. Money boy says the users get sick and then start attacking people, biting them and eating them. Weird, no?"

Minty swallowed. The stink of blood and sweat in the car was making him feel nauseous.

"I've seen weirder," he said into the phone. "You need us back at the yard?"

"No rush. It's quiet here. How did the recovery go?"

"Fifty-fifty," Minty replied. "We ran into some fucked-up nigger crackheads. Took care of it. Comin' back by the yard now."

"Come see me when you arrive." Jethro hung up.

Minty reached into his jacket pocket and pulled out the ounce of cocaine. Leaning over, he opened the glove box and dropped the packet inside, closing it tight before wiping his hand on his jeans.

"What did he say?" Fish asked.

"Nothing we didn't already know."

CHAPTER 2

"**B**am!" Freak crowed. "And did you see that fucker's head?" Fish sat in the front of the Crown Victoria, grinning and saying, "Nah it was nothing," but looking pleased at the adulation that Freak was giving him.

Minty kept quiet. In all his years he had never seen anything like that. Even the most strung-out dope fiend didn't eat people. Angel dust made people do crazy things. Maybe that was what the drugs were laced with? Some kind of PCP batch gone bad?

"Hey," he broke his silence. "Didn't that guy cut his face off one time, high on angel dust?" Freak and Fish looked at him blankly.

Freak's face suddenly lit up. "Yeah, man. He sliced it off and then ate it. I saw pictures of him on the net."

"You think those crackheads were on PCP?" Fish chewed his lip.

"Yeah," Minty replied. "Seems the only way to explain the crazy shit they were doing." *But what about the baby? That kid wasn't high on dust . . .* In spite of the warm night air, Minty shivered.

Chops had been quiet until then, slumped against the rear passenger door, not responding to Freak and his excited reenactment of the fight against the crazy crackheads. Now he stirred and coughed, a deep phlegmy rattle deep in his chest.

"Chops ain't looking so good," Freak announced. "Oh man! Jesus, Chops! You just pissed yourself!"

Minty looked over his shoulder. Chops would have to be in a bad state to let Freak get away with giving him shit like that. The big biker's skin had gone grey, his eyes were sunken, and an oily sheen of sweat had soaked through his T-shirt, clumping his long hair into dark ropes.

"Hang in there, buddy," Fish said without looking round.

"I could use a beer," Chops managed, his voice a husky whisper.

The Locusts headquarters lurked behind a high fence of corrugated roofing and barbed wire. A sign declared it to be LUCKY'S SALVAGE YARD, several acres of rusting car hulks, stripped household appliances, and unidentifiable piles of twisted metal. To Minty and the Locusts it was home. The bikers owned the business and did well out of buying and selling salvage materials. Their "no questions asked" policy made them popular with those who were looking to sell freshly cut copper wire and pipe.

The Crown Victoria bounced through the open gate; the dry ground of the yard was a lunar surface of potholes and dirt packed as hard as concrete.

"Freak, close the gate," Minty said as he parked the car in a pool of halogen light and went to stand by the rear passenger door. Fish worked his way out of the car and hitched his jeans up.

"Maybe we should take Chops to the hospital?" Fish's courage faded when he was faced with a problem he couldn't solve with a baseball bat.

Minty spat on the ground. "Let's get him inside. It's probably just the flu."

"What if we all get sick?" Fish asked, stepping back.

"Then we'll have an excuse to drink more. Give me a hand." Minty opened the car door. Chops slid out, his head hanging down near the ground, his feet caught up under the front seat.

"Look at his arm, Minty." Fish pointed but Minty could see it. Chops' forearm was black with deep bruising. Some kind of yellow pus was oozing from the bite mark, and the veins along his arm were rising in hard, white lines.

"Chops, how you doin', brother?" Minty didn't touch him. Chops lifted his head and tried to speak; instead he twisted away and vomited a dark mix of black blood and bile onto the ground.

"Box of fucking birds," Chops muttered, spitting puke out of his mouth. "All shit and feathers."

"Fuck me." Fish took another step back.

Freak came wandering back from the gate. "Wow, Chops is really sick, huh? Fuckin' crackheads. We should go back there and burn the whole fuckin' place down!"

"Freak," Minty's voice cracked like a gunshot. "Go find Jethro, ask him to come down here."

Freak swallowed hard. "Uhh, sure. Sure thing, Minty." The kid took off into the two-story building that housed the Locusts Motorcycle Club's offices and living quarters.

"He's real sick," Fish said.

"No shit." Minty swept a hand through his greasy hair. Chops slithered out of the car, crawling through his puke and moaning as he went.

Jethro arrived a few minutes later. Chops had dragged himself to his feet and leaned against the car, sagging like he was dead drunk. Minty and Fish kept their distance.

"What's up with him?" Jethro asked.

"He got bit by some fucked-up crackhead," Minty replied.

"How you doing, Chops?" Jethro lit a cigarette and took a long drag. Chops didn't respond; he stood, drooling and glassy eyed, staring at the ground. Jethro exhaled through his nose, then drew a pistol from his belt and shot Chops in the chest, twice.

"The fuck!?" Fish hollered.

Chops shuddered and collapsed, his legs twitching.

"Come inside. You'll be interested in hearing what the kid has to say." Jethro's pulse barely twitched. Minty admired and feared that about him. The Locusts leader was always calm. Nothing fazed Jethro; he just killed one of his oldest friends without blinking.

"C'mon," Minty said and walked away.

They gathered in the boardroom, a den of leather couches, flags, bike posters, and a display wall of members who had died or been put away for at least a ten-year stretch. A black kid with both eyes swollen shut and blood dripping from various cuts and abrasions sat tied in a chair in the center of the room. Minty sent Freak to the bar for beers and waited for Jethro to speak his piece.

"Kid, tell them what you told me."

The black kid lifted his head and regarded Minty through a stinging film of sweat and blood. "You fucked," he said. "We all fucked."

Jethro drew his pistol again; this time he smacked the kid in the side of the head with the butt.

"Y'all went into the house on Garden? Y'all see what those mo'fuckers turned into?"

"We saw some fucked-up shit," Minty admitted.

"Y'all ain't seen shit, mo'fucker. Y'all din't open no locked doors did you? Y'all din't go into the cellar? Fuck, shit you din't." The kid shook his head.

"What if we did? What the fuck is going on down there?"

"We gotta line on some good shit. Weapons-grade coke, straight outta the Colombian jungle. Goin' cheap. Some Chinese mo'fucker wanted to dump it. We paid a K a key." The kid shook his head again.

"You paid a grand a kilo in California?" Minty said. That price for Colombian cocaine was unheard of.

"Tested pure as a nun's piss," The kid said, his beaten lips splitting into a bloody smile.

"We made so much fucking money. We cut that shit down with everything we could lay our hands on. Then people started gettin' sick. They got to pukin', and turned grey. Then . . . they started fuckin' shit up. I had to lock Tyrell and Maggie in the bedroom. They tried to fuckin' eat me, man."

"We met them, and the kid," Minty said. "The kid was as fucked as the rest of them."

"Yeah, Junior din't do no coke. His momma went crazy and bit him."

"So anyone snorting this shit got sick?"

"Naw, man, they din't get sick! They got fucked up! Started tryin' to eat every muthafucka!"

"Like zombies?" Fish said.

"Naw, man, zombies are like dead people. These fuckers are just fuckin' crazy."

"So a few crackheads chew themselves up," Minty said. "So fucking what?"

"Y'all need to open your fuckin' ears and listen, muthafucka! I am telling you that this shit is spreading. Once those crazy fucks bites you or pukes their shit on you, you fucked."

Jethro spoke up. "What our friend is trying to say is that if someone is infected, they are contagious. Bites, body fluids, shit like that." He cracked open a beer and took a long swallow.

"So what are the cops doing about it?" Minty demanded.

"I'm sure the police are doing what they do in every emergency situation: telling people that everything is going to be fine." Jethro took another swig of beer and blew smoke out of his nose.

"Fuck da police, man," The kid sneered.

"What if the kid's infected?" Fish backed up to the wall.

"He's fine. He's been a fount of information. But now the well has run dry." Jethro stubbed out his cigarette and finished his beer. The pistol in his other hand had more killing to do.

Minty didn't want to see it. "We'd better put Chops in the car crusher. Freak, give me a hand.

They walked out into the night. Two shots sounded from inside the clubhouse. Freak jumped, then hunched his shoulders and kept walking. The two men approached the Crown Vic and stopped short. Chops had vanished from beside the car.

"Fuck me," Minty swore. "Chops? Where the fuck are you, man?" Freak danced around the car, peering under it and venturing into the fringes of the heaps of rusting junk.

"Minty . . . Minty . . . I don't feel so good . . ." Chops lurched out of the shadows. His grey skin glistened with oily sweat, his chest stained with blood and the black vomit that still trickled from the corners of his mouth. Tendrils of white, like dried mucus, spilled around his lips and raised pale welts on his skin.

"It's okay, man." Minty's mouth felt like it was filled with ashes. "I'll take you to the hospital. Freak! Help me here!"

CHAPTER 3

The ER had the usual smells of disenfectant and pain. Olfactory fatigue meant that Dr. Callie Blythe didn't smell it after a while. She took a moment between cases to splash cold water on her face in the staff bathroom. Four hours into a shift and the deadbeats they called GOMERs (*Get Out of My Emergency Room*) were just warming up.

Callie regarded herself in the small mirror over the sink and swept a hand through her strawberry blonde hair. Cut to just below her ears, her hair spent most of its time pinned back or under a surgical scrub's cap. Her face was narrow and defined by sharp cheekbones under hazel eyes. A common color, *like the scum on a stagnant pond back home in Alabama,* she always thought. She stood at an average height, and hidden under the shapeless lime-green scrubs and white coat she wore, her body was lean and fit. On nights like this, she wished she smoked; the adrenaline hit would help keep her alert.

The door opened and a nurse stuck her head into the room. "Doctor Blythe, we have three ambulances inbound."

"Be right there," Callie said. Looking her reflection in the eye she thought, *You're only thirty years old, Callie. You can still save the world.*

Callie pushed away from the sink and exited the bathroom. The chaos of the ER engulfed her like a flash flood. Information on cases came from all directions. The paramedics, the attendings, the medical students, the nurses, and occasionally the patients themselves. During the rest of her shift she assessed patients with the usual fractures, abrasions, concussions, food poisoning, suspected heart attacks, and a heavily pregnant woman who had overdosed on drugs and died in the ER. The tox screen would confirm what drug had killed the woman and her unborn child, but Callie didn't have time to care. The living needed her now.

"Who's next?" she said to the inbound patient board. Cases were triaged and cataloged here. She marked off a male Caucasian, presenting with flu-like symptoms and a bite wound on his right wrist. A walk-in. Picking up the chart, Callie went to one of the curtained-off cubicles.

"Mister Ericksen?" she said to the trio of sullen-looking men in the cubicle. A long-haired biker in stained jeans and leather stood up before helping a second man, who sat slumped on the bed, to his feet—the patient by the look of him. A third, much younger guy bounced to his feet with them.

"Get Mister Ericksen on the bed, please," Callie said to the nurse who had appeared beside her. "What can you tell me about your friend?" she asked, her eyes flicking over the admission chart: febrile, vomiting, and an infected bite on his arm.

"Some fucking crackhead bit him. He got sick real fast," The older guy said.

"Yeah but we got him good, eh Minty?" The scrawny kid looked like he might be jacked up on something. He was grining and could hardly stand still.

"The human mouth is filthy. Though it's not common for a bite to draw blood. We'll get some tests done, prescribe antibiotics, and a nurse will clean and dress that wound."

According to the admissions chart, his temperature was 104. Callie regarded the black oil staining his shirt. Two holes in the center of the mess looked like bullet wounds. Callie ordered scissors from the nurse and together they cut the patient's shirt off.

"What the hell? This man has been shot. Nurse, send an urgent request to surgical. We have a male, Caucasian, presenting with two

GSW, center chest." She turned to Minty. "Care to explain how your friend came to be shot twice?"

"Nope," Minty replied. The doctor slipped an oxygen mask over Chops' face and wondered what the hell was keeping him alive. As long as the patient had a pulse, bullet wounds like that should be bleeding all over the place. Instead they were oozing at best, which could mean he had been wearing some kind of armored vest when he was shot. Each wound had a strange white fibrous material, like spider's web, trailing out of it.

Callie pressed a stethoscope against Chops' chest and listened to the fluid gathering in his lungs. "Has he been vomiting?" she asked.

"Yeah," Minty replied. "Dark though. Like blood or something."

"Is he going to be okay?" The younger biker asked.

"We won't know for a while yet. We'll do everything we can to take care of him."

Callie updated the patient's chart and signaled one of the ER security guards for assistance. When he stood next to her she said, "You two, stay right here. The police will need a statement from you." She left the bedside and headed back to the administration desk.

Screaming erupted from the critical care cubicle, where a team of physicians treated the most seriously injured patients.

A woman jerked up from the gurney, her arms flailing. She ripped lines out of her arms. The medical team were shouting and trying to restrain her. A flood of black vomit sprayed out her mouth. Callie winced as it splattered against the glass of the door, blocking the view. Callie stepped forward and the door burst open, a nurse stumbling out, one hand clutched to her throat. Bright red spurts of blood jetted out between her fingers.

"Shit!" Callie shouted. "I need some help here!" The nurse collapsed, shuddering on the floor. Callie applied pressure to the wound and kept yelling for assistance. All available staff came running. They scooped up the wounded nurse and laid her on a gurney. Callie called for a surgical kit and ordered blood typing as they wheeled her into a critical care station. Lines went into the woman's body and plasma bags drained into her to replace what she was losing through the ragged wound in her neck.

"What the fuck happened?" Clint Pascoe, a chiseled young doctor, asked as he inserted a breathing tube down the gurgling nurse's throat.

"Patient in four went berserk and attacked her," Callie said. "Give me more suction here." With her view of the wound site cleared, she pressed a clamp against the spurting artery and the flood slowed to a trickle.

Somewhere behind her, another woman started screaming. Callie glanced up from her work and saw a nurse running past the cubicle. The sound of equipment crashing to the floor and more yelling added to the confusion.

"Clint, go and find out what's going on. Get security over here," Callie ordered. The injured nurse was stabilized and the call went through to the OR to expect an emergency transfer for surgery. The shouts and screams from the ER were getting louder. Callie stripped off her bloodstained coat, dropped it into a biohazard container, and went to check on her gunshot patient. Pulling the curtain back, she saw her biker jerk back from a wrestler's embrace with Clint. The screaming doctor's face was awash with blood and the biker chewed a bloody mouthful of his cheek.

Stunned, Callie stared at the carnage. The security guard lay writhing on the floor, blood spurting from his maimed arm. The injured biker's friends were nowhere to be seen, but another patient stumbled into view. This one was trailing IV tubes, his hospital gown soaked in blood.

"Sir? Sir, I need you to return to your bed." Callie's voice sounded muffled over the rush of blood in her ears. The bloodstained man turned toward her voice and then opened his mouth to shriek at her. Black, blood-filled fluid vomited from his mouth, splashing on the floor. Pale fibers, like the feelers of some cave-dwelling insect, waved between his lips. He came at Callie, legs jerking as he began to run. She realized that he had a gaping wound in his calf.

The entire ER was going crazy. People screamed and fell in blind panic, slipping in the blood and gore as they tried to escape. A young boy stood howling in the middle of the waiting area until a woman with a raw and seeping wound where her scalp should have been leapt over a row of chairs and knocked him down. The scalped woman snarled and tore at the boy with her teeth. His screams joined the cacophony of the others trapped in the waiting area.

As Callie staggered backwards, a gunshot sounded. Then another. She ran down the hallway, past the staff that came out of emergency cubicles to ask what the hell was going on. She ran until she hit the elevators. Bloodstained handprints were smeared on the buttons. Recoiling from the grisly marks, Callie headed for the stairs. The air in the stairwell was cooler; she ran down, taking the steps two at a time. Twisting at the landing, she threw herself down the final flight and hit the door to the underground parking lot. It burst open and she reached her car before realizing she had left her keys and bag in the locker room upstairs.

"Shit," she sobbed and turned to face the door again. Whatever was going on up there, she wanted no part of it. In her three years working in the ER as an emergency physician, she had seen it all. But not this. Nothing like this.

The adrenaline faded from her system and Callie sank to the ground. The concrete under her butt was icy cold and the door of her car pressed into her back. She closed her eyes and fought for control over her panicked breathing.

The stairwell door boomed open, the older of the two bikers tumbling through it, closely followed by the hyperactive kid. Throwing themselves against the door, they almost got it shut again before something heavy struck the other side.

"Push!" Minty yelled. Freak threw his weight against the door. It clicked shut but shuddered under repeated blows. Callie could hear howling and shrieking in the stairwell. Climbing to her feet, she ran toward the vehicle exit. *Call the cops*, she thought. *They will make it all better.*

The vehicle exit barrier needed a card swipe to activate. Callie ducked under it and pulled open the heavy pedestrian door. Outside, the street had filled with people running. Sirens from three different emergency services wailed in all directions, and gunshots echoed off buildings. Callie could hear screams and cries for help. Whatever was happening, it was bigger than one hospital ER.

A line of people, most drenched in blood, came around the corner. Those on the street fled before them. The blood-soaked line broke into a shambling run, howls and snarls ripping from their throats. They brought down their prey the way lions do on the nature documentary shows. Callie stared as three of them ripped and tore at a woman, tearing her clothes off and then biting into her flesh. Lumps of bleeding meat were excised from her back, buttocks, and legs. No one stopped to help; they just ran. Other blood-soaked predators sprang and attacked. A cop fired three rounds into the chest of one of them before two others dragged him off his feet. They clawed at his face, ripping his eyes out and shredding his lips with their teeth.

Callie pushed the door closed with numb fingers. There was no escape that way.

The door at the other side of the hospital parking lot had been abandoned. The two bikers had wedged it shut and vanished. Callie winced as the doorframe at her back shook under the weight of something heavy landing against it. Over and over again until the latch started to give. The doctor ducked behind a car as bleeding hands first shattered and then tore the mesh-reinforced glass from the door's window.

Desperate for another way out, Callie ran down the exit ramp and away from the street. She heard the sound of a car engine turning over as the door latch behind her gave way, spilling a horde of gore-stained people into the parking lot.

They climbed over each other, snarling and staggering. The car engine roared and Callie ducked behind a pillar as the howling mob moved down the ramp. Car tires spun, spewing white smoke into the air and squealing loud enough to drown out all other noise. Callie peeped out, squinting in the bright lights, and watched the seething mass of bloodstained people go deeper into the parking lot.

A Crown Vic sedan exploded out of a bay and hit the advancing group. Bodies broke and flew over the hood. As the car roared through the parking lot, Callie stepped out and waved her arms frantically. "Stop! Stop! Please! Stop! Please!"

The car skidded to a halt, the rear door opened. "Hey, Doc! Need a ride?" The scrawny biker kid said, grinning up at her. The older guy was at the wheel. Callie nodded and threw herself inside the car, slamming the door as others who survived the initial strike reached the car and began to pound on the panels.

"Got the ticket?" Minty asked the kid as they gunned it toward the exit.

"Uhh . . . yeah." The kid pulled a parking ticket out of his jeans pocket. "Damn, if we'd lost this we'd be walking, huh?"

"You paid, right? You put the money in the machine?" Minty asked as he threw the Crown Victoria around a corner and bore down on the exit barrier and ramp.

"Yeah, you owe me two bucks, man."

"Just stick the fucking ticket in and hurry up!" Minty slid the car to a halt; the kid lowered the window, leaned out, and fed the ticket into the slot. The barrier and the after-hours door began to rise.

"More of those crackheads coming up behind us," The kid said. He slid back inside the car and closed the window. "Hi," he beamed at Callie. "I'm Francis, but you can call me Freak. Everyone does."

"Callie," she replied. "Can we please get out of here?"

"Your wish is my command," Minty growled. He revved the engine and dropped the transmission into drive. The Crown Victoria sprang up the ramp like a shot from a cannon. The front of the heavy car went airborne at the top of the ramp, crashing down in a bone-jarring impact. The tires squealed and gripped the roadway. Minty turned right, a woman bouncing off the hood as they accelerated away.

"Please take me home," Callie said from the backseat, her voice cracking.

"Sure, where's home?" Minty said, the streets and cars flashing by in a blur of lights and screams.

"Gadsden, Alabama," Callie said. "My daddy is the county sheriff."

"Alabama is going to be a little out of our way." Minty swerved the car and avoided a waving pedestrian.

"Hell, a road trip could be fun!" Freak slouched down in the wide seat and fished a battered cigarette packet out of his jeans. Lighting two, he handed one to Minty, who took it without looking away from the road ahead.

"Where do you live in LA?" Minty skidded to a halt as a convoy of fire and police vehicles shot through the intersection in front of them. The night lit up with their flashing lights, and sirens drowned out Callie's response.

"I got a better idea," Minty said. He turned the Crown Victoria, cutting across traffic, ignoring the horns of other drivers.

"You can come back to our place. If this all settles down, we'll drop you home."

"I'd rather go home!" Callie said, leaning forward to tug on Minty's shoulder.

"No can do, sister. Not tonight anyway."

"Goddamn it, this is kidnapping!" Callie slapped at the back of Minty's head.

"Hell no," he replied, ignoring her flailing hands. "This is a rescue."

CHAPTER 4

The doctor had gone quiet by the time they reached the junkyard. The place was lit up with floodlights, the harsh halogen bulbs illuminating the gate and surrounding fences. Freak had been waving to the bikes that roared past them, all heading the same way, for the last few miles.

"Looks like Jethro got the word out; all the chickens are coming home to roost," Freak said. Lowering the window, he slid out to sit on the sill, whooping and hollering at each hog that passed them.

The yard gate stood open, Harleys passing in and out. The parking area inside was filling up with bikes and bikers. An oil-drum fire blazed and a crowd of old friends were drinking and catching up with each other as they stood around the fire.

Freak scrambled out of the car as soon as it stopped. Like an excited dog he ran up to everyone, jumping around and blurting out the story. Minty took a moment to light up a fresh cigarette.

"You're our guest here, Doc. You did what you could for Chops. You got nothing to worry about here. These assholes are just good ol' boys. You'll get the respect that's due ya from the Locusts."

"You take me home tomorrow morning. I need to speak to the police, they'll need witness statements."

"Sure, whatever you want." Minty climbed out of the car. Callie followed him, not wanting to let the old biker out of her sight. These people looked little better than animals—unwashed, tattooed lowlifes. Back home, her father would have put a stop to their partying. He would have deputized every man in the county into a posse and forced every one of these freaks to run for the state line.

Harley engines roared as bikes surged around the yard like Indians circling a wagon train. Callie stayed close to Minty, who made his way directly to a tall, slim man with long blond hair and a matching beard that reached his chest. The guy looked like a blond Jesus from an old Sunday school picture book. He stood next to a picnic table loaded with an ice-filled cooler and an array of open bottles, beer and cheap bourbon mostly.

"Hey, Jethro, this is a doc from the hospital. She did her best to save Chops. But he went crazy, like the crackheads, started tearing up the ER, along with a bunch of other fuckers."

"Pleased to meet you, Doctor . . . ?"

"Blythe, Callie Blythe." Callie folded her arms and regarded Jethro with clear distrust.

"Welcome to our sanctuary from the world at large, Doctor Blythe. Can I get you a drink?" Jethro regarded the attractive woman with the short hair and bloodstained hospital scrubs. "You look like you could use one."

"Thank you. Do you have a phone? I left my cell at the hospital."

Jethro poured a glass of bourbon and handed it to Callie. She shook her head, a pharmacy list of date-rape drugs that could be dissolving in that drink scrolling through her mind.

"Try this one." Jethro handed her a cell phone. She dialed 911 and got an overloaded signal. She dialed the hospital and got the same steady blip.

"It's not working," she said, handing the phone back.

"We rely too much on advanced technology," Jethro said calmly. "Our infrastructure is so fragile. Look around you. This is a junkyard; a graveyard for all mankind has built. A reminder of the temporary nature of empires."

"You aren't bothered that some kind of riot has broken out in the Los Angeles? That people are killing each other out there?" Callie's ire rose in the face of Jethro's placid expression.

Jethro smiled gently. "I am concerned. Gravely concerned. I know that the best thing to do right now is to wait. The situation is out of control. Soon the forces of authority will come to bear and they will regain control. They will force their view on the situation. The guilty will be punished. The causes will be investigated. And finally blame will be laid at the feet of those least able to adequately defend themselves."

"So in the meantime you are just going to sit here?"

"Yes," Jethro replied, smiling at her apparent understanding. "That's exactly what we are going to do. We have stockpiles of food and supplies. We can last a week easy if we have to." Jethro's voice rose to a speech-giving volume. "And we will welcome our brothers and sisters of the Locusts to the yard. The call has gone out. All those who are able are to come and join us. Let the world outside deal with its problems. They are of no concern to the Locusts." His words were answered with a cheer from the twenty or so bikers and women gathered in the yard.

"Do you have a shower somewhere around here and some clothes I can borrow?" Callie asked Minty.

"Yes, ma'am. Come with me." He led her inside. The two-level building was a bizarre mix of college frat house and armored bunker. From the outside it looked nondescript. Inside Callie saw concrete-block walls and metal bars that could be slid into place across doors, steel shutters that could be locked over the windows and a well-polished wooden bar. The shelves behind it were packed with a range of liquor that would not look out of place in an upmarket neighborhood bar.

Minty guided her upstairs and showed her the dorm rooms and the showers—separate cabinets with lockable doors, she was relieved to note. "Towels are in here. Soap and all that shit is in the showers. You can put your laundry in that bin; one of the chicks will take care of it."

Typical, Callie thought. *Even in countercultures women are still domestic slaves.* "I have nothing to change into," Callie reminded him.

"I'll get one of the chicks to take care of that too."

Callie waited until Minty had left and locked the door after him. She collected a towel from the cupboard and stepped into the shower cabinet. Running the water until it was scalding, she stripped and washed under the hot stream using the shower gel hanging from the faucet.

Back in the yard, Minty cracked a beer. "You don't stop for hitchhikers of her caliber, Minty," Jethro said, opening a beer of his own.

"Special circumstances. Downtown is going crazy, Jeth. This coke plague is like a disease. The kid said it makes you crazy and then you start attacking people. The hospital was filling up with them. They all started going fucking psycho, even Chops. We were lucky to get out of there alive."

"We have dreamed of anarchy, Minty. It's what the Locusts were founded on. A dream of freedom. Freedom from society's laws and rules. The chance to live on our own terms. To make our own rules and to live and die by our wits and the providence we bring to ourselves."

Minty nodded. Jethro talked like a college professor from the 1960s, and his vision was an odd mix of hippy dropout philosophy and punk-esque anarchy. It attracted the usual losers and ex-cons. The core group believed in the Locusts philosophy like it was a religion. The rest were looking for something to be a part of. It had always been that way. Some stayed, others drifted away. Only Jethro had been a constant guiding force for the group since Minty had met him all those years ago.

"The providence has been good," Minty said and took a slug of his beer. "Shame we didn't get the rest of the money from the crack house. They were sitting on a gold mine. Would have been a few million dollars cash in there easy."

"We have plenty of time to get that. The television is catching up, the police and National Guard are mobilizing to quarantine those infected. The CDC is investigating. No one will be going back to get the money before we do."

"I hope you're right. It would be a sweet deal to score that much cash. We could lay low for a while on that kind of nest egg."

"Do we want to lay low?" Jethro stared out into the night sky, watching the sparks from the fire rise and vanish into the dark. "Laying low feels like defeat to me. Why not take the money and rise? Become a force for change. Real, effective change in the world."

"Maybe," Minty shrugged and crushed the empty beer can. "Tonight, I'd just like to drink and get laid."

"A worthy aspiration," Jethro said and tossed his own empty can in the trash.

The doctor emerged into the firelight. She was wearing tight jeans, boots, and a Harley-Davidson tank top that accentuated the best aspects of her athletic figure. She didn't look comfortable with the amount of skin she was showing, and Minty admired her look, even as she pulled the tank top down to cover more of her smooth abs.

"Hey, Doc, feeling better?" Minty called. Callie rubbed her hands through her short hair; it spiked and fell where it may.

"Do you have any tops with long sleeves?" she asked.

Minty looked around and picked a grey hoodie off the picnic table. He tossed it to the doctor and she pulled it on, her nose wrinkling at the smell.

"We have beer. Did Minty show you where you can crash for the night?" Jethro passed a cold can from the cooler.

"Yeah, quite the setup you have here." Callie cracked the can and took a long swallow. She never drank, a mix of the memory of her father's angry ranting about the effects of alcohol and the fact that she never had time these days. Tonight, it was just a cold, wet drink that made her throat rejoice.

"We believe in being prepared." Jethro lit a cigarette and exhaled away from Callie as she frowned at the smell.

"For . . . ?" She left the question hanging.

Jethro gave his calm smile. "Every eventuality."

A chill always went up Minty's spine when Jethro smiled like that. Minty had seen that smile after Jethro finished smashing the narc's head to mush in the bathroom of that Seattle bus station.

"Hungry?" Minty asked to break the silence.

"Sure." Callie gave him a smile that made her eyes light up.

"We've got a barbeque happening. C'mon and get yerself a plate." They sat and ate, steaks and hamburgers with all the sides. The bikers came, loaded their plates, and moved away. To Callie it seemed no different than a family barbeque, one with lots of greasy, long-haired, scary-as-hell uncles and a lot of trailer-trash aunts slipping in amongst them.

"You have family in the city?" Minty asked as he swiped mayonnaise off his plate with a heel of bread.

"No. I work long hours. I had a houseplant. It died. I had a roommate, but she moved out. I think." Callie gave a shrug.

"You been a doctor long?"

"For most of my life. It feels like it anyway. How about you? Been a rebel biker outlaw for long?"

Minty chuckled. "For most of my life, it feels like it anyway." They grinned at each other. The beer sat easy in Minty, mellowing his mood and making the events of the evening seem distant and easily forgotten.

Callie finished her beer, the only one she'd had, and stifled a yawn.

"Sun'll be up in a few hours," Minty said. "Best get you to bed. Just take any empty bunk in the upstairs dorm."

Callie didn't argue; she could have slept on the ground at this point.

"Don't let me sleep too late," she warned. "I need to make some calls tomorrow, when things are back under control."

"I'll wake you early enough, don't worry." Minty stood up with Callie.

"Thanks. For everything I mean." She ducked her head and headed into the building. Minty sighed and watched her ass as she walked away.

CHAPTER 5

Edward Gibbon watched the late news on TV with growing delight. The local channel had terminated a live report from an on-the-scene reporter. There was some kind of riot breaking out downtown. The police were firing into a crowd who were attacking people and tearing the place up. The reporter and her camera crew left it too late to run.

Two women and one man charged them. Shrieking and howling they knocked the reporter down, bloodied hands tearing at her hair and clothes. The cameraman tried to pull them off, the view skewing as the camera fell. It kept rolling from the ground. Edward and ten million other viewers saw the reporter screaming as a fat chick tore her throat out before the newscast cut back to the studio where the anchor sat in stunned silence.

With shaking hands Edward flicked the TV off. The elation bubbling up through him threatened to blow his head off. He took a deep, calming breath and flexed his soft, flabby fingers. *Remember the plan.*

Yes, the plan. Edward walked through the house, turning off power switches and unplugging all the electronics. Then hurrying outside, he turned off the gas and water.

Back inside he unlocked the door to his basement. Flicking the light on, he descended the stairs and unlocked his emergency cabinet. Pulling out three heavy bags, he stacked them on the workbench. Everything

. 33 .

he needed was in those bags: food, medical supplies, fuel, and, most importantly, thousands of rounds of ammunition.

Puffing with exertion, he carried the bags upstairs and went through the internal door to the garage. A Hummer he called "the Tank" was parked inside. Edward had spent hundreds of man-hours preparing for this very day. Heavy-gauge wire mesh in steel pipe frames had been painted black to match the paintwork. Edward had learned MIG welding from watching YouTube videos, and each mesh panel was welded to the chassis. This protected the glass from projectiles. The tires were heavy-duty mud and snow types. The back of the vehicle and the luggage rack on the roof were loaded with camping equipment and more survival gear. A black tarp tied down with cargo straps covered the roof rack. A row of spotlights stood in their own mesh cage at the top of the windshield.

They said you were crazy. Who's the crazy motherfucker now? Edward stifled a giggle. It came out as a squeak and he clenched his fists until he got his emotions under control.

After he loaded the three bags into the backseat of the truck, Edward returned to the basement. Unlocking another cabinet, he pulled out four AR-15s, a pair of semiautomatic pistols, and a webbing harness. Clipping it on, he holstered the pistols and checked that the spare magazines were snug in their bandolier. The last items he took out of the second cabinet were a katana samurai sword, a sharpened entrenching tool, and a brush cutter. The brush cutter had a pickax handle and a wide, curved blade, like a short-bladed scythe.

Arms full of weapons, Edward hurried upstairs again. This load went into the back of the truck too.

By now he was hungry, so he turned the electricity back on, microwaved a pizza, and drank a bottle of juice while sitting at his computer. Edward checked the forums and news sites—only a few people were making the connection. Most were repeating the CDC and local law enforcement announcements. Stay indoors. Remain calm.

At 5:00 a.m., he opened his laptop and posted his final *"fuck you"* To an online troll who wouldn't accept what Edward was telling him. Standing up, he hurried through the house making his final checks and turning the power off again. Finally he locked up the basement, turned off the electrical mains, and opened the garage door manually. The street was deserted, and in about an hour the sun would be up.

Driving the bulky H1 Hummer out, Edward left the engine idling as he went back to close the garage. Locking it, he took a sign from the passenger seat and hung it on the front door of his house.

Warning! This property is boobytrapped! Do not enter!

When all this was over, Edward hoped to come back, but not for a while. First he had a plan to enact. Years of preparation had come down to this.

Driving out into the street, Edward kept his eyes peeled for signs of infection in the few pedestrians he did see. The panic hadn't happened yet, the news was still breaking; people would still be in doubt and trusting the authorities to protect them.

Give them twenty-four hours and they would be too late. But not for Edward—he could read the signs. The media and Hollywood talking up zombies. The books, comics, movies, and TV shows. Edward had never forgotten the day the CDC—*the fucking Centers for Disease Control and Prevention!*—had put up a website warning about the coming zombie apocalypse.

That was when he knew he had to be prepared. As a child Edward had lived in fear of the zombie apocalypse. Watching *Night of the Living Dead* on VHS had given him nightmares for months, made worse by the bedwetting and beatings he got for making a mess.

Finally the day has come! The Hummer purred along the quiet suburban streets.

Edward flicked on the radio and moved through the channels. A talk radio station gave him the unfiltered information the normal media wouldn't.

A woman was screeching over the phone. *"They's gone crazy! Crazy! Lord have mercy!"*

"May? May? Could you tell us what you are seeing from your apartment, May?" The DJ sounded like he expected he was being pranked. But a hysterical woman on the phone made for good radio in the early morning.

"They are fighting people! They are hurting them! Oh Lordy! Jesus save that child!" Edward could hear the muffled screams and occasional gunshots coming down the phone line and then being broadcast out by the talk show.

"May, can you tell me, are the police on the street?" The DJ was cool under fire.

"They's eating the police! Oh my God! Oh my God!" May broke down and started sobbing.

The DJ disconnected the call, or at least switched off the live feed. *"Well folks, we are getting some strange reports of a riot in the downtown area. I suggest you avoid the blocks between Fourth and Mayfair on your commute this morning. Take an alternate route to work today maybe? Now we have Charlie on the phone. Hi Charlie, what's on your mind?"*

Edward tuned out as Charlie started to complain about the government. By the end of the week the government would have bigger issues than Charlie's missing pension check.

Heading toward the freeway, Edward bypassed the early morning commuter traffic. They were heading into the city, and the city was going to become a death trap by lunchtime.

Edward had made a study of the effects of a zombie outbreak in the city. *Epidemiology* they called it. The science of disease spread. Pandemics, massive outbreaks of uncontrolled infection. *The fucking CDC tried to warn us!* No one listened. Even the members of the survivalist forums and other websites that Edward joined. They laughed him off the Internet. *Who's laughing now, assholes?* Edward's hands gripped tighter on the wheel.

For the next two hours he followed the route preprogrammed into his GPS. Printouts of Google maps were in the glove box. All the back-road routes were clearly marked. Edward would not be one of those dumb asses who got caught in a traffic jam and died because he tried to travel on a highway.

He almost missed the girl. She had her thumb out and only started waving when he was within twenty feet. Normally Edward wouldn't pick up a hitchhiker. This morning though, he needed to share his glee with someone. He needed someone to know just how damn *right* he was.

Another thought struck him as he pulled up. A pretty blonde teenager like that, he could take care of her. She would be *grateful* for his protection. She would let him do anything as long as he kept her safe. Edward's cock twitched as he pulled over to the sidewalk and unlocked the passenger door.

"Morning!" he called cheerfully. The girl shrugged a pack off her shoulder. A cowboy hat with a rolled-up brim was perched jauntily on her head. The yellow tank top she wore stretched tight against her breasts and left a tantalizing gap between its hem and the belt of her jeans. Edward nodded; there was no way she was older than eighteen.

"Hey, mister, where you headed?"

"Somewhere safe," Edward grinned.

"You headin' east?"

Edward smiled. "Yes, I am."

The girl smiled back. "Sounds fine to me. Can you give me a ride?"

"Sure I can. Hop on in."

The girl hesitated. "Got room for two in there, baby?"

Edward's grin faded. "I guess. I mean there's not much room . . ." An equally young, blond, and pretty boy popped out of the dawn shadows.

"Really appreciate the help, mister," The kid said, sliding past the girl and into the front seat.

"I'll ride in back, sugar." The girl tried the Hummer back door but it didn't open.

Edward pressed a button and the door clicked. "Try it now," he said, the charm deflating from his voice.

"Great truck," The boy said as they drove off.

"It's an essential part of my survival plan," Edward said. *Goddamn it,* he thought. He knew what was coming next: the boy would laugh and the girl would think he was a dork too. They always laughed.

"I'm Todd, that sweet thing in the back is my fiancée, Jessie." The boy smirked and slouched down in the passenger seat.

"Edward," Edward said.

"We really appreciate your stopping for us, Eddie." Jessie curled her arms around the headrest of Edward's seat and purred in his ear. "We're running away to Vegas. Gonna get married in a little old chapel. Then me and Todd are gonna live happy ever after."

Edward swallowed hard. *Who talks like that?* "Sou-sounds like a fun trip." Edward clenched his teeth. He didn't sound suave and cool. He sounded like a dork.

"Yeah, sugar!" Jessie squealed and flopped back against the cases of supplies that took up most of the space in the back of the Hummer.

"Going on a trip yourself, buddy?" Todd looked with interest to the rear of the vehicle.

"Kinda," Edward replied. He didn't want to share anything with these people. This wasn't how it was supposed to go.

"Put the radio on, baby," Jessie crooned from the backseat. Todd reached out and Edward bristled. *I'm driving! No one should touch that but me!*

"Hey, don't touch that," Edward said, but Todd ignored him and flicked on the radio. The talk channel blared in the cab with a woman's voice, calm and full of authority.

"*. . . is under control. We are advising people to stay at home today. Under no circumstances should any person who is acting aggressively be approached.*"

The DJ cut in over her monologue. "*Can you tell us if the National Guard or any other federal units have been dispatched?*"

"*All city residents are advised to stay at home. The situation is under control. Conserve water and food supplies. Updates will be provided by television and radio. Do not be concerned by rumors and information broadcast from unofficial sources, particularly on the Internet.*"

The DJ sighed. "*Well there you have it, folks, the situation is concerning many of our listeners. But the city authorities have it under control. So by all means head back to bed, and keep it here on KDIJ News Radio, we'll be right back after these messages.*"

"Sounds bad," Jessie said. "Hey, can we stop to eat somewhere?"

"What? Maybe." Edward was feeling warm in his heavy leather coat. It was meant to make him feel cool and tough. Like Neo in *The Matrix*. With the two teenagers in the car he just felt like a fat nerd in a Halloween costume.

"Looks like it's going to be a beautiful day," Todd said, slipping a pair of dark glasses on as the sun rose higher above the horizon.

"Yeah," Edward said. He had sunglasses. Prescription lenses, but he was wearing contacts and taking them out to wear his dark glasses would mean pulling over and it just seemed like too much hassle. More than anything he wanted the two kids out of his truck. They were ruining everything.

"Where are you headed?" Todd asked again.

"Out of town. There's a disaster coming. It's happening now in fact."

"What kind of disaster? Like an earthquake? Or a tornado?" Jessie sounded concerned.

"The people that are rioting downtown. They are just the beginning." Edward warmed to his favorite subject. "The outbreak we are seeing now is in the early stages. The virus is currently transferred by contact with bodily fluids. All those people who get bitten, they are going to turn. They are going to turn and then attack the living. Everyone who gets bitten will become one."

"Become one what?" Todd pulled his sunglasses down and peered at Edward.

"Become a zombie," Edward announced.

They both laughed.

"Zombies?" Todd said.

"Yes." Edward was used to people laughing at him. Soon they wouldn't laugh. Soon everyone would know just how right he was.

"It's happening. It's happening right now," Edward said firmly.

"Dude, it's some kinda occupy protest. Remember those? People got pissed off and camped out in downtown. They did it in New York, they did it here." Todd waved dismissively.

"The ninety-nine percent didn't start eating people!"

"Shit, mister, you are crazy. Zombies aren't real!" Todd was laughing at him. Edward could feel the mocking coming through those dark glasses.

"The CDC put up a website. They knew this day was coming!"

"Oh my God, are you serious?" Jessie looked genuinely frightened now.

"The CDC zombie page was a joke," Todd said. "They simply took a popular horror idea and used it to illustrate disaster preparedness. You took that seriously?" Todd laughed out loud and slapped his thigh. "You are fucking retarded, man!"

"Todd, don't be an asshole," Jessie said immediately.

Edward clenched his fists around the steering wheel. *Always laughing at me.* "You are going to die. You know that, right?" he barked at Todd.

"Whatever, man. There's no fucking zombie apocalypse happening right now or ever!"

Edward's rage boiled over. Turning in his seat he slapped the shiny sunglasses off Todd's face. "Listen, you little fucker. The world is ending. It's starting right now. If you are smart you will listen to me. You want to survive? You will listen to me. If you want to be a smart-mouth punk-ass, then *get the fuck out!*" Edward kept slapping at the smirking kid as he screamed all his rage and hate at him. People like Todd had been ruining things for Edward his whole goddamned life. But not anymore. *Now I am in cont—*

Jessie screamed. Todd yelled and Edward looked forward in time to see a blur of red and blue flashing lights. A cop car had powered through an intersection, coming straight at them. As he was beating on Todd, the Hummer had drifted into the path of the oncoming vehicle. Edward screamed and twisted the wheel. The cop car swerved and fishtailed. The military styled Hummer struck it a glancing blow. The heavy-steel bars tore the front fender off the police car and bounced it into the curb. Edward fought to keep control of the truck and it spun around. The heavy tread on the tires caught on the asphalt as Edward overcorrected and the truck flipped. Turning onto its roof in midair, the heavily loaded Hummer crashed down on the driver's side. Supplies flew through the cabin and Jessie screamed louder.

The truck rolled up onto its rubber feet and came to a halt in the middle of the road. The stalled engine ticked as it cooled. A trail of exploded storage containers from the roof rack lay strewn down the road behind them.

"Holy shit," Todd muttered.

"Tooooodd!!" Jessie wailed.

"Gughhh . . ." Edward moaned, blood streaming from his face. He reached out with fumbling hands and patted at a strange bulge in his black T-shirt.

"The fuck, man?" Todd whispered. Edward groped at the lump in his chest. Todd unclipped his seatbelt and climbed up on the seat. Leaning across Edward, he pulled the man's T-shirt up. A round tube of steel jutted out of Edward's torso. The broken weld at the end held shredded clumps of lung tissue.

"Oh Jesus . . ." Todd moaned and clambered backwards out of the truck. Jessie slid out from under the boxes in the backseat and joined Todd next to the Hummer. She hugged Todd, crying hard.

"We gotta call an ambulance, baby. Eddie's hurt bad."

"Th-the cops! They'll call for help!" Todd pointed a trembling hand at the police car. The lights were still flashing but no one had gotten out of it. Someone in the back was thrashing around. The two teens could hear a weird yowling sound, and something wet was thudding against the car's rear window.

Todd ran over to the car as a bare foot kicked at the Plexiglas of the rear passenger window. The two cops in front were slumped in their seats. Jessie banged on the driver's window.

"Hey, officer! Our friend is hurt bad. Officer?"

The prisoner in the back twisted around. Howling and snarling, he slammed his head and shoulders through the starred Plexiglas of the car window. Shrieking and slavering as the window tore his flesh off, the bloodied thing snapped and gnashed at them.

"Jessie, get back, honey!" Todd grabbed her by the arm and pulled her away. The prisoner slithered out of the window and landed like a worm, his belly slapping against the dust. His hands had been cuffed behind his back in the patrol car. Now his face was a mask of dust and congealing blood. Naked above the waist, the prisoner arched his back and shrieked at them.

"What the fuck . . . ?" Jessie wailed. The prisoner twisted and thrashed, rolling until he got to his feet.

"Run!" Todd screamed. Jessie bolted back toward the Hummer. Todd threw the front passenger door of the vehicle open and pushed Jessie inside. The prisoner staggered and screamed, his body arching forward as if he was sniffing the air.

"Hurry up! Hurry up!" Jessie screamed. Todd raced around the front and got the driver's door open. Grimacing, he reached past Edward's flabby, pale belly and unclipped the seatbelt. Grabbing the man by the coat, Todd yanked him out of the truck. Edward fell forward and caught on the homemade roll cage pipe that had impaled him.

"Jessie!" Todd hissed. "Come here and gimme a hand." Jessie sobbed and leaned over. Together they pushed Edward forward enough to slide him off the pipe. Heaving backwards, Todd dragged the fat bastard out of the truck and let him land with a wet splat on the shoulder of the road. The prisoner shrieked and like some kind of armless dinosaur as he darted forward from the back of the vehicle. Todd leapt into the driver's seat, narrowly avoiding gashing his arm on the broken pipe as he scrambled past.

The prisoner dropped to his knees and sniffed at Edward's corpse. The half-naked man's mouth opened wide and he hissed like an angry cat. Thick black drool sprayed out, splattering over the dead man. White strands that looked like blades of ghostly grass writhed out of the prisoner's mouth.

Todd slammed the Hummer door shut. Twisting the key in the ignition, the engine turned over and over . . .

"Get us the fuck out of here!" Jessie squealed. Todd slammed his palm against the steering wheel. The prisoner launched himself at the truck's window, bouncing off the heavy steel mesh on the other side of the glass. With a howl of rage, he jumped to his feet and charged again.

The engine caught and fired. Todd jerked the transmission into drive and floored the gas pedal. The Hummer leapt forward as the prisoner smeared his face against the mesh, pushing himself against the steel until his skin tore as if it were on a cheese grater. Todd spun the wheel and narrowly avoided driving straight into the crashed police car. Facing the right way, he stomped on the accelerator and they roared off down the road.

Jessie wept tears of relief. "Oh God! I love you, baby! I love you so much!" Todd responded to her passionate kisses and tried to keep an eye on the road.

"Vegas here we come, baby!" Todd whooped.

CHAPTER 6

Minty slept until after dawn. The air inside the communal sleeping room was thick with a cloud of farts and snores. Most of the bikers hadn't made it to a bunk, instead having passed out where they stood, lying facedown in pools of spilt beer and in one case with his face buried in the naked crotch of a stripper, also passed out drunk, lying naked on her back on the bar. Empty cans, bottles, and broken glass were everywhere. Minty yanked the front of the cigarette vending machine open and selected a pack of Lucky Strikes from the rack. Lighting up, he stepped out into the morning sun. Squinting, he slid on sunglasses and stepped around the corner to take a piss.

The yard was a wreck. Cars and bikes were lined up and the die-hard party animals around the oil-drum fire were asleep on the ground. Minty zipped up and inhaled his first smoke of the day. *Just another night in Locust Land.*

"Can you take me home?"

Minty turned around; the cute doctor from the night before stood there. She looked pale, and the circles around her eyes were darker now.

"Sure thing. Can I buy you breakfast along the way?" Minty patted his pockets. The Crown Vic's keys were in his leather jacket with his wallet. They drove out of the junkyard, Minty getting out to open and then close the heavy gate.

"Where to?" he asked the doctor.

"I have an apartment, on Bolero Avenue," Callie said.

"Nice." Bolero Avenue had a reputation for being the home of successful people. Ones who did a lot of business with the Locusts, but wouldn't piss on a brother if he were on fire.

They drove in silence and Minty flicked on the radio. He liked classic rock and Delta blues. Those old black bluesmen like Blind Lemon Jefferson, Howlin' Wolf, and Robert Johnson. They cut right to the heart of life's great truth: Shit happens to the best of people. Best just get on with living.

The radio hissed with static, Minty flicked through the channels, nothing but white noise until an official recording came on. "*All residents are advised to stay in their homes. A state of emergency has been declared across the city. Conserve water and food. Stay tuned to official broadcasts and news reports. If a member of your family is injured by one of the rioters, keep them secured in a locked room and file an incident report at the emergency response website. Limit calls to 911 for life-threatening emergencies only. Do not under any circumstances attempt to restrain or communicate with a person or persons who are acting in an aggressive way or have recent injuries. This is a recorded message and will continue broadcasting until the emergency state has been lifted.*"

Minty flicked the radio off. "Guess people finally had enough, huh?" He almost laughed, but the memory of the crackheads and what they did to Rim and Chops killed it in his throat.

"I should go back to the hospital; there will be casualties." Callie looked ill at the idea of going back. She took a deep breath. "Can you take me back there instead?"

"Sure, if that's what you want."

Callie picked up Minty's cell phone as they drove into the city. The streets were filled with abandoned cars and people stumbling around. Most of them were covered in blood and gore. Sirens wailed and emergency vehicles crossed the car's path, racing through intersections and paying them no heed.

"Fuck me . . ." Minty breathed as he pulled up outside a McDonald's. "They are closed. Can you believe that? The fucking world must be coming to an end for McDonald's to not be open. Have you ever seen a McDonald's that wasn't open?"

Callie shrugged. She'd been pushing buttons on Minty's cell phone for a while. "I can get a signal, but none of my calls will connect. It might be your phone; this thing looks older than I am."

"It's a phone—you call, you text. What more do you want?"

Callie looked at him with a raised eyebrow. "Internet, Wi-Fi, apps, music, a camera?"

Minty grunted. "I'm not sure the hospital is such a good idea. When we left the place was going to shit." Minty pulled out into the street again. The abandoned cars were eerie and he drove slowly, watching the people who jerked and thrashed as they stumbled around.

In the passenger's seat the doctor stared at the people. "We should go past, see if they need help. Security should have gotten the situation under control again. If it was a riot, then they will have moved on or gone home. These people are going to need help."

"You really think what we saw last night was rioters? Doc, I saw crazy crackheads. They ate my friend Rim last night. They ate him like he was a cheeseburger and fries. Chops got bit, then he went crazy too. Rioters, no matter how pissed off they are, they don't do that. They don't fucking eat my brothers."

Callie shuddered. "I'm sorry about your friends. I don't know of anything that could have caused this. The authorities will work through the emergency. They will quarantine anyone infected and research a treatment or a vaccine. We just need to do what they say."

"They are saying we should stay home and watch TV," Minty scowled. "Fuck that. We are not sheep. We need to look after ourselves."

"People are likely to be sick and injured. I have to do what I can to help. The hospitals will be overrun with casualties."

"Hey, I said I would take you there!" Minty lit a cigarette, ignoring Callie's grimace of disgust. She pressed the button and the window hummed down. She put her face out and the biker thought she might be crying. He drove down the street, slowing for and then driving through red lights. As they got closer to downtown, he smelled smoke, then saw a burning car. A fire engine was parked to one side, but no firefighters attacked the blazing vehicle.

People stumbled along the street—some in small groups, others on their own. All were shuffling, stunned, dazed, and lost.

Minty slowed down. "Roll the window up," he said, leaning over and tossing the cigarette out past the doctor's ear.

Smoke drifted around them, and Callie closed the vents on the air conditioner. "How can these people still be walking?" She twisted in her seat as they rolled past a woman with a missing arm. The raw bone of her elbow stuck out the end of her shirtsleeve. "She should be dead from blood loss, or at least unconscious." Callie's eyes went wider as the crowd of seriously injured but still walking people thickened ahead of them.

The Crown Victoria turned a corner, the hospital two blocks down the street. Minty stopped the car. Ahead a rough barricade of police cars and other vehicles blocked the road. Piles of something burned with an oily black smoke in front of the barricade.

"It doesn't look like the authorities have everything under control to me," Minty said. One of the injured walkers thudded against the car window. His teeth bared and bloody spit sprayed over the window as he hissed at the occupants. A hand, cut and missing two fingers, clawed at the glass. Minty watched carefully, seeing those weird white strings feeling their way out from the oozing stumps of the man's amputated fingers.

"Get us out of here," Callie said, shying back from the ghoulish vision. Minty kept staring at the freak. "Get us out of here!" Callie shouted louder.

Minty shrugged, staring deep into the bloodshot eyes of the bloodstained man. Raising one hand, he pointed a finger gun at the center of the man's forehead.

"Pow," Minty said and slowly drove forward. They turned around, the Crown Victoria tires crushing the burning bundles as they swept over them.

"Oh, God . . . they are people, those are burnt people." Callie drew her feet up off the floor of the car, pulling herself as far away from the charred remains as possible.

They were almost back at the corner when a National Guard Humvee roared up. The hatch on top was open and a soldier in a cloaked helmet and gas mask manned the mounted M240B machine gun.

"Stop your vehicle! Turn off your engine! Remain in your vehicle! Keep your hands visible at all times!" an amplified voice boomed at them.

"Busted," Minty said and grinned. Callie raised her hands; Minty kept his resting at the top of the steering wheel.

"Turn off your engine!" The voice boomed again. The people on the street snarled and spat, moving closer to the noise, the crowd building around the armored truck.

"How the hell can I turn off the engine and keep my hands visible at all times?" Minty muttered. Moving slowly, he lowered one hand and switched the ignition off. The silence was broken by the moans and growls of the crowd building outside. Rioters or crazed crackheads or God knows what were now walking past the car. Most were injured, chunks of flesh missing from arms or legs. Entire limbs missing from some. A girl of maybe high school age, with her hair burned away and half her face melted like extra cheese on a pizza, reached the Humvee and raised her hands to the soldier visible in the top hatch.

"These poor people," Callie whispered. Her voice dry and husky.

"Now what do they expect us to do?" Minty had both hands back on the steering wheel. He watched the ones around the Humvee with interest. He also watched the only visible soldier with a very careful eye. The guy behind the machine gun was yelling something and then the amplified voice started up again.

"*Move back! Move back or we will open fire! Move back now!*"

The soldier in the hatch jerked the cocking handle back on the M240B and swept the muzzle over the gathering crowd. They started banging on the panels of the Humvee. A couple pulled themselves onto the hood and slowly stood up.

The first one to reach for the soldier disintegrated in a burst of gunfire. The soldier in the hatch twisted and fired again, tearing the second climber in half. Both pieces of her body fell into the crowd. The noise drove the crowd into a frenzy. The Humvee started rocking and then reversed while the mounted gun sprayed the howling crowd with lethal force.

"Jesus," Minty said. He started the car and dropped it into reverse as a hail of gunfire tore into the mob. They didn't seem fazed by being shot and Minty didn't expect them to run away.

Bullets tore up the roadway, a line of dust puffs and the scream of ricochets zinging past the Crown Victoria.

Minty skidded the car to a halt at the barrier. It would take a tank to get through that. Shifting into drive, he floored it, feeling the heavy car's back end shimmy as the tires spun. With a lurch, they got traction and the car shot forward. Minty sailed it around the crowd and past the Humvee that was still reversing from the slavering rioters.

Bodies bounced off the fender and hood of the car. The engine roared as they drove over the fallen and the wheels lost traction again. Rocking over the soft obstacles, they broke through and turned back into the street away from the crowd and the Humvee. A final blast of machine gun fire tore up the street and the rear window of the Crown Victoria exploded.

"Fuck!" Minty yelled and swerved the heavy car among the abandoned vehicles that lined the road. He pressed down hard on the accelerator and the car shuddered. "We lost a tire," he said to Callie, who hunched down in the front seat, her eyes wide and face pale.

At fifty miles an hour the remaining rubber shredded off the rim and the Crown Victoria slid in a shower of sparks, coming to a thudding halt against a lamp post. Minty sniffed the air. "Get the fuck out!" He leaned over, popped the car door open, and pushed Callie out. The biker slid across and out the same door.

Pulling the doctor to her feet he yelled, "Car's on fire! Run!" They took off down the road, flames flicking up behind them. A dull *WUMPH!* and a blast of heat washed over their backs. A moment later flaming shrapnel and debris rained down.

"That's going to attract attention," Callie said as she scanned up and down the street. There were a few crazies staring in mute astonishment at the blaze.

"We need to get off the street." Minty took the doctor by the arm and dragged her to a shattered department store window. "In here."

They knocked a mannequin aside and Minty kicked in a panel at the back of the window display. Dropping into the store, they looked around. "Place is closed," Callie whispered.

"We don't have much time," Minty replied. "Alarm syst—"

The silence was shattered by the sudden screeching of an alarm.

"Why didn't it go off with the broken window?" Callie yelled over the noise while pressing her hands against her ears.

"Different system. Glass break isn't the same as motion detectors! Move!" Minty pushed her through the women's wear department and into menswear. They reached the other side of the store and pushed open a door labeled STAFF ONLY. Beyond the door was a narrow concrete-floored corridor.

"Wait for me in there," Minty said. He waited until the doctor had closed the door and then he turned and dashed up a flight of stairs. On the second floor, he jogged through housewares and furnishings. A second zone alarm burst into life as he tripped the sensor.

Reaching sporting goods, Minty snatched up an aluminium baseball bat from a display rack. He grabbed a hockey mask and some thick gloves. Sliding the mask over his face, he pulled the gloves on and swung the bat. It felt too light. He grabbed a second one on the way back to where he left Callie.

Minty stopped at the landing halfway down. Over the earsplitting shriek of the alarm, he could hear the howls and snarls of fucked-up crackheads. Two men and a woman came prowling through the kicked-in panel by the window display. They leapt on a mannequin, knocking it down, snarling and gnashing their teeth at the plastic form. Minty used the opportunity to get down the last of the stairs and duck behind a rack of suit pants.

The two males pushed the female away, sending her flying back against a display case. The glass shattered, and the woman shrieked in rage more than pain. Whatever these junkies were on, it made them immune to pain.

The biker took a deep breath behind the hockey mask and made a run for the door to the back hallway. A triumphant howl behind him made his hair stand up. Minty hit the door and spun around. One of the guys crouched, half naked and filthy, facing the biker.

"Come on!" Minty snarled. The freak leapt. The bat swung; if it had hit a ball it would have been a home run. The sweet spot of the bat connected with the freak's jaw, shattering the bone and dislocating it into a slack-jawed look of surprise. Minty took a step forward and swung the second bat overhand, bringing it down with a wet thud on top of the junkie's head. The man's skull cracked and a bloody fluid dripped out of his ears as his eyes rolled up and he slumped. Minty kicked him away. Behind him, the door to the corridor opened.

"Come on!" Callie called. The biker backed through the door as the second male and his girlfriend came charging at it. The doctor slammed the door shut as the two rioters on the other side thudded against it.

"What's down there?" Minty indicated the dark corridor.

"What the hell are you wearing?" Callie replied.

"Protection."

"What about me?" She folded her arms.

"This is so I can protect you," Minty said, clumps of wet hair and blood dripping off one of his baseball bats.

"Well then, you go first," she said, indicating the corridor. Minty snorted and marched off, Callie close on his heels.

At the end of the corridor, they found another door. This one opened out onto a loading bay with a single, half-ton delivery truck parked up in front of a large garage door.

"We'll take that." Minty hurried across the concrete floor. The truck was unlocked; he opened the passenger door and helped Callie up into the cab.

"Are the keys in the ignition?" he asked. The doctor leaned over to the driver's seat and then nodded.

"I'll get the door." He turned a key and pressed a button. The overhead door began to creep upward, chains rattling. Heading back to the truck, Minty climbed into the driver seat. They backed out, turned, and pulled into the street. A crowd of freaks had gathered at the shop window now, most of them tearing at the broken glass and trying to force their way inside. Minty revved the engine. A group of the fucked-up crazies turned away from the window and stumbled toward the truck.

"Go! Just go!" Callie slid down in the seat, trying to pull herself as far away as possible from the advancing horde. Minty pushed the transmission into drive and the truck growled forward. He pressed down on the gas and the vehicle was doing thirty miles an hour when it hit the first line of rioters. Some were torn apart by the impact, others slid under the wheels and chassis. Minty kept his foot on the gas and punched through to the clear street on the other side. The stink of blood boiling on hot engine parts wafted through the AC vents.

A helicopter whooshed in low and buzzed through the intersection ahead of them. Callie could see the heavily armed soldiers crouched inside, all wearing full-face gas masks, helmets, and protective clothing. The chopper waved its tail, twisting against the rotor wash, and then it lifted away and vanished down the street.

"Why didn't they help us?" Callie yelled.

"I don't think they are on a rescue mission," Minty replied and got the truck up to forty, swerving through the people and the abandoned vehicles as the sound of gunfire erupted behind them.

CHAPTER 7

Jessie ate chips and Todd drank soda as they drove. She'd climbed into the back and rummaged through Edward's supplies. "There's enough food here to feed us for a year," she remarked.

Todd grinned. "Baby, we just need enough to get us to Vegas."

Jessie climbed back into the front passenger seat. "I found this," she said, holding up a pump-action shotgun with a sleeve of shells strapped to the stock.

The boy nearly leapt out of the driver's seat when he saw it. "Holy shit! Are you crazy? Put that back!"

"Aww, sugar, it ain't nothing. I been handling guns since before I could walk." Jessie slid the gun down between her thighs. "I love a long hard barrel. Makes me think of your *thing*," she purred.

Todd grinned. Jessie gave him blue balls on a daily basis. Sometimes when they were making out she would give him a hand job. If they were really going hot and heavy, she would let him slide his hands up under her shirt. Cupping those perfect apple-sized breasts with nipples as hard as peach pits. She liked to talk dirty, but protected her precious virginity like her pussy was a bank vault.

"Damn, baby, we are so close to getting married, we could just pull over somewhere and do it. No one would know." He tried not to whine, but his cock throbbed like it was swollen and burning up with some kind of infection.

"God would know," Jessie said gravely.

Fuck God. Todd grimaced, an almost physical pain radiating from his nutsack.

Jessie didn't pay much more than a passing acknowledgment to God. She hadn't been to church since she was a kid. There was just no way she could tell Todd that she didn't feel safe, giving herself to him. Not that way. Not yet. She cranked up her seductive smile another notch. "Sugar, once we are married, you can have this body. You can do anything you want . . ." Jessie ran her hands down her front, dragging the edge of her tank top low enough to show the lace edge of her bra. "I'll do it with you all day and all night. I'll even . . ." She leaned in close and whispered, "suck your thing." Todd groaned, one hand dropping from the steering wheel to squeeze his throbbing shaft through his jeans. "*Fuuuuuuck!*" He shuddered and slumped in his seat.

"What the hell, Todd? You animal! That is so gross!" Jessie pushed herself away and regarded her fiancé with a look of disgust.

"Sorry, baby, but you talk so hot and you're wearing that outfit . . ." Todd trailed off mumbling.

"You're sick," she said. Her final word on the matter. Todd sighed. The pressure had eased in his pants. Instead, he had a cool, damp feeling. It was as uncomfortable as the shame flooding his face.

He looked at the side mirror; the road behind them was filling up with low-slung motorcycles. Bikers riding across both lanes were bearing down on them fast.

"Shit." Todd straightened up and put his foot down. Jessie looked back and then twisted in her seat.

"Go faster! Jesus, do you think they've seen us?"

"Of course they've seen us." Todd shook his head. They both watched as the Harleys pulled up alongside. Grim-looking men in leather and filthy denim turned to stare at them as they rode past.

Todd breathed again as the last of them opened the throttle and pulled ahead, the Locusts Motorcycle Club logo on their patches vanishing around the next bend.

"Oh my God," Jessie breathed. "Did you see the way they looked at us?"

"Forget it, they're gone now. We won't see them again."

Edward's GPS guided them along the back roads, heading out of town. They were driving through industrial estates, past empty truck stops and deserted lots. The GPS spoke up, telling them to take the on ramp to the freeway, follow it a mile, and then take an exit. Todd turned the Hummer and they drove up the ramp.

"Shit," he swore and skidded to a halt. The five lanes of freeway were blocked by rows of Harley-Davidson motorcycles, all parked. Beyond the bikes was empty space up to an overpass. In the shadows under the bridge stood a row of concrete barriers. Beyond the barricades, he could see the vague shapes of a lot of soldiers standing in front of two tanks.

"What the fuck?" Todd muttered.

"Toddy, stay in the car." Jessie grabbed his arm as he killed the engine, but he ignored her warning and slid out of the cab. The bikers stood around their machines, watching the Hummer with intense interest. Todd went to the shoulder of the highway, unzipped, and took a piss. A shadow loomed over him, and a cold circle of steel pressed against the back of his neck.

"Morning, kid." The shadow had a voice scoured to gravel by years of hard drink and hard living.

"Hello," Todd squeaked, the last few drops shivering onto his shoes. He gingerly zipped up.

"Interesting ride you got there, kid," The voice said.

"It's not mine. But we didn't steal it or nothing." The words came out in a rush. "We were hitching, and we got picked up by this guy, called Edward. Then we crashed into a cop car, and Eddie got hurt real bad. I think he died. The cops were either dead or unconscious. They had this guy in the backseat who was going crazy. He busted out and tried to attack us, so we jumped in Eddie's truck and got the fuck out of there. We were going to call an ambulance as soon as we found a phone. I swear!"

"You killed a couple of cops?" The voice sounded like death.

"Jesus, I hope not. We didn't mean to crash; they hit us."

The unseen shadow laughed, and the sound sent a chill up Todd's spine. It sounded like bones shaking in a tin cup at the bottom of a well.

"Shit, cop killer, you may be alright." The pressure at the back of Todd's neck vanished. He slowly turned around. The man holstering the pistol stood well over six feet, and close to three hundred pounds rested in his massive steel-capped boots. He had long black hair and a beard that curled down over his chest. "They call me Tag," The giant growled.

"I'm Todd, and that's my fiancée, Jessie. We're going to Vegas, to get married."

Tag walked back to the group of bikers who were gathering around the Hummer. Todd followed him.

"Here kitty, kitty, kitty." One of the bikers leaned in against the mesh over the truck side window and patted the wire, while Jessie recoiled.

"Lady's name is Jessie, this is her fiancé, Todd." Tag said it in a way that made Todd feel stupid. "They're on their way to Vegas. Gonna get married."

The bikers laughed, and one of them tried the door of the Hummer. "What say you open the truck and let us introduce ourselves to the little lady," a blond biker with tattoos up his neck said. He curled his fingers through the mesh and gave it a shake.

"Todd's a cop killer; he's alright," Tag announced. They all turned and looked at him then.

"No shit?" The blond asked.

"Yeah, I guess. Couple of them tried to run us off the road. They're fucked now." Todd lifted his head a little.

"Cool," The blond said and the rest of the bikers nodded in agreement. Someone slapped him on the shoulder. A broken chorus of "Right on, man" and "Fuckin' A" came from the rest of them.

"Is there some other way we can go?" Todd nodded toward the concrete barricade and its armed guard.

"To Vegas? Sure. All roads lead to the desert," Tag said cryptically.

"We gonna go round?" The blond biker asked.

"Not much choice. We can get to the yard on another route. Looks like no one gets to leave the city just yet. Jethro will be interested to know about this. Cop killer, you follow us. We'll get you to where you need to be."

Todd nodded in appreciation. Walking around the Hummer, he tried the driver's door. Jessie had locked it the moment he stepped out of the car.

"Jessie, come on, open up. It's okay, baby." The bikers mounted their machines and the air filled with the growling rumble of twenty motorcycles coming to life.

Jessie leaned over and popped the lock, and Todd slid back into the truck. "They're okay," he said. "The leader, his name is Tag. They're going to show us a better way to get to Vegas." Jessie looked at the bikers as they turned their bikes around. Something about the way they looked at her sent butterflies tumbling through her stomach.

Todd started the engine and turned the vehicle around. They followed the bikers down the off ramp and out into the industrial wasteland of the city's edge.

CHAPTER 8

"Rules of engagement are to use lethal force if attacked." The squad in the helicopter looked at each other, and Garrett tapped his mic. *"Sergeant, did you say we should shoot unarmed civilians?"*

Sergeant First Class Dukes activated his throat mic. "At ease that shit, Garrett. You had the same briefing we all did. Local PD can't cope. Martial law is in effect until this disturbance is brought under control. We aren't going to be shooting civilians. We are going to be containing a volatile situation."

"Sixty seconds to LZ," The chopper pilot's voice cut in. Dukes liked the way she sounded. First Lieutenant Swimsuit Model; nothing could beat that. SFC Dukes had seen her around. She was younger and an officer, which made her forbidden fruit. Dukes could tell she liked what she saw. He was a bad boy infantry special ops kind of guy. Ranger, Airborne wings, Combat Infantryman Badge. He looked the part. He made sure that whenever she looked his way he had his *"I am a bad motherfucker"* face on. If they completed this mission successfully, he decided he would take the risk and try for a hookup.

The helicopter banked and Dukes stared down at a fast-moving delivery truck. The chopper hovered for a moment as the pilot dropped through an intersection, lining up the approach between two buildings. They were close enough that Dukes could see the driver, a broad-shouldered guy in leather with long hair and a beard shot with grey. The younger woman beside him looked clean-cut and terrified. The chopper ducked into the next block and the truck vanished from view.

"Thirty seconds out. Get your shit straight. We are doing this by SOP. Alpha team at nine and Bravo at three. Stay sharp."

The team's standard operating procedure for airmobile insertion was for the Alpha team to unload from the left door of the Blackhawk helicopter while Bravo team unloaded from the right. The nine soldiers double-checked their equipment and squared away their ammunition. They readied their weapons and prepared to unass the bird. "Masks on," Dukes ordered and they pulled their gas masks down and secured their helmets.

The city block they were putting down in was awash with smoke from burning cars. A fire truck stood abandoned near a burning wreck.

"Dismount in three . . . two . . . one . . . *go go go!*"

The pilot held the chopper a couple feet off the deck and the squad dropped out of the open sides, landing on their feet and running to defensive positions, covering their assigned quadrants.

Dukes was the last to leave. "Good luck, Sergeant," The chopper pilot said. *Yeah, when we get back I am looking you up,* he thought.

"We'll see you in twenty-four hours!" The copilot gave a thumbs-up and Dukes dropped to the concrete. Less than ten seconds after the exit order, the chopper lifted away and turned back toward the temporary base camp beyond the city limits.

Dukes scanned the area. High buildings, abandoned cars, some drifting trash. Civilians were in the area, but none of them seemed to be actively rioting. "Report," he said into his microphone.

"*I have twelve Charlies scattered between the next intersection and us,*" Sanchez came back. The others also reported varying numbers of civilians, no active threats.

"Okay, people, by the numbers. We are moving to rally point Juliet eight." The squad came out of their positions, double-timing it in pairs to the beginning of the westbound street. "Sanchez, check that fire truck; Valentino, cover him."

The two men approached the abandoned vehicle at a wary trot. First Sanchez and then Valentino moved up. Sanchez gave the signal and with Valentino covering, he stepped up and looked in the cab.

"Fire truck is empty, Sergeant."

"Roger that. Everyone keep an eye out for FD casualties. They are a priority recovery. Medevac will want their locations."

They assumed positions on both sides of the street, staggered right and left with their weapons facing out toward the possible threat. All the soldiers kept an eye on the civilians, who mostly stared at them or shuffled after the squad as they moved down the road.

"Sergeant, we are pulling local talent," Corporal Milquist spoke up from the back of the group.

"Are they aggressive?" Dukes looked back; the thick smoke obscured his view of Milquist and the rear guard.

"Negative, Sergeant. Some of these people are injured. Seriously injured."

"We aren't a medevac unit, Milk. This is a recon only mission."

"I roger that, Sergeant, but these people are walking when they should be lying down or dead." Milquist sounded distinctly uneasy.

"Keep an eye on them and keep moving."

The squad walked through the dark smoke of burning cars and smoldering trash, the gas masks they wore keeping it out of their eyes and lungs but severely limiting their vision.

"Close up, maintain visual contact," Dukes said into his throat mic. A short burst of gunfire erupted from the front of the squad. "Report?" Dukes barked immediately.

"Tango contact!" Sanchez came back immediately. *"We have multiple targets advancing on us!"* The rest of the squad moved to cover, ducking behind cars and into doorways. The smoke cleared enough for Dukes to see a group of five rioters running at Sanchez and Valentino. The soldiers fired, red spray bursting from the chests of two men. But they kept running. *What the fuck?*

"They aren't going down!" Valentino yelled. He fired again, a longer burst. The stream of bullets tore through the lead rioter's abdomen. A twisted tangle of intestines bulged and slithered out of the ragged gash in his belly. The man kept coming. One foot caught on the hanging ropes of guts and yanked the whole mess out of him. Dukes shouldered his rifle and aimed. The weapon kicked in his hands. The disemboweled rioter's head exploded.

"Head shots. Head shots will put them down!" he said into the mic. The street filled with the sharp crack of M4 rifle fire. The rioters came on even when riddled with bullets. Those with shattered legs crawled on their arms.

"*This is fucked up!*" Milquist yelled. "*Sergeant, we have a large group inbound on our six!*" The transmission was cut off by a surge of gunfire from Milquist's position.

"Keep moving to the target location," Dukes transmitted. The squad worked the way they were trained. Covering fire was laid down and they moved forward. Their destination was the seventh floor of a masonry office building, one of the older constructions that had been renovated inside, modernized, and camouflaged to blend in with the rest of the beige block of office space in the inner city.

The squad laid down a field of fire; the rioters kept moving into it. The shots were sporadic, the team taking time to find their targets and lay them out. Headshots from their weapons made a mess of a dozen skulls, and more were coming from all directions.

"*We are about to be overrun back here!*" Milquist sounded adamant but not panicked—not yet anyway.

"Keep it tight," Dukes said. A black woman, her clothing torn to rags, lunged at him. He fired from the hip, blasting holes in her from stomach to shoulder. She barely flinched. Correcting his aim, Dukes fired again, three shots—jaw, bridge of the nose, and the final round blew the top of her head off.

"*Valentino!*" Sanchez shouted over the comms. "*Get off him, you sons of bitches!*" Through the comms came a noise like a pack of wild dogs tearing Valentino to pieces.

"*Valentino is down.*" That was Garrett. "*We are at the entrance to Juliet eight,*" he continued. Garrett didn't get bothered under fire. Dukes anchored his sense of calm to that voice.

"Good work, Garrett. Secure the entrance," Dukes said. "Bravo team, fall back to Garrett's position. Covering fire. Watch your flanks."

"*I'm going for Valentino,*" Sanchez advised. Dukes didn't order him to stand down. These men would rather die than leave a comrade behind.

"Alpha team, support Sanchez, bring Valentino back," Dukes ordered.

"*Roger that, Sergeant.*" They moved into the street, their covering fire answering the howls of the rioters as the team made its way to Valentino's body.

"*Valentino is secured,*" Sanchez reported.

"Good job, get back to Juliet eight," Dukes ordered.

Before they reached Dukes' position, Timberson, a corn-fed kid from Idaho or Nebraska or some place they grew crops and soldiers, went down when a child leapt on him from the roof of a car and tore out his throat with a savage growl.

Standing in the doorway, Dukes didn't hesitate. Two rounds shattered the child's skull and sent him skidding across the bloodstained concrete. Timberson choked to death on his own blood as Alpha team dragged him toward their destination.

Dukes held the door open as the team charged through the gap.

"Close the fucking door!" Milquist yelled, rolling to his feet, eyes wide and shocked. The squad fired, bringing down four more rioters while Garrett and Drake carried a reception desk from a side room to barricade the entrance.

"The fuck, Sergeant?" Sanchez demanded. "They took out Valentino and the Tree."

Dukes lowered his M4 and took what felt like his first breath since they landed. The two bodies on the floor had been savaged—Valentino's chest had been ripped open like an autopsy and Timberson's neck was a mess of blood and exposed bone.

"We gonna fucking stand here all fucking day?" Garrett was looking bored already.

"Milquist, take Garrett and search this floor. The rest of you, upstairs. I want a floor-by-floor sweep." They moved without question; shit had suddenly got real.

Dukes followed the squad up the stairs. The power was still on and they had the alarm codes for each office space. No one in the squad expected any of the rioters had made it into the building, but they were doing a lot of things that were unexpected.

"They fucking ate Valentino," Sanchez said as they climbed.

"Are we fighting fuckin' zombies, Sergeant?" Drake spoke up.

"Hell no. We are fighting a terrorist threat. American civilians have been compromised and are posing a clear and present danger to our nation's security. You keep that in mind and shoot anyone who tries to bite you. Do you understand, Drake?"

"*Fuckin' hooah, Sergeant!*" The two fire teams responded.

"Milquist, you and Trow, find somewhere quiet for Timberson and Valentino to wait for evac. Stay frosty, men." Dukes tapped Walburn on the shoulder and indicated he should head out on the second floor. A second tap sent Sanchez with him.

Dukes took point and covered the third floor while the remaining squad members came up to that level. "*First floor clear,*" Garrett came over the comms.

"Come up the stairs; we are on the third-floor landing," Dukes replied.

"*Second floor clear,*" Walburn announced immediately after.

"Are you sure, Private?" Thirty seconds was a fast sweep and clear of an entire floor.

"*Yes, Sergeant, this place is empty. Looks like it's been locked up since folks went home last night.*"

"Alright, form up on me. Third-floor landing. Keep frosty, people."

The squad moved up through the floors. Each one was dark and locked down. The men started to relax, the rush of adrenaline from the fight outside starting to fade. Now they were almost casual. Dukes keyed in the access code on the seventh-floor office. The door opened and he ushered his men inside. Motion-activated lights flickered and came on.

"Secure the door," Dukes said. "Garrett, come with me. The rest of you—"

"Stay frosty," They all echoed at once. Drake laughed and then looked guilty.

Dukes headed deeper into the office, Garrett silent and watchful beside him. They walked past various doors, all marked with numbers. The sergeant stopped outside door 17. "This is us," he said. Extracting a key card from a belt pouch, Dukes swiped the card and entered a code. The door clicked and opened.

Beyond the door was a large room. Rows of computer terminals and large screens stood in a space without windows.

"We good?" Garrett asked.

"Roger," Dukes responded, scanning the room. Finding the right terminal, he sat down and booted it up. "Watch the door," he ordered. Garrett swung around and hunkered down.

Using a laminated card he carried, Dukes logged into the system and inserted a thumb drive into the USB slot. He waited while the program activated. While images and documents flashed on the screen, Dukes glanced around. Garrett was still watching the door. Intelligence reports, sealed off from the outside unless an authorized user was logged in to approve the transmission, streamed past Dukes' eyes. He saw detailed intel reports coming out of Colombia, disturbing updates of some kind of inter-cartel violence escalating in the jungle. Investigators reported finding mutilated remains and trashed cocaine factories deep in the green. The violence in the jungle had moved to the villages and then cities across South America. Now, it had moved north, through Central America and Mexico and crossing the US border. Dukes stood up as the sound of gunfire echoed through the building. "Sit rep," he said into his mic.

"Rioters, they are coming through the windows on the first floor. We have multiple contacts," Drake replied.

"Fall back to the second-floor landing. We will meet you there. Everyone else move back to the second floor. We will secure and exit the building from that point."

The screen flashed, indicating the program had completed its transfer. Dukes pulled the thumb drive out and tucked it in his jacket. "We ready to roll?" Garrett asked.

"Affirmative, let's go." Dukes followed Garrett out of the office and down the stairs. The gunfire increased in volume and intensity.

"Get that crazy bitch," Sanchez said over the comm.

"Drake, cover that door!"

"I've got three Tangos inbound!"

Garrett readied his automatic rifle and thumbed his mic. "Garrett and Sergeant Dukes, we are on the third floor and are coming down, do you copy?"

They arrived at the back of the squad without being shot. The air over the stairs was filling with the stink of cordite. A squirming mass of shattered corpses blocked the way down.

"How many?" Dukes asked.

"All of them, I think," Walburn replied.

"Sergeant, we need to find an alternative exit." Milquist squeezed off a three-round burst. It disintegrated the skull of a man in a grey suit. Others came up the stairs, howling and snarling.

"Put 'em down," Dukes ordered. The squad unleashed the full power of their collective arsenal. Windows shattered and wall paneling disintegrated along with the heads and bodies of rioters.

Dukes had to shout over the noise. "Garrett, find us a way out of here. Fire exit or something."

"Roger that, Sergeant." Garrett backed up the stairs and vanished.

"Hold this position," Dukes ordered, firing over the stair rail and dropping a couple of rioters before they were close enough to be a threat.

"*Fire exit secured,*" Garrett said in Dukes' earpiece. "*Turn left at the top of the stairs, then straight to the end of the office. I'm at the fire exit window.*"

"Follow me, fall back, covering fire!" Dukes yelled. They withdrew from the stairs. "Sanchez! Drop a grenade on those motherfuckers!"

Sanchez was the last to leave the stairwell. "Frag out!" he yelled and a moment later the *WOOMPH!* and flash of a grenade explosion obliterated the rioters storming the stairs.

Garrett waited, crouched on the fire escape. "Go, go, go!" Dukes dropped into a covering position behind a desk. No rioters came through the swirling smoke and ruin of the stairs. The squad went out the window, down the fire escape steps, and dropped into the alleyway below.

"Sergeant, you're the only one left!" Garrett called through the open window. Dukes climbed through the window. "After you, Sergeant," Garrett said, indicating the steps leading down the side of the building.

On the ground, the squad reloaded weapons and took stock. "We have what we came for," Dukes said. "Until our pickup arrives we are to maintain minimal contact with enemy forces and provide intel."

"We should have stayed upstairs," Drake announced.

"At ease that shit, Drake. Trow, get on comms, advise the TOC that we have the package. Now heading to rally point for phase two."

Trow nodded and pulled the radio handset from his pack. "*Alpha three-seven, this is Delta two-two. Do you read me, over?*"

Dukes pulled out a laminated map. "We are here. There are three marked secondary sites for us to wait out the shit storm. Here," he pointed to a red dot on the map two blocks away from their current position. The others were four and five blocks away.

"Closest gets my vote," Sanchez said.

"Well, it does my heart good that I can please you, Sanchez. Now shut the fuck up," Dukes replied curtly. "We aim for the nearest site. If it's too hot, we go for the secondary site, and so on."

"What if they are all fucked?" Milquist asked.

"Then we double-time it back to the freeway perimeter."

Sanchez looked startled. "The fuck? What about calling in a bird to pick us up?"

"All airborne assets are on priority missions. We sit tight until our scheduled evac, or we walk out. Those are our choices."

"We could take a car," Drake said.

"Negative. As of ten-hundred hours, any civilian vehicles seen in transit are to be disabled."

"That's fucking bullshit!" Sanchez retorted. "We can flash an IR signal, or a flare or some shit."

"That's the way the fucking world works right now, Private. Do I make myself clear?" No one else commented or raised an objection. "Okay, keep your sectors clear and move with a purpose."

The squad gathered their shit before heading down the alleyway and into the chaos of the city.

CHAPTER 9

The truck made good time through the streets. The unrest was spreading to the suburbs, and they drove past crowds of infected crazy people attacking screaming innocents. Police and soldiers ignored the truck, focusing their attention and firepower on the howling masses that fell upon them, shrieking and ripping at their living flesh.

"This is insane," Callie said for the fourth time since they had left the downtown area.

"I've seen worse at motorcycle rallies," Minty said and swerved around another multicar pileup.

"How much further to the junkyard?" Callie asked.

"Not much further. The fast route was blocked off," Minty reminded her. Callie remembered the scene. An army blockade on the freeway. Cars that had tried to get too close lay torn open and burning. An army helicopter had swooped down, and machine gun fire had stitched a line of small craters through the concrete ahead of their vehicle. Minty had done a hard turn, slewing the truck around and almost rolling it. They wasted no time in getting the fuck out of there and now found themselves driving through a suburban landscape straight out of a Romero film.

"An infection causing a fever that severe, it should debilitate anyone. The fever itself should kill the infection. It's why our body temperature goes up so damn much when we are sick." Callie didn't expect Minty to keep up with her thinking. There was so much going through her mind, if she didn't process it out loud, she would never get a handle on things.

"We have an infection that is transmitted by what . . . by bite? Contact with infected bodily fluids? The sick weren't sneezing or showing respiratory distress. Why not? Sneezing mucus would be a far easier vector for transmission. So assume it's a viral infection. It causes a psychosis, some kind of infection of the brain. You've heard of CJD?"

Minty shook his head.

"Creutzfeldt-Jakob disease. It's sort of similar to mad cow disease, but it takes years to manifest itself. This is happening fast. Full-blown symptoms within an hour? What's the prognosis? How long until the infected burn themselves out? They can't be getting sufficient energy from the meat they are eating. And how can they live with such massive injuries?" Callie pressed her hands to her face and gave an angry sigh. "Feel free to chime in with any ideas you may have," she said to Minty.

"Maybe God did it," he replied. "Maybe this is divine judgment. Maybe something in the food supply got mutated and started to fuck things up. Maybe the genetic engineering finally connected two wrong parts in a way that turned us all into time bombs. Maybe this is our one chance to decide where we really stand. Our one chance to make a stand, make a difference, and if we die, we die fighting for our most basic instinct. Survive so we can fuck enough and make the next generation."

"Survival of the fittest? The replication of our genetic material? Well, thank you, Richard Dawkins."

"Something I learned in prison: if you give up hope you will die." Minty lit another cigarette. "The situation you are currently in may be bleak as shit. But as long as you have something to focus on, you can get through it."

Callie gave him a long look. "What were you in for?"

"Which time?"

They drove on in silence after that. The helicopters flew overhead, but too high to cause concern.

"Hungry?" Minty said eventually.

"Starving," Callie admitted. Minty slowed and drove the truck off the road and into a diner parking lot. They climbed out of the cab and looked around. The place seemed deserted. A couple of semis were parked beside the diner, and the lights were still on inside.

"Stay behind me," Minty said and led the way. The diner was warm inside; the smell of fresh coffee and bagels and bacon set them both salivating.

"Anyone here?" Callie said loudly.

"Keep your damn voice down," Minty growled. He had left the gloves and hockey mask in the cab, but carried a baseball bat. A door clattered somewhere in the back. Minty hefted the bat and waited. A Chinese man in cook's whites came into view as he walked past the serving hatch on the kitchen side.

"He looks okay," Callie said.

"Morning!" Minty called and leaned the bat out of sight against the counter. A pot crashed down in the kitchen and the swing doors flapped open.

"Good morning! What we get you?" The Chinese cook beamed, handing them two menus plucked from a stand.

"Coffee, and then . . ." Minty scanned the menu. "The works plate."

"Coffee, wheat toast, and jam on the side. No butter," Callie said.

"No problem!" The cook tapped at the register. "Twelve dollars," he said. Callie looked at Minty.

"Can you get this?"

"Sure." Minty pulled a roll of bills from his pocket and peeled off a twenty. "Keep the change."

"Sorry, no waitress today. She no come in to work this morning!" The cook shook his head. "You take any table, I bring you food."

They sat in a booth overlooking the parking lot. Minty smoked and Callie stared out the window at the sun heating up the parking lot.

"It's a beautiful day," she said.

"If you say so."

"You no smoke in here," The cook said when he brought their food.

"How about you bring me an ashtray?" Minty replied.

"No smoking. State law. You smoke outside now."

Minty shrugged, dropped the butt on the floor and crushed it.

The food was good and hot. They ate, he with fork loads of eggs, bacon, and fried potatoes one after the other; she with a delicate precision, never losing a crumb.

Minty sat back with a sigh and belched a long rolling call like a frog deflating. "Hey, fella, how about a refill on the coffee?" They were still the only customers in the diner, so the cook brought more.

"Phone not working. I pay bill. Can't even ring phone company to say why phone not working," he told them as he poured the coffee.

"There's trouble in the city. People are being told to stay at home today. Didn't you see it on the TV news?" Callie asked.

"I no watch TV. Radio all rap music and too-fast talking. I have jukebox. Elvis, he tell me all I need to know." The cook left their table and fed quarters into the Wurlitzer at the other end of the diner. Elvis started crooning and their host went back to the kitchen, singing along with the King.

"A guy like that could come out of this completely unscathed," Callie said wistfully.

"Or he could end up dead and have no idea why. Come on, let's get moving." Minty stood up; Callie swallowed the last of her coffee and followed him. They stepped out into the warm morning air as a truck and trailer unit trundled into the parking lot with a hiss of air brakes and a low rumble of a sequential downshift. The rig stopped and a squat man in jeans and a sweat-stained T-shirt hopped down.

"Goddamned motherfuckers!" he yelled.

"Stay behind me," Minty said quietly. "What's up, mister?" he called to the driver. The guy advanced on them.

"Eighteen thousand pounds of shrimp! Eighteen goddamned thousand pounds! Goddamned motherfuckers!"

"Never been that keen on seafood myself," Minty said, nodding.

"You being a smart-ass? I will fucking kick your ass if you are, boy!" The driver came up to Minty's chest. He was bowlegged like a cowboy, his torso thick and sagging with beer and long hours in the saddle. When the biker didn't respond, the driver seemed satisfied. "Goddamned roadblock. They've sealed off the damned freeway! How in the hell am I supposed to deliver my goddamned load of shrimp with the goddamned motherfucking roads closed?!"

"They?" Callie ventured.

"The goddamned motherfucking army!" The driver stamped his booted foot and slapped his thigh with a baseball cap.

"It's just the freeway. There are other roads out of town," Minty said.

"An' every goddamned motherfucking one of them has a goddamned motherfucking army blockade on it!"

Callie and Minty looked at each other. The concern was evident on her face.

"I suggest you head on inside and get yourself some breakfast. The cook in there, he does a nice plate of bacon and eggs."

"You don't think I know that? Hell, I been coming here for seventeen years! Every goddamned motherfucking week! This is the first goddamned motherfucking time that I have not delivered a refrigerated load. Someone is going to get their goddamned motherfucking ass kicked!" The rig driver was purple faced and spitting in his apoplectic fury.

"Good luck with that," Minty said and led Callie back to their truck.

Back on the road they flicked through the radio stations, but they were all off the air. The recorded message about staying home and conserving supplies was the only transmission they could pick up. Minty switched it off again and they drove on, winding their way through side streets and avoiding military vehicles, wandering groups of the bloodied and insane, and the fleeing survivors.

Lucky's salvage yard seemed to be under siege when the truck arrived and stopped outside. Harleys of all shapes and models drove up and down the road outside the fence. Inside, bikers stood around drinking beer and talking in small groups. The smell of barbeque filled the air.

"Who are all these people?" Callie asked Minty.

"Hell, these are just the other chapters. Jethro put out the call last night. Got them all to come on in and bring their brothers." Minty grinned. Jethro had an army of the baddest sons of bitches around standing with him now. Let those crazy crackhead motherfuckers come out to this part of town. These guys will destroy them.

They left the truck out on the road; there was no room inside the fence for a vehicle that size anymore. Walking to the gate, Minty shook hands and was clapped on the back by everyone they passed. Most of the new arrivals were Locusts he hadn't seen in a year or more. Callie felt relieved to see that her escort was so well respected. A beer was thrust at him and everybody greeted him warmly. Minty didn't stop, though he acknowledged everyone and knew their names.

Inside the yard, a hundred bikers had gathered with their women and some kids. Everyone was armed: pistols, clubs, knives, machetes, semiautomatic rifles, and shotguns. A table had been set up under a tarp and a production line was making Molotov cocktails.

Minty found Jethro in the boardroom of the clubhouse. The leaders of seven chapters from five states were sitting around the table. Jethro stood at one end, preaching to them.

"You see now how the government has failed us. They are cordoning off the city. They are closing down all lines of communications. They are quarantining the uprising. Why do you do that? You do that if you are trying to contain the uncontainable. A war has begun here, brothers. Right in our metropolis. This city is going to be ground zero for the real revolution. Nothing can be achieved by words or peaceful protest. We must meet force with force! Armed resistance! Take what is ours by right of conquest!"

The men around the table pounded its surface with their fists in a thunderous applause.

"We are with you, man!" someone shouted.

"The first thing we must do is know our enemy. There is an infection loose upon this city. A plague sent by the government to destabilize and terrify the population. People faced with an enemy that could be a friend or family member will give up their freedom in order to have salvation. The federal authorities are counting on that terror. They have unleashed an act of terrorism upon us! But we will not be cowed! We will destroy anyone who is infected. We will break the government's vanguard. Let them know that we will not be frightened by their freaks! This is our time! This is our anarchy!" The applause exploded.

Jethro waited till the noise subsided. "You have your assignments, you have my message. Freedom is yours, but you have to get out there and take it!"

Minty stood aside as the room broke up. The chapter leaders all greeted him with the same warmth as the bikers outside. They looked Callie over too, curiosity evident in most of their faces.

"Welcome home," Jethro said to Minty. "You brought her back with you."

"Yeah, we went through town. The situation is worse. It's pretty much complete shit. Whatever set those people off, it's spreading."

Jethro raised a hand. "I know. We have had reports of rioting and attacks on civilians from every part of the city. The government-sponsored plague has a purpose. A percentage of the population is infected. They create terror. The rest of the population gives up their last freedoms, reliant on the protection of the state."

"There is no evidence that this is a government plot!" Callie spoke up.

"Doctor Blythe isn't it?" Jethro drawled. "You worked in a big hospital. Right in the epicenter of the outbreak?"

"Yes, but we had nothing to do with it. We are the primary care facility for a massive population. Statistically if there is a disease outbreak, it would appear to begin there simply because people come in to the hospital with early symptoms. Your friend is a classic example of that." Callie looked to Minty for support. He lit a cigarette and made no comment.

Jethro smiled. "Open your eyes, Doc. This is our chance to bring about real change. We can make something new here. We can steal the opportunity from the government and brand the future with our own legacy."

Callie looked him straight in the eye, her expression grim. "You have to survive the present first."

CHAPTER 10

The all-terrain tires of the Hummer rolled along the concrete roadway. Jessie wasn't speaking to Todd; she'd curled up in the passenger seat and now stared grimly out the window. She'd accused him of abandoning her, and demanded to know what she would have done if the bikers had killed him. Todd felt cocky after his encounter with Tag and his band of nomads. They belonged to some interstate biker community that called themselves the Locusts. They thought Todd was a cop killer. That carried a lot of weight with these guys. They respected him for that.

After about a minute of Jessie screaming at him, Todd turned around and slapped her. He didn't mean to hit her in the face. He meant to slap her in the arm, the same one she was hitting him with. Instead, with a resounding crack, he hit her across the cheek. The pink print of his palm had faded now. But the hurt and shocked look on her face still lingered.

He wanted to say he was sorry. He wanted to beg her for forgiveness, but he was a cop killer and that meant never saying you were sorry, especially not to some cock-teasing bitch like Jessie.

The bikers led them through back streets and past empty factories. They saw plenty of rioters. The crazy people seemed to be spreading out, looking for something else to destroy, Todd reckoned. They turned and followed the convoy, maybe a hundred of them, but all were left in their dust.

The clock on the dashboard said it was 10:00 a.m. when they heard the helicopter. The others they had seen were flying high and going somewhere. This one buzzed overhead and then immediately banked and came back around. The sunlight glinted off the glass cockpit. Todd thought it might be an AH-64 Apache. It had pods with slots in the front mounted on stubby wings and a square shape to the chassis.

The chopper settled in the air, its face angled down toward the oncoming pack of motorcycles and the Hummer at the rear. Todd saw a flash come from the front of the bird and then dust kicked up in a line, bursting down the road toward them. The sound came a fraction of a second later, a thudding *chunk-chunk-chunk* noise. The bikers were already splitting up, careening their Harleys out of the oncoming stream of bullets. Todd and Jessie watched in horror as the line of dust cut through a motorcycle, detonating it in a fireball, sending the rider tumbling like a broken doll.

Jessie screamed. Todd yanked on the wheel of the Hummer. The tires screeched and the loaded truck bounced off the road and onto the cracked sidewalk. The chopper roared past and vanished for a moment as it flew behind a warehouse.

Four bikes lay torn and burning along the road. The rest were circling, the riders waving and yelling at each other.

"Get us out of here!" Jessie shrieked. Todd noticed the sliding sheet metal door covering the delivery access to the building across the street. Driving forward, he turned the Hummer to face the street. Putting it in reverse, he floored the gas and rammed the truck backwards. The door boomed and ripped away from its runners. The vehicle bounded backwards into an empty warehouse shed the size of a small hanger. Leaving Jessie screaming, Todd leapt out and ran to the doorway.

"In here!" he yelled at the bikers. The chopper drowned out his second shout, coming in from the south on the same attack angle. This time rockets fired from its stubby wings. Explosions tore apart more motorcycles and cratered the roadway. The remaining bikers took off, some driving under the chopper as it flew past. Seeing Todd waving, they turned sharply and skidded to a halt inside the warehouse.

The helicopter made another pass, and the M230 auto cannon mounted in its nose opened up again. A steady *chunk-chunk-chunk* of cannon fire pulverized the concrete road. A wounded biker fired a full magazine from his pistol into the chopper's armor before the cannon's stream of death disintegrated him. Of the two dozen who rode a few minutes before, only ten had made it into the warehouse. The helicopter flew off. Everyone stood in silence, listening for its return.

"What the fuck was that?!" Tag suddenly roared. "Are we not law-abiding citizens exercising our constitutional rights to travel the roads without harassment from fucking helicopter gunships?!"

"Shit on me," The blond biker with the neck tattoos said. "They tore the shit outta us, Tag."

"No fucking shit!" Tag yelled. "You!" He pointed a finger at Todd, his eyes blazing with fury. "You! Cop-killing motherfucker!" Todd winced. Tag was going to kill him. Tag was going to blame him for the unprovoked attack by the helicopter and would stab him and then they would all rape Jessie. *Fuckfuckfuck.*

"You saved our fucking asses!" Tag seized Todd by the shoulders and shook him. "You are a fucking miracle!" Todd blinked. Tag started laughing. Then the rest of them joined in. They clapped him on the back so hard it hurt. Rough hands tousled his hair and he tried to grin through it.

Tag set the survivors to pushing the door back up over the empty space in case of a return patrol. Todd opened up the Hummer and unpacked a cooler filled with soda and chocolate bars. The bikers drank the soda and complained about it not being beer.

Jessie got out and announced she needed to pee. They found a bathroom near an office and Todd had to stand outside while she went in and used the facilities. He listened to the laughter of the bikers. The sudden attack had become a joke now. They were retelling it, all sharing their versions of how their brothers were taken down and laughing at the faces and the crazy antics. Todd didn't know how much of it was true. From what he saw, no one had died in any way that could be seen as funny.

Jessie came out of the bathroom. She'd been crying and pressed back against Todd when he hugged her.

"It's going to be okay, baby. I'm going to get you to Vegas and we'll get married. I promise."

Jessie lifted a tearstained face and said, "I don't want to go to Vegas. I wanna go home."

"We can't go home. You wanted to run away. If we go back now, John will kick the living shit out of me and your mom."

Jessie paled at the mention of her latest "father." He was a cold-blooded asshole.

The bikers worked on their machines and drank more sodas while bitching about the lack of beer. The warehouse stank of piss as they relieved themselves in the corner. They helped themselves to the various firearms Edward had packed and regarded some of the homemade melee weapons with interest. Tag gave the order to mount up as the sun was going down.

The bikers grabbed their new weapons. Todd drove the Hummer out, then looked both ways and up into the sky. The airspace was clear, but the street had started to fill with the rioters who they passed hours before.

"Tag!" Todd yelled back into the darkness. "We got a bunch of freaks out here!"

The motorcycles fired up and poured out of the warehouse, making a noise like the sky falling. The freaks hissed and snarled, while the ones with their legs intact began to run toward the group. Tag leveled a .50-caliber Desert Eagle semiautomatic pistol at the fast-approaching freak. The gun boomed and its head exploded.

"Head north!" Tag shouted. "We'll be right behind you!"

The other bikers unloaded their guns into the approaching rioters. They discovered that a body shot didn't stop them. A shot in the leg only slowed them down. The headshots, they counted, but the remaining freaks were almost on them when they learned this lesson, and the bikers were running low on ammunition.

A slavering woman, her drool spraying like a slashed artery, leapt and knocked a fat biker off his ride. Hollering, he punched her in the face. She caught his fist in her teeth and bit down hard. He bellowed in pain. Clawing at her with his other hand, he ripped chunks of hair and scalp off her head. The woman just bit harder. Blood gushed into her mouth and drove her into a frenzy. The other bikers fought from the back of their bikes. The rioters leapt at them, bloody saliva spraying through clenched teeth, the heat of their fevered bodies burning so hot the air almost shimmered around them.

"Get the fuck out!" Tag yelled. The bikers hesitated; none of them had ever backed down from a fight or bailed on a brother. But there was something deeply wrong about the mob attacking them. Tito went down, squeezing the trigger on an MP5 that had spewed its full magazine into the belly of a fat man who didn't even pause in his rush to tear at Tito's tanned hide. Shots rang out thick and fast. Pistols, shotguns, and a few automatic weapons tore chunks of bleeding flesh from the rioters. But they kept on coming.

"We ride! Now!" Tag yelled. The remaining Harleys roared and headed up the road into the gathering dusk. Riding around the wreckage and the craters in the road, they left the remaining freaks to follow along at their own pace.

The bikers caught up with Todd and Jessie a few blocks further along the road. Todd wound down the window for Tag.

"Jethro is waiting for us. Jethro will show us the way," Tag said. Todd wondered who Jethro was and couldn't wait to meet him.

CHAPTER 11

The steady chatter of M4 rifle fire drew more rioters down on their position. Sanchez suggested engaging them with knives and bayonets. It was grim and bloody work, but faced with insane terrorists with cannibalistic tendencies, the soldiers got on with doing what they had been trained for. Destroy the enemy. Use every means at your disposal to put him down. Break his will, destroy his ability to fight back. Complete the mission even if it kills you.

The soldiers hacked, stabbed, and bludgeoned the waves of fevered flesh that hurled themselves at the steadily retreating group. They had fought every step of the way, two hundred meters from the nondescript office building that was their next target position.

"One hundred meters to Bravo point," Dukes said over comms. Using the butt of his rifle, he smashed a teenage girl's face in. She spewed blood on his boots and toppled forward. He risked a shot and splatted her brains over the sidewalk.

"Keep it moving, people!" With the gas masks and full NBC protection on, the microphones inside the masks were the best way to communicate. The heat of the day was building, and the full gear was heavy and stinking hot. Sweat stung Dukes' eyes as the gas mask filled with pools of sweat and the glass fogged up with the sauna of his breath. He wouldn't take his mask off. Not if whatever was affecting these people was a pathogen transmitted by air or bodily fluids. Dukes would sooner die of heat exhaustion than take a breath of unfiltered air.

They fought on, smashing and tearing their way through the growing crowd. *Infected*—that was how Dukes thought of them now. *Diseased*. It made it easier to kill them. Like maybe a bullet would be a mercy.

Two female freaks grabbed Drake while he was reloading and he went own. The first one tore his mask off. The second one ripped chunks of his face away with her teeth. Drake, the kid from Rhode Island, screamed, twisting and spraying blood. His teeth glistening through a lipless mouth like he was snarling.

Dukes shot him through the head and then killed the two women. With the fight raging around the squad, they could not stop to recover the body of their fallen comrade this time. Gunfire, the claustrophobic heat of the masks, and the unending onslaught of the raging rioters meant they fought or they died.

A car engine roared and tires screamed. A florist van skidded sideways through the blood-maddened crowd. The side door slid back; a small figure with a blue bandanna tied across his face was crouched in the back. "Come on! We gotta get out of here!" he yelled.

A hundred freaks were advancing from all sides on what remained of the squad. "Get in the van!" Dukes hollered into his comms unit. "Stay sharp! We do not know the status of these people!"

The soldiers broke and ran, weapons ready, to the van. A quick check inside and Sanchez waved the others in while he covered their escape.

"Get in the van, Sanchez!" Dukes yelled, emptying his magazine in a series of single shots that took out four more freaks.

Sanchez dived into the back of the van and rolled to his feet. He fired past Dukes, who ducked and ran, jumping the last few feet as the bandanna-wearing kid yelled, "Go, Maria!"

The van took off with the tires squealing. The door slid shut and the air was filled with the stink of hot blood and the panting of the soldiers lying on top of each other.

The florist van drove fast, weaving through crashed cars and around obstacles. The driver swerved to avoid larger groups of freaks and ran down lone ones at forty miles an hour, breaking bones and spraying blood as they were cast aside. Walburn shuddered and sat up. Dukes recognized the symptoms of panic and struggled to get close enough to grab the private. Walburn tore his hood back and pulled the mask up onto his head. He panted, gasping for air, the sweat streaming off his face.

"Put that mask on, soldier!" Dukes yelled.

"Can't-can't breathe in it. I think the filters are gummed up with shit and blood," Walburn wheezed.

"Kid's okay, Sergeant," Sanchez spoke up and nodded at the boy crouched at the back of the van. The blue bandanna wouldn't stop a pathogen, Dukes realized. But would their gas masks?

The rest of the squad pulled their hoods back and lifted their masks.

"I'd rather die fighting than suffocating, Sergeant," Garrett said as he gasped for air.

"Fuck," Dukes muttered and pulled his hood off. The air inside the van was stifling, but it felt cool compared to being under the protective film of the NBC headgear. The mask slid off and he finally wiped the sweat from his eyes.

"If we get an officer showing up, tell 'em I gave the okay to take the masks off," he warned. Five sweat-stained and grimy faces grinned back at him.

"Thanks for pulling us out back there," Dukes said to the driver. She turned her head, a fine-boned Latina face, black hair pulled back in a ponytail. Her eyes were large, warm, and brown as chocolate.

"You are welcome," she said, turning back to watch the road. "I hope you can help us now," she added.

"Depends on what you expect us to be able to do."

"We have family, friends, and some neighbors. They are trapped in their apartment building. We are not sick, or crazy. We have not gone loco like these people. You can help us get out of the city."

"You should stay in your homes. This situation is being contained."

"That's bullshit, man!" The kid with the bandito bandanna blurted. "People are going crazy!"

"The army is taking action to suppress the terrorists. We will be back in full control of the city within twenty-four hours." Dukes remembered Drake's screams and the way his head came apart when the sergeant shot him. *Yeah, we are in complete control.*

"My brother is right, this is complete bullshit. Whatever madness is gripping these people, it is spreading. You and your men will die with the rest of us if we stay here."

Dukes swallowed hard. "Vehicles aren't safe anymore. We need to travel on foot. How many civilians do you have in your group?"

"We have no civilians," The Latina woman replied as she spared him a quick glance. "We have sisters and brothers, grandmothers and grandfathers, aunts and uncles, women and children."

"How many?" Dukes asked again.

"Forty," The woman said.

"They all mobile? They can walk?"

"Some are old and frail, others are just babies. They can be carried," she said.

"Then they will die," Milquist said from the back of the van.

Dukes shot him a look. "At ease that shit, soldier."

"He's right," Sanchez said, not looking Dukes in the eye. "We need to keep moving. We need to head to the nearest perimeter and report on what is happening. This situation is beyond the intel briefing. The chain of command needs to be advised."

"They will be," Trow said. "We are supposed to secure ourselves and observe."

"Trow, shut up. We are among civilians," Dukes said.

"Like they give a fuck!" Trow kicked the steel side of the van. "We lost people out there, Sergeant. We had friends get taken down and fucking eaten!"

"Shut the fuck up, soldier." Dukes rolled to his knees and grabbed Trow by the jaw and they swayed as the van turned a corner. "You are professional soldiers, so fucking act like it. Remember your training and you will get out of this alive." He released Trow and moved back.

"Sergeant, it's ten twenty. We need to be away from this vehicle," Walburn spoke up. Dukes took a look out the front. The road was clear, almost peaceful.

"How much further to the apartment building?" he asked the driver.

"A couple of blocks up and one block over," she said.

"Pull over, we need to walk."

"Why?" She looked fearful at the idea of being a pedestrian out there in a city being overrun with the infected.

"The military are flying air missions over the city. Any civilian vehicles seen moving after ten o'clock are to be destroyed."

"Oh Jesus," The woman replied. She leaned forward and scanned the sky, looking for airplanes.

"They will come in helicopter gunships. They will be armed with rockets and chain guns. They will shred this van and anyone inside it. They will find you. They will not miss. You, your brother, and all of us will die if we stay in this vehicle." Dukes spoke plainly. There was no way to sugarcoat it.

The van skidded to a halt, and the woman turned and shouted at her brother to get out. He pulled the side door of the van open and stumbled out into the morning sun.

"Move out, squad!" Dukes pulled his NBC hood and mask on and followed the troops out of the vehicle.

"Which way?" he said to the woman, his voice muffled by the heavy mask. She pointed and with the squad covering every approach they started walking in that direction.

"What's your name?" Dukes asked her as they walked.

"Maria," she replied.

"Common name I guess," he said. Maria shrugged.

"What is your name?"

"Sergeant Dukes."

"Was Sergeant your father's name?"

"No, my first name is Kyle, my dad's name was John."

Maria looked sideways at him and smiled.

"What is happening? The army must know," her brother said.

"If they do, they aren't telling me," Dukes replied. He had orders, and until ordered otherwise he would be as ignorant as the civilians they were now escorting.

Milquist's transmission crackled in Dukes' ear: "*Sergeant, we have a bogey, six o'clock, eighty meters.*"

"Do not engage unless it attacks," he replied.

"What's your name?" Dukes asked the boy.

"Carlos. It was my father's name and his father's name."

"How old are you, Carlos?"

"Twelve. Maria is eighteen." Carlos grinned like he had confessed a great secret.

"I'm nineteen in a couple of months." Maria wouldn't look Dukes in the eye.

"We'll do everything we can to make sure you get to your birthday party," Dukes said. *Great, now I sound like a recruitment poster.*

"Have you killed many people?" Carlos asked.

"Not many, and only when I had no other choice." Dukes didn't feel comfortable talking about his experiences in war. Afghanistan had been the hardest.

"Carlos, you don't ask him those kinds of questions," Maria chided.

"Why not? I want to be a soldier when I'm old enough."

"Why not go to college, become a doctor or something?" Dukes asked as they walked.

"Doctors don't get to go to war and protect America," Carlos announced.

Dukes had a flash of the platoon medic, Donny Sanderson, up to his elbows in the blood of screaming men. Sanderson did more to protect

America than the rest of the platoon with their rifles and grenades. When an IED had detonated and torn his legs off, the minute it took Sanderson to die was the longest of Dukes' life. "Sometimes they do," Dukes said. "Sanchez, give me a sit rep."

Sanchez's transmission came through in a steady rhythm with his breath as he walked. *"We're being followed. They aren't close enough to charge. I think they can't see so good, or can't tell we aren't like them."*

"Copy that. Keep your eyes on and watch the sky as well."

"Will they send helicopters to rescue us?" Carlos asked.

"Maybe." Dukes knew that the only birds flying now were gunships. Maria looked at him, the fear in her eyes making him walk faster.

The squad reached the next corner. Dukes crouched and took a long look at the street ahead. He saw nothing but abandoned cars and a scattering of bodies lying torn and bloodied in the road. Somewhere a dog was barking. A shrill, angry sound muffled by imprisonment behind a door it could never open.

"Clear ahead," Dukes said into his mic. "Follow my lead," he added and stepped around the corner, scanning every doorway and vehicle for movement.

CHAPTER 12

The biker convoy rolled down the empty road as the sun went down and the shadows grew long. Chain-link fences on each side warned that trespassers would be prosecuted. Industrial sites, workshops, heavy trucks, auto-repair and body shops all stood silent. The thudding bass note of the Harley engines echoed off the walls. They rode in a wedge formation, spread across the road, and Todd followed them at the wheel of Edward's tricked-out Hummer. The junkyard fence started at the corner of a large wasteland block. A totem pole had been erected on the corner, twenty feet high and made from salvaged car parts crudely fashioned in caricature of Native American spirit totems.

Outside the fence a street party of sorts was gearing up. A bonfire of burning trash and oil threw thick shadows against the evening sky. A crowd of rough-looking bikers were riding and drinking and fighting. Women screamed in mock fear and slapped at groping hands. White smoke from spinning tires mixed with the cigarettes and joints that passed from hand to hand. Into this near rioting crowd the convoy descended. Bikes were backed into a line and parked up. Todd stopped in the middle of the street and killed the engine. Jessie pulled her knees up and hugged them tight to her chest. The roughhousing going on out there reminded her of the shark tank at SeaWorld during feeding time.

Todd grinned. "Fuck yeah! C'mon, Jessie, let's get out there." He reached for the door handle when she grabbed his arm.

"No, please. Let's just go. Vegas, remember? We're gonna go to Vegas and get married in one of those Elvis chapels."

The boy watched the girls dancing under the spray of foaming beer, tight T-shirts turning translucent under the amber liquid. "Sure," he said. "We'll get on in a bit." Todd ignored Jessie's demands and slid out of the Hummer. Slamming the door behind him, he walked up the road, grinning at the party animals slaking their thirst and lust in the light of the bonfires.

Todd found Tag with a woman under his arm and a bottle of whiskey in his hand. "Cop killer," Tag said, and offered the bottle. Todd hesitated a moment and then took it. The liquor burned his throat and stomach and then filled his limbs with warm caramel. He handed the bottle back.

"Wanna fuck her?" Tag said. Todd shrugged, not sure if the biker was referring to the woman burrowing into his side or commenting on Jessie.

"We were thinking we would head on out to Vegas," Todd said.

"The fuck?" Tag said, pushing the woman away and leaning forward.

"Vegas, me and Jessie. We're getting married."

"Well goddamn." Tag spat on the ground and took a long draw from the bourbon bottle. "We gotta give you a goddamn bachelor party before you fuck off into the wild-blue fucking yonder." Tag put an arm like a railroad tie made of meat around Todd's narrow shoulders. "Come and meet the rest of the family," he said and walked Todd past the bonfire and into the darkness beyond.

Jessie watched Todd vanish into the crowd and swore under her breath. It had started getting cold in the Hummer. She climbed into the backseat and opened the bag she'd stuffed with a few changes of clothes the night before. This wasn't how she had imagined running away. *Eloping with Todd,* she reminded herself. She loved him. He was nice, and kind and caring. But she had lied about how old she was, and these people terrified her.

Pulling out a light jacket, she twisted into it and sat there with her arms folded, glaring at the dancing heathens around the fire. They had no business messing with her and Todd. Out there, in the drifting smoke, music started. Todd was out there, getting tempted by other women and alcohol. She could see it in her mind's eye. Women who would let him do everything he wanted. Women with experience that meant they weren't afraid. Women who were old enough to know what they wanted.

Jessie grabbed the door handle, filled with an urge to bring Todd back to where he could look only at her.

Something wet slapped against the window. Jessie screamed and squirmed backwards. A bloodstained face smeared its torn lips against the mesh. A man, the top of his scalp flapping like a loose toupee, banged his raw fingers on the window. Clawing at the metal wire he snarled, red foam splattering on the glass, and Jessie screamed again. The bikers had stripped the weapons from the Hummer, leaving her defenseless as torn fingers curled around the mesh and ripped it away from the driver's side window.

Other freaks came into view, pounding on the windows and panels, rocking the vehicle and ricocheting off it to blunder onward into the circle of firelight and partying bikers. A shout went up, and then a gun went off. The air exploded into a popping staccato symphony of gunfire and yelling. The freaks moved toward the firelight—a crowd of them, enough to climb over the bonfires and tear at the living flesh of the drunken crowd beyond.

Jessie scrambled into the driver's seat. The key was in the ignition— she twisted it and pumped the gas. The big engine roared into life. The girl slipped her seat belt on and put the vehicle in gear. The Hummer leapt forward; a line of bodies cracked and toppled as she drove through them. Under the heavy wheels skulls burst, and the tires glistened with blood. The gore dripped down the mud flaps and left a wet trail in her wake. A burning woman ran screaming and flailing at the air in front of the truck. Jessie didn't have time to swerve or brake. The woman came apart when the brush guard mounted on the grill hit her.

Outside, chaos reigned. The infected howled and tore at the living. People screamed and fought against the enraged onslaught. Jessie looked for Todd and steered around the knots of bodies that were using fire, guns, and metal bars to defend themselves. The bikers were backing up, herding the women and a few children behind them through a large gate into the junkyard.

On battlements at the top of the sheet iron and barbed wire fence, others fired into the advancing mob with rifles, pistols, and shotguns. Spotlights jabbed ghostly fingers through the smoke and stroked over the confusion. Jessie rolled the window down and screamed "Todd!" into the twilight of smoke and shadows.

A slavering freak grabbed at her, his fingers gripping the mesh covering the window. He yanked the mesh away, falling back and under the wheels.

Someone jumped onto the Hummer's running board. Jessie shrieked and swerved left.

"For fuck's sake!" The passenger bellowed. "Get inside the fence, you dumb bitch!" He reached in and jerked the wheel to the right. Jessie beat at the stranger's hand as the vehicle swung in a wide circle. The truck rode up on the pavement and bore down on a thick crowd of rioters who came on through the burst remnants of the bonfire, scattering glowing embers and burning trash across the road. Jessie put her foot down and the truck ploughed into the infected crowd. They howled and pressed forward, a thickening wall of smoldering clothes and bloody flesh. The biker on the running board cursed and scrambled up onto the roof of the cab.

Jessie leaned away from the open window as hands thrust through the gap and clawed at her face and hair. Screaming, she twisted the wheel again. The Hummer turned, wheels squealing on the slick asphalt, and tilted up on two wheels. The biker on the roof let out a yell and scrambled onto the side of the vehicle that was now pointing toward the sky at a forty-five-degree angle. Wrenching the passenger door open, he leaned back like a sailor on a yacht in a gale. "Hold it fucking steady!" he yelled and after an agonizing moment the truck shuddered and dropped back onto all four wheels.

The biker fell to the road and rolled. The crazies outside the junkyard fence turned and charged at this unprotected source of meat. He came to his feet and ran after the vehicle. Jessie slammed on the brakes. Wrenching the transmission into reverse, she came hurtling back. The biker twisted aside and then jumped on the running board again. He pulled the passenger door open again and slid inside as Jessie skidded to a halt; the soft crunch of bodies being mauled by the rear of the truck sounded muffled to her ears.

"Drive in there." The biker pointed and she nodded. Roaring forward, the Hummer plunged through the open gate. The bikers on the other side pushed it shut and barred the entrance against the remaining rioters. Hands pounded on the steel gate and torn shadows milled in the light of the dying fire.

Jessie brought the Hummer to a halt. Her hands clenched on the wheel, her breath coming in tight, asthmatic wheezes from her chest, her blank gaze staring into the distance.

"My name's Freak," The biker said. "Welcome to Lucky's Salvage."

CHAPTER 13

The residents of the Oasis Apartments complex were gathered in the communal courtyard, the late morning sun beating down on their upturned faces. The surviving members of Dukes' squad crouched at the gate, covering the street. Dukes himself spoke with authority to the frightened civilians, pausing regularly to allow Maria to translate his words into rapid Spanish.

They asked questions, mostly in rapid-fire Spanish and translated by Maria.

"No," Dukes replied. "I don't know when help will be coming. But it will be coming." He sounded more reassuring than he felt. Picking up noncombatants was not part of their orders. He had no business risking his mission and his assets by playing fucking Mother Teresa to the locals. They should be moving on to the next checkpoint and contacting the tactical operations center—what all soldiers simply called the TOC—with an update.

Milquist came hurrying back from the gate. "Sergeant, we have Tangos coming around the corner."

"Do they have our position?"

"I don't think so. They're just wandering around. It's like they're looking for something to fuck up."

"We need to move to site Echo and make contact for an extraction," Dukes said quietly. "Get the squad ready to move out."

Milquist nodded and ran back to the waiting troops. Maria folded her arms and glared at Dukes. "You are going to abandon us here?"

"You need to secure yourselves in your homes. There is no risk to you if you stay off the street."

Maria swore in Spanish. Dukes watched her steadily until she had finished. "You know I'm right. Out there, it's a war zone. In here, you have water, security, and your people. Once the situation is brought under control, an evacuation and medical assessment team will come through and help you."

"I hope they have plenty of body bags," Maria said. "We may all be dead by then."

"I cannot help you," Dukes said firmly.

"No, you *will* not help us. You are making this choice. You come here! You are the US Army. We trust you to protect us. Carlos thought you were heroes coming to save us and now? You leave us behind?" Maria threw her hands up in disgust.

"This city is full of people who are in the same situation. If I take you, your friends, and your family out there, you will be in real danger. There is a high likelihood that someone will get seriously injured or die."

"If you do not help us, we will die. Those people will get in here and they will kill all of us. You have seen what they can do. Please, take Carlos with you at least."

Dukes looked into Maria's eyes for a long while, then turned on his heel and marched back to the gate. She stood silently watching him go. The soldier reached the gate and tapped Sanchez on the shoulder.

"Find me a vehicle. A bus, a truck, something large enough to move all of these civilians."

Sanchez exhaled smoke from his cigarette and looked at him, one eyebrow raised. "You sure you want to do that, Sergeant?"

Dukes checked his watch: eleven-hundred hours. "Be back here in fifteen minutes. With or without transport." Sanchez nodded and slipped out the gate, vanishing into the sunlit haze.

The sergeant walked back to Maria. "I've sent Specialist Sanchez out to look for a bus or a truck. He has fifteen minutes. You need to know that there are helicopter gunships flying around up there. If they see a moving vehicle, they have orders to destroy it. If Sanchez doesn't find a vehicle that can take all of you, you will return to your homes and barricade yourselves in. Are we clear?"

"We are not afraid," Maria replied.

"You're not scared because you have no idea what you are going in to. You tell your people if they leave here with me, they follow my rules. They will obey the orders given by me and my men. They will move fast and keep track of each other. Anyone goes down or falls behind, they are on their own. We will not be going back for stragglers."

Maria nodded. Dukes could see the fear dancing in the corner of her eyes, but her grim determination masked it well.

The squad watched the street from cover. A few dazed rioters stumbled past, missing the huddled civilians in the courtyard. Dukes watched the sky, looking for surveillance aircraft and helicopter gunships. So far, so clear. Sanchez returned as the sergeant's watch ticked over on fourteen minutes. The city bus Sanchez was driving had some badly smashed panels down the driver's side, but seemed to be rolling okay. The door hissed open right outside the gate. "I've got crazies on my tail! Move!" Sanchez yelled from inside.

"Everyone, on your feet and get on the bus!" Dukes barked.

The civilians gathered themselves, their young, and the few possessions they were carrying and hurried on board. "First Squad, mount up." Dukes followed his men onto the bus. Rioters were flowing up the street toward them in a rising tide of enraged humanity.

"Milquist, keep an eye on the sky. Sanchez, get us out of here." Dukes took up a position near the front of the bus and pulled a folded map from a pouch on his webbing. The heavy vehicle ground forward, slowly picking up speed. The first rioters bounced off the flat face of the bus fender, and others closed in from all sides. A hundred blood-soaked faces, caked in dried gore, stared up at the meat trapped inside.

"Turn right," Dukes ordered, his eyes scanning the map.

"Roger that," Sanchez replied. Twisting the wheel, he sent the bus careening around the tight corner. Smoke from a burning car blew across the street ahead.

"Pick up speed, Sanchez," Dukes said. "We can try and bust through anything in our way. Stay on this street for . . . three blocks, then . . ."

"Where are we going, Sergeant?" Milquist asked.

"Get us back to the perimeter. We'll get a medevac for these people and get the intel to the TOC."

"Colonel Byrd is gonna shit a brick when he hears about this," Sanchez said without taking his eyes off the road.

"Colonel Byrd can eat a dick. This is my fucking mission and his fobbit ass can eat shit and die," Dukes said.

A gasp from behind him made Dukes turn his head. A young girl, maybe seven years old, sat in her mother's lap and stared at him with eyes as wide as saucers. Her mother's hands were clamped firmly over the girl's ears.

"*El diablo va a tomar las almas de los que maldicen*," The woman scolded.

Sanchez grinned. "With all due respect, Sergeant, the colonel is gonna be all of our problem."

"I'm taking responsibility. You get this fucking bus back to the fucking line. Do I make myself fucking clear, Sanchez?"

"Hooah!" Sanchez barked. Dukes ignored the attitude. Everyone's nerves were tight right now. They had already lost good men, and they risked losing a lot more.

"Sergeant, we have half the city on our asses." Walburn had taken a position at the back window, warily watching the sky for aerial attack and the street for infected rioters. He spat a stream of tobacco juice onto the floor.

"Which way?" Sanchez kept the bus moving at a steady forty miles an hour, and they were now bearing down on a tangled barricade of ruined and burnt-out vehicles.

"Ahh shit." Milquist scanned the map. "Go right! Go right!"

Rioters sprang over the cars, their clothes singed, burnt faces blistered and oozing bloody fluid. They threw themselves against the sides of the bus, leaving smears of gore down the windows as they bounced off. The civilians cried out in terror and the whispered murmur of prayer sounded up and down the bus.

Sanchez heaved on the steering wheel. The bus tires squealed and slowly turned. Dukes grabbed hold of a rail and hung on. The vehicle tilted, the heavy chassis bearing down on the suspension springs until they groaned.

"Hang on to something," Sanchez yelled as some of the passengers cried out in terror while the rest prayed louder. The bus skidded around the corner; Sanchez spun the wheel, the passengers almost flying out of their seats.

"Keep us on the fucking road, Sanchez!" Dukes yelled. Rioters shrieked and howled as the bus roared past. They reached out and had their arms shattered and torn off. Bodies spun around and crashed into the sidewalk.

"Sergeant!" Walburn yelled, but Dukes only nodded. He'd seen it too. In a swirling cloud of smoke and dust, an AH-64 Apache attack helicopter broke the horizon view out the side window.

"Whadda we do, Sergeant?" Sanchez's eyes were wide as he kept glancing toward the approaching chopper.

"Stop the bus!" Dukes yelled. The Apache was turning in a slow circle to come at them head-on. On all sides of the bus the crazed rioters were closing in.

"What are your orders, Sergeant?" Sanchez and Milquist were looking at Dukes.

"Walburn! Get the emergency exit open. You and Trow watch the rear and get the passengers out. Secure a building and barricade yourselves in! Garrett, Milquist, Sanchez, give them cover."

Milquist pushed the button on the door controls and they hissed open. Dukes stepped out and scanned left and right. A dozen rioters lunged out of the smoke. The soldier squeezed off a three-round burst, the final round punching a hole through a charging man's head. "Go!" Dukes yelled and crouched beside an abandoned car at the side of the street. His rifle fired steadily, headshots dropping the snarling mob.

Sanchez bailed out the front door. The passengers at the front of the bus followed him.

"No, go back, out the back!" Sanchez waved and started shouting orders in Spanish. The panicked civilians surged forward, knocking Sanchez aside.

"Let 'em through, Sanchez!" Dukes could see they had mere seconds to evacuate before either the crazies or the Apache swooped down on them. Passengers tumbled out of the bus from both ends. At the rear of the bus, bursts of gunfire and screams told Dukes the rest of the squad were engaging the rioters. The whining shriek of a helicopter's turbine filled the air. Then came the *whoosh* of Hydra rockets and the shriek of 30mm chain-gun fire.

"Down! Down!" Dukes yelled. A giant fist of hot air picked him up and threw him over the hood of the parked car. He rolled into shelter against the front of a building as glass rained down and chunks of burning bus smashed into the concrete around him.

"First Squad! Report!" Dukes shouted into his mic, the ringing in his ears drowning out any immediate response.

The air filled with smoke and fire as the Apache passed overhead in a rhythmic thudding of turbine-driven rotors. The crowd bearing down on Dukes had mostly disintegrated in the rocket attack, though a few blackened amputees writhed on the ground, teeth glowing white through the charcoal of their faces.

Voices babbling in Spanish came through the smoke, and then over the noise Milquist yelled, *"Sergeant, you copy?"*

"I copy, Milquist. What's your situation?"

"Couple of civilian casualties, and Trow's hit."

"Is he still alive?"

"Yeah, Sergeant. He's a tough hombre."

"*Sergeant,*" Walburn cut in. "*We've got multiple freaks closing in on our position.*"

"Get to cover, Walburn. Secure a position and get the civilians inside," Dukes replied.

"*No can do, Sergeant. Nowhere to go. We're going to have to fight our way out.*"

"Hold your position. Take your time and aim for the head. I'm coming from behind on your left." Dukes double-timed it down the side of the burning bus. Dropping to one knee at the rear, he scanned the street ahead. Lots and lots of civilians, all moving toward the remains of his squad and picking up speed. Sanchez, Garrett, and Walburn were laying down a steady stream of fire. Trow lay propped up against a parked car, an emergency field dressing pressed against his crotch with one bloodstained hand.

Dukes pulled the pin on a smoke grenade. The colored smoke would tell the helicopter crew that friendlies were down here in their strafing line. The hissing grenade rolled into the street, green smoke gushing from it in a streaming cloud.

For every rioter that fell, two more came rushing forward. Dukes took stock of the civilians. Maria was huddled with other survivors on the ground on the other side of the burning bus. Carlos looked terrified but wasn't crying. Dukes gave him a quick nod.

The sergeant spoke into his mic. "Okay, this is what we are going to do. Walburn, you take point. We keep going the way we were headed. Making our way back to the quarantine perimeter is our best chance. We have what we came for. Let's hope it's enough. Sanchez, you and Milquist flank our civilians. Keep them moving. Keep them together, and keep them safe. Garrett, you're with me. We'll cover the rear."

"Sergeant! Chopper's coming around!" Sanchez half rose from his crouch and then twisted around to stare at Dukes. The whites of his eyes showing stark against the dirt on his face.

"Move, people! Right side of the bus. Then straight up the street. Walburn, on point. Go!"

Walburn kept low and ran up the side of the bus. The rioters were closing in. Milquist, Sanchez, and Dukes resumed fire, dropping half a dozen men, women, and children who shrieked and frothed at the mouth as they approached.

"Sanchez, get these people out of here!" Dukes shouted. Sanchez reassured the civilians in Spanish and got them on their feet. "Milquist, get Trow and move out!"

The late morning sun gleamed off the AH-64 Apache's cockpit glass as it dived in on an attack vector. The 30mm chain gun tore the road into dust and concrete chips. Dukes backed up, his rifle firing steadily at the approaching horde, taking out one crazed rioter after another. Garrett was crouched on one knee, sighting down his rifle, firing single shots with calm certainty. The Apache's chain-gun rounds sprayed through the crowd and Garrett rocked to his feet, tossing his last grenade into the center of the heaving crowd before running back to take a position next to Dukes at the corner of the bus. The rioters heaved forward through the marker smoke as the Apache howled overhead. A second stream of chain-gun rounds tore into the advancing bodies, tossing them into the air and ripping them into bloody chunks and red haze.

Milquist got Trow on his feet. The wounded soldier was limping badly, barely conscious, his weight bearing down on the smaller man. Milquist heaved his comrade onto his shoulders in a fireman's carry and jogged after the retreating civilians.

Dukes emptied a magazine and ejected it. Spent shell casings clattering around his feet, he slapped another magazine into place and released the bolt, chambering a round before he aimed down the sight. Squeezing off another single shot, he took his time, calmly dropping the rioters who were now coming at him at a brisk trot. Garrett paced him shot for shot. The stink of cordite and blood filled the air.

The Apache came back around and tore a wide swath through the crowd, thinning their numbers by half, tearing limbs off and shredding others with chain-gun fire. The chopper flashed overhead, now climbing again. Dukes took the moment to slap Garrett on the shoulder. "We are leaving!" Leaving the smoldering bus behind, he took down two more rioters who lunged at him with blood-soaked mouths and ragged wounds in their chests and throats.

"*How we doing, Sergeant?*" Milquist's voice crackled in Dukes' ear.

"Apache strafed the Tangos. Garrett and I are moving out. How's your progress?"

"*We are moving steady, Sergeant.*"

"My last order still stands. Secure a position where the civs can barricade themselves in. We can send evac for them once the situation is contained."

"*Fuck, Sergeant, this shit is a long way from being contained.*"

Gunfire sounded from up the street. It echoed off the buildings, sounding loud and close in Dukes' ear.

"What's going on up there, Milk?"

"*We're taking fire, Sergeant. Single-shot weapons and handguns. Permission to return fire?*"

"Negative. Find cover and try to talk to them. Clearly they aren't infected."

Milquist muttered something and disconnected. Dukes and Garrett moved down the street. From behind them, the howls of the rioters grew louder as they massed again.

CHAPTER 14

Sergeant Dukes risked a glance around the corner of the building. A shot rang out immediately, shattering concrete an inch away from his face and showering him in cement dust.

"Third floor, second window from the left, copy," he said.

"Mark," Milquist replied from behind him.

"This is Sergeant Dukes, US Army! I am ordering you to cease fire immediately!" Dukes waited until the barrage of small arms fire launched in response to his shout tapered off.

Sanchez's voice crackled in Dukes' earpiece. "*We got rioters closing in, Sergeant.*"

"Roger that, Sanchez. Stay out of sight and move back to our position."

"*Sanchez out.*"

The civilians were crouched along the wall of the building behind Dukes and Milquist. Trow sat with them, leaning against the wall, white-faced and pressing his hand against the seeping wound at the top of his thigh.

Sanchez had taken cover, keeping watch back along their trail. Walburn lay facedown and unmoving out in the street. The shooters had ambushed Dukes' squad and their civilian baggage, cutting Walburn down before he had a chance to make cover.

"We got no more time for this bullshit. Milquist, put a grenade in their laps."

The soldier stepped out with the M320 launcher attachment on his M4 locked and loaded. The stubby barrel belched a puff of smoke and with a soft *thunk*, the heavy explosive slug arced across the street and vanished through an open window as Milquist ducked back into cover.

A second later they heard a dull *whumph*. The breeze of the explosion swept over the squad. Dukes poked his head out; smoke poured from the building and no more shots were fired.

"Clear," he announced. "Take the civilians and head around the back. I'll recover Walburn and follow you."

Milquist nodded. He got the civilians moving down the wall of the building toward the distant corner where Garrett crouched, covering their advance.

In a quick dash across the street, Dukes scanned the windows looking for movement, the glint of steel, or the flash of a shot. Barely pausing his stride, he grabbed Walburn's limp body by the back of his body armor and started dragging him back to cover. The bullet had hit Walburn in the neck. Dukes collected the dead man's short-chain tag. Lifting the second tag on the long chain around his neck, Dukes pried Walburn's mouth open and pushed the tag past the dead man's teeth. He noted that Walburn had gone down and stayed down. Whatever was affecting the civilian population didn't seem to be giving Dukes' men immunity to bullets.

With the tags secured for graves registration and recovery, Dukes stripped the soldier of his ammunition and weapons before moving on to check on Trow.

The soldier was pale, his breath coming in shallow pants, and his eyes barely flickered when Dukes shook him by the shoulder.

"How we doing, Trow?"

"I feel like shit, Sergeant," Trow whispered.

"Getting shot will do that to you."

"Damn bus bit me." Trow's eyes rolled up in his head as he passed out again. Dukes lay the soldier down. Sanchez had already stripped him of weapons and ammunition. Medevac would be a long time coming. In the quarantine zone they were on their own, at least until he reported the mission complete. There seemed little chance of that now, with rioters closing in and the target positions overrun.

"On your feet, Trow. We have a way to go." Staying here would get them both killed.

Sanchez came running in, keeping low and ducking from abandoned car to doorway. "*There's a crowd thirty seconds behind me, Sergeant,*" he transmitted.

"Roger that. Move up to cover Milk and Garrett." Dukes staggered under Trow's weight as he got the soldier to his feet. Trow moaned and the sergeant felt fresh blood seeping through his fatigues.

"We're walking, Trow. One foot after the other. Just like your momma taught you."

Looking ahead, Dukes saw the last of the civilians vanishing around the corner. Sanchez ran up and took a position next to Garrett watching the intersection.

"Come on, Trow," Dukes said, picking up the pace. The soldier stumbled, his feet dragging.

"*Sergeant,*" Sanchez warned. "*You're going to have to leave him, man.*"

Dukes didn't respond. He could hear the shrieks and howls of the enraged freaks crashing into the intersection they had just left. With any luck, Walburn's body might distract them for a few precious seconds.

Garrett's voice came over the comms. "*Can't get a shot past you, Sergeant.*"

"Hold your fire, you'll just attract attention. Get out of sight. Your priority is to find a secure position for the civilians."

"*No can do, Sergeant. You've got a crowd of those fuckers coming up your ass.*"

Dukes felt his skin crawl. He had lost too many men today to abandon Trow to the ravening mob. The wet gurgling of their bloodlust became louder. The click and slap of shoes and bare feet against the concrete sounded right on his heels.

"Fuck!" Dukes let Trow slip to the ground. Spinning and lowering to a crouch in one movement, he leveled his M4 and fired a round into the face of a man in a torn police uniform.

"Semiautomatic fire only," Dukes ordered as a burst of covering fire came from behind him. Supplies were limited and the enemy was not.

The street filled with the infected, all hungry and screaming for his blood. Dukes fired again and took down a fat woman who skidded on her face to within a few inches of Trow's feet, a spray of broken teeth spilling out of her mouth like candy corn.

Dukes reached out with one hand and dragged Trow backwards by his combat webbing.

"Sergeant." It was Trow, but Dukes could barely hear him over the noise of the rioters. The wounded soldier's hand came up and grabbed his wrist. Dukes glanced down. Trow held a grenade in one trembling fist.

"Fuck 'em all, Sergeant," he whispered and let go of Dukes' arm.

Dukes dropped Trow's webbing. Stumbling back, he shot the first freak to reach for him, then turned and ran for the corner. The flash and roar of the grenade split the air behind Dukes a few seconds later. He threw himself flat and felt the blast pass overhead. Scrambling to his feet, he joined Sanchez and Garrett at the intersection. All three soldiers charged around the corner and ran for their lives. Milquist had the civilians moving at a steady pace down the street. The three remaining squad members ran after the straggling group.

"Milk! Pick up the pace. We have Tangos inbound." Milquist looked back and then scooped up one of the younger kids, settling her on his hip as he encouraged the others to run.

"Sergeant, Apache." Garrett was looking back and skyward as he ran.

"Sonovabitch," Dukes swore. No time for a friendly marker smoke grenade.

"Get off the street! Apache inbound!" Dukes yelled at the group ahead.

The group broke, running blindly past crashed cars and drifting trash.

"Milk! Left side!" Dukes gestured at a solid stone building, maybe a bank or a library. Either way, it looked strong enough to hold everyone and keep them safe.

The Apache came in on its first strafing run. Dukes flicked a strobe light on and prayed the chopper crew would see the friendly signature flashing.

The helicopter twisted and laid rows of hot death down the street where the crazed rioters were advancing in a murderous rush. The air filled with the hot copper stench of spilt blood and the burning smell of heavy weapons fire.

"We should signal them for extraction!" Garrett yelled.

"Civilians!" Dukes yelled back. Evacuating Maria's people would be tricky, even with a Blackhawk summoned to aid their escape.

Dukes herded the survivors up the wide stone steps of the towering building. The gold lettering on the glass frontage said it was the First Capital Investment Bank. Garrett tried the door, and to Dukes' surprise, it swung open.

"Inside." The civilians didn't need telling twice; they bustled through the doors and gathered in a terrified group in the banking lobby.

"Secure those doors," Dukes ordered, scanning the stairs and balcony above for the infected.

Garrett snatched up a line stand and jammed it into the door handles, effectively barring the exit.

"We can still get out this way in a hurry, but it should slow down anyone coming in," he reported.

Dukes nodded. "Sweep and clear this place. Keep everyone away from the windows."

The squad moved out, leaving Garrett and Dukes to herd the civilians.

"Okay, everyone, quiet down." Dukes raised his hands and made lowering gestures at the noise of crying and sniffling. "We need you all to move into the building. The soldiers will find some office space where you will be safe. Then we will get some food and water distributed."

The thudding roar of the Apache helicopter swung overhead and then faded as the chopper moved away. In the sudden silence Dukes took a long, slow breath. The civilians sank to the floor, holding each other and watching fearfully as the soldiers moved around them. Within minutes the building was confirmed clear. The upstairs offices were empty, having been vacant since the end of business the previous day.

Dukes ordered distribution of water and rations to the civilians. Milquist jimmied a vending machine open and loaded up the kids with candy and soda.

They kept quiet, fearing discovery by the marauding mobs outside. While they rested, the sound of helicopters passed overhead, though none of them hovered over the building.

"Sergeant, how long we planning on staying here?" Sanchez asked from his overwatch position at the mezzanine-floor window facing the street.

"Oh-five-hundred. Then we move out, leave the civilians with food and water. Keep them secure."

Garrett's voice cut in on the comms channel. "*What about the mission?*"

"Mission is still active. We just have to get to an evac point. Then we can request a medevac to this location once we report back to the TOC."

"And if they salute an' say fuck you?" Garrett asked softly.

"We burn that bridge when we get to it," Dukes replied. "Now get the civs tucked in. Sanchez, you and I are on first watch; Garrett and Milk, get chow. This day is a long way from over."

CHAPTER 15

"You left Trow with a grenade?" Dukes asked Sanchez when the last of the civilians had been escorted to a back room office.

"He didn't want to get eaten, Sergeant."

"Trow gave us the time we needed," Dukes replied. "He died right."

"Hooah," Sanchez replied and went back to watching the shambling crowds that moved in a restless tide up and down the street outside.

The remaining hours of the day passed slowly. Dukes and the three survivors of his squad were used to waiting. They each caught a few hours sleep and rotated guard shifts, at least one soldier guarding the civilians and another watching the street out front. Whatever fury gripped the rioters still simmered. They moved constantly, like hungry animals looking for something to eat. Whenever anything moved that wasn't one of them they exploded into furious action, catching and tearing apart the occasional dog, cat, or civilian that strayed too close.

"You think that intel is going to tell us what happened, Sergeant?" Milquist asked around three in the morning.

"I guess so. The TOC made it clear that the intel was the priority."

"If it ain't worth shit, then our buddies died for nothing," Milquist replied.

"Soldiers never die for nothing, Milk. They die protecting people like those holed up in the back, they die trying to complete fucked-up missions like this, but most of all they die for the guys to their left and right. Trow died covering our asses. He died giving us a fucking chance to get out of this alive. So how about you don't waste the chance that your buddy gave you. I know I plan on making the most of it."

"It ain't worth shit if we're all dead and they get stuck inside the quarantine perimeter," Milquist said.

"Then don't fucking die," Dukes snapped.

"*Hooah*," Milquist replied.

Dukes dozed fitfully for the next two hours. Sleeping in a war zone was always a challenge for him. Out of the shit, he would sleep like a baby. On a patrol or a mission like this one, he was too amped. Too wired for the slightest sound or change in the environment.

When Garrett crouched down next to him, Dukes' eyes were already open and alert.

"Oh-five-hundred, Sergeant," The private reported.

"Roger that. Make ready to move out in two minutes."

Garrett nodded and slipped away to where Milquist watched the street.

The squad merged at the front doors of the bank. Crouching low, they made an estimate of the numbers outside. The passing hours of night had done nothing to thin the crowd.

"How about we distract them?" Garrett asked.

Sanchez grinned. "Sure, Garrett, get your ass naked and run down the street. The few it don't kill on sight will surely follow you."

"Fuck you, man," Garrett replied.

"Both of you, shut the fuck up," Dukes said.

"Anyone got any cigarettes?" Sanchez asked. The others shook their heads.

"There's too many of them, Sergeant," Milquist reported.

Dukes nodded. "I believe you may be right, Milk. We're going to have to find another way out of this box."

"This is a bank, right?" Sanchez asked.

"Not really," Milquist replied.

"It says it's a fucking bank. Right there on the fucking door." Garrett pointed to the gold lettering on the glass panels in front of them.

"I can read, asshole," Milquist snapped. "It's not a bank, like where you go in and cash your fucking paycheck or stand in a fucking line waiting for a fucking fag to tell you that your fucking loan application is declined. This is one of those big money banks. They do it all with computers and shit."

Garrett frowned. "Fine, fuck you anyway."

Dukes looked away from the street. "What's chewing your ass, Garrett?"

"Nothin', Sergeant." Garrett scowled at Milquist.

"So quit your fucking bitching," Dukes replied.

"There's a fucking garage in the basement," Garrett said. "We could check it out and find a fucking truck or something."

Milquist gave a snort.

"How the fuck do you know that, man?" Sanchez asked.

"There's a sign on the wall in one of those back offices, next to the stairs. Says garage on it."

"Garrett, take Sanchez and check the stairwell. If you find anything, come back and let us know."

"Roger, Sergeant." Garrett stood up, Sanchez on his heels as they headed deeper into the bank.

"You think there's anything down there?" Milquist asked Dukes.

"No fucking idea," Dukes replied. "The basement should have been checked and cleared in their initial sweep."

"*Hooah,*" Milquist nodded.

"Cover," Dukes ordered and ducked down as a wandering group of infected shuffled up to the glass doors.

"You think they know we're in here?" Milquist whispered.

"They would be breaking the doors down if they knew."

The two soldiers watched from cover for another three minutes. The crowd outside butted against the doors, snapping and snarling against each other.

"We're cool," Dukes said. "They can't see us."

The silence shattered with the muffled chatter of gunfire from inside the building. The infected outside the door went still and then the entire crowd turned and stared intently at the glass doors.

"Fuck," Dukes said.

⚜

Garrett covered the door to the stairs while Sanchez reached out and turned the handle. The door swung open onto darkness and the cold concrete of stairs going up and down.

Garrett tapped on his helmet light and activated the rail light on his M4 before ducking through the doorway. His rifle swept up the stairs and then down, checking for movement in both directions. With his back to the wall, he sidestepped down the first flight of stairs. Sanchez followed, again checking above and below as he shadowed Garrett to the next landing.

One more flight of stairs down, they came to the door that led to the basement parking lot. Their lights illuminated the darkest space under the stairs. Both soldiers' weapons tightened in their grip as the bright beams reflected off the pale skin of a man in a suit.

"Down on the fucking ground," Sanchez barked. "Eyes down, spread eagle. If you so much as look at me I will waste you, motherfucker. We are not kidding around here. We are United States soldiers and we are here to help you." The man cowered back into the corner, his leather shoes skidding in a pool of spilt blood.

"Is he infected?" Garrett asked. "Are you bit?" he asked the man.

Something thudded against the door beside the two soldiers. They leapt back, rifles jerking from covering the blood-soaked man to the shuddering door.

"Help me! Please! Help!" a muffled voice screamed through the door.

The man in the suit whimpered and burrowed deeper into the corner.

"Get his ass out of there, man," Sanchez ordered.

Garrett let his rifle hang loose from his single-point harness and grabbed the suit by his feet. Walking backwards, he hauled the man out of the corner as he howled like a baby.

"He looks okay," Sanchez suggested while covering the pathetic figure.

"Can you walk?" Garrett asked. "If you don't get up and walk out of here, we will leave you behind. We do not have time to play games with you, motherfucker."

The man rolled onto his hands and knees, snot and drool dripping from his face as he wept.

Garrett watched him with an expression of disgust. "Fucking useless," he said. Garrett grabbed the suit by the arm and jerked him to his feet.

"Let's go," he said and frog-marched the man up the stairs.

Sanchez took one last look at the door. The screaming voice behind it could be male or female. But the choice had been made, and they would live with it.

Emerging into the hallway on the first floor, Sanchez heard Garrett yell, "Back off, motherfucker!"

The suit was grappling with Garrett, pushing him back and howling like a madman. Garrett smashed the man's nose with the butt of his rifle, knocking the drooling crazy back.

As the man bounded up again, Garrett fired, two shots, both in the head. The man dropped and lay still.

"The fuck happened, man?" Sanchez asked.

"Fucker went fucking crazy."

"He musta been bit." Sanchez covered the corpse with this weapon.

Dukes and Milquist appeared around the corner, sweeping the corridor with their rifles.

"Clear!" Sanchez yelled.

"The fuck happened?" Dukes asked as they came together over the fresh corpse.

"Civilian, downstairs, went nuts. Garrett had to put him down," Sanchez explained.

"Fuck me," Dukes muttered. "Did you find anything in the basement?"

"Door's closed and someone was beating on it. We brought this guy up. He was okay till we got here," Garrett said.

"Sergeant," Milquist warned from the corner. "We gotta move. Fuckers are coming in hot. They're going to breach the doors soon."

Dukes turned to Sanchez and Garrett. "Get your damn asses downstairs. Open that fucking door and find us a way out. Move!"

The two soldiers headed downward. The sounds of the front doors breaking could be heard clearly now.

"What about the civies?" Garrett asked as they double-timed it down the first flight of stairs.

"They aren't mission critical," Sanchez replied.

At the bottom of the stairs the door shuddered and cracked as something hit it from the other side. The latch pushed out of the frame. A heartbeat later the door was struck again and it flew open.

Sanchez and Garrett opened fire, shooting the figure that lunged at them out of the darkness.

Blood and bone splattered across the walls. The infected thing shrieked and flailed as the rounds punched holes in its chest and neck. The body fell and Sanchez fired a last round into the convulsing figure's head.

"Switch to NVG," Sanchez whispered. Garrett killed his lights and flicked the AN/PVS-14 night-vision goggles on his helmet down, then turned the spring-loaded wheel to the IR setting. The 14s emitted an infrared beam and gave him a clear view to three meters in darkness. Now prepared, he ducked through the door. Sweeping the space beyond, he waved Sanchez through. The darkness of the underground parking lot lit in a bright green. Two armored cars, used for transporting high volumes of cash, were the only vehicles parked here.

"Check that the fuck out," Sanchez breathed, waving a hand in Garrett's peripheral vision. A bank vault stood open in the concrete wall. Marked by a circular door at least five feet thick and as tall as the two men, it opened on to the secure parking lot for the armored cars to make deliveries of cash. Blocks of currency, bundled in plastic wrap, were stacked up on pallets inside. A load of cash had been torn open and piles of notes lay in a deep drift across the floor, stained with fresh blood.

"Fuck me . . ." Garrett stared at the fortune spilled out on the concrete.

They approached the vault, trying to make sense of the millions of dollars just lying there.

"Fuck me," Garrett said again. Sanchez sank into a crouch, checking the open vault for threats.

"You thinking what I'm thinking?" Garrett whispered.

"Sergeant would skin us alive," Sanchez said.

"Only if he found out," Garrett replied softly.

Sanchez licked his lips. Even a fraction of the money lying there would solve all his problems. Get his mom's house back from the bank. Put his niece and nephews through college. Shit, he could even stop selling blood for beer money before payday.

"Cover me," Garrett said, and stepped up to the ruptured pallet of cash. Tearing at the plastic, he pulled a bound stack of crisp notes free and stuffed it inside his assault pack.

"Hurry up, man," Sanchez whispered.

Garrett stuffed the bound wads of cash into his assault pack.

"Back up, my turn." Sanchez shouldered his weapon and snatched up blocks of hard currency. Packing them into empty ammo pouches and pockets, he moved as fast as he could.

A bloodied hand rose out of the crumpled storm of notes drifting across the floor and grabbed Sanchez by the boot.

"Tango!" he yelled, snatching his rifle into a ready position.

Garrett shouldered his own weapon, aiming for a clear shot. "Get out of the way, man!" he yelled.

"Fucker," Sanchez swore and squeezed the trigger on his M4. A single round punched a neat hole in the crazy's head. The body slumped back into the drifting pile of loose bills.

"Okay," Garrett said and scanned the underground parking lot outside the vault. "Okay. Now we get on those fucking trucks."

The two armored trucks were parked nearby and the driver's door on one of them hung open. A smear of blood across the floor suggested the driver had been pulled out.

"We gotta secure that vehicle, man," Sanchez said. Garrett went first, covered by Sanchez. They checked the cab of the first truck and took the keys out of the ignition. Opening the back door, they confirmed it was empty. They completed a sweep of the rest of the underground parking lot. The other armored truck was locked up tight, but they found no more infected or survivors.

They both spun around as the door to the stairs banged open. "Friendlies coming in," Milquist called from the other side of the door.

"In here, Milk," Sanchez yelled back. "Place is clear." He cracked a chem-light and shook it until the luminescence lit the area. He tossed it on the floor closer to the door.

Milquist came through the doorway and a stream of terrified-looking civilians followed him. They hesitated in the sudden gloom and deep shadows. Many reached out with spread fingers and wide eyes, trying to feel their way.

Up the stairs a loud boom sounded. A moment later Dukes came leaping down the stairs. "We clear?" he yelled as he hit the ground.

"Clear, Sergeant!" Milquist replied, pulling the last of the civilians through the doorway.

Dukes pulled the broken door closed and backed away from it.

"Vehicles?" he asked.

"Armored truck, Sergeant," Sanchez reported.

"Keys?" Dukes asked, still covering the door.

"Check!" Garrett yelled from the cab of the open truck.

"Get these people on board. Milk! The door to the street gonna open?"

"On it, Sergeant!" Milquist dashed into the darkness.

"Maria, get your people into the back of the truck."

The civilians moved forward under Maria's guidance. Sanchez had climbed into the back of the truck and was tossing heavy canvas bags out onto the parking lot floor.

"Exit's ready to go, Sergeant*!"* Milquist reported over the radio.

"Roger that. Now get your ass back here."

"No room!" Sanchez yelled. *"No hay espacio! No hay más espacio en el camion!"*

Dukes pushed his way through the crowd. "What is the fucking holdup, Sanchez?"

"We're full up, Sergeant!"

"So, open the second truck." Dukes glanced back to the closed door at the stairwell. Half of the city's infected would be coming through that door any minute now.

"We don't have the fucking keys," Sanchez said.

"Fuck." Dukes looked to the stairwell door one more time. It was moving.

"Squad, on the truck," Dukes ordered. "You people, back up! You need to stand over there!"

The civilians responded in a chorus of Spanish. They were talking so fast Dukes only caught about every third word.

He hopped up on the back step of the rumbling truck. "We will send help! You are safe here! Ahh, *vamos* ahh *ayuda.*"

The bodies pushing against the broken door managed to force it open. The infected crammed into the stairwell howled and blocked the gap with their squirming bodies.

"Shit," Dukes said. "Tangos inbound. Time to work."

Firing over the heads of the civilians added to their panic. Dukes and his men focused on the horde charging toward them. For every infected that fell, another would clamber through the gap. For an insane moment Dukes was reminded of a meat grinder. Chunks of bloodied flesh squeezing into a funnel and coming out in a stream of ground beef on the other side.

"Get in the vault!" Dukes yelled. The civilians pressed forward, reaching up, thrusting babies and themselves at Dukes. Desperate for a place on the last ride out.

Garrett's voice came over the comms. "*Sergeant, we are out of time.*" Dukes could see it. At the back of the crowd, the infected were tearing people apart. The air filled with the stink of weapons fire and hot blood.

He emptied a magazine. His last shot took out a man whose throat was being torn out by two others.

"*Squad secured, Sergeant,*" Milquist announced over the comms.

"Get us out of here," Dukes ordered. The remaining civilians screamed and surged forward, everyone desperately reaching for the truck that started to roll forward without them.

Dukes pressed into the back of the truck, heaving on the heavy steel door until it swung shut, closing him in with the civilians and Sanchez.

"Where are the others?" Maria demanded. "Where are they?"

Dukes slid his helmet off and rested his forehead against the cold steel of the truck door. The screams from outside didn't fade until the vehicle was on the street and Garrett had them rolling.

CHAPTER 16

Todd stood staring down into the street. Infected people kept on coming, joining the monstrous crowd outside the Locusts' steel wall. He wondered if they were attracted by the noise, the smell, or some kind of crazy cannibal code. The space outside the junkyard was now a seething mass of angry bodies. The bikers had gotten bored watching them hours ago. The high wall of roofing iron, reinforced with car bodies and junk, kept the crazies at bay. The few who managed to start climbing got shot down. The rest seemed content to simply seethe.

"Morning, cop killer," Tag said as he appeared at the top of the ladder.

"Morning," Todd replied. Tag handed him a steaming mug of coffee. Todd wrapped both hands around warm cup. "Thanks."

"Where the fuck do they keep coming from?" Tag scratched a match on the corrugated iron battlement and lit his cigarette. He flicked the burning match out into the crowd below them. Todd watched it float down into the shifting sea of upturned faces.

"You been up here long?" Tag snorted cigarette smoke into the chill morning air.

"A while." Todd shifted on his feet. He'd been up here all night. The noise and the partying of the bikers had gotten to be too much for him. He was sure that the freaks outside were going to tear through the walls, climb up over the barricades, and rip him apart at any moment.

Up here at least he could face his fear and not let them take him by surprise.

⚔

Jessie woke up with a start and clutched a camouflage jacket around herself. She looked around in fearful confusion. Then the events of yesterday washed over her in a sickening wave.

"Todd?" she asked. It seemed clear that he wasn't in the truck. She unlocked the door and slid out, pulling the jacket on and zipping it up against the early morning chill.

Stepping around and over the sleeping casualties of the party from the night before, she crept into the two-level building and followed a sign to the bathrooms.

Coming out she shuddered. Finding Todd and getting out of here was the only thing she wanted right now. Outside, she looked around. Todd was nowhere to be seen.

"You hungry, Jessie?" Freak broke her reverie. Jessie glanced up at him and tried to smile.

"A little, I guess."

"Well, we've got toast, bacon, eggs, oatmeal if that's your thing. And the coffee is pretty good." Freak indicated the direction of trestle tables loaded with pots steaming in the morning air.

"Sally, a plate for me and one for my friend here," Freak said to a hungover-looking blonde.

"Here, hold this and I'll load you up." Freak shoveled food onto Jessie's plate. They got coffee and walked to a vacant spot on one of the picnic tables.

"I didn't get a chance to thank you for what you did last night," Jessie said quietly.

"Weren't nothing," Freak said, ducking his head and smiling. Jessie pushed beans around on her plate.

"What's going on, Freak? What is wrong with those people?"

"I dunno. What I do know is that they bite you, you end up like them. Crazy and pissed off and wanting to bite other people."

Jessie shuddered. "I'd rather die."

Freak looked up from his plate, "I won't let that happen. I reckon I saved your ass last night. Which means I've got a responsibility to look out for you."

"I have a boyfriend. A fiancé actually." Jessie felt embarrassed as soon as she said it. Todd hadn't saved her last night. This rough-looking boy with the cute smile had.

"Is that right?" Freak split a fried egg and poked it with a piece of toast. "Where were you two headed? That truck of yours looks like you were ready for World War Three or something."

"Vegas, we were going to Vegas. To get married. It seems like a week ago now."

"Time flies when you're having fun." Freak grinned and slurped his coffee.

"You call this fun?" Jessie swept her hair back and gave Freak her best smile. Freak grinned again, egg yolk and crumbs sprinkled on his lips.

"Hell yeah. This is the revolution, man. This is when the old system falls and the revolution truly begins."

"It's awful," Jessie said, shivering slightly in the morning air.

"It's freedom," Freak said and tapped a cigarette out of a packet on the table. He offered Jessie one and she shook her head. Lighting up he added, "You stick around and you will come out of this on top. You go heading off to Vegas or some other city, and you'll end up dead, or worse."

"You think we should stay here?"

"You should definitely stay here. Your fiancé can do whatever the hell he wants." Freak blew smoke in the air and sipped his coffee. Jessie pushed her plate aside and took the cigarette from Freak's fingers. She took a slight drag on it and tried not to choke.

⚔

Minty woke up with a snort. A warm weight stirred against him and he blinked in the darkness. After a moment, he slid out from under the blanket and set his bare feet on the concrete floor. The chill of the cement woke him right up, bringing on an urgent need to piss. Standing up, he shuffled out of the dorm and into the bathroom. It felt like heaven. Afterwards he splashed water on his face and stared into the streaked mirror. An old man looked back at him, lines of grey streaked through his hair and beard.

"You are getting too old for this shit," he muttered. Back in the dorm he found his boots, jeans, and shirt. He was buckling the jeans belt when the slim shape under the covers stirred and one lithe leg slipped into view.

"Morning," Minty said. The covers froze and then a tousled blonde head appeared over the top.

"Where am I?" Callie asked.

"The dorm. We partied hard last night."

"I don't drink . . ." she muttered, patting around the side of the bed looking for her underwear.

"So you said. Last night I mean. We were doing tequila shots by then."

"I need my clothes." Callie sat up, gathering the covers of the narrow bed against her naked chest. Minty conducted a quick search and found a bra, panties, jeans, and the borrowed T-shirt Callie had been wearing the day before. She slipped the underwear on without a glance in the old biker's direction. He tried not to stare, but in the dim morning light she looked as fit and fine as any woman he could remember being with.

"Did we . . . ?" Callie looked at him over her bare shoulder.

"Fuck? No. You took off your clothes and passed out. I put you to bed."

Callie blushed. "Jesus . . ."

"Some things you never get too old for," Minty muttered while lighting up his first cigarette of the day.

"What are you talking about?" Callie stood up, straightening her shirt and sweeping her short hair back off her face.

"Getting old and how to avoid it," Minty said, grinning at her around the Lucky Strike.

"You can start by quitting smoking." Callie took the cigarette and snapped it in half. She tossed the butt end into the shadows and crushed the burning tip under her shoe. "I think a cat crawled down my throat and choked me last night," she added.

"Coffee'll cure that. Coffee and a good breakfast."

Callie blanched, "I'll take the coffee. But the rest, I don't think I could . . ."

"Bathroom's that way." Minty stepped aside as Callie dashed out the door.

Her color improved by the time they got outside. He slipped a pair of dark glasses out of his pocket and offered them to her. "Thanks," she said and put them on, then quickly pulled them off, frowning at the lenses. "These are prescription?" she asked.

Minty snatched them back, his face coloring. "Sorry, wrong ones, try these." He handed her a second pair and she put them on with a sigh of relief.

"Morning, Minty; morning, Doc." A trail of people emerged from various sleeping places and queued up for breakfast in the yard. Callie watched the sheet-metal fence. The moans and snarls of the sick could be heard over the sounds of babies crying and the morning conversation of those inside.

"This is a nightmare. I want to wake up now," Callie said.

"It's not so bad," Minty said. "You're safe here. We have food, booze, friends, and no freak is going to get through that wall."

"The CDC and FEMA will be containing the outbreak. The city will be fully quarantined now. They will have emergency medical centers set up. They will need someone with my skills. I should try and find them."

"Doc, we saw the city yesterday. FEMA couldn't even save New Orleans from a hurricane and flood. What the hell d'you think they're gonna be doing about now?"

"They'll probably nuke us," a heavily tattooed guy said, half turning in the line ahead of them.

"They won't nuke an entire city. That's insane," Callie replied.

"FAE, fuel air explosive. Same bang, no radiation," Minty said.

"Either way we are fucked, man," The tattooed guy said.

"Jethro will see us through," a woman spoke up. Others murmured their agreement.

"Yeah . . ." Minty echoed, but didn't look convinced. They got their food, sat, and ate in silence. Callie nursed a large mug of hot coffee and refused offers of anything other than a single slice of dry toast.

Minty ate enough to stay alive for another day. The food here wasn't half bad. He'd had worse. In the joint, in the Marines, in any number of shithole diners along a thousand miles of empty highways. He lit a cigarette and finished his coffee. At the next table Freak was smiling at a young blonde girl. She didn't look like the usual half-burned young whores with cold junky eyes who warmed the beds of the club. An air of innocence hung about her, and she kept on glancing toward the high metal fence that shielded them from a view of the crazed freaks.

"Hey, Freak," Minty called. The boy's head jerked around. "Who's the tail?"

Freak actually blushed. "Uh, this is Jessie. She came in last night."

"Jesus, what is she? Sixteen?" Callie muttered over the rim of her coffee cup.

"Hey, Jessie, how old are you, girl?" Minty called across the picnic table. The girl swallowed hard and ducked her head. "Eighteen," she said and tried to glare defiantly at him.

"Bullshit." Callie twisted out of the bench seat and walked over to sit down next to the girl.

"Where is your family, Jessie?"

"At home I guess. I'm here with Todd. We're going to Vegas."

"They're getting married," Freak added, rolling his eyes.

"You can't be serious? How old are you? Really?" Callie said.

Jessie's chin lifted. "We love each other, we want to get married. Todd has a job, he will look after us and we are getting our own place."

"Yeah, Mom," Freak said, grinning. Callie ignored him and lowered her voice, leaning in close to Jessie.

"I get that you think he is the greatest guy in the world. He probably is. But you're maybe sixteen. You need to live a little, meet other guys, find out what life is really like. No one should get married so young. It's a guarantee of misery."

Jessie opened her mouth to respond, and then blinked and closed it again.

"I'm an ER doctor," Callie said. Then her voice dropped to a low murmur and she leaned in to speak privately to the girl. "Can I ask you, have you had sex with him? If he is pressuring you to get married so you can have sex, that's not cool."

Jessie flushed. "It's not like that. We love each other." Blushing, she clambered out from the picnic table and hurried off toward the main building. Callie stood up and followed her.

"Chicks, huh," Freak said with a sage grin at Minty, who just snorted in response and cleared the empty plates.

The sound of a gunshot rang out. Minty scowled and headed up to the ledge atop the wall overlooking the road outside.

The freak show had gotten larger overnight. Tag watched them with his usual frown, a .45 semiautomatic pistol steady in his hand. A clean-cut-looking kid stood beyond the biker, watching the crowd with an expression of intense focus.

"Morning," Minty said and flicked a cigarette butt over the wall.

"Hey, man." Tag didn't take his eyes off the moving mob below.

"Jethro is going to want a report," Minty said.

"Blonde chick, behind the fat man," The kid announced, pointing down into the sea of blood- and dirt-smeared faces. Tag raised the pistol and squeezed off a round. The shot was muffled by the snarling crowd, and one face among the hundreds came apart in a spray of blood and brain matter.

"The fuck are you doing?" Minty asked.

"Cop killer here reckons some of the crazies are dead. Like they should be laying down and getting body-bagged. But they're still up and walking around. We're shooting ones that shouldn't be alive."

"You got a reason for doing that?"

"If you were so fucked up that you should be dead, wouldn't you like someone to end your life? Quick and painless?" The kid asked.

Minty shrugged. Yeah he'd been there. Jethro had saved his life more than once during their tour of the assholes of the world. In those days Jethro's dream of the Locusts had just been late-night bullshit in a foxhole or a sentry post in some desert assignment.

"They don't seem relieved," he said after a moment's observation.

"They'd thank us if they could," Tag said with a grin.

"You eat?" he asked the boy.

"Not hungry. Thanks." Todd kept scanning the crowd of upturned faces. Each one turning to watch him as he moved along the narrow walkway at the top of the wall. Minty didn't think they would break through, but he wondered. The corrugated iron and old car chassis piled up against the fence were designed to withstand a full frontal assault from police SWAT units. That had never happened, and maintenance on the fence had been ignored for years.

"Tag, anyone checking on the fences around the back?" Minty peered across the crowded junkyard. Something wasn't right back there, beyond the rows of stacked car bodies and rusting parts. A sense of unease was growing in Minty's gut.

"I guess. Hey kid, the nigger with his jaw ripped off," Tag said.

"Dead, dead, dead," Todd agreed. Tag aimed and fired, the crack of the shot making Minty frown.

"You're just going to attract more of them," he warned.

"Flies on shit. Nothing else to do here." Tag grinned and saluted Minty with the gun. The older biker climbed back down onto the hood of a gutted Honda and then jumped to the ground. Walking through the people gathered for breakfast, he noted the number of women and children. Civilians, the families of the Locust chapters who had answered the call to rally.

"It's breaking out everywhere," a woman with a mewling baby nuzzling at her bare breast said.

The woman she spoke to nodded. "The radio says the army has it under control. But I got a text from my friend in Tucson yesterday. She said that people are going crazy and attacking each other in the streets there too."

"Is she okay?"

"I hope so. The phone went dead after that. I'm so glad Charlie made us come with him."

The voices faded as Minty walked inside. He unlocked a steel cupboard and took a .50-caliber Desert Eagle pistol from the collection of guns inside. He checked and loaded the magazine from a box of ammo on a shelf. A second loaded magazine went into his jeans pocket. He hesitated and then slipped an extra handful of rounds into the same pocket. Walking out of the clubhouse, he tucked the handgun in his belt and stepped around the first row of car bodies. It was a maze back here. Any sense of order had long since collapsed as Jethro became more invested in the business of drugs and gunrunning than managing an actual salvage yard.

He followed the twisted path, walking through the knee-high weeds pushing up through the oil-stained dirt and curling around the crushed and rusted skeletons of Japanese steel. The back fence came into view. This one was eight-foot-high mesh, topped with three strands of barbed wire. This far back through the strata of mechanical corpses, the makes were mostly American and the weeds were higher.

Minty paused at a stack of flattened Fords and Chevys wedged up against the fence. They were rocking as if pushed by an unseen hand. A snarling growl rose on the other side of the pile, and the stink of drying blood and shit came to him on the air.

"Motherfuckers," Minty muttered. Pulling the pistol from his belt and keeping low, he moved closer. He peered between the twisted pillars of metal until he came face-to-face with a lunging freak. The man's lips peeled back and blood gushed from his mouth as he slammed his face through a ragged tear in the mesh fence. Minty leapt back. The freak twisted its head and strained against the mesh snare around his neck.

Minty raised the gun and aimed down his arm. A single shot boomed and the freak's head jerked upward, the back of his skull spreading down his spine.

The corpse shuddered; then filth-stained hands reached and tore, yanking the body away. Fingers curled around the edges of the mesh fence and started tearing at it, desperate to get inside the fence and tear the life out of the warm meat inside.

"Fuck me," Minty swore. Backing away, he watched the pile of auto carcasses topple over and six slavering crackheads reaching through the widening tear in the fence. He fired the remaining five rounds, taking an infected out with each one. The last remaining freak snarled and the biker took to his heels and ran.

CHAPTER 17

Jethro's room was shrouded in darkness. Minty didn't bother knocking; he just barged in and started talking to the lumps in the bed.

"We have a problem. With the fence. Out the back. Freaks are breaking through."

Female heads emerged from the covers. Bleary eyed and mussed, they staggered out of the bed like the start of a bad joke: a blonde, a brunette, and a redhead.

"Jethro, for fuck's sake. Are you listening to me, man?"

The bed sighed and Jethro waved a dismissive hand. "Quit freakin', man."

"Fuck you. I am telling you those cracked-up motherfuckers are breaking through the back fence!"

"How many of them?" Jethro put his feet on the floor and lit a cigarette. His lean body was a writing mass of tattoos and scars.

"Enough. They've torn a head-sized hole in the mesh fence and pushed over a stack of wrecks."

"Anyone hurt?" Jethro pulled a pair of stained jeans on over the image of a dragon that coiled up from his knee to breathe fire onto his balls.

"Not yet, but we've got to get the women and kids inside and fortify the defenses."

Jethro stood up, exhaling smoke and setting his shoulders back. "We built this place to withstand any kind of assault. Pigs, soldiers, and even a crowd of insane crackheads."

Minty shook his head. "We need to get the back fence shored up. Get some guards on that sector."

"Sure, sure. Damn, Minty, we're not in the Haj now."

"Maybe not, but we're still in the shit."

Jethro pulled on a shirt and spread his hands wide. "Embrace the suck, brother."

"Fuck that," Minty said and stalked out of the room. Jethro had always been a leader. Even when they were in the Marines he had been an engineer, which meant he thought he was above the grunts like Sergeant MacInnes.

Outside, the last of the breakfast remains were being cleared away. Children ran around in the oil-stained dirt, shooting each other with finger pistols and shrieks of laughter.

Minty approached a group of three Locusts who were getting an early start on their drinking. "Hey, you guys packing?"

"Sure," They replied, showing the butts of pistols tucked in their belts.

"Come with me." Minty led them through the twisting maze of car wrecks. The sound of the freaks scraping and tearing at the mesh fence and steel barricades got louder as the sounds of children at play faded behind them.

The hole in the fence was larger, as was the crowd of raving and bloodstained faces gathering on the other side. The bikers drew their weapons and started shooting.

Shrieking faces shattered under the hail of bullets. The fence rocked as the mob frenzied, shaking and tearing at the mesh while guttural howls roared from a hundred bloodied throats. Fingers bled as the flesh tore from them, strips of skin caught in the diamond mesh. Minty and the three bikers fired until their guns clicked dry. Reloading, they fired again. Bullets blasted skulls open, sprayed brains, and smashed faces to pulp.

"We gotta get some more fortifications on this fence!" Minty yelled over the sound of gunfire.

"Get the forklift!" one of the shooters yelled. Minty nodded and backed away. The hole in the fence was growing. A woman pushed her way through the gap, slicing her skin and pissing blood from the long gashes the broken wires tore in her back and breasts.

Minty jogged back to the center of the salvage yard. The forklift was actually a tractor, a John Deere, with a front-end loader and forks attachment on it. He swung up into the saddle, turned the key, and pressed the ignition. The engine coughed, turned, and then roared into life.

Pulling the throttle, he lowered the forks and twisted the wheel before engaging the gear. The tractor rumbled forward and Minty navigated it through the gaps between stacked walls of car wrecks. A crowd of cheering kids followed, excited by the roaring thunder of the machine.

Driving through the narrow alleyways between car stacks, Minty couldn't avoid banging the tractor into debris and wreckage. The forks on the front of the tractor tore a silver gash in the rusting hulk of a crushed Ford truck and ripped the side mirror off the remains of a Pontiac Firebird. Reaching the back fence, Minty reversed and slid the forks under the toppled pile of crushed cars. Twisting the throttle, he pulled the hydraulics lever and the forks took the strain, lifting the slabs of twisted metal off the ground and tipping them back against the mesh fence. One of the infected thrashed in the noose of torn fence, shrieking and twisting until a car body slammed down on him, crushing his body into a red paste.

The bikers shooting into the crowd storming the fence had run out of ammunition. They backed up as Minty lifted a fresh load of stripped car chassis, and the back wheels of the tractor rose off the ground until he slammed it down on top of the growing stack. He worked until the barrier was two cars deep and stood as high as the forks could reach.

"Why the hell did they try busting in through there?" The bikers looked shaken, and Minty could only shrug in reply.

"I don't think they even know anymore. Completely out of their fucking heads," The second biker offered.

Minty gave orders from the driver's seat of the tractor. "I want you guys to arm up, then patrol the fence, all the way around. Do it in pairs. If you see any sign of weakness you come back to the yard and find me, alright?" The bikers nodded and ran ahead while Minty turned the tractor around.

"You kids, get the fuck back to your mommas!" he yelled. They hesitated a moment, then broke and ran.

Minty gunned the tractor back to the central yard, where Locusts were gathering on the concrete pad next to the clubhouse.

Jethro stood on one of the picnic tables, addressing his people. They raised their weapons and cheered every few seconds, and Jethro looked to be in fine oratory form.

Killing the engine, Minty climbed down. The three bikers he had sent to patrol the fence were stuffing extra magazines into their pockets and looked to have two more recruits for their mission. Looking over at Minty, one of them gave him a nod. He nodded back. They wouldn't fuck this up.

Jethro's voice rose again. "Everything we believe in has come to pass! The system has collapsed in on itself, and only those who are prepared to fight for their future and the future of their children will rise!" Another spontaneous cheer from the crowd. "We are prepared to fight any motherfucker who gets in our way! We stand strong and united! We are the cleansing plague! We are many! We are the Locusts!" They roared again. Women and children screaming in adulation along with the bearded, the leather-clad, and the fresh-faced probies.

"If we want to inherit the world, we have to keep it together! Believe in each other! Believe in the dream of the Locusts! Believe in what we can do!" The roar of the small crowd became nearly deafening. "Stay strong! Very soon the world will be ours for the taking! A new world order has dawned! This is the age of the Locust!"

Minty turned away sharply at the first gunshot. He drew his own handgun as more shots rang out. Jethro stopped evangelizing and frowned at the interruption. Mothers gathered children and men started moving to where they had stashed their gear and weapons.

The first of the fence patrollers came running out of the alleyways of wrecked cars. Blood streamed from a deep wound in his shoulder, the side of his face had been splashed with red, and his eyeball shone as white as a hard-boiled egg in the middle of all that blood.

A freak girl with long blonde hair, stiff with blood and gore, no older than a child, appeared on top of the wrecks behind him. The infected kid wore the bloodied remains of a pink pajama top and cotton underwear. She crouched there a moment and then lifted her head and shrieked as if the horror of it all had burned her mind to ashes.

The running man fell and lay still. Two of the crowd went to help him, and Minty swore and rushed forward. "Get back!" he yelled. "You get bit, you get infected with whatever it is that's fucking them up!"

The child screamed again, a fine spray of bloody saliva raining down and beading in the dust. With a savage howl she leapt. Minty smashed her in the head with the butt of his gun as she flew at him. The kid crashed into the dirt and sprang up, screeching and slashing with her filthy hands. Minty fired, and the bullet punched through the little one's forehead and blew out the back of her skull. Red gore and bone fragments splattered against the car wreck as she staggered and fell backwards.

The biker's hand was steady when he aimed the pistol and fired again. This shot took the wounded man in the side of the head, blowing his ear off and spraying blood on the ground. He dropped and lay still.

The others looked at the corpse in stunned silence. Then they immediately grabbed Minty and started to kick the shit out of him for killing one of their own.

"Get back! Stand clear! Let him be!" Jethro's voice slashed through the crowd like the lash of a whip. Minty got to his hands and knees, spitting blood and feeling one eye swell shut.

"We do not fight amongst ourselves, brothers and sisters!" Jethro declared while pulling Minty to his feet. "We fight the enemy only!" He took a look at Minty's battered face, "Christ, man, find that lady doc and get yourself cleaned up." Looking to the seething crowd he yelled, "You guys arm up and check the fences. The kid came in from somewhere!" They moved then, in twos and threes, armed with pistols, shotguns, rifles, submachine guns, baseball bats, and axes. The yard emptied of all but the women and children.

Callie came hurrying over. "Minty, what happened?" Her hands were as cool and refreshing as a cold beer on Minty's skin.

"I fell down," Minty muttered.

"Can you walk? Come on, I'll get you cleaned up." She gave Jethro a furious look. "You can't allow this sort of thing to happen. Someone is going to get killed."

Jethro blinked and then threw his head back and laughed. People would die all right. The dying was only just beginning.

CHAPTER 18

"W e gotta get the fuck outta here," Minty muttered. He pushed Callie away; the way she was dabbing at the cut on his cheek was embarrassing.

"The infected people have us surrounded," Callie reminded him.

"We are the fucking Locusts. We will overcome." Minty stood up and went to look for his cigarettes. He found them in the bar that made up a good portion of the first floor of the Locusts' clubhouse. The space around them was filling up with people looking for a drink to appease their hangovers.

"Where do you plan on going?" Callie asked. Her arms folded and she regarded the older man with a clinical gaze.

"Wherever. The fucking army has the main exits from the city cordoned off. They can't be everywhere. We've been running guns and shit for long enough. We can find a way through."

"It would be safer to stay here. Wait until the army or whoever gets the situation under control," Callie said.

Minty lit a cigarette and inhaled deeply. "Army will just burn the infection out. Anyone alive inside the city limits is going to die. FAEs, gas, and shoot anything that moves."

"We are American civilians," Callie replied. "There is no way the government will allow the US Army to murder civilians. There's the Posse Comatose Act."

"Posse *Comitatus?* The National Guard are professional soldiers. They have the same equipment and firepower as the regular army. Most of them have combat experience overseas now too. They'll just label us as terrorists or collateral damage. Either way, if we stay, we will die."

Callie stood up, ready to argue, to say that Minty couldn't be right. This sort of thing just did not happen in America. *But it could,* she thought. *God help us all.*

"Okay." She moved closer and kept her voice low. "The truck that came last night. It's loaded with supplies. We can take that and find one of your back routes out of the city. Once we are out of the city, we can assist the government with medical advice and reports of what is happening here. We can contact the media; they will be crying out for any news."

"Cable is out. Radio's not broadcasting. I think we are in a news blackout," Minty said.

"Then we get to a place where we can get in front of a TV news camera, on a radio station, or the Internet. They can't block the entire Internet."

"Maybe they can, I don't fucking know," Minty replied.

Callie looked around. "Jessie, that young girl? Her and her boyfriend have the keys to that truck. I'm going to find them and we can work on getting out of here." She pulled on a beaten leather jacket and walked out of the club.

Minty stubbed the cigarette out and scowled. In his world, women didn't start giving orders. The ones that did were hardly ever taken seriously. He liked the doctor; she was smart as hell and tough. The shit they had been through already had proven that. Sure she was young enough to be his daughter, Minty grinned ruefully. Callie was way too pretty and educated to be his, though.

Checking that the revolver he carried was loaded with the hammer down, he headed outside. Callie was talking to Jessie, the tight little cherry going to Vegas to get married. Minty approached slowly. His appearance tended to startle kids, the elderly, and good, God-fearing folk.

"Hi, Jessie, where's your fiancé?" he asked.

"Todd?" Jessie looked worried.

"I'm hoping he can help with something." Minty didn't smile. A couple of missing teeth made him even more disturbing.

"He was up on the wall. I think." The girl looked to Callie, who smiled reassuringly.

"I saw him up there earlier. I thought he mighta come down to get some breakfast," Minty said.

Jessie looked around. All the men in the yard were armed now. Women gathered their children and headed inside. The bikers gripped their weapons with grim determination and regarded the stacked piles of scrap and crushed car bodies with suspicion.

"I don't know where he is, sorry."

Minty nodded and walked away. Jessie folded her arms and stared at the dust.

"You okay?" Callie asked.

"Why didn't he come and find me?" Jessie looked close to tears.

The look of betrayal on Jessie's face was familiar, and Callie could almost read her thoughts.

"He's scared. He's going to want to protect you and take care of you. He's like the rest of us. Just trying to make sense of things and keep safe," Callie said.

"I want to go home," Jessie said.

"Me too," Callie said. "Do you have the keys to that truck you came in on?"

Jessie nodded. Pushing a hand into her jeans pocket, she pulled a heavy key ring out. "It's not our truck. We didn't steal it though. Just borrowed it. The guy who owned it, he died in a crash."

"I'm sorry," Callie said.

"I didn't know him. We were hitching a ride."

"If you want, we can still get you to Vegas for your wedding," Callie said.

Jessie sniffled and looked at her with bright eyes. "Really?"

"Sure. You, me, Todd, and Minty, we can get in the truck and get out of here."

"I'd like that," Jessie said.

"Great. Find Todd and don't tell anyone else about the plan, okay?"

Jessie nodded and hesitantly walked into the crowd.

Climbing the ladder to the top of the wall, Minty scowled at the rank of spectators. The weight of so many on the high deck was making it creak.

"Todd?" he called out.

"Yeah?" The kid pushed his way through the leather and denim crowd.

"Get your ass down here."

Todd nodded, a flicker of guilt dancing across his face.

Minty descended the ladder. Todd followed him.

"We're pulling out," Minty said quietly as they walked together across the dusty yard. Todd gave him a sharp look.

"But we're safe in here. They can't get in."

Minty shook his head. "They will, eventually. It would be better for us to fire up that truck of yours and run for Vegas."

"I dunno if I want to get married," Todd muttered, a blush rising on his cheeks.

"Then don't. But if you stay here you'll likely never have the choice."

Callie stood next to the Hummer, watching everyone and looking tense. Minty brought Todd over.

"Where's the girl?" he asked.

"She went looking for Todd," Callie replied.

"Here she comes." Todd gestured toward the clubhouse. Jessie emerged, Freak loping at her heels.

"Jessie, we agreed it was just the four of us, right?" Callie said calmly.

"Freak helped me out last night," Jessie replied. Her gaze flicked to Todd and then back to the ground. "He's coming too."

"It's okay," Minty said. "Y'all ride in the truck. I'll take my hog."

Callie raised an eyebrow. "You mean a motorcycle? You're going to ride a motorcycle through a crowd of highly contagious, bloodthirsty psychotics?"

Minty shrugged. "Ride or die."

Freak grinned. "Yeah, man."

"We can't get out," Todd said. "There are too many people outside. They're pressed up against the walls and the gate. Any one tries opening the gate, they are gonna die."

"Is there another way out of here?" Callie asked.

"Nothing that the Hummer would fit through," Minty replied.

"So we are stuck here?" Jessie asked.

"Not stuck—safe," Minty said.

"For how long?" Callie asked.

"If something stirs them up"—Todd glanced toward the reinforced wall and the bikers on the high parapet—"they will climb over each other to tear the wall down."

"We need a distraction," Minty said.

"We need one of those helicopters, like what shot at us yesterday," Jessie suggested.

"Was it the army?" Minty asked.

"Umm, they were flying so I guess it was the air force?"

"They were US Army. Apache gunships," Todd said. "I watch Discovery Channel," he added.

"Well, if someone has a phone that works and the number for the local general in charge, then we can call in an air strike," Minty said.

"You're not helping," Callie said.

"We need to sit tight and wait," Minty said.

"For what?" Callie asked. "Jethro to completely lose his mind? Or for your buddies to run out of alcohol?"

"The Locusts are family," Minty reminded her.

"We don't run out on family," Freak said.

"You were the one telling me that when the army comes they would probably burn us out. Now you want to stay put?" Callie asked.

"No. I want to get out of here, but I want us to do it right," Minty replied.

"How about we burn the fuckers?" Freak suggested. "With some of those Molotov cocktails."

"People don't burn very well," Callie said. "Spreading burning gasoline around isn't going to make us any safer."

"Jethro," Minty said and lit another cigarette. The others looked and then stepped apart, making their group seem more casual as Jethro approached.

"The fences secure?" he asked Minty.

"Yep, got guys doing a perimeter patrol," Minty replied.

"Good. We're going to thin the herd a bit. Get some heavy guns up on the wall and create a free-fire zone."

"There's a lot of them," Todd said.

"Their numbers aren't a problem. We have many guns. We have crates of ammunition. We have ordnance that will bring God to His knees." Jethro grinned in a way that sent a chill up Callie's spine. *He is loving this.*

"I'm thinking about doing a run," Minty said. "Find out how far this shit has spread."

Jethro nodded. "I need you here, brother. You're my right hand. The one that wears the gauntlet."

Minty grimaced inwardly. He had always been the blunt end of the club that Jethro wielded. Doing his dirty work, loyal to the cause and the Locusts philosophy of anarchy, freedom, and fraternity.

"We're going to need to do something about all the people outside the fence," Todd said.

"When there is no peril in the fight, there is no glory in the triumph," Jethro said cryptically and raised his arms before pirouetting away, his boots kicking up puffs of dust.

"He quotes seventeenth century French poets. I'd say that is a clear sign of an altered mental state," Callie said.

"Is he crazy?" Jessie asked.

Freak chuckled. "Jethro is as crazy as a motherfucker."

"He's okay," Minty said.

They stood and watched as Jethro gave orders and a group of Locusts came out of the clubhouse with two LAW rockets, an antique-looking M60 machine gun, and several crates.

"They cannot be serious?" Callie said, staring at the weapons as they were relayed up the ladder to the high parapet over the gate.

It took five minutes for the weapons to be made ready to fire. The voices of those giving advice at the top of the fence grew louder and the crowd of spectators in the junkyard swelled as people came out to see the show.

Finally the first of the M72 LAW rockets was deemed ready. Tag shouldered it and after waving to the cheering crowd, he sighted down into the howling mass of infected and squeezed the trigger.

Smoke jetted from the back of the launcher's tube and a dull *whoosh* sound echoed over the yard. The watchers on the wall cheered.

"I thought the explosion would be bigger," Todd said.

"The rockets are designed to take out armor," Minty explained. "The bang isn't big, but if one of them hits a tank, it penetrates the skin and the shrapnel inside the machine kills everyone."

"I didn't see any tanks out there," Callie said.

The crack of the M60 caught their attention. One of the bikers stood behind the gun, his arms vibrating as the machine gun chewed through its ammo belt.

Tag launched another rocket; this one ricocheted off the road and blew a basketball-sized hole in an abandoned vehicle on the other side of the street. The gas tank on the car exploded in flame, sending black smoke billowing skyward.

Minty shook his head in disgust. "He's too close to the target; you need about ten meters to arm the rocket."

On the wall the M60 jammed. Bikers clustered around the weapon and someone swore loudly as he burnt his fingers on the hot barrel.

"These people are amateurs," Callie said. "They are going to kill themselves and a lot of other people."

"Shut up a second. Do you hear that?" Minty cocked his head. Too many years of loud music, loud engines, and combat had knocked the edge off his hearing, but he knew the sound of an approaching helicopter gunship when he heard it.

They came in a formation of three, two Apaches and a Blackhawk bringing up the rear. The gunships had their noses down, ready to attack ground targets. They split up, one chopper going left along the front of the yard and the other breaking off to the right. The Blackhawk swept low overhead and Minty could see the reflection of the fires in the dark visors of the crew behind the heavy guns.

"Shit," Minty muttered. "Callie, Todd, Jessie, get in the truck. Freak, keep your fucking head down."

The helicopters swept over the yard. Minty waited for them to complete their surveillance sweep. *Nothing to see here; just move along . . .*

Another five seconds and things would have been different. Instead one of the bikers on the fence raised his AR and unleashed a burst of automatic weapon fire at the Apache.

"Fuck!" Minty yelled as the armor plating of the chopper rang with the patter of bullet fragments.

The flight crew turned the bird away, rocketing across the junkyard and gaining altitude. They turned around and came back.

"Ahh shit," Minty said and ducked down behind the Hummer. The Apache's 30mm chain gun made a sound like a metal tongue blowing a raspberry. A line ran along the ground at a rate of 625 rounds per minute. The dust trail spanged up the wall and the armed bikers scattered in a spray of blood and panic.

The second attack chopper jetted flame as it fired into the infected crowd. Unlike the LAW ordnance, these Hydra 70 rockets exploded with devastating force. The fence disintegrated in a flash of expanding fire and shards of twisted metal. Minty pressed himself into the dirt as chunks of concrete and steel rained down.

Standing up, he stared through the clouds of smoke and saw shattered bodies writhing and burning.

"Get the fuck out of here!" he yelled, pounding on the door of the Hummer.

Behind the wheel, Todd nodded and the engine roared.

"Freak, time to go," Minty shouted and ran for the Crown Victoria. The car had been hit by explosive debris, leaving it with a flat tire and a web of shattered safety glass for a windshield. Minty yanked the door open and opened the glove box. He pulled out the packet of cocaine, a little seed money if he really got stuck, and then he ran for the garage.

The Locusts' Harleys were lined up in neat rows. Minty swung into the saddle of his bike; seniority in the club meant his was in the front row.

A moment later the heavy bike tore out into the yard. Screams and gunfire sounded in a discordant chorus across the front of the yard. The Hummer was gone, and the surviving bikers were fighting the swarm of infected that had crawled through the blasted hole in the fence.

Minty twisted the throttle and the motorcycle leapt forward and blasted through the shattered gateway. Freak should be right behind him, he figured. If not, he was on his own.

CHAPTER 19

The civilians in the armored truck had gone quiet. Dukes could feel Maria's eyes burning into the back of his head. There were a lot of things he wanted to say to her, but none of them would take that horrified expression of grief out of her eyes.

"Sergeant?" Garrett called from the driver's seat up front.

"Yeah?"

"We're flashing a chopper patrol. They're signaling back."

"Apache?" Dukes was grateful for any interruption to his thoughts.

"Yeah."

"Keep your strobe light on, let them keep track of us. Head towards the perimeter, exit point Delta X-ray."

"Delta X-ray, copy that, Sergeant."

Soon they would be back in the hands of the TOC. The civilians would be taken away and processed and the officers in charge would ream Dukes' ass. He hoped the intel they had recovered would be sufficient to prevent a summary court-martial.

⬧

At fifty feet above the ground, Lieutenant Samuel Dawson tilted the AH-64 Apache helicopter into an easy turn to starboard. The city below a seething anthill of chaos. Pillars of smoke rose hundreds of feet into the air from the fires of crashed vehicles and damaged buildings. National Guard units were pulling back in all sectors. The Blackhawks were having a hard time keeping up with the demand for evac.

Behind Lieutenant Dawson, his copilot and only other crewmember, Lieutenant Christine Jackson, was making her radio report to the TOC.

"Yes, sir, positive ID. Friendlies, they are westbound in sector J13."

"Roger that. Maintain contact and provide air support with friendly unit."

Throughout the night the Apache crew had been flying support and escort missions for ground troops going in to recover key assets and complete assessment missions on the ground. They had already come under fire from various small arms. Earlier that morning some idiots in a junkyard with an arsenal of weapons had tried shooting them down.

If you are engaged, return fire was one of the parameters of the flight missions. They returned fire all right.

"Hey, Dawson," Jackson said over the flight comms.

"Yeah?"

"What do you think those grunts are doing down there?"

"Running away?" Dawson grinned.

"Sure looks like it. I don't think an armored car is standard issue from the motor pool."

"Nothing about this situation is standard. We're in the fucking Twilight Zone," Dawson replied.

"Amen," Jackson agreed. "Crowd ahead," she reported a minute later.

"Looks like civilians," Jackson said.

"Roger that. Rioters. They are attacking that building."

"Any sign of friendlies?" Jackson asked.

"Negative," Dawson confirmed.

"I would not want to be down there," Jackson said quietly.

"Our cash truck is coming up on them, two blocks," Dawson said, bringing the helicopter around in a wide circle.

"Ready to provide fire support," Jackson confirmed as she checked the weapons systems.

"Light 'em up," Dawson ordered. The rockets mounted in the wing pods fired, streaking smoke and fire in contrail lines toward the ground. The fireball of the explosions shattered window glass the length of the block and shredded the hundreds of bloodstained people who raged against an unseen enemy at ground level.

A minute later the cash truck drove through the wreckage, maneuvering around the rocket craters and crushing the few squirming bodies that still reached and clawed at the air.

⚔

"What the hell was that?" Dukes asked.

"Apache sweep," Sanchez reported. "That was a big crowd of motherfuckers."

"Not anymore," Garrett added.

"Keep moving," Dukes ordered.

The truck rolled on, grinding corpses to paste under its wheels and driving in a careful slalom around the debris. Dukes rocked on his feet as the truck slowed and stopped.

"What's happening?" Dukes asked.

"Route is blocked, Sergeant."

"Shit. Any Tangos?"

"Negative, Sergeant."

"All right, I'm getting out. Milk, with me. Maria, please keep your people inside the vehicle."

The rear of the truck opened and Dukes stepped down into the rubble and smoke of the ruined street. A moment later Milquist stood beside him. The two soldiers scanned the street and buildings, alert to any threat or movement.

"Okay, Milk, I'm going up front." Dukes moved up the side of the truck and stopped beside the cab door. Ahead of them a burnt tangle of vehicles blocked the roadway.

"Everyone out," Dukes ordered into his throat mic.

The truck disgorged its military and civilian cargo.

"Why don't we just go back?" Milquist asked.

"Side streets are jammed up worse than this," Sanchez reported. "Too many fucking cars in this fucking city, man."

"On foot we can make better time. Head through buildings and get to the perimeter ASAP."

Maria separated from the huddle of civilians. "We need water and bathrooms," she said.

"We will take care of your people as soon as we can," Dukes replied.

Maria relayed Dukes' words in Spanish to the frightened group of survivors.

Dukes pulled out the map. "Sanchez, on point. Garrett, cover our six. Try to keep as close to two-seventy as you can; that is the way home. Keep the civies together. Keep them quiet."

"Roger, Sergeant." Sanchez stepped out of the shadow of the truck and started leading the group toward the nearest building.

The recent attack by the Apache gunship had blasted windows and doors open. The view through what had been an art gallery was clear halfway through the building.

"Structure looks stable," Sanchez reported.

"*Stay in contact*," Dukes replied.

The rest of the squad took positions at the edge of the shattered windows. The civilians crouched against the wall behind them.

Sanchez scanned the interior, stepping carefully; he settled each step on the shattered glass covering the floor. Moving without a sound he went deeper into the building.

Milquist followed, sweeping the space in front of him with his weapon, ready to fire at any target that presented itself.

"*I'm on the other side. There are infected all over the street*," Sanchez reported.

"Okay," Dukes replied. "Come back and we'll find another way."

"*Sanchez, I'm five meters behind you*," Milquist said.

"*Roger that, coming back.*"

Sanchez retraced his steps. The eerie silence of the city amplified every slight sound and had him freezing at every shadow.

"Milk? That you?" he whispered.

Something scraped on the floor, sliding through glass and concrete dust. The soldier raised his weapon. There was enough ambient light to make night-vision gear useless.

"Milk, there's something in here," Sanchez whispered into his mic.

Milquist clicked an affirmative response. "*I have eyes on you,*" he murmured.

Sanchez glanced to his right and then gestured toward an open doorway.

Moving together, Milquist and Sanchez reached the door and took up positions on either side.

Milquist went first, ducking into the room and sweeping the corners. Sanchez followed him and stepped to the right.

"Clear," Milquist said.

"Clear," Sanchez confirmed.

There were no obvious exits from this room, so the two soldiers straightened up.

"Must be the building settling, after the rockets and shit," Sanchez said.

Milquist turned to cover the open doorway, knowing not to leave an open exit at their backs unsecured. "Nah, man. There is something in here with us. What the fuck is that smell? Jesus, did you fart?"

"Let's move, there's nothing we need to see here." Sanchez backed up to the door. Overhead the ceiling panels creaked. Milquist and Sanchez looked up. A second later the roof collapsed, obscuring everything in a cloud of dust.

An obese mass squirmed in the heap of broken plasterboard and dangling cable ducting. Sanchez thought the man might once have been human. Now he looked like he had eaten someone and maybe the couch they were sitting on too.

The thick rolls of fat were grey and oozing yellow pus. The smell that came rolling off the thing made Milquist choke.

"Fuck," Sanchez managed, but he held his fire. He had an aunt who weighed over four hundred pounds. This guy might need medical assistance.

The grey-skinned mountain mewled a high-pitched whine, rocking until it got into an upright sitting position.

"Sir! We are United States soldiers. Keep your hands where I can see them," Milquist ordered.

A wet ripping sound, like Velcro parting underwater, came bubbling out of the figure's belly. Milquist and Sanchez backed up another step as the skin on the man's stomach split. Yellow curds of fat spewed out of the spreading wound. The man's mouth gaped open and he shrieked in agony.

"The fuck is that shit!" Sanchez yelled.

White fibers reached out of the wound like skeletal fingers and crept across the dying man's quivering flesh. A white ball covered in a translucent skein of pale tissue bulged out of the man's stomach wound. It swelled, as if being pushed or inflated from deep inside the corpse that now sagged in death. The dead man's grey tongue lolled as the distended lump burst with a soft *whoof* and filled the air with fine white dust.

Milquist and Sanchez opened fire, the rounds punching into the man's body and head. Sanchez raised his weapon and stepped out of the room. Milquist followed him, both soldiers checking their surroundings for signs of approaching infected.

"What the fuck was that shooting about?" Dukes asked when they emerged a few seconds later.

"Rioter," Milquist replied. "We took him down."

"That way is fucked, Sergeant," Sanchez reported.

"We could walk over those wrecks," Milquist suggested.

"Negative," Dukes replied. "We go around."

They approached the pileup in three groups. Sanchez and Dukes at the front, Milquist with the civilians who huddled together like sheep, and Garrett bringing up the rear.

On the other side of the street, the wreckage was only one car high. Dukes crouched down and watched the street beyond for a long minute.

The way ahead was choked with traffic. Cars had been abandoned as panic swept through the city. Many stood with their doors open and their owners' personal belongings strewn on the ground.

"We gonna walk through that?" Sanchez asked.

"It's the most direct route," Dukes replied, never taking his eyes off the way ahead.

"*Sergeant, we have Tangos inbound on our six,*" Garrett called over the comms.

"Roger that, Garrett. Get the civilians up here, on the double." Dukes slid over the crumpled hood of the car that blocked their way. "Guess we have no choice."

The civilians were herded through the narrow gap. Small children and the elderly were lifted up and helped down the other side. Garrett came over last, moving at a near sprint.

"Lots of them coming into the street, Sergeant."

The sound of an approaching helicopter came on the still air.

"Keep moving," Dukes ordered and the group hurried through the maze of traffic.

$$\blacktriangle$$

"There's that bank truck," Dawson said. "Looks abandoned."

"Where're our boys?" Jackson asked. The Apache flew slowly twenty feet above the rooftops of the nearest buildings, Dawson alert to crosswinds and any sign of attack.

"Big crowd, coming from three directions," Jackson said. "I think they're following the truck."

Dawson glanced down. "They might get bored when they find it empty. Why the fuck don't they just go home?"

"There's the friendlies," Jackson said. "On foot and westbound."

"Are those civilians?" Dawson lifted the chopper to rise above the skyline. They passed through a drifting cloud of smoke and turned to fly back over the traffic jam.

"Why are they escorting civilians?" Jackson asked.

"Could be assets," Dawson said.

"I see women, children, and old people. Regular goddamned humanitarian mission going on down there."

Dawson sighed. "We'll continue to provide air support. They can explain themselves to the TOC when they get back to operations."

"Dumb motherfuckers," Jackson said.

The Apache swooped low, roaring over the heads of the soldiers and civilians, who cowered at the noise. Rockets fired and the piled-up wreck of vehicles went flying in a blast of fire and twisted metal that shredded the front ranks of the approaching infected.

They pulled up, turning in a sharp arc to retrace their flight path. The ground troops were hustling the civilians along. They ran down the block, and the few infected who lunged at them from between the cars were shot.

"We're getting low on fuel," Jackson advised.

"Roger that. I guess they're on their own. Call it in to the TOC."

"Good luck, you crazy bastards," Jackson said.

"Are they trying to kill us?" Maria asked.

"Who? The chopper?" Milquist asked.

"Si."

"If they wanted us dead, we would be dead. They are giving us air cover."

"Keep moving," Dukes called.

Sanchez signaled that the intersection ahead was clear. *"Which way, Sergeant?"*

"Turn left, then take the first right," Dukes replied.

They were nearing the edge of the center of the city. Beyond lay the tangled veins of freeways and sprawling suburbs and satellite towns.

The roads ahead could be choked with abandoned cars, so Dukes kept his people moving, knowing that on foot they had a chance; at least until they could signal a Blackhawk to land and pick them up.

CHAPTER 20

Minty pulled up alongside the racing Hummer and waved at Todd to slow down.

The kid had a white-knuckled grip on the steering wheel and was tearing down the road at over sixty miles an hour. It seemed a good way for them to end up dead.

"Ease up, Todd! Lift your foot, man." Minty didn't know if he could be heard over the roar of both engines. But the Hummer started to slow down.

Callie was leaning in from the backseat and speaking intently to Todd.

Slow the fuck down, kid, doctor's orders, Minty thought. He let his Harley drop back, giving Freak a chance to catch up on the other hog.

The Hummer rolled to a halt, the bikes pulled up beside it, and Todd climbed out of the cab. Minty watched in silence as he doubled over and threw up, thin bile and coffee.

"Fuck me," Todd said. "What a fucking mess."

It wasn't clear if he was talking about the charred wreckage of several hundred infected people and the salvage yard fence they had left a mile back, or the spreading pool of puke.

Jessie walked around the front of the truck. She had her arms folded tight across her chest and she stared at Todd like he was an alien.

Callie lowered the window. "You're going to be fine," she said from the backseat. "We shouldn't stay here though; there might be infected people attracted by the noise."

"Todd, are you okay?" Jessie asked from a safe distance. She looked like she didn't want to touch him, maybe ever again. The howls of the infected and the crunching, splattering sound as Todd drove the Hummer through the crowd would haunt her for the rest of her days.

"Yeah, I'm okay." Todd straightened up, wiping his mouth and breathing hard.

"Where the fuck are we going?" Freak asked.

"I need to find the authorities. Military, FEMA, someone in charge," Callie said.

"Whaddya reckon, Mint?" Freak asked his superior.

"Yeah, the doc has a point. Our best chance is to find a way out of the city and let her go back to fixing people."

"We're going to Vegas," Todd said, some of his previous confidence returning.

"Sure, we can go to Vegas. Hell I'll walk your girl up the aisle myself. The doc and Freak can be your witnesses," Minty said. "Now follow us. Honk once if you see more of those choppers and shit."

Minty and Freak rode ahead, Callie took the wheel of the Hummer, while Todd and Jessie sat together in the back. She heard them talking quietly, giving each other support the way close couples did. Callie wished for that kind of relationship sometimes. It seemed that her focus on high school, college, medical school, and now her career left little time for people. Her father was the only other person in her family and he had always been strict, but loving. She wondered if the reason she had never had a serious relationship was because no man could live up to the standard of decency and strength that she saw in him.

On any other day, a drive like this would be pleasant. They wound their way out of the light industrial wasteland of the city and headed toward the eastern arterial routes that headed up into the hills. Beyond lay the arid states of Arizona, New Mexico and then into the Deep South.

The two Harleys cut through side streets and avoided any roads that might be carrying troops or funneling the infected toward them.

Callie wished Minty had told her where they were going. His vague references to knowing ways to get in and out of the city without being detected by law enforcement bothered her. He seemed trustworthy, so far at least. Every instinct she had told her to find the authorities. Find the police, the army, anyone who was in charge and who could make her part of a controlled system again. There was no sign of control here. Just abandoned cars, torn bodies, and out of control fires.

Minty and Freak stopped their bikes. Callie slowed and stopped behind them. She was about to get out to ask what the holdup was when she saw the first of a group of tattooed Hispanic men. They were armed with a mix of handguns and wearing their gang colors like a uniform.

"Shit," Callie said softly. The men facing them wore sunglasses and heavy gold chains. With the police otherwise occupied, it seemed that the gangs were patrolling their turf and enforcing their own law.

A figure stepped up on the hood of a car and gestured with a flick of his pistol for Minty to come closer. Callie watched as Minty lowered the kickstand on his bike and slid off to stand beside the machine.

"I got your back, man," Freak said softly. *Fucking gangbangers.*

Minty approached the barricade of cars with a casual swagger. He oozed an air of easy confidence that said *Everything is cool . . .*

"Hey," he said and gave a slight wave to the man on the hood of the car.

"The fuck are you doin' in this neighborhood, ese?" The Hispanic replied.

"Just passing through, heading out of town till this shit blows over."

The Mexican nodded. "*Sabes que, ese?* This street belongs to me. I'm a bad motherfucker. You come through here, you gotta *pagar el peaje.*"

"How much is the toll?" Minty kept smiling, but not too much. Show them that he was taking this shit seriously.

"Whatchu got, ese?" The Mexican grinned, the gold caps on his teeth matching the gold around his neck.

"Sorry, man, I ain't got shit," Minty said and gave a self-mocking grin.

"You got some pussy in that wagon back there?"

Minty turned, regarding the Hummer as if noticing it for the first time.

"No pussy in there, amigo."

The Mexican hopped down from the car. He strode toward Minty, the heavy pistol in his hand coming up and aiming straight at the biker's face.

"I ain't your fuckin' amigo, ese," he snarled.

Minty slowly raised his hands, his gaze fixed on the face a foot from his own. "No, you're the bad motherfucker. Just like you said."

"Thass right, ese. Bad Motherfucker. That is my name."

"Bad motherfucker," Minty agreed, nodding and smiling. His grin never faltered as he knocked the gun upward. It went off and Minty twisted Bad Motherfucker around as a shield, one arm locked around the smaller man's neck. Minty wrenched the gun out of the Mexican's hand and fired three times in quick succession.

The first shot took out the gang member hiding in a doorway with a shotgun. The second shot went through the window glass of the car blocking the road and hit a second gangster in the chest. The third shot hit a kid in the arm. The kid screamed and dropped the pistol he was holding.

"You may be a bad motherfucker," Minty said in the squirming gangster's ear, "*yo soy el mismo Diablo.*" But I am the Devil himself. He brought the gun down and pushed it hard into the kid's back. He fired once and felt the gangster's legs give out. The biker stepped back, letting the body fall, blood streaming from the Mexican's mouth. "Adios," Minty said and shot him in the head.

Minty dropped the body and walked back to his Harley. The semiautomatic hanging by his side. Ready to shoot anyone else who challenged him.

Instead of bouncing around and making smartass comments, Freak was subdued for once.

In the back seat of the Hummer, Jessie whispered, "Oh my God."

Callie swallowed hard. The situation was bad. She knew that society had changed, at least here, within the quarantine zone. But the calm brutality with which Minty destroyed the gang members shocked her. The tissue-thin veneer of civilization tore easily. If the infection could not be contained, the entire country would be lost in a new Dark Ages.

Minty and Freak exchanged brief words and then they walked back to the car blocking the road. Working together, they pushed it aside. Freak gathered the weapons from the dead and brought them back to the Hummer.

"Minty says you should hang on to these," he said.

Callie nodded. The shotgun smelled of fresh blood.

"Where are we going?" she asked.

Freak shrugged. "Minty knows."

Minty knows. In Minty we trust, Callie thought. She wanted to start the Hummer and do a U-turn. Get as far away from Minty and Freak and whatever was out there as quickly as possible. If she just went home, she could be safe until the nightmare was over.

A calm, rational part of her spoke up. *Nowhere is safe. Not anymore.* If Minty could get them out of the city, then she could catch a flight, or hire a car or something and head to Alabama. Home would always be the kitchen table where she did her homework while her dad fixed dinner and tested her on math questions.

Todd leaned forward. "Are you okay, Doc? They're leaving us behind."

Callie blinked. "Yeah, fine. Sorry." She started the engine and drove around the blockade. The two squat motorcycles were cruising up the street, going around crashed vehicles, the blast of their engine noise echoing off the buildings.

The hills were clearly visible. With so few vehicles on the road, the smog had cleared. Only the smoke of the fires turned the sky to haze now.

The Hummer drove past a high mesh fence reinforced by sandbags on the edge of a barbeque restaurant parking lot. A military Humvee rolled out and blocked the road. The two Harleys were stopped further up the street by armed soldiers wearing gas masks and hoods.

"Exit your vehicle," an amplified voice boomed.

Callie killed the engine and slid out of the truck. Todd and Jessie climbed out and stood beside the Hummer as soldiers approached, their weapons covering the three civilians.

"Lie down on the ground, with your hands above your heads," The loudspeaker ordered.

They obeyed immediately, stretching out on the warm concrete as the soldiers stepped over them and secured their wrists with plastic ties.

"Have you experienced any flu-like symptoms or nausea in the last seventy-two hours?" a muffled voice behind Callie demanded.

"No. We aren't infected. I'm a doctor," she replied.

"Get 'em up," another soldier said. Callie, Todd, and Jessie were pulled to their feet and marched toward an open gate in the fence.

Snarling German shepherds on short leashes approached, the handlers keeping a firm grip on the dogs.

"Stand still," a soldier ordered. The three of them froze as the dogs sniffed their hands and passed by them.

"Okay, take them through," a guard ordered. The civilians were pushed forward through the gate and into a crowded parking lot.

Vehicles and tents filled the space behind the fence. Machine gun posts were set up behind sandbags and soldiers moved with a purpose in all directions.

Callie looked back and saw Minty and Freak being pushed through the gate. The dogs sniffed and immediately went berserk, snarling and snapping at them both. The soldiers stepped back, weapons ready to fire. The two bikers went to their knees, hands behind their heads. Figures wearing white, full-body biohazard suits emerged from a large tent and came hurrying over to the gate.

Callie watched as they took swabs and did a quick examination of both men. A white, golfball-sized packet was removed from Minty's pocket and placed in a larger ziplock bag. She walked back to the closed gate in time to hear the soldiers asking Minty questions.

"I have a prescription," he said and Freak giggled.

The bikers were stood up and marched into a tent draped in clear plastic sheeting.

"In there," one of the soldiers ordered. The civilians moved into the tent and Callie felt a sense of relief. Here at least were signs of modern medicine. Blood samples and DNA swabs were taken, while they answered questions ranging from name and date of birth to details of their movements in the last three days.

"It's okay," Todd said quietly to Jessie. "There's no sick people here. The army has it contained."

Minty caught Callie's eye. He glanced at the arrayed equipment and security and then frowned. She nodded in return. They weren't completely safe here, but it was better than being out there in the storm.

"I'm an ER doctor," Callie repeated to the blank glass visage of the person in the biohazard suit.

"So you said." It was a woman's voice that came through the mask.

"I'm volunteering. To help," Callie added.

"Thank you. We will let you know if we need assistance."

Soldiers, hidden under the protective hoods and gas masks of their NBC suits, pushed them into a fenced-off area with a tarpaulin providing shade.

"We are not infected," Callie insisted.

Minty didn't protest or provide resistance. He just went where he was pushed and stood calmly, smoking a cigarette as the mesh gate was closed and padlocked behind them.

"Why are we being detained?" Callie said to anyone who would listen.

"They are just following whatever orders they have," Minty said. "There's nothing we can do except wait. Whatever tests they have done will come back negative and they will move us to some refugee processing station."

Jessie looked pale, but calm. Todd stood close to her, the fear just as evident on his face.

Freak strutted along the short fence, linking his fingers through the diamond mesh and almost hanging off the wire.

"Hey, man," Freak called to a passing soldier. "I want my phone call."

Jessie giggled and looked embarrassed. Freak turned his head and grinned at her.

Callie folded her arms and walked over to Minty. "This is not what I had in mind."

"You've always been private sector then, huh?"

"What does that mean?"

Minty finished his smoke and crushed it under his boot. "You've always had it easy. College, medical school, your job. Never been hassled by the police, never been locked up, never been in the military."

"So?" Callie could not believe that being a good person could somehow count against her.

"When you have been in the service or prison, you get used to being pushed into a hole or a cell until the powers that be complete their paperwork. It takes time. There's nothing to do but relax and wait for the wheels to turn."

"I thought you were some kind of rebel outlaw?" Callie replied.

"I am." Minty regarded her with a Zen-like calm. "I just know when to resist and when to go with the flow."

Freak started hooting like a chimpanzee and climbing along the mesh fence, making faces at the soldiers outside.

Jessie had a hand over her mouth, her shoulders shaking with suppressed laughter.

Todd scowled. "Don't encourage him. He's going to get us in trouble."

"No, he's funny," Jessie said and pulled away from Todd's reach.

"He's an asshole," Todd replied.

"Don't be such a dick, Todd," Jessie replied, the expression of amusement evaporating from her face.

"What the hell, Jessie?" Todd grabbed her by the arm and pulled her toward him. The girl jerked free.

"Leave me alone," she snapped.

"What the fuck is wrong with you?" Todd demanded.

Jessie stepped hurriedly toward the fence. Freak went silent and hopped down, turning to face Todd as he advanced.

"Chill out, man," Freak said, his grin loose enough to almost fall of his face.

Todd pointed at Freak. "You, back the fuck off."

Callie started to approach, but Minty caught her hand. "Let them sort it out," he said.

"I'm cool, man." Freak continued to grin, his eyes shining so bright they seemed to glitter.

"I'm telling you, stay the fuck away from Jessie."

"Excuse me?" Jessie asked in disbelief.

"Lady can make her own choices," Freak said.

Todd exploded, lunging at Freak and swinging a white-knuckled fist at his head. Freak's grin widened and he ducked under the blow and thrust upward, the strength of his legs driving his fist. He hit Todd under the ribs, knocking the wind out of him and lifting the teen off his feet.

Todd gasped for air, his face going grey as he collapsed.

"Stop it!" Jessie shouted. Freak's grin had a cold, masklike quality to it now.

"Freak," Minty said in the same tone he would use to call a dog to heel.

The Locust prospect lowered his hands and walked away from Todd. Jessie started crying and walked to the back of the enclosure. She sank down, drew her knees up to her chest, and sobbed.

Freak went back to walking up and down the fence. Todd lay on the ground until Callie went to him and checked if he was okay. She got him on his feet and he went and found a corner to sit in and look miserable.

CHAPTER 21

Garrett approached Dukes. "Sergeant?" he said in a way that made it a question.

"Yeah?" Dukes sat on a table and watched over the civilians as they lined up for the bathrooms in a burger joint while those who had relieved themselves drank bottled water raided from the fridges.

"Sumthin's up with Sanchez." Garrett didn't like ratting out a squad member. But worry and sweat had etched lines through the dust on his face.

"Sanchez?" Dukes called. There was no response. The sergeant stood up and walked over to where Sanchez was watching the empty parking lot through the window.

"Sanchez?" Dukes said again. The soldier had pulled his hooded gas mask down over his face and appeared to be crouched in silence. Dukes wondered if he had gone to sleep.

"Sanchez, wake up, you asshole." Dukes reached out and shook him by the shoulder. Sanchez toppled forward, his helmet striking the glass as he slid down to fall on his face.

Dukes pulled the cover of the gas mask up from the back of Sanchez's head. The skin of the soldier's neck had gone mottled grey and the veins stood out in stark white welts.

"Shit. Milk, get over here." Dukes grabbed Sanchez by the boots and laid him out flat. Sanchez coughed, dark snot spilling out of his mouth and dribbling down his cheek.

"Sergeant?" Milquist asked.

"Did Sanchez get bit?"

"Nope." Milquist regarded Sanchez with a scowl of unease and disgust.

"Are you okay?" Dukes stared hard at the private.

"Good to go, Sergeant."

"This shit must be airborne. We need to get an evac."

"That Blackhawk's flown over us a few times now," Milquist suggested.

"When it comes by, get out there and pop a red smoke. We'll cram the civies in to the Blackhawk and get Sanch to a medic."

"Hooah," Milquist said and stepped outside, scanning the skies and the empty parking lot.

Dukes knelt on one knee, not touching Sanchez. "Hang in there, Sanchez. We're getting you out of here."

"He's got it, hasn't he?" Garrett asked.

"We're calling in an evac. See if we can get the civies out at the same time," Dukes replied, carefully ignoring Garrett's question.

The pop and hiss of a smoke grenade caught their attention a few minutes later. Milquist threw the streaming can out into the parking lot.

While the smoke hissed out into the atmosphere, Milquist took a one-meter-square VS-17 signal panel out of his assault pack to mark the center of the pickup zone. The high-visibility nylon-cloth panel was orange on one side and magenta on the other. Milquist spread it out, orange side up, and weighted it down with a couple of rocks from a well-tended landscaping bed.

The helicopter lowered in a hover and Milquist waved until the pilot signaled he had visual contact. The pilot assumed guidance from the corporal, who used his Air Assault School training to guide the Blackhawk down safely in the tight space.

Milquist sank into a crouch, head down to avoid getting a face full of grit and trash being blown around by the rotor wash. He looked up far enough to wave at the two gunners behind the M240H machine guns that covered the flanks of the craft.

Dukes came out and ran to the open side of the chopper. "We have fifteen civilians, three troops, and one squad casualty!"

"We can't take civilians," The flight chief shouted.

"It's women and children. Take them and our wounded. Come back for us."

"No can-fucking-do, Sergeant."

"They aren't sick," Dukes yelled.

The crew chief leaned forward. "There is a large force of rioters bearing down on our position. So we are lifting off in fifteen seconds, Sergeant. If you have US military personnel in need of medical assistance, you get them on this bird. Anyone else approaches, we will shoot them as an identified threat. Do I make myself clear?"

Dukes felt a surge of nausea roll up from his gut. "Give me one minute." He backed away from the helicopter. "Milquist, get on board. Do not let them leave without us."

"Roger, Sergeant." Milquist climbed onto the passenger deck and crouched there, watching as Dukes ran back to the restaurant.

Inside, the civilians were gathering and Maria came forward, her eyes filled with hope. "You did it, Sergeant Dukes? You got a helicopter to come for us?"

"Garrett, get Sanchez's mask back on. Get him out to the chopper. Do not let anyone take his gas mask off. Are we clear?"

"Yes, Sergeant." Garrett covered Sanchez's head and then lifted him onto his shoulders. He carried his buddy's limp body out into the swirling smoke and dust.

"Everyone, please sit down." Dukes raised his hands and motioned for silence.

"Maria, translate for those who don't speak English." He turned to the others. "We need you to stay here. There is water, food, and we know where you are located." Dukes paused while Maria repeated his words in Spanish.

"This helicopter cannot take you to safety. You will be picked up later. So until then you will need to stay here. This is the safest place we have found so far."

Maria's eyes went wide. She translated and stood staring at Dukes as a chorus of cries erupted from the women and old people gathered around her.

"We can give you guns, ammunition. You can protect yourselves until we return."

"Guns? We are not soldiers, we do not know how to use your guns," Maria scolded.

"Fuck." Dukes pinched the bridge of his nose.

"Take the children," Maria said. "Please, take Carlos and the other babies." She pulled Carlos out of the group and stood behind him.

"How many?" Dukes asked.

"*Qua* . . . Four, there are only four other children left," Maria said.

"Bring them out," Dukes said.

As well as Carlos, there were two girls, both under five, and two babies still in diapers, who screamed at their mothers' sudden wails of alarm.

"Carlos, carry a baby for me, okay?" Dukes asked him. The boy nodded and cradled a shrieking bundle.

Dukes gathered up the second baby and, with his rifle hanging, he took each of the two little girls by the hand.

"*No te olvides de nosotros,*" Maria said. "Do not forget us."

Dukes nodded and led the small group toward the chopper.

"The fuck is this shit?" The Blackhawk crew chief demanded when Dukes handed the baby to Garrett.

"We are taking them with us," Dukes said.

"No fucking civilians on my fucking bird, Sergeant," The crew chief said.

"They are gonna fucking die here." Dukes lifted the second baby and the crew regarded him with cold expressions. Milquist climbed onto the deck and took the baby.

"We are taking them with us," Dukes repeated. He lifted the two girls onto the deck and then lifted Carlos up as well.

"It's your ass, Sergeant," The crew chief said.

"Damn right." Dukes sat on the edge of the passenger deck, his feet hanging out of the chopper.

The Blackhawk's rotors were powering up to flight speed. Sanchez was strapped down and Garrett crouched nearby. Milquist simply nodded at him.

"Tangos inbound," The gunner on the restaurant side called out and aimed the heavy machine gun.

Dukes saw a woman burst through the restaurant door, breaking free of Maria's grasp and running toward the chopper.

"No, go back!" Dukes yelled as the bird twitched and started to rise off the concrete.

Maria ran after the screaming woman as the downdraft of the rotor wash blinded them with dust and tossed paper trash. The Blackhawk rose into the air, and Dukes stared down at the two small figures as they fell away. The last of the red smoke curled in tendrils around the few abandoned cars.

Milquist tapped him on the shoulder. "Sergeant, trouble's coming." He pointed toward the street, where a crowd of at least a thousand rioters were closing in on the restaurant parking lot.

Dukes nodded. He didn't trust himself to speak. Instead he packed the emotion down under a cold layer of training. He followed orders. They all did. When you didn't, shit got fucked up. Maria, Carlos, and the others were proof of that. The civilians were a complete fuckup on this mission. Even worse, they were his fuckup.

CHAPTER 22

Minty opened his eyes. Callie sat next to him, her head warm and soft against his shoulder. Freak and Jessie were whispering together, suddenly thick as thieves. Todd sat in his corner, the scowl of his sulk warning everyone else away.

For a moment Minty relaxed and enjoyed the warmth of the woman leaning against him. The soldiers outside the enclosure fence were still ignoring them, instead focusing on unpacking crates of equipment and securing their location.

"I need to pee," Callie mumbled.

"Yeah," Minty agreed. The doctor sighed and lifted her head. Looking around, she stood up and brushed the dust off the seat of her pants.

"Hey, we need a bathroom," she said to the nearest soldier.

The troops gave no indication she had been heard, until a minute later, three biohazard-protected soldiers approached.

"Step away from the fence," The first soldier said, his voice muffled by the heavy gas mask.

Callie stepped back. Jessie and Freak scrambled to their feet and stood with her; Minty sauntered over as well.

The mesh gate was unlocked and they were escorted at gunpoint to where portable toilets stood in a neat row at the back of the camp.

When they emerged a few minutes later, a woman with grey hair in a tight bun stood waiting them.

"Our tests have concluded you are not carrying the infection," The woman said.

"I could have told you that," Callie said.

"As civilians you will be relocated to an emergency containment camp until the current crisis has passed."

"Told you," Minty said as he stepped out of one of the green plastic boxes.

"This is bullshit. I am a fully qualified medical doctor. I have current practicing licenses and ER experience. I should be helping people in need."

"Your skills are noted, Doctor Blythe. However this is a military operation. You will find more demand for your skills in the civilian containment camps."

Callie's retort was lost in the sudden thudding of a helicopter that came swooping in from the east.

"Back in the cage," The soldiers ordered. The Locusts and the civilians were pushed back through the gate and into the enclosure. A military helicopter floated down and settled on the roadway outside the perimeter fence.

Soldiers hopped out and then reached back into the machine and lifted children out.

The final figure to be lifted out was a soldier in full NBC gear, who lay motionless on a stretcher.

Minty regarded the new arrivals with curiosity. They were dirty and bloodied. These men had seen combat today, and Minty wondered how many brothers they had left behind.

Dukes' squad approached the gate. The children shied back from the German shepherds, and Garrett crouched down and comforted a little girl who screamed in fear when a dog approached to check her scent.

The squad and the children were ushered through the gate. When the stretcher approached, the dogs were brought forward to check the patient. The noise of the chopper winding down was drowned out by the sudden frenzied barking of the dogs. The handlers strained on their leads, keeping the animals back as the stretcher-bearers set Sanchez down and moved away.

Dukes came hurrying back, but the gate guards blocked his way.

Minty watched as words were exchanged. More soldiers converged on the gate, until specialists in the white biohazard suits came on to the scene with a body bag. Sanchez was sealed into the bag before being taken through the gate and into the medical tent.

"Tangos inbound!" a guard yelled. The crews at the machine gun posts manned their weapons.

The infected came in ones and twos at first. Wandering up the street, drawn by the noise of the helicopter and the barking dogs.

A command was given and the soldiers opened fire. After the first few seconds, they adjusted their aim and focused on headshots. Bodies were torn apart by the chattering stream of bullets. In the lee of the building, Minty and the others couldn't see what was coming up the street; instead they watched as the helicopter crew leapt back on the chopper and the bird lifted into the air.

The Blackhawk's machine guns joined the massacre, cutting down the growing mob of howling infected.

"Oh God, that noise," Callie said, her face pale.

"We don't want to stay here," Minty said. "Freak, Todd, Jessie?"

They came together in the middle of the enclosure.

"We need to get out of here," Minty said.

"Fuckin' A," Freak agreed.

"I left the keys to the truck in the ignition," Callie said.

"We can get back to the Hummer and get the hell out," Todd said.

"The trick is going to be getting out of here without getting killed by soldiers or crazies."

"What do you suggest?" Todd asked.

"Aren't we safe in here?" Jessie interrupted. "If the army can't keep us safe, where are we going to go?"

"It's okay, hon," Todd said and then his jaw tightened as Freak put a comforting hand on Jessie's shoulder.

"Stay together," Minty said. More soldiers ran to the fence along the street. The steady crack of their rifles added to the machine gun fire as the number of advancing infected swelled.

"We could climb the fence," Freak suggested. "Go up that corner and then onto the building of the store."

"They will see us," Jessie protested.

"It's better than staying here and getting eaten," Minty said.

"Eaten . . ." Jessie shivered.

Todd walked over to the corner and started climbing. The mesh fence was only ten feet high, but topped with three strands of razor wire. The others gathered underneath him, casting cautious glances at the soldiers who now had higher priorities.

"Throw me a jacket or something," Todd said. Freak stripped the filthy denim and leather vest off his shoulders and tossed it up. Todd caught it and draped it over the bladed wire. Squirming through the narrow gap between the tarpaulin and the fence, he vanished from sight.

"Up you go," Minty said and gave Callie a boost. She climbed quickly, following Todd up to the roof and out of sight.

"Your turn," Freak said to Jessie. He went to put his hands on her and lift her up.

"Back off," she warned.

Freak grinned that kicked puppy look he usually wore. "Damn, you're not like other girls."

"What the fuck is wrong with other girls?" Jessie snapped.

"I . . . what?" Freak grinned in confusion.

"Jessie, get up the fucking fence," Minty ordered.

Jessie scrambled up and wriggled through the gap.

"You want me to give you a leg up, old man?" Freak wisecracked.

"Watch your fucking mouth, maggot."

Freak went still and stared at the ground.

"Get up there, look after the others."

Freak bounced on to the mesh and climbed up, unhooking his jacket and draping it over his shoulder.

"Come on, man," he said, looking down.

"Quit your damn bitching and go," Minty snarled.

Freak climbed out of view, taking his jacket with him.

Minty sighed. The voice in his head that liked to remind him he was getting too old for this shit sat back and cracked open a cold beer, content to watch in silence for once.

"Fuck," Minty muttered and reached up to grab the mesh.

"Hey. What are you doing in there?"

Minty let go and turned around. A soldier was standing at the gate, weapon ready to go.

Minty shrugged. "They tested me for the crazy and when it came back clean, they put me in here until I could get shipped out to some safe place."

"This camp is being evacuated," The soldier said. He had the blood and dust coating of someone who had been in the shit all day. Minty could barely make out the sergeant stripes on his uniform.

"Well, that's great, Sergeant," Minty replied.

"Come out, we'll get you on a truck with the others."

"Sure thing." Minty walked out the gate.

Babies were crying and the medical personnel in their white suits were loading children and heavy suitcases into the back of a truck. Out at the roadside the firefight was intensifying.

"You've got the numbers. Aren't you going to just stay put?" Minty asked the sergeant.

"No, I've seen what the rioters can do. They are going to overwhelm this position and kill anyone they can reach."

"Well, my truck is out there on the road. You can drop me off," Minty said.

A dull boom of exploding ordnance made them both turn to look. A spreading cloud of smoke and fire erupted out of a building across the street.

"Propane tanks musta been hit," Dukes said.

Minty nodded. He could see the infected now tearing at the fence line. The mesh was already ripped open in places from the gunfire going through it.

"Time to go," Minty said and clambered up into the back of the truck.

Dukes lifted the tailgate and secured it. Running up to the cab, he climbed in the passenger side. "Get us the fuck out of here," he told the driver.

The truck started up and ground through a lumbering three-point turn until it faced the street. The driver, young enough to still have fresh acne, went pale.

"Drive," Dukes ordered. "Drive!" he repeated.

The kid pressed down on the gas and the truck rolled across the parking lot. Abandoned equipment cases shattered under their wheels and he hit the mesh fence full on, tearing through the wire like it was paper.

Out on the street the crowd seethed and snarled. A hundred pairs of hands reached for the truck as it crawled through the mob.

In the back, Minty grabbed an M4 and joined the two soldiers crouched at the tailgate.

"What the hell, man?" The nearest private snapped, jerking his rifle around to cover the suddenly armed civilian.

"First Marine Division, Desert Storm," Minty announced.

"Try not to hurt yourself, old man," The kid replied and went back to aiming at the freaks that followed.

They only fired when an infected person started climbing up the back of the truck. The rest flowed in to fill the empty space left in the wake of the truck's crushing passage through the crowd.

"There's a Hummer just ahead. I need to get to that truck!" Minty yelled.

"Can you fucking fly?" a soldier with the tag GARRETT on his fatigues asked.

"Just get me to it. I have friends who are going to need to be picked up before your camp is overrun."

"The camp is already overrun," The soldier tagged as MILQUIST said.

"Hooah," Garrett agreed.

Minty went to the front of the truck, rummaging through the hastily loaded piles of munitions and equipment.

He gathered up grenades and extra magazines for the M4, stuffing them into an assault pack. Under a pile of wool blankets, he found a flamethrower. Minty came back to the tailgate. "You boys ever used one of these?" He held up the flamethrower.

"Fuck, old man, put that down before you barbeque yourself," The one called Milquist said.

Garrett reached out and took the flamethrower. With casual expertise he checked the pressure regulator, ignited the primer flame, and lit a cigarette off the propane pilot light.

"Flamethrowers aren't military issue," Minty said, shrugging the assault pack onto his back and tightening the straps.

"Hell no," Milquist agreed.

"Fucking cool though," Garrett said. He pushed the nozzle out into the open air and squeezed the fuel release trigger. A jet of burning liquid sprayed out over the infected crowd. The stench of scorched skin and burning fuel filled the air.

"Where the fuck did you find this?" Garrett asked, looking both pleased and perplexed by the chaos he had wrought.

"Someone had it stashed up front. Can you use it to clear a path for me to get to the Hummer?"

"If you want to commit suicide, we can probably just shoot you right here," Milquist said.

"Just get me close to the truck."

"This is some fucked-up shit," Garrett declared and sprayed the crowd with liquid fire for a second time.

Dukes' voice came over the comms. *"What the hell is burning back there?"*

"Just doing a bit of field clearing, Sergeant," Milquist replied.

"If you're gonna go, now is the time," Garrett said. Minty looked out. The ten feet between the Hummer and the back of the slow-moving truck was now clear of infected, though burning bodies were thick on the ground.

"Thanks for the ride." Minty jumped down and ran. Stepping as lightly as he could on the crisped bodies underfoot, he made straight for the Hummer.

Dragging the door open, he tossed the assault pack onto the passenger's seat and slid in behind the wheel, slamming the door shut against the smoke and the moans of the dying.

"Thanks, Doc," he said and turned the ignition key. The engine roared into life and the Hummer executed a slow turn, grinding the burnt corpses under the wheels.

As the smoke cleared, Minty smashed through the few remaining infected. He pulled up next to the building that the others had climbed on to and honked the horn.

"Minty!" Freak yelled, his grin flashing from the store roof.

"Get your damned ass down here!" Minty called back.

They lowered Jessie down first. She flinched at every step but got to the truck and climbed in. Callie came next, then Todd and Freak, both hanging on to the edge of the roof and dropping the last ten feet to the ground.

The Hummer filled up with people, all talking at once.

"We thought you were dead," Callie shouted and punched Minty in the arm.

"Can we please just get out of here?" Jessie asked.

"What about the bikes?" Freak asked.

"Forget the damn bikes, just go," Todd snapped.

"A Locust never leaves his hog behind," Freak said.

"Callie, you drive. Freak and I will follow on the bikes. Head west, follow the truck. They are going to be heading to those civilian camps they were talking about."

The Hummer stopped next to the two Harleys; one had been knocked over. Callie slid over to the driver's seat as Minty got his bike upright. After a quick check and a couple of attempts, the bikes both started.

"Get going," Minty said. "We're right behind you."

Callie didn't argue; she hit the gas and drove off up the street.

"A Locust never leaves his hog behind?" Minty said, looking at Freak. "What kind of fucking horseshit is that?"

Freak grinned, blushing in sudden embarrassment.

"You're a dork, Freak, but you've got balls of fucking steel." Minty laughed and the two riders gunned the engines. They picked up speed and a few seconds later they had left the burning desolation behind.

CHAPTER 23

A strange convoy drove through the desert that evening, a green US Army LMTV truck, followed by a black civilian Hummer and two Harley-Davidson motorcycles.

The sentries guarding the hastily erected perimeter fence around the camp were on high alert. Spotlights flicked on and pointed, like the accusing finger of a spiteful God, at the vehicles as they approached.

Dukes stopped the truck and slowly climbed down from the cab. He was bone tired—it had been a long day, and they'd run out of cigarettes an hour down the road.

"Sergeant Dukes, US Army. First Squad, Recon Platoon, one-two-five Infantry, designation Echo. I have my men and civilians ready for processing and debrief," Dukes called to the shadows at the fence.

"Everybody get out of the vehicles, and keep your hands up," The order came back.

"Okay, people, everyone out. Milk, help Garrett with the kids."

The children who had cried themselves to sleep began to fuss again as they were lifted out into the cold night air.

After the civilians were lined up, a squad came through the camp gate, dogs and weapons ready to take them down at the first sign of infection.

German shepherds sniffed everyone and then sat beside their handlers.

"Alright, walk through that gate," a sergeant ordered. The civilians started walking.

"Sergeant Dukes," Dukes said with a nod.

"Sergeant Fuller," The other man replied. "You look like shit, Sergeant."

"Traffic in the city was bad," Dukes said.

"We'll get these vehicles parked and see about getting you and your squad some chow." Fuller regarded the two soldiers who stood behind Dukes. "Where's the rest of your men, Sergeant?"

"Dead," Dukes replied. "I need to report to your CO."

"Fuck me. Sorry to hear that. They were good guys. CO's this way." Fuller led them through the gate and into a larger version of the camp they had seen in the city.

"We have fifteen hundred soldiers here, with facilities to support five thousand civilians. We have electricity, medical support, food, water, and sanitation. Hell the cable guy is coming tomorrow and we'll have ESP-fucking-N."

"This place is nicer than my apartment," Dukes said.

The camp was divided into two parts. The army side, with vehicles and men and women in fatigues, buzzed with activity. Behind a high mesh fence, rows of tents—with more being set up—marked the civilian compound.

"Your civilians will get escorted to their side of the camp. There they will be given a physical checkup, food, water, and a billet."

"How many civilians do you have here already?" Dukes asked.

"846. Most of them were intercepted trying to enter the city. The rest were picked up as outbound traffic. We—"

Fuller was cut off by the flare of a fire south of the camp.

"Body disposal," he said and spat on the ground. "We have been isolating anyone showing signs of infection and then we burn the bodies."

Dukes nodded. *Isolating* seemed like a polite way of saying *terminating.* "If what is happening in the city spreads, you're going to need a bigger grave."

"Exactly how bad is it?" Fuller asked.

"It's worst-case scenario," Dukes replied.

Fuller let that roll around in his head for a moment. "TOC is this way."

A modular network of domed, tent-like structures, covering hundreds of square feet, made up the tactical operations center. Interconnecting passageways connected the five largest structures and gave quick access to the various operational divisions of supply, intelligence, and operations.

Outside, trucks carrying huge generators provided electricity to the systems within: lighting, computer, communications, even air-conditioning.

Inside the air hummed with voices and the whispering of laser printers. Data arrived in a well-orchestrated wave via radio, satellite, air surveillance, and on-the-ground observations. A hundred reports were collated into useable information, giving the command structure a clear view of just how bad things were getting.

Dukes saw a monitor showing a map of the area, with infected zones marked in red. The lines had moved steadily, with new shaded areas appearing in the north and west of the city.

"Major Kiro, this is Sergeant First Class Dukes from recon team Echo here to report," Fuller said and both men stood at attention three steps in front of the desk as they snapped a salute at an Asian officer who regarded them steadily.

"Thank you, Sergeant Fuller. You are dismissed. Dukes, you were sent on an intel recovery op?"

"Yessir," Dukes replied.

"And was it successful?"

"Yessir." Dukes retrieved the memory stick from his shirt pocket and handed it over.

"Lieutenant Bell," The major said. A young officer leapt from his chair.

"Yes, sir?"

"Have this data analyzed."

"Yes, sir."

Dukes watched with a sense of anticlimactic disappointment as the memory stick that had cost most of his squad their lives, was handed over to the lieutenant. *Valentino, Timberson, Drake, Walburn, Trow, and Sanchez.* All good men who died to protect whatever secrets were hidden on that tiny slab of plastic.

"Get some food and some sleep. You will be required to attend a debriefing at oh-six-hundred. You are dismissed."

"Yessir." Dukes saluted again and half-stumbled out of the TOC. He followed his nose to the mess tent and ate without appetite or enthusiasm. Sleep came because he forced himself to shut down.

When his eyes snapped open, his watch said it was 0530. He rolled out of bed, gathered the shaving kit that was issued with his bunk, and went to the shower block. Refreshed, awake, and dressed, he grabbed a hot coffee and reported to the debriefing session.

Inside the tent, various soldiers and officers sat on chairs until Major Kiro entered; then everyone leapt to their feet in a stance of attention.

"At ease. As you were," Kiro said before most of them were fully standing. Everyone settled back into their seats and the major began his briefing.

"Ladies and gentlemen, we are responding to a serious threat to our domestic security. While this situation is vastly different from any that has ever been encountered before, our mission is the same. We will support and defend the Constitution against all enemies. Unfortunately, this time the enemy is domestic, and they pose a grave threat to our nation and our way of life.

"The United States has always been victorious. We have never allowed victory to become complacency. We have remained vigilant against all threats, and that vigilance has prepared us for this day. Joining us now is Doctor Stahl, from the CDC in Atlanta. She is going to provide you with an update on what we currently know. Doctor?"

The major stepped aside and a woman who Dukes concluded looked too young to know shit stepped into his position. She had dark hair tied back in a ponytail and pair of glasses on that gave her a sexy librarian vibe.

"Good morning, I'm Doctor Evelyn Stahl, from the Centers for Disease Control and Prevention. My specialty is epidemiology, the study of how diseases become epidemics." Stahl paused and seemed to collect her thoughts for a moment.

"What we are dealing with is an infectious agent, the specifics of which were previously unknown to science. It is not a bacterium or a virus. This is both good news and bad. It's good news because viruses cannot be treated with antibiotics, and it's bad news because we do not have a cure or a vaccine for this type of infection."

"What the hell is it?" someone called from the back of the room.

"Good question," Stahl nodded. "We believe it may be a fungus. Fungi spread by means of microscopic spores, which are like tiny seeds. When a host ingests a spore it germinates, like a seed, and spreads through the body. We think it uses the vascular system as a conduit to colonize the host body until it reaches the brain. There it causes changes to the neurophysiology of an infected person, resulting in extreme personality changes and aggressive behavior."

"Some kind of mushroom is making people crazy?" another voice from the rear of the tent called out. There were a few laughs. Dukes stayed silent.

"At ease!" The major ordered and the murmurs snapped off.

"Yes and no," Stahl said. She paused and pushed her spectacles up her nose. "From data gathered in the quarantine zone, we have concluded that the infection source is South America. We believe that cocaine manufactured in the jungles of Colombia became contaminated with fungal spores. There are collaborating reports of drug cartel workers fighting and killing each other. Entire villages have disappeared in the last month.

"The contaminated drugs appear to have been shipped to the US and then distributed. We are still investigating how many ports of entry were used and just how far the contaminated drugs have been distributed."

"This is bigger than one city?" Dukes asked.

"Yes. In the last twenty-four hours there have been outbreaks in Tucson, Dallas, Atlanta, Phoenix, New Orleans, and as of four hours ago, Miami."

"How do we stop it?" a captain asked.

"We quarantine anyone showing signs of infection. This includes flu-like symptoms and discoloration of the vascular system—typically, white or black lines on the skin, which follow the network of blood vessels."

More voices erupted, all asking questions and demanding answers. Dr. Stahl just shook her head and stepped aside. Major Kiro glared at the men. "At ease! This is my briefing, not some damn town hall meeting. You will conduct yourself accordingly." He waited until the silence had reigned for a few seconds.

"We are the US Army. We will defend this great nation of ours against all foes, foreign and domestic. This is a terrorist attack on our nation, and we must stand together to win the day. Specific assignments will be given by oh-nine-hundred. You will maintain a clear focus and remember what you are fighting for. Am I understood?"

The tent erupted in one voice. "*HOOAH!*"

"Dismissed," The major ordered and snapped a salute.

"Sergeant Dukes?" Dr. Stahl asked as the briefing room emptied.

"Yes, ma'am?"

"I need to talk to you. I understand you were the team leader in the mission to recover the data on the contaminated drugs."

"I have no recollection of any such mission, ma'am. If I did have any knowledge of such a mission, I would not be at liberty to disclose any details to you."

"I appreciate your security concerns, Sergeant, so allow me to be blunt. We have completed a preliminary examination of a small quantity of cocaine contaminated with the infectious agent. We need to find more of it. Without a larger sample, we cannot ensure that any other caches of the material are identified when they are found."

"Sorry, Doc, I'm all out of coke."

Stahl gave a thin laugh through her nose. "Sergeant, how about you stop fucking with me and cooperate? The sample was brought in from the forward operating base on what was the eastern edge of the city quarantine zone until yesterday afternoon, when it was overrun and destroyed. You were there, perhaps you saw who brought it in?"

"No, ma—" Dukes stopped, remembering the old biker and the civilians he was riding with. "I may have a lead on that, ma'am. However, I will need a direct order from Major Kiro to discuss any details of any such mission with you."

"Thank you, Sergeant, come with me," Stahl said.

⚔

Staring up at the canvas over his head, Minty felt the memories of his time in Iraq during Desert Storm cycle through his mind.

He sat up and put his feet on the bare ground. Freak snored softly in the next cot and Todd had left already. The women were housed elsewhere.

Pulling on his boots and jacket, Minty stepped outside and patted himself down for cigarettes. He looked around the neat rows of tents. The smell of hot food was carried on the steam wafting from a chimney on one side of the camp.

He headed that way, diverting briefly to following a sign that indicated the toilet block. The mess tent was like he remembered them from his days as a gainfully employed US Marine. The coffee was hot and the food plentiful. The biker took a seat and ate, ignoring the mix of white, Hispanic, and black civilians who were having breakfast around him.

"Hey," a soldier said.

Minty looked up; the soldier who let him out of the enclosure the day before stood on the other side of the table. A dark-haired woman in civilian clothes stood next to him.

"Hey," Minty replied.

"Sir?" The dark-haired woman broke in. "I'm Doctor Stahl, with the Centers for Disease Control and Prevention. I understand you may have some information about a sample of cocaine that was confiscated at a forward operation base yesterday?"

"Sorry, don't know anything about it," Minty said.

The woman pushed past Dukes and sat down. Leaning forward she whispered, "It's really important. You're not in trouble. We have bigger problems than your drug habit right now."

"I don't have a drug habit," Minty replied and sipped his coffee.

"Great." Stahl smiled brightly. "Do you know where the cocaine came from?"

"Colombia?" Minty guessed.

"No shit?" Stahl's smile became more masklike. "I was thinking more along the lines of where in the city did you get it. The name and location of the distributor. Or maybe the dealer who sold it to you."

"Why do you want to know?" Minty asked.

"There is evidence that the infectious agent arrived in the country in a contaminated shipment of cocaine. We need to find a larger sample of it for testing and evaluation."

"This shitstorm was caused by some bad blow?" Minty asked.

"Seems like it," Dukes said.

"If I tell you what I know, you can't use it in evidence against me?"

"There is no criminal investigation happening here mister . . . ?" Stahl trailed off.

"MacInnes. Call me Minty."

"Could you please come with us, Mister MacInnes." Stahl stood up. Minty finished his coffee and got to his feet.

"I remember details a lot better with a pack of cigarettes," he said.

"I'll take care of it," Dukes said.

The interrogation took place in a prefab building with a video camera and Dr. Stahl taking notes.

Armed guards were outside the door. Apart from when Dukes delivered a sealed pack of Lucky Strikes, they were alone.

Minty told Stahl the whole story, how they had gotten a lead on a major shipment of cocaine being distributed in the city. They went in to claim it and found a gruesome scene of ghoulish slaughter and horror.

"There was a substantial quantity of the drugs still on the premises?" Stahl asked.

"Yeah, shitloads," Minty agreed.

"Mister MacInnes, would you be able to guide a squad of soldiers to that location?"

Minty laughed. "Fuck no. The whole area is overrun with psychos now. Shit, it was bad enough before they started eating each other."

"This is a matter of national security, Mister MacInnes. As a representative of the US government, I am requiring you to assist."

Minty regarded the doctor with a half-closed eye as he lit a fresh cigarette. "Sorry, Doc, I'm a civilian. You can't legally compel me to enter a conflict."

Stahl's lips thinned. "Your *cooperation* could save thousands, if not millions of innocent lives. This is a life and death situation, Mist . . . Minty."

The biker exhaled a stream of smoke. "Doc, level with me. Just how bad is this going to get?"

Stahl swallowed hard and sat back in her chair. With a sigh she rested her fingertips against her temples and remained silent for a moment.

"And I saw another sign in heaven, great and marvelous, seven angels having the seven last plagues; for in them is filled up the wrath of

God." Stahl spoke quietly, without looking up. "We are talking about a plague on the extreme high end of the biblical End of Days scale. Maybe not the wrath of God, maybe just a random coincidence of nature. It could have just as easily been Ebola, or a variant flu strain, or an asteroid strike or a nuclear war."

"Aren't you guys supposed to save us from shit like that?" Minty asked.

"There are thousands of known viruses that have no cures or vaccines. They evolve and adapt. What worked last flu season doesn't work this year. Places like South America, the jungles are filled with organisms, parasites, microbes, and God knows what else that has yet to be discovered by science. The only real surprise about this outbreak is that it didn't happen sooner."

"But the CDC is working on this one, right?"

"Of course we are." Stahl sat up. "But we need to trace its origins. Can we develop an antifungal agent? Create an immune response? Can we cure those already infected with the later stages of the disease? What about FDA approval? Testing? Development of a drug could take years."

"I don't think we have years," Minty replied.

"I know. We have resources, but we don't have time. We need to move against this and we need to do it right now. Before more people are infected and we have a full-blown pandemic on our hands."

"Okay. I'll take you to where the coke is. Provided we can go in by helicopter, with enough firepower to level a city block, and we don't stick around."

Stahl stood up. "We will be leaving as soon as possible Mister MacInnes. Please wait here until you are collected."

The doctor turned the video camera off and gathered it up. The door opened at her knock and she slipped out of the room.

Minty went to the door and knocked. The guards outside opened it.

"I can go back to my tent now," Minty said.

"Our orders are you stay put until advised otherwise," one of the soldiers said.

"Yeah? That's weird. I was told different." Minty scratched his ear and the door closed in his face. Knocking on it again had no effect.

⚔

"Have you seen Minty?" Callie asked Todd when they found each other at the mess tent.

"I saw him heading towards the military side of the camp. He was with a soldier and some woman who looked like a lawyer," Todd replied.

"Do you know where they are taking him?"

"Nope." Todd sipped coffee. Sourced from the lowest bidder and brewed in a big steel vat, it didn't taste like much, but it was warm. "Hey, how is Jessie?"

"She's okay. She volunteered to help with the children. There are quite a few that need looking after."

"Oh." Todd looked disappointed. "Did she ask about me?"

"Umm, no. Honestly? She'll find you when she is ready to talk. Until then, maybe give her some space."

"I thought you were supposed to go after a girl who was upset with you. Show her that you care," Todd said.

"You could do that. But Jessie has a lot to process right now. She has been through a lot, just like you. Give her a while to work things out. Then be there for her. Listen to what she has to say."

"Sure." Callie watched as Todd left the mess tent. She hoped he would follow her advice, but if he didn't, she really hoped Jessie would set him straight.

The day was warming up, the clear sky marred only by the flight of military aircraft and helicopters flying west toward the city.

Callie walked around, looking for signs of Minty. She found Freak in the vehicle compound; he had scrounged some tools and was doing something with the engine of his motorcycle.

. 185 .

"Nah, I haven't seen Minty since last night," Freak confirmed.

"If you see him, tell him I'm looking for him," Callie said as she walked away.

Jessie showed up shortly after that, a baby in her arms and a little olive-skinned girl holding her hand, staring at everything past a fist pushed against her mouth, her thumb anchored inside.

"Watcha doin'?" Jessie asked.

"Maintenance," Freak said and gave her one of his loose grins. "You a momma now?"

"Heck no, just helping out. This here is Lucy, and my friend Sophia."

"Well hello, senorita," Freak said. The little girl pressed against Jessie's leg and sucked her thumb harder.

"This guy's name is Francis," Jessie said to Sophia. "He's a nice man."

"Nah," Freak mumbled and blushed.

The baby girl stirred and started to whimper. "We'd best be getting back. Someone needs a diaper change," Jessie said.

"All right, see you later then." Freak watched Jessie walk away. She was pretty and her fiancé was an asshole. The prospect hadn't given much thought to math since sixth grade, but he could see how this added up in his favor.

◬

Callie approached the guards at the gate that separated the civilian compound from the military side.

"I'm looking for a friend of mine, older guy, wearing leather and denim?" she asked. "He has a Locusts Motorcycle Club patch on his back."

"Sorry, ma'am, we can't help you," one of the soldiers replied.

"He went through here?" she pressed.

The two soldiers just stared at her with blank expressions.

"Thanks, you've been a big help." Callie walked along the fence. The army compound was a mix of tents and prefab buildings, and the purpose for most of them wasn't obvious.

A familiar mane of greying hair passed between two tents. "Hey! Minty!" Callie jumped and waved.

Minty turned and started toward her. Two soldiers flanking him started after him and he calmed them with a gesture and a few words.

They stayed on his heels as he made his way through the tent lines to the fence.

"Hey, Doc," he said.

"What are you doing over there?"

"It's a long story." Minty lit a cigarette, "Listen, I have to run an errand with these guys. I want you to keep an eye on Freak. Don't let him be an asshole. I'll be back later."

"Come on, man," one of the soldiers behind Minty said.

"Those things will kill you," Callie said.

"I sincerely hope so." Minty gave a half wave and headed back into the compound, flanked by his escort.

"What the hell are you doing, Minty?" Callie asked the empty air.

Feeling distinctly uneasy, she went back to the clinic tent. It was spartan in its supplies and facilities, but the military confirmed they would be setting up a prefab in the next few days, with proper lab and treatment facilities. Until then, treating some basic injuries and illnesses would keep Callie busy.

She paused outside the child-care tent where the children of refugees were being kept occupied and cared for during the day. Jessie was making her way slowly down one of the avenues toward the tent, a little girl walking with her.

"Hey," Callie said as the girl approached. Jessie smiled; the hand Sophia wasn't holding cradled a well-wrapped baby. There was a naturalness about Jessie's way with kids that gave Callie a sense of peace. In all the madness, there was still humanity.

Todd marched out from between two tents and broke the spell, appearing between them and facing Jessie. Callie walked closer, ready to intervene.

"Where have you been? I've been looking everywhere for you," Todd said.

Jessie held the children tighter. "I've been busy. I'm looking after the kids."

"Where are their parents?" Todd asked.

"They got sick. Can we not do this now?" Jessie asked.

"Hey," Callie said, announcing her presence. "Everything okay here?"

"Fine," Todd said with a glare.

"Jessie, can I get some help over at the clinic?" Callie asked.

"Sure."

Jessie twisted past Todd and walked away with Callie, leaving the boy scowling behind them.

"Is he bothering you?" Callie asked.

"No," Jessie replied. "He's just annoyed that I'm not talking to him."

"Does he have a history of violence?" Callie asked.

"You mean has he ever hit me? No, of course not." Jessie seemed surprised at the suggestion. A voice in the back of her mind reminded her that Todd had hit her when they were in that weird guy, Edward's, truck. But that was an accident, right?

"Well, that's good. This is a uniquely stressful situation we are in. People can do strange things," Callie replied.

Jessie almost smiled. "Yeah, I've seen plenty of people doing really strange things in the last couple of days."

Callie giggled, a stress reaction. The grinding terror and confusion of the disaster unfolding around them made for gallows humor. Laughing at ghoulish things could be one way to release some of the tension.

The baby in Jessie's arm began to cry. "Lucy's going to need a change and a bottle," Jessie said.

The two women returned the kids to the child-care tent. Callie answered some questions about colic and examined a child with a mild respiratory infection. Jessie delivered Sophia to a group being read a story and changed baby Lucy before leaving her with a woman who was preparing bottles of formula in a regular cycle of feeding babies who all had their own schedule.

"Minty's being taken somewhere by the army," Callie said to Jessie when they left the tent.

"Is he in trouble?" Jessie asked.

"Probably." The women both smiled at the joke.

"We can't stay here, can we?" Jessie asked, her face serious again.

"No, this is a temporary sanctuary. If the infected don't break through, there are going to be shortages of food, clean water, and essential supplies. Maintaining order in a population of refugees is going to require a lot more troops than they can spare."

"I don't want to be here when things get bad," Jessie said.

Callie nodded. When the military order collapsed as it no doubt would, women would be among the first targets, along with food, weapons, and water.

"We have to be ready to run," Jessie said.

"With Minty, Todd, and Freak?" Callie asked.

Jessie frowned. "We don't wait for anyone who isn't ready to go when we are. If we do, we all could end up dead."

Jessie's calm objectivity struck Callie. The girl had been thinking over the last few days. Her teenage princess persona was being scoured away by experience and underneath, she was steel.

"We stand a better chance with friends," Callie said. "Friends who know how to fight, shoot, and drive."

"I can shoot and drive," Jessie reminded her.

"Just talk to me before you do anything about leaving, okay?"

Jessie nodded. "Sure."

Callie stopped and turned to look at Jessie, who came to a halt and regarded her back.

"I have to ask, what is your story?" Callie asked.

"Whaddya mean?" Jessie folded her arms.

"Let's start with how old you are. I mean really."

Jessie swallowed. "I'm nearly sixteen."

"Nearly? Are you running away from home?"

"Kinda." Jessie shrugged. Callie waited for the girl to speak again. "I . . . I've been around foster homes and shit all my life. I got a letter once from my mom. I don't remember what it said. I never knew shit about my dad."

"I'm sorry," Callie said.

Jessie shrugged again. "You get old enough and the foster system drops you. But if you're smart, you get out before that happens."

"You are protected by law until you are eighteen," Callie replied.

"Law can't protect you from foster dads who keep coming into the bathroom when you're in the shower. Or want to give you a kiss goodnight after their wife's asleep."

"Shit," Callie murmured.

"Todd was my ticket out, you know? He had a job at a sandwich place. We were going to get married in Vegas and live happily ever after."

They stopped walking and watched as an army truck rolled into the civilian compound. Soldiers jumped down from the back and lowered the tailgate.

"Everyone out," The soldiers ordered. The group, mostly women and old people, climbed down and were pushed into a line. They looked scared, bloodied, and dirty.

"These people are going to need medical attention," Callie said.

"Is that a problem?" Jessie asked.

Callie shrugged. "The army seems to have good hospital facilities set up. I just hate feeling useless."

"You could always volunteer," Jessie said. "I could help too, I guess."

Soldiers with dogs came through the gate. The people were checked over the by the animals under the watchful eye of armed men.

It didn't take long for the dogs to start barking and snarling. The people started screaming and talking loudly in rapid Spanish as they tried to move away. In the middle of the group an old woman with a bandaged arm collapsed. The dogs would have attacked her if their leashes weren't held firmly.

"Back up! *Mover hacia atrás!*" a soldier shouted.

The dogs were reined in and the civilians moved away in a tight huddle of crying people. The soldiers stepped up and gunshots rang out. The old woman's head came apart and her blood soaked into the dust.

"Bag it!" one of the soldiers ordered. A black plastic body bag was pulled off the truck and the old woman was loaded into it. They even scraped up the dirt where she fell, and it looked like they were burying her as they shoveled the dark sand in on top of her.

"I should go and help," Callie said, her voice sounding strained and distant. "You can help me."

Jessie stared at the bloodstained ground. The shock of the sudden execution left her feeling cold, but strangely unmoved.

The two women went to the area where the new arrivals were being processed. Army medics conducted the initial tests and checks. Callie was allowed to dress wounds that weren't caused by bites. She spoke a little Spanish and was surprised when Jessie started to translate fluently.

"I've lived in California my whole life," she explained.

"We did not think we would survive. This truck, it was sent by God," a young Mexican woman said.

"I'm Doctor Blythe," Callie said. "What is your name?"

"Maria."

"Do you have any family here, Maria?"

"There is only my brother. We were helped by soldiers. They took the children to safety and told us to hide in the burger restaurant. We locked the doors and hid. The rioters came but did not see us, and we went up to the roof and waved the orange flag the soldiers left behind.

A truck was going past. They came and killed the rioters and brought us here."

Maria's story came out in a rush, her eyes red rimmed and dry. Any tears she had to shed were long dry.

"Did you see many of them? Rioters, I mean?" Jessie asked.

"*Si*. So many. Many times we thought they would drag us out of the truck and kill us. They are marching this way, following trucks and helicopters I think."

Callie and Jessie exchanged concerned looks.

"You seem to be okay," Callie told Maria. "Drink lots of water, and try to get some sleep. The army will give you a place to rest and help you find Carlos."

Jessie dragged Callie aside by the arm as soon as Maria had offered her thanks and moved on.

"You heard what she said. We have to keep moving."

"I know, but I'm not leaving without Minty," Callie said firmly.

"Minty? Why him?"

"He saved my life and yours. More than once. We owe it to him to wait till he gets back."

"But what if he doesn't come back?"

Callie had no answer to that.

CHAPTER 24

Flying in a Blackhawk on a combat mission wasn't as much fun as the movies made out. No one talked or played Creedence over the PA system. Most of the guys crammed into the chopper looked focused, preparing themselves for what was to come.

Minty rested his palms on his knees, letting his jeans soak up the nervous sweat. He hated flying, and flying into the shitstorm to end all shitstorms freaked him out even more. The army had offered him clean clothes, or a uniform. He refused, knowing that if was going to die, then he would die wearing the patch of a Locust. They hadn't offered him a weapon, which made his palms sweat even more. He was wearing the body armor and kit that came as standard issue. It was eerily familiar.

"Sergeant," Minty had greeted the soldier when he climbed into the back of the Blackhawk.

"Hello again," The sergeant had replied.

"The name's Minty," The biker said. He hadn't offered to shake hands, already conscious of the moistness on his palms.

Dukes had nodded. "This is Corporal Milquist; we call him Milk. That's Garrett. The rest of these guys—well, they can introduce themselves."

"You lose some people today?" Minty asked.

"I lost some fine soldiers yesterday," Dukes replied.

The conversation stopped and the rotors started to wind up. The chopper was signaled to take off, and with a lift and a tilt, they were airborne. Minty wished he could smoke. Some of the soldiers around him were chewing tobacco.

"Sergeant," Garrett yelled over the noise of the turbine, the whine of the transmission, and the sound of the rotor. "What's with the old lady?"

Minty gave a half smile; he was used to jokes about his hair from redneck assholes.

"Just like you were briefed, Garrett. He's a consultant. Has key intel on the mission location. We cover his ass like it was your momma's."

Garrett spat tobacco juice into the empty water bottle he carried. "My momma din't have no beard like that."

"Sure she did," someone else on the bird said.

The chopper flew on through the smoke of a hundred fires. From what Minty could see, the situation on the ground was shit and getting deeper. Anyone alive down there was fucked. The idea of going back into the city made his balls crawl up into his belly.

"What's the plan if we encounter Tangos?" Milquist asked.

"Infected civilians?" Dukes shouted over the noise of the rotor. "If you see any, you put those motherfuckers down. Once we have secured the sample, then we pop smoke and bug the fuck out."

"Yeah, cuz that worked out real fucking well last time," Garrett said.

"How about you keep your fucking mouth shut, Garrett," Dukes snarled.

The other soldiers watched the exchange and steeled themselves. They had heard the reports, the stories, and even seen the early news footage. But they were based in Nevada, and they had not yet been into the infected metropolis.

"*Two minutes to LZ,*" The pilot reported. Dukes leaned over and handed Minty a comms set. "So you can hear me when I say run like fuck."

Minty nodded; he had never used this gear, but kids working in fast-food drive-thru windows could make a radio headset work. He slipped it on and gave Dukes the thumbs-up.

The remaining ninety seconds crawled for Minty. He concentrated on breathing as the chopper sank to the ground.

Dukes tapped him on the knee. "Stay right behind me."

Minty nodded and the squad bailed out of the aircraft as the wheels touched down. Dropping to the ground, the biker checked their surroundings. The street hadn't changed much in the last few days—it still looked like an abandoned slum.

The Blackhawk lifted off again, retreating to a patrol perimeter until they called them back for a pickup. Overhead a pair of Apache gunships circled like distant buzzards. Above them, hidden in the darkening sky, an AC-130 Spectre completed the trinity of close air support.

Dukes used hand signals and vocal commands to direct the squad into position. "Which house?" he asked Minty.

"Ahh . . . that one." Minty pointed toward the house he had visited only a few nights before. *Christ, has it only been three days?*

"Last time I was here, there were people in the basement. Seriously fucked-up people."

"How many in total?"

Minty did a quick count in his head. "Four? Maybe more? I didn't stick around to count."

Dukes passed on the warning to the squad as they entered the dirt-and trash-strewn yard. A sagging wooden fence ran down each side of the lot, keeping the soldiers out of sight from any freaks who might be nearby.

"*Ready to breach, Sergeant,*" Garrett said over comms.

"Go ahead," Dukes replied.

"*Knock-knock, motherfuckers,*" Garrett said. The door opened when Garrett tried the handle. He stayed low, sweeping the dark interior with his night vision.

"*Christ, it smells like ass in here,*" Garrett reported.

Down the street a dog howled. Minty narrowed his eyes. Shapes were emerging from the derelict houses and filling the streets.

"Sergeant, we might want to get off the street. The neighbors are coming."

Dukes took stock. "Alpha team, move inside and secure that premises. Bravo team, take cover outside the building and stay out of sight. Do not engage unless necessary."

Minty followed the sergeant. He knew staying out here would be suicide. Going in that house didn't make any sense either.

The smell hit them like a wall. Rotting diapers, blood, and decaying flesh.

"I'm closing the front door," Dukes advised and the door clicked shut. "Flashlight, on your six," he warned. A moment later Minty could see again as a narrow beam of high-intensity white light probed the room.

Dark splatters ran up the walls, and the maggots were thriving in the open cavity of Rim's putrefying chest where he lay in the doorway to the kitchen.

"One of yours?" Dukes asked, seeing Minty staring at the corpse.

"Yeah," Minty said.

"*First floor clear. No one here, Sergeant,*" Milquist reported.

"The drugs are upstairs," Minty whispered.

"Garrett, head upstairs, softly now," Dukes ordered. "Here," he handed Minty a semiautomatic pistol. "You can use this, right?"

"Fuckin' A," Minty said. He took the gun, checking it was loaded and the safety was on.

Garrett went up the stairs sideways, his back to the wall and rifle raised, ready to eliminate any threat. The stench coming down the stairs felt as thick as fog, so he breathed in slow, shallow breaths.

Darkness closed in on the narrow hallway at the top of the stairs. Garrett listened for movement, the green luminescence of the night-vision goggles giving everything a strange alien hue. The NVGs gave clarity in pitch darkness, and the contrast brought out details in stark relief. Trash and the glowing eyes of rats stood out along the floor.

"Stairs are clear, Sergeant," Garrett reported. He moved a few steps closer. An open doorway loomed like a cavern to his left. White powder and a drifting pile of bills had spilled out of the room.

"*Jackson, on your six,*" a voice said in Garrett's earpiece.

He glanced back and saw the soldier give a quick wave from the top of the stairs.

Garrett indicated the open doorway on the left and waited for Jackson to join him.

"Ladies first, man," Jackson said. Garrett ignored the jibe and sank down to one knee. Checking around the door, he saw two bodies, a lot of white powder, and money that had fallen out of an open closet.

"Two Charlies, both dead," Garrett reported.

"*Is the room secured?*" Dukes asked.

"Affirmative, Sergeant."

"*Jackson with you?*"

"I'm here, Sergeant," Jackson confirmed.

"*You have the sample containers?*"

"Roger that, Sergeant. We got all the flavors up here. Which one you want?"

"*Double chocolate fudge.*"

Jackson entered the room while Garrett kept watch. Taking a steel canister the size of a thermos flask from his assault pack, Jackson scooped up white powder until the container was full. He screwed the lid shut and sealed it with yellow plastic tape that bore the biohazard symbol.

"*Tangos are closing in,*" Sergeant Pierce, who led the second squad, spoke over the comms. The support squad was set up outside the house, with a sniper team on the roof. They were ready to raise hell if any infected strayed too close to the recovery operation.

"Your call on the CAS," Dukes replied.

"*Roger that.*"

"Hammer, Hammer, this is Anvil Bravo. Fire mission, over."

"Roger, Anvil Bravo."

"My position is the target residential building, marked on roof by IR strobe. Target location is the street, south of IR strobe. Target is enemy personnel, marked by IR laser, over."

"Fire mission confirmed."

"Hammer, you are cleared danger close."

"Roger, Anvil Bravo. We are inbound, ten seconds to contact, over."

Jackson and Garrett made their way downstairs as the sudden roar of an incoming Apache added to the noise outside.

Rocket fire and a long burst from the chopper's chain gun tore a hole in the night. The infected came running. They hit the fence around the yard, knocking it down and falling over each other as they stumbled. Rocket shells exploded in tight clusters down the street. Body parts flew as the stench of burnt flesh and blood came wafting on the air with the sharp chemical stink of explosives residue.

"Top Hat, Top Hat, this is Anvil Bravo. Fire mission, over. My position is the residential building, marked on roof by IR strobe. Target location is street south out to five hundred meters. Target is enemy personnel, marked by IR laser. Top Hat, you are cleared danger close."

The stream of minigun fire came in so fast from the A-130, it looked like a laser beam tearing through the crowd. The 105mm howitzer rounds that followed came shrieking in and detonated in a tight cluster of fire that burned away the darkness, sending shadows writhing up the walls.

"Did anyone check the basement?" Minty asked Dukes from where they crouched to the side of the front door.

"Milk, you covering the basement door?"

"Roger that, Sergeant. Other than a stink like a fucking latrine, it's quiet."

"You think the tenants are still in there?"

"They had a bunch of infected down there, when we last visited. I guess they're gone now."

"Dukes, we have multiple Tangos inbound. They are approaching from the north and south. We're engaging."

"Roger that, Pierce," Dukes replied. From outside came the sudden chatter of two M249 SAWs as the belt-fed machine guns laid down field of 5.56mm fire.

"That should help with crowd control," Dukes said.

"Masks on, we're firing CS," Pierce advised.

Minty pulled down the heavy rubber faceplate even though his beard would prevent the rubber from sealing against his skin. He took a few slow, steady breaths. His vision was obscured, and it took a minute for the smell of tear gas to drift inside.

"Gas having any effect?" Dukes asked.

"Awaiting confirmation . . ." Pierce replied. A moment later he came back online. *"Negative. Tear gas is affecting their vision, but not slowing them down any."*

"Garrett and Jackson, coming down, Sergeant," Garrett reported.

"Roger that, Garrett. Pierce, do we have a clear PZ?"

"Negative. Space out here is filling up. Adjusting Top Hat via ROVER. Alpha squad, pull back to the rear of the property. Bravo team, hold your positions. Repeat, hold your positions."

"Top Hat, this is Anvil Bravo. Move sparkle fifty meters north. Roll sparkle ten meters west, over."

"Christ, that's going to bring it right in on us," Dukes muttered.

The house creaked and groaned, fine white powder and plaster dust raining down on the soldiers as the fire mission poured death in many forms on the unprotected rioters swarming from the street and into the yard.

"Top Hat, this is Anvil Bravo. Freeze sparkle, over."

The night flared again with the explosions of rockets and aircraft-launched ordnance. Minty scrambled back as a smoldering corpse sailed through the window, sending broken glass cascading across the floor.

"Pierce, sit rep?" Dukes asked.

"They're still coming. Fire at will!"

A storm of gunfire broke outside. The bang of grenades punctuated the clatter of small arms. The infected were coming in greater numbers. They climbed over the charred corpses and crawled through the smoking craters left by the air assault.

Minty peered over the sill of the shattered window. The darkness was lit with tracer fire and the burning buildings further up the street. Silhouettes of rioters, jarred by the impact of automatic weapons fire, danced in the swirling smoke.

Pierce came over the comms. *"Alpha squad, are you able to assist, over?"*

"Roger that. Garrett, Milk, Jackson, Potenski, get the others and provide suppressive fire for Bravo squad."

A chorus of affirmatives and clicks on the comms sounded as the squad found windows and started shooting the targets that presented themselves.

"Home Run, Home Run, this is Anvil Alpha. Two squads are moving to secondary PZ, repeat, two squads moving to secondary PZ. Could use a pickup."

"Anvil Alpha, this is Home Run, affirmative. Pickup at secondary LZ. Awaiting your signal beacon."

"Where's the pickup zone?" Minty asked.

"Four hundred meters west, about a block. We light a red flare in the center of the intersection."

"Sounds easy. But how do you plan on getting us there?" Minty waited while Dukes fired at incoming targets.

"Alpha squad, we are moving to secondary PZ. Be advised, artillery fire is scheduled to target concentrations of infected. They are going to start raining on our parade in nine minutes."

"The fuck?" Minty asked.

"We were given a window to get in, get the sample, and get out. That window is closing. We need to leave."

Minty spat plaster dust from his mouth. "After you, man."

"Bravo team, Bravo team. Alpha squad is moving out to secondary PZ. We will provide cover fire while you relocate, over."

Pierce's response was lost in the howls of the infected and the screams of the dying.

"Alpha squad, covering fire. Bravo, get out of there."

Dukes' squad opened fire and buried the advancing rioters under a pile of their own bullet-shredded bodies. The men of Bravo retreated, running from cover to cover. They headed toward a fence behind the house, stopping only to fire at the advancing rioters who shrieked and slavered in the drifting smoke and clouds of tear gas.

Minty stayed on Dukes' heels as he went through the kitchen and out to the six-foot-high back fence. Soldiers were climbing over it, and those on the far side were firing through gaps in the wooden slats.

"Eyes on your six," Dukes warned. They had no way of knowing what might be waiting in the houses behind them. Once they were on the street, they could hustle to the intersection, set off the signal flares, and be picked up.

Minty went over the fence, adrenaline giving him wings. The house on the other side lay shrouded in darkness. The flare of weapons fire, tracer shells, and the burning neighborhood made the dark house as creepy as Hell.

A shape thudded down beside him. "How you doin', granma?" Garrett asked.

"I'm just fine," Minty replied.

Garrett's grin evaporated as he raised his weapon and fired past Minty. The biker ducked and turned, the pistol he carried feeling next to useless in the fight.

A naked man, dark skin grey with the infection, skidded on his face the last few feet and came to a halt at Minty's boot.

"Keep your head down," Garrett said. He moved forward, covering the narrow path down the side of the house. More soldiers tumbled over the fence. Minty jogged to the corner of the house and hunkered down.

Glancing back, he saw Pierce vault over the fence with a rugged-looking laptop case in his hand. Landing in a crouch, Pierce sprang to his feet and dashed to a position next to Minty against the wall.

"Did you get it?" he asked Minty while flipping the case open.

"The sample? Yeah, Garrett and, uh, Jackson? They got it."

Pierce nodded and focused on the screen in front of him.

"You're bleeding, man." Minty gestured at his own forehead.

The soldier didn't look up from the screen. "It's how I know I'm still alive," he muttered while typing fast.

The sniper team was the last over the fence. The shooter, with the heavy-looking M24 rifle, was followed a moment later by his spotter. The second soldier howled in sudden pain. "Get the fuck off me!" he shouted as he struggled to get over the fence. The other squad members grabbed his arms and pulled.

"Fuck!" The spotter screamed. A soldier aimed his weapon over the fence and fired blind, spraying rounds into the yard and at the crowd of attackers clawing at the spotter's legs.

The screaming man was dragged over the fence. The legs of his fatigues were torn and stained with blood.

"Medic!" The sniper yelled. The squad had one medic and he got to work trying to stop the bleeding from the multiple cuts and bite wounds.

"We need to evac," The medic reported.

"*Dukes to Pierce*," The sergeant's voice spoke in Minty's ear.

"Pierce here, go ahead."

"*Clear to the street. Move out*," Dukes advised.

"I have five minutes till cluster fuck," Pierce said.

"*Affirmative. Five minutes until hard rain.*"

"All squads, make ready to move out. Cover fire, by the numbers. Am I clear?" Pierce barked.

The soldiers began an orderly retreat. Two men gathered up their wounded comrade and carried him down the side of the house. Minty fell into step with the others. A loud thudding from inside the house they were passing made him nervous. The soldiers covered the windows as they passed.

A pitched battle was taking place in the street on the other side. Dukes knew that the pickup was now three hundred meters away from their current position. The crowd of infected on this side of the block was growing steadily.

"Do not stop!" Dukes yelled. Grenade launchers coughed and the explosive projectiles slammed into the mass of raging humanity. The explosions tore limbs, shredded flesh, and sent shrapnel into crashed and abandoned vehicles. A Nissan Sentra parked across the sidewalk exploded in a ball of flame, adding to the chaos.

"Samples secure?" Dukes asked.

"Yes, Sergeant," Garrett confirmed.

"Casualties?"

"Flynn, the spotter, his leg's fucked. Bravo team lost three guys before we got the fuck out."

The two squads worked their way out into the street. The rioters had no firearms so there was less need to find cover. Instead the soldiers jogged down the street, covering their fellows in all directions and putting down anyone who came too close.

"Three minutes!" Dukes advised. Minty wondered what it was going to be like, dying in the middle of an artillery barrage.

The two squads kept up the pace, firing in controlled bursts as they moved toward the pickup zone.

Pierce called in another fire mission from the circling Apaches. The gunships howled across the sky, laying fire and death into the midst of the raging crowd.

For Minty, this was insanity, a desperate struggle to survive against an enemy that had lost all reason, and all understanding of anything, except the need to tear flesh and kill. The soldiers around him had an eerie calm; they communicated in quick phrases and their aim remained steady. When the killing was done, they might shake. But not now, not in the thick of a fight for their very lives. To break in this moment would be to shame those friends who had already given their all.

The biker's hand shook. He took a deep breath and sighted down his arm, all the way to the end of the pistol. He waited a moment and then squeezed the trigger, the noise of it lost in the cacophony of gunfire. The gun kicked and blood sprayed from the neck of a man charging toward them. A second shot put him down.

"Star cluster, going up!" Dukes called over the noise. A streaming red light rushed skyward, where it burst in a halo of red phosphorous that cast a blood-like filter over everything.

The infected responded with renewed vigor, or hatred. The light seared them and they pressed forward. Minty fired in a steady cadence of aim and shoot. He counted the shots and was still surprised when the pistol's slide locked to the rear when the magazine was empty.

"I'm out of bullets," he said to Dukes, who handed him a fresh magazine.

Minty dropped the spent magazine on the ground and slapped the loaded one into the butt of the pistol. A Blackhawk helicopter roared over their heads, coming down in the middle of the intersection, the pilot skillfully landing between overhead wires and the abandoned wrecks of cars.

"On board! Go! Go!" Dukes called. He waved to his troops and they ran for the chopper.

"Get on there!" Dukes yelled at Minty, who was covering the soldiers clambering onto the chopper.

"There's another one coming, right?" Minty shouted over the rotor noise.

"Ten seconds," Dukes replied. Minty wondered if he meant the second chopper or the artillery fire that they were counting down to. The biker stayed where he was and continued to lay down covering fire as the Blackhawk leapt skyward. The gunners in the doors fired down into the advancing crowd. For every body that fell, two more seemed to fill the space.

Minty felt real terror for the first time in a long time. The remaining troops—Dukes, Pierce, and the last of their squad—were backing into the intersection. Infected civilians came at them from all four streets. Minty moved with them, the troops firing on the advancing mob as the second Blackhawk descended into their midst.

Minty didn't wait for instructions. As soon as the chopper touched down he climbed on board, making as much room as possible for the soldiers who leapt on around him.

Dukes was the last. He knelt on the deck and fired into the rioters who reached toward the chopper. The snarling freaks fell back as the Blackhawk rose into the air.

"Deadline!" Dukes called out. The chopper rose above the streets and buildings. Minty stared as thunder roared and clouds of explosive fire erupted on the distant edge of the neighborhood. As the helicopter gained altitude the artillery barrage moved across the ground. An inferno of fire and exploding fragments destroyed everything. By the time the chopper had turned toward the east, Minty could see that the dragon had swallowed the entire block they had just left.

They flew over a city tearing itself apart, fires raged everywhere and air-to-ground missiles launched from National Guard aircraft detonated in pulses of lightning and rolling thunder. As the Blackhawk climbed over the eastern hills, Minty sat back in his seat and closed his eyes and almost slept through the forty-minute flight back to the base.

The Blackhawks unloaded. Minty climbed out and realized his legs were trembling. He felt cold and in desperate need of a cigarette.

Garrett, his face stained black with dust and grime, grinned around a lit butt and offered Minty the open pack.

"Thanks," Minty croaked. He lit the cigarette and inhaled deeply.

"You did all right, old man," Garrett said. Minty nodded. He didn't feel all right. He felt like the shit had been kicked out of him while soldiers around him had died. He sure hoped it was worth it.

Dukes noticed that Minty had pocketed his Beretta, but didn't comment. The old guy could hold his own in a firefight and he'd earned the right to carry a weapon.

▲

The debriefing felt like an interrogation. Minty answered questions while a blank-faced clerk tapped away at a stenography machine, like they were in court.

Afterward Minty drank coffee. He had no appetite for anything but coffee and cigarettes.

It was after midnight by the time he was escorted back to the civilian compound, and the biker went into his tent to crash. Freak was sound asleep, his face as peaceful as a child. Todd lay awake on his own cot, arms folded behind his head, a dark expression on his face.

Minty greeted him with a nod and stretched out. Sleep came easily.

CHAPTER 25

Private Larko wriggled in the dirt. A stray rock had been digging into his hip for the last hour and he squirmed with the discomfort.

"You got something up your ass, Lark?" The camouflaged figure to his right hadn't so much as twitched since they took position four hours earlier.

"Fuckin' rock. Digging into me."

"You want me to get you a donut cushion?"

"Gee, Sergeant Houston, would you?" Larko asked.

Houston didn't reply. Instead, with a slow and deliberate movement, she adjusted the telescopic sight she was using to scan the horizon ahead of their observation post.

Being partnered with a female soldier had earned Larko a lot of shit from his comrades. He had been skeptical too, until the first time he went on a field exercise with her. His smirk had evaporated within a few hours. Houston kicked ass and by the end of their first three days in the field, Larko thought he might be in love.

"Movement," Houston murmured.

Larko adjusted his scope. Staring out into the darkness, he scanned the ground and roadway. Then he saw it, heads moving as they crested the horizon of the road.

"Call it in," Houston said.

Larko lifted the handset of their radio. "Home Plate, Home Plate, this is Redbird, over."

"Redbird, this is Home Plate, go ahead, over."

"We have unidentified personnel inbound to sector Mike Lima oh-nine-seven."

"Confirmed, maintain visual contact only."

"TOC says sit tight and watch the parade," Larko murmured.

"I could have stayed home and watched this on the news," Houston replied.

The observation team didn't move as they watched the road below them fill with a crowd of shuffling people. They looked normal until you got close. Then the ragged wounds, the drooling mouths, and the streaks of white veins pulsing under their skin became obvious.

Larko kept counting, a hundred, five hundred, now he was just estimating, a thousand, two thousand . . . Still they kept coming. The crowd on the road spread up the embankment, walking close to the hidden watchers' position. The two of them were invisible under camouflage and dirt and they went completely still as people of all races, ages, and states of injury shuffled past them.

A woman in high heels, one broken and making her limp, stepped squarely on Houston's arm. She held her breath, teeth gritted against the stabbing pain of it. Even after the woman moved on with her awkward gait, the soldier remained frozen and barely breathing.

⚔

"Major Kiro, sir," Lieutenant Bell came to attention.

"Go ahead, Lieutenant," Kiro replied.

"Reports are coming in from multiple sectors. The infected have reached the forward observation posts."

"Rate of movement?"

"Walking pace, estimate two to four miles an hour, sir."

"Advise all perimeter security, high alert. They are going to arrive here by morning and we are going to be ready. Dismissed, Lieutenant."

"Yessir." Bell saluted and hurried back to his station.

⚔

Todd waited until Minty was snoring gently, then he rolled off his cot and slipped on his boots. Walking out into the cold night air, he had one thought: *Find that bitch Jessie and make her sorry.*

He had been keeping an eye on her all afternoon. He had waited, given her the fucking space she fucking wanted, and instead of coming back to talk it out, she had been slutting all over that biker asshole.

The time for talking and being nice was past. Now she would listen to what he had to say.

Jessie shared a tent with three other women and two babies. The tent was quiet, still with the sleeping air of the innocent.

She stood out, her fair skin and blonde hair, tousled in a way that took his breath away. Todd crouched down and gently placed a hand over Jessie's mouth. She squirmed, whimpering, her eyes flicking open.

"It's me," Todd whispered.

"What the fuck are you doing?" she murmured through his hand.

"I gotta talk to you. Come outside."

Jessie nodded and Todd released his grip. He moved back as she pulled on a hoody and crept after him.

"What do you want?" she asked, her arms folding across her chest.

"We need to be together again. Like things were."

Jessie frowned, her gaze slipping to one side.

"It's what we both want, right?" Todd reached out and touched her arm.

"I don' know," she said. Her eyes flicking up to his and away again.

"You and me. Las Vegas. We're going to start our new lives together."

"Things have changed." Jessie met his gaze and held it this time. Her chin lifted slightly.

Todd's eyes darkened. "Nothing has changed."

"I don't want to talk about this. I-I don't want to go to Vegas with you, Todd."

"Of course you do." Todd seized Jessie's arm and tried to pull her close. She resisted, twisting away. He meant to slap her, to make her listen to him. Instead he caught her in the face with a clenched fist. Jessie gave a cry and fell back, clutching her bleeding nose.

"Fuckin' bitch," Todd swore. "Fuck you and that asshole you are fucking."

He stormed off, leaving Jessie crying in the dirt. The noise roused the other women and they came, helping Jessie to her feet and offering comfort and damp cloths to staunch the flow of blood from her face.

Callie arrived, first-aid kit in hand. She took Jessie to the clinic and confirmed her nose was not broken.

"Stay away from him," Callie said.

Jessie nodded, the throbbing pain of the rising bruise on her face speaking for her.

"I'm going to talk to the soldiers," Callie announced. "They can make sure he stays away from you. Maybe put him in jail or something for assault."

"No, just leave it. I can take care of myself." Jessie pulled away. "It'll be light soon, I'm leaving. Going east. You can do whatever you want."

The girl walked out of the tent, leaving Callie to clean up.

By dawn it became clear that something was happening in the camp. Choppers had been flying in and out all night, and the traffic intensified after sunrise. Trucks with troops were coming in from the west. Many of the soldiers looked battle-shocked and exhausted. They climbed down, smoking cigarettes and not speaking.

Callie watched as they were escorted to the command compound, for debriefing and whatever she guessed.

She found Minty with Freak, both men kneeling beside their motorcycles, engine parts arranged on a rag in front of them.

The doctor knew the internal workings of the human body intimately; she could diagnose and prescribe, treat serious injuries, and even perform emergency surgery with confidence. The internal-combustion engine, however, was as alien to her as the bottom of an ocean trench.

"Morning," she said.

"Hey, Doc." Francis, the one they called Freak, waved a greasy hand.

"What time did you get back last night?" she asked Minty.

He looked up at her with a half-closed eye. "Around midnight."

"Todd attacked Jessie early this morning," Callie said.

"Sorry to hear that," Minty replied.

"Is she okay?" Freak bounced up, wiping his hands on his jeans.

"She's fine. Just a little shaken up," Callie said.

"Where is that asshole?" Freak asked.

"I don't know. You should leave him alone. He's angry and unpredictable right now."

"He's an asshole," Freak said. "I'm gonna fucking bury him when I find him."

"Chill out, Freak," Minty ordered. The prospect glowered. "We will take care of it, but not like that."

Freak frowned. The Locusts believed in their own brand of justice: harsh, brutal, and final. Freak had seen it dealt out more than once.

"Jessie's leaving," Callie said. "Heading east, she said."

"How far does she think she's going to get?" Minty asked.

"I don't think she even knows where she is going. She doesn't want to stay here. Frankly, I agree. We stay here, we are going to get trapped when the infection spreads. All it's going to take is one person to get past the dogs and we will have an outbreak here."

"We'll be ready to roll in an hour. Just need to put this lot back together," Freak said.

"Find the girl, don't let her leave on her own," Minty said.

"I'll find her, then we pack. We can meet you back here in an hour, okay?"

"Sounds good," Minty replied.

When the first lines of sunlight crept over the horizon, Private Robinson pushed up his night-vision goggles and rubbed his eyes. Hours of staring into the starlit darkness had made his eyes ache.

"Coffee?" Private Harding asked from where he crouched over a tiny gas stove and bubbling pot.

"Fuckin' A," Robinson agreed.

Harding poured the coffee into two metal cups and killed the flame. The two soldiers sat and savored the brew, watching the desert over their wall of sandbags.

"You think it's as bad as they say?" Harding asked.

"Nah. We've had riots before. Ferguson, Missouri, that time in Kentucky, and LA, that guy, Rodney King?"

"Before my time," Harding admitted.

"The point is, shit like this happens all the time. People blow off a little steam, then things go back to normal."

"They are saying it's different this time. There's some kind of disease that is making people crazy."

"You know what is driving people crazy? The heat, the government, the shit in their water supply. That is what is driving people crazy."

"What if it's Ebola?"

Robinson swirled the dark liquid in the bottom of his cup. "Ebola is different. Besides, they have a vaccine for that now."

"Maybe it's the vaccine that's making—movement, two o'clock."

Both soldiers dropped their cups and lifted their rifles. Sighting down the scope, Harding zeroed in on the lone figure running toward them through the brush and sand.

"The fuck is that?" Robinson muttered.

"Friendly?" Harding asked. "They're in army-issue gear."

"Shit. Call it in."

Harding lowered his rifle and picked up the field radio. He reported to the TOC and was advised to only engage if the approaching figure showed signs of aggression or infection.

"He's within shouting distance," Robinson advised. "US Army! Halt! Or we will fire!"

The figure stumbled, looking back over its shoulder and nearly falling.

"He's armed," Harding confirmed.

"Shit, they're from our LPOP," Robinson murmured to Harding. "Keep your hands up! Advance slowly!" he yelled.

Out in the desert the figure raised its arms, the rifle held in both hands above his head.

Harding and Robinson covered the soldier until he was within thirty feet of their position.

"Halt, who goes there," Robinson called out.

"Sergeant Lara Houston, One-eighty-seventh MP Battalion."

"Plywood!" Robinson shouted into the dim light.

Without hesitation, Houston replied with the password. "Dog house."

"Advance and be recognized," Robinson ordered. Houston came walking toward them

"I need to report. Don't have much time."

"Come forward, slowly," Robinson ordered.

Houston did, lowering her rifle until it lay across her shoulders. She looked bloodied and broken.

"Home Plate, Home Plate, this is Harding. We have friendly inbound. Sergeant Lara Houston, one of the Designated Marksmen from the LPOP, she's asking to report."

"*Keep her there, escort imminent,*" The voice on the end of the radio replied.

"Sit down, Sergeant, take a load off," Robinson said. Houston sank down in the dirt, her head lowering to rest in her hands.

"Where's the rest of your squad?" Harding asked.

"She's LPOP, they don't have a squad. Just her and her little fuck-buddy, dumbass," Robinson said.

"Private Larko. He was with me and he's dead," Houston said without looking up.

"Sorry to hear that," Harding replied.

A Humvee came driving over and two soldiers with medic armbands dismounted. They covered Houston with their weapons as they approached.

"Sergeant, I need you to raise your hands and lift your head."

Houston didn't respond. The medic spoke again. "Houston! Look at me! Do it now!"

Houston's head lifted. She swept a fringe of dark hair back from her face and squinted into the morning sunlight.

"Are you experiencing any flu-like symptoms?" The medic asked.

"No," Houston replied.

"We should wait for a dog," The second medic said.

"She looks clean. Are you bitten, Houston? What happened out there?"

"We were dug in, providing surveillance. Our mission was to simply observe and not engage. There are thousands of civilians. Wounded civilians, all coming this way. They have filled the roads and spilled out on to the hills and desert."

"What happened to you?" The medic asked.

"One of the rioters tripped over right in front of me. Looked me right in the eye. Larko, that stupid sonovabitch, he broke cover. Shot the Tango in the face with his rifle. Then he led the others away from our position. It gave me a chance to escape and evade. I had to fight a few but I've been running ever since."

"Come with us," The medic ordered. "We'll get you checked and debriefed."

Houston nodded. Rising to her feet, she shouldered her rifle and followed the medics to the vehicle.

"Guys," she said, half turning back to Harding and Robinson. "You're going to want to bug out. There is a massive enemy force coming down on your position. They're not armed, but they don't need to be."

Houston got into the back of the Humvee and the two medics drove her back to the gate.

"The fuck was that shit?" Harding asked.

"Fuck knows." Robinson lifted his rifle and scanned the shimmering horizon again. "Shit, see that?"

In the mirage on the horizon, wavering figures moved and twisted.

"Call it in," Robinson ordered.

⚔

Jessie and Callie finished packing. They took as much as they could—MRE ration packs, bottled water, medical supplies—without arousing suspicion.

"We can go on the bikes," Callie had explained. "They are fast and easier to maneuver around traffic jams."

"I've been wondering, where are we going to go?" Jessie asked. "But then I realize, it doesn't matter. Nothing is ever going to be the same again. If we hesitate, we will die. If we move sure and fast, then we can survive."

The girl's fatalistic calm raised the hairs on the back of Callie's neck. In times of crisis, some people became hysterical and others got practical to the point of psychotic detachment.

"Ready to go?" Callie asked.

"Yes."

The two women headed back to where the bikers waited with their machines. They had packed the saddlebags with supplies, but Callie was concerned to see that neither man was armed.

"What are we going to use to defend ourselves?" Callie asked.

"We'll find what we need on the way," Minty said. "Where are we going?"

"East," Jessie said. "Find a place away from other people. Somewhere we can hide and wait this out."

"Sure, because it's not happening all over," Minty said.

"We need to leave. Right now. If we stay here, we will die," Jessie replied.

"I agree with her," Freak said. "We can't stay here. This place is a fucking time bomb."

The air split with the sound of a wailing alarm. On the army side of the fence, soldiers started running, vehicles fired up, and shouted orders rained down.

"Too late," Jessie said. "Too fucking late."

"What the fuck is that?" Freak asked. Minty looked around, scowling at the noise.

"Geddon," he said, swinging into the saddle. The Harleys roared into life and Callie pressed up against Minty's back. With Freak and Jessie on the second bike, they rode toward the gate between the compounds. The soldiers who guarded the gateway were gone, leaving the gate locked. A group of troops were hustling toward the main entrance.

"Is there a back way out of here?" Freak asked.

"There is. Trucks come through a gate, with supplies," Callie said.

"Where?" Minty asked and Callie pointed. Minty gunned the engine and the heavy bike roared down the narrow avenue between tents, the bikes' straight pipe exhaust sounding like artillery fire. The entire compound was coming to life now, civilians coming out of their tents, wondering at the noise and ducking aside as the two machines bellowed past them.

The rear gate was locked and under the guard of two army personnel. They leveled their weapons as the bikes came to a halt in a spray of dust.

"You're needed up front," Minty called.

"You need to turn around and go back to the civilian compound," The nearest soldier ordered.

"You don't understand." Callie slid off the motorcycle and came toward the two men.

"Halt!" one of them yelled. Their weapons trained on the doctor and she froze.

"Go back to the civilian compound. Go now, or you will be detained."

"Callie, come on. We'll find another way," Minty said. The doctor backed away from the soldiers, her hands up. A Humvee appeared through the tent town and came to a halt behind the bikes.

"What's going on here?" The familiar voice of Sergeant Dukes asked as he climbed out of the cab.

"Civilians attempting to leave the compound without authorization, Sergeant," The nearest soldier advised.

"They're with me. Open the gate," Dukes ordered.

"Yes, Sergeant." The troopers ran to unlock and open the gate.

"Follow me. If you don't I'll shoot you myself," Dukes warned Minty. The Humvee rolled through the gate, the bikes followed it, and the camp gates closed behind them.

Minty followed the Humvee's dust down a trail and onto a secondary road. They followed it for a few miles before turning onto a paved road that advised the town of Bowen was a mile further on.

The Humvee pulled over in front of the WELCOME TO BOWEN! sign and the bikers parked behind the truck.

Dukes, Milquist, Garrett, Jackson, and two other soldiers—Potenski and Dawes—exited the vehicle. They were all heavily armed and armored.

"Where the fuck are you going?" Dukes asked Minty.

"Not sure, Sergeant. Like the song says: anywhere but here."

Dukes nodded. "We're on a priority mission. We need to get the samples on to a flight to Atlanta. Priority one. The CDC needs to do their thing, find a cure for this shit."

"They're sending you?" Minty tried not to look too surprised.

"We're meeting a cargo plane outside of Las Vegas. We drop the samples off there and they fly them out to Atlanta. From there our orders are to assist Nevada state authorities and report to the local TOC."

The Humvee passenger door opened and Dr. Stahl looked out. "Sergeant! We are behind schedule!"

"Yes, ma'am," Dukes called back. To the bikers he said, "Thankfully, she's going on the bird too. Stay with me and I'll see if we can get you somewhere secure."

"Did the infected attack?" Jessie asked.

"As we were leaving a large force of walking infected were closing in on the western side of the camp, yes."

"Jesus," Callie muttered. "Jessie? Todd is still in there."

Jessie, still sitting behind Freak on his bike, shrugged and looked away.

"Sergeant!" Stahl called again.

"Mount up. Next stop Nellis," Dukes ordered.

CHAPTER 26

Driving on blacktop they made good time. The bikes purred as they cruised, and the Humvee tires hummed at sixty miles an hour. Small towns, little more than gas stations in the desert, fell under the wheels. Faces watched them from windows, kids on bikes stared and waved excitedly as they drove past. It almost looked normal.

Traffic along the road had been pulled over and the occupants of each vehicle were gone. Military trucks drove on both sides of the roads, and several times they had to thread their way around burning wrecks.

Minty saw no infected, just miles of brush and sand. The trip to Nellis Air Force Base would take them at least four hours. The fuel that Freak scavenged had filled the bike's five-gallon tanks, but even cruising on the highway, they wouldn't make it all the way.

Helicopters and fixed-wing aircraft passed overhead. Minty assumed there were no civilian aircraft in the airspace above California. The risk of infection transmission would be too high.

The small convoy slowed as they approached the cluster of buildings that marked Jean, Nevada. There were no houses here, just an airstrip, a post office, and to Minty's relief a gas station. He signaled the Humvee to pull over and then dropped back. The bikes rolled into the station and stopped at the pumps.

"I really need the bathroom," Callie said. She slid off the bike and hurried inside. Minty filled the tank and handed the pump hose to Freak, who filled his too.

The soldiers parked the Humvee at a diesel pump and climbed out. Dawes filled the tank while the others walked up and down, stretching their legs and surveying their surroundings.

"Radio comms from Nellis," Dukes said, approaching the bikes. "Las Vegas is turning to shit. They've had to blockade the roads and it's turning ugly in there."

Minty frowned, staring out into the desert. Vegas had always been a resort town built on a fantasy. At its core he always felt the place was a house of cards. Waiting for something, natural disaster or a terrorist attack, to destroy the façade and let the cockroaches spill out into the daylight.

"So what do we do now?" Minty asked.

"We sit tight. They are sending an aircraft over to pick up the sample and get it to Atlanta. My squad is escorting it."

Minty looked around. The desert stretched to the mountains.

"There's a landing strip here, not a big one, but it's long enough."

"And after that?" Minty lit a cigarette.

"You're on your own. We go to Atlanta; there's no room for civilians."

"What about the women? You can take them? Callie, she's a doctor, might be useful."

"The CDC is filled with doctors," Stahl said as she stepped out into the desert heat. "Specialist doctors; anyone else is just going to be in the way."

"You're going then?" Minty asked.

Stahl continued. "We thank you for your assistance, Mister MacInnes. Your contribution has possibly saved the lives of millions."

"Could you maybe leave us some weapons?" Freak spoke up.

"That won't be possible. We need to account for any weaponry," Dukes replied. "I know it's a shit situation, so I suggest you get to shelter, stock up on whatever food and supplies you can find in there, then head into the Rockies. Get deep in the wilderness. Get off the roads and start walking. Find a cabin or a lodge. Stay there. Survive until this is over."

"I don't think any of us are really prepared for an extended camping trip, *Sarge*," Minty said.

"Do what you can," Dukes replied. "This will pass. Order will be restored. We will need people like Doctor Blythe. Stay with her and keep her safe."

"It's the End Times," Jessie said, her head resting on Freak's back as she stared out across the shimmering landscape.

"There's no one here," Callie said, coming out of the tiny store and approaching the group. "Looks like they left in a hurry. There's something I think you might want to see, Sergeant."

Dukes indicated for Milquist to follow him and he went with Callie as she disappeared back into the store.

"The fuck are we gonna do, Minty?" Freak asked.

"Locusts survive. We keep moving. Fight when we have to. There's Nevada chapters, we can fall in with them."

Minty walked after Callie and the soldiers. Anything she thought they should know about, he wanted eyes on too.

He found the three of them through the store and the empty workshop. Out the back where drums of waste oil shimmered in the heat, they stood looking at a rectangular hole cut in the ground. Drag marks showed where a buried cover had been pulled aside.

"Nothing in here now, Sergeant," Milquist reported from inside the hole.

"It seems a bit bigger than your standard gun cabinet," Callie said.

Dukes stared into the gloom thoughtfully. From the marks in the dirt, it looked like crates had been lifted out and loaded onto a pickup. That could mean ammunition, or something more heavy duty. The idea of anything support weapon–size or above, in working condition, in the hands of some kind of paramilitary survivalists, sent a chill up his spine.

"Like the fucking Taliban all over again," Milquist said as he climbed out of the empty cache.

"Some kinda survivalists?" Minty asked.

"Could be anything. Drugs, weapons, supplies. Maybe just a meth lab," Dukes said.

Minty shook his head. "Doesn't smell like a meth lab."

"All right, back to the Humvee. Nothing to see here," Dukes ordered.

"Do I want to ask how you know what a meth lab smells like?" Callie asked Minty as they made their way back to the bikes.

"We visited one on a community college field trip," Minty said with a straight face.

Callie's only response was a snort. Minty helped himself to sodas and snacks on the way through the store. The four bike riders sat in the shade and ate jerky and Doritos, washed down with ice-cold Cokes.

Dr. Stahl stood outside the vehicle now. She looked agitated at the delay, and Dukes was talking her down.

Garrett leaned out of the Humvee cab. "Sergeant, Nellis called in. Our bird is inbound."

All eyes went to the sky as the sound of an approaching prop plane reached them.

"There," Dukes pointed.

Minty shaded his eyes and then let out a harsh laugh. "You are fucking kidding me! Look at the size of that thing. We can all fit on that easy."

Coming in low from the north was a C-27J Spartan, a midsize twin-prop cargo plane.

"Orders are orders, Minty," Dukes replied. "No civilians on this ride."

"That is bullshit, Dukes, and you know it."

Stahl lifted a cooler bag bright with biohazard labels out of the back of the Humvee. She stood, watching the plane as it turned and lined up with the airstrip.

"Do you think I fucking like this? I don't get to make that call. It is way above my pay grade."

Minty stepped up into Dukes' face. The two men scowled at each other like heavyweight contenders at a pre-fight meet and greet.

"You can't leave us here. Take the women at least. They have the skills that are going to be needed. Me an' Freak, we can manage on our own."

"I'm not leaving you behind," Callie said, and then looked startled at her own words.

Dukes ignored her. "Orders. You were army? Marines? You know how it works."

"Marines, back when you still thought your dick was for pissing."

"Is there a problem, Sergeant?" Garrett and the other soldiers stood poised, ready to leap in and kick the shit out of the bikers in support of their leader.

"No problem, Private. Mount up, we're heading out to the runway. Get the samples loaded up and we'll be on our way."

Dukes stared at Minty while he spoke, then stepped back and turned away, the spot between his shoulder blades twitching, waiting for a blow.

The Spartan came in on its final approach, four hundred feet, three hundred, two hundred, one hundred . . .

From somewhere in the cluster of buildings that made up Jean, Nevada, came a whooshing sound and a streak of smoke. The aircraft was too low to evade the rocket. The projectile impacted and detonated forward of the wing. The aircraft frame bucked and tore before exploding in a searing ball of fire and black smoke.

An A-10 Thunderbolt streaked overhead and released an AGM-65 Maverick missile. The watchers on the ground stood in shocked silence as the missile homed in on its ground target, detonating on impact.

"Fuck me," Minty muttered.

"Holy shit! Did you see that shit? Fuck!" Freak was just about dancing in delight at the sudden airshow.

"Sergeant," Garrett called from the Humvee. "Nellis command advises us to keep moving. They'll reschedule a pickup at an alternative landing site."

"What are they thinking?" Stahl demanded. "We are trying to save you, you morons!"

"Doc, get in the Humvee. You"—Dukes gestured at Minty—"follow us. I'll see what we can do about getting everyone to safety."

The strange convoy packed up and rolled out of the gas station. Where the rocket had fired at the Spartan, only a smoking crater remained. To Minty, it seemed insane that anyone would fire on an aircraft like that. Though if you were paranoid enough to believe that your worst nightmares of a military takeover of the government had taken place, then shooting down anything that looked like it might be carrying troops or weapons would make sense.

Dukes plan called for them to approach the Las Vegas blockade, then turn northeast. Avoiding the center of the city as much as possible, circling around and try to get to Nellis AFB on the northern side of the city.

Callie was warm and comforting against his back as Minty rode the last few miles. That the world had gone to shit so fast astounded him. It wasn't what he had imagined when Jethro preached about his revolution of anarchy and freedom from the state. This was savage and wild, a dirty reality compared to the romantic vision of lunatics like the leader of the Locusts.

Wherever Jethro was now, Minty hoped he was dead. Having the Locusts alive in this rapidly emerging world of chaos would be a very bad thing indeed.

The Nevada National Guard were out in force on the highway leading into Las Vegas. Tanks, Humvees, and support weapons were covering the roadway, and the line of empty cars parked on the side of the road stretched for over a mile.

Sentries leveled weapons at the approaching convoy. They rolled to a halt and identified themselves. The four civilians were described as consultants, essential to the current crisis.

They were given food and a place to nap while Dukes and his men attended a briefing, giving their own report on the changing situation both in and on the outskirts of Los Angeles. Minty was ordered to attend to represent the civilian "consultants" in the group.

Vegas appeared to be infection-free at this time. Martial law was in effect across the state. The National Guard was patrolling in support of civilian law enforcement. So far their biggest problem had been looters and armed civilians shooting each other.

"Airport and roads are closed," Colonel Gresham advised. "We are maintaining a secure perimeter. No one leaves, no one gets in without my authorization."

"Understood, sir. We are escorting essential data and personnel to CDC, Atlanta. We were supposed to get a flight from outside the city. Now we're looking to get to Nellis AFB and fly out from there." Dukes stood at attention, the document detailing his orders held out in one hand.

Gresham took the paper and frowned as he read it. "All right then, Sergeant, what do you need from me?"

"Nothing, sir. We are fully supplied and mission ready."

Minty coughed and shuffled his feet. Dukes and Gresham both shot him a look.

"Sir, we could use some additional weapons," Minty said.

"The hell kind of operation do you think I'm running here? This isn't a goddamn Dick's Sporting Goods store."

"Understood, sir," Dukes replied.

"Understood. Sir, I'm a retired US Marine. I fought for my country in Desert Storm. I'm part of a group of four key civilian personnel on this mission. With all due respect, we have survived LA and everything between here and that shitstorm. I'd be a lot happier going on into an uncertain situation with some firepower on my person."

"Goddamn Marines," Gresham muttered. "Captain Rhodes."

"Yessir?"

"Process a requisition order for weapons and ammunition for Sergeant Dukes. Any supplies issued to him are to be taken from the ordnance confiscated from civilians. Is that clear?"

"Yessir," The captain saluted.

"You are dismissed, Sergeant."

"Yessir." Dukes snapped a salute. Minty did the same and the colonel just shook his head in disbelief as they marched out of his command center.

The confirmation of Colonel Gresham's authorization got Dukes and his squad access to a locked shipping container packed full of AR-15s and other weapons. They shopped, checking each weapon was clean and well maintained before adding it to the selection. Within half an hour they had a good selection of semiautomatic rifles, handguns, and ammunition.

⚔

The fence erected across Las Vegas Boulevard opened and the Humvee drove through. Minty and Freak followed on their bikes. Civilians camped out in their cars watched them pass. This part of the city had an eerie sense of tension about it. The people were almost pressed up against the fence, desperate to leave as soon as possible. These are the smart ones, Minty figured.

The map they had pored over had them going along the St. Rose Parkway as far as the Bruce Woodbury Beltway. Then all the way out through Henderson, along Lakeshore Road, left onto Lake Mead Boulevard, which took them away from the city until it wound back into the northeast corner of Vegas. They would end up at Nellis Air Force Base. Hardly a direct route, but Dukes declared it to be the safest option.

"Just how bad is it in the city?" Callie asked.

"Looting mostly, and lots of unhappy civilians. Many of them armed. I'm not prepared to risk my squad or the samples driving through the middle of a potential firefight."

"Stay close to the Humvee," Minty said to Freak. The boy grinned; he was having an adventure. The kind of batshit crazy stuff he had dreamed of when he joined the Locusts. He didn't feel like a lowly prospect anymore. He had a hog, admittedly a stolen one, and he was riding through chaos like a total badass biker.

The bikes roared through the outskirts of Las Vegas, the Humvee giving them a clear path through the army patrols. They were stopped regularly, but the signed orders from the colonel that Dukes carried were sufficient paperwork to get them waved through roadblocks and checkpoints.

Everywhere they saw civilians, many armed with handguns, shotguns, hunting rifles, and AR-15s. Painted signs warned looters of lethal force awaiting anyone who dared to invade their tiny kingdoms. A vocal subset of people on the streets was carrying placards calling on the sinners to repent; Judgment Day was upon the earth. A man wearing only shorts was being whipped while he marched up and down a block, dragging a full-size wooden cross over his shoulder.

Jessie stared in fascination at the bloodstained figure until they were through the next checkpoint and out of sight.

It was getting dark by the time they reached Nellis Air Force Base. The entire site was lit up with bright halogen beams that gave the compound an almost sterile whiteness.

Getting in took a lot of negotiation and reporting. The documentation went up the chain of command and the message at every level was the same: The US Air Force has bigger issues right now than some National Guard mission. Take a number and we'll get to you in due course.

Dukes argued and demanded. Stahl lost her cool and started screaming at an impassive captain. They were assigned tent space for the night with a promise that their request for air transport would be reviewed in the morning.

"Seems that they are losing more aircraft to ground fire," Dukes reported. "Command is sensitive about sending unarmed aircraft up when there are units of assholes hiding in the hills ready to fire at anything that is moving slower than a jet."

"What you are saying is that we are going to have to go by road," Minty said.

"Seems that way." The group clustered around a map Dukes spread out on the table. "Atlanta, Georgia, is nearly . . . two thousand miles from here. That's gonna be at least thirty hours driving."

"Thirty hours on empty roads. If the shit keeps hitting the fan the way it is, it could take a week," Minty said.

"We don't have a week. We go back to the damned officers in charge around here and demand that they get us a flight," Stahl snapped.

"With all due respect, Doctor Stahl, the air force don't give a flying fuck about your demands. They have lost contact with our previous TOC. That means no refresh on our authorization. No one is able to confirm the priority of our mission."

"Christ," Minty muttered.

"Lost contact?" Callie asked. "What does that mean exactly?"

"They aren't saying. But it seems that it means there has been a breakdown in communications between the base to the west and those further east. It could be a technical fault. Or it could mean that they are up to their assholes in infected and are too busy to pick up the phone right now."

"Tell them that. Tell them that the longer they delay us the more likely it is that there will be an outbreak in Las Vegas," Stahl insisted.

"Doc, they are containing the situation and relying on the intel they are receiving from multiple channels. The CDC is issuing updated reports. Dallas, Houston, San Fran—this shit is happening everywhere but here."

"That's weird," Minty said. "Plenty of people looking to buy drugs in Las Vegas."

"Well fuck, maybe it's a logistics issue," Dukes said. "It doesn't fucking matter. The important thing is that we need to be moving. We either wait and try to get a plane and crew to fly us to Atlanta, or we stock up on fuel and supplies and get moving."

"We're on a sinking ship." Jessie spoke for the first time in hours. "We keep moving to the next dry part, but the ship is sinking anyway. Sooner or later, we're going to drown."

"She's right," Callie said. "What we need is the equivalent of a life raft."

"Atlanta is our only destination," Stahl said.

"Sure, but after that?" Callie asked.

"The situation will be contained. The fungal agent will be identified and a cure developed. In a few weeks, months at best, this crisis will be resolved."

"Are you even listening to yourself?" Callie snapped. "Have you seen what infected people are doing? This situation is about as contained as a hurricane. In a few weeks, there will be nothing left of the southern states of the US. Any treatment developed will take months to test and then it has to be mass-produced, distributed, and administered. There will be no one left to treat!"

"Okay, everyone stand down," Dukes ordered.

"We get to Atlanta, then we work out what our next move is," Minty said.

"Sure, but let's try and keep a realistic perspective," Callie said.

"Get some sleep," Dukes advised. "We'll be moving at oh-five-hundred."

CHAPTER 27

As they loaded the Humvee the next morning, smoke could be seen rising from the direction of the Strip, the world famous party-central area of Las Vegas. The sound of sirens blared as emergency services responded to the blaze.

Dukes gathered the civilians and his soldiers for a briefing.

"We have spare fuel, weapons, food, and water. We will stop every six hours to refuel. If we encounter resistance of any kind, civilians will not engage. Leave the shooting to the professionals. Our priority is getting the samples to Atlanta. If you get lost or go off on your own, we will not be coming back for you. Am I clear?"

Everyone nodded.

"Any questions? All right, let's go."

Leaving Nellis by the same route they came in, the sun rising in their faces, the group made good time clearing the built-up areas.

Boulder City's population had swelled with people trying to get into Las Vegas and points west. With the closure of the main highway, the traffic had doubled back to Boulder and store shelves had been stripped of everything. National Guard units were present on the streets; local police and sheriff department officers were out in force.

Dukes and his group were ignored and they kept driving, aware that all it would take was for one infected person to arrive in the middle of a population like that for a wildfire of death and terror to erupt within hours.

At the bridge over the Colorado River, just south of the Hoover Dam, they went through a military checkpoint.

"We cannot advise you to continue," The sergeant in charge of the roadblock said. "We do not have up-to-date intel on the security of any areas beyond this point."

"I understand, Sergeant. We will proceed with caution," Dukes replied.

"Stay safe out there. We've heard reports. Not sure how much of it is true, but there seems to be some kind of widespread rioting in many of the major population centers across the south."

Dukes shrugged. "It's not that widespread. The Guard are simply out supporting local law enforcement. I can't tell you anything more than that."

The squad leader didn't look comforted. They stepped aside and opened the way for the Humvee and Harleys to roll past.

Following Route 93 as it headed southward, they turned east at Kingman, Arizona, and continued along Interstate 40. They passed through Flagstaff, Winslow, into New Mexico and through Gallup until, by early evening, they had reached the outskirts of Albuquerque.

The city seemed quiet, a few cars on the road. Store windows showed signs declaring they were out of food and bottled water.

The gas stations they passed were under National Guard control, and signs indicated a ration of ten gallons per vehicle was in effect.

"I bet they all wished they had bought a Prius," Callie yelled into Minty's ear over the roar of the Harley's engine as they rode past.

He laughed. "I'd rather slam my damn balls in a door than drive a fuckin' Prius." It was true, and he needed a good reason to laugh. Callie pressed up against his back, a silent squeeze that felt as intimate as a kiss. Minty wondered what the doctor's plan was. Did she simply see him as a bodyguard? A shield against whatever insane dangers the world was coming up with? Or maybe she actually liked him, in a genuine way.

You're old enough to be her father, he reminded himself. *No, fuck that,* he mentally replied. *She's a grown woman. A fuckin' doctor for Chrissakes. She can make her own decisions. If she's just using me as a shield, well okay. At least it means you have a purpose. If she wants to take it further, a little sweet lovin' before I die wouldn't be so bad, would it?*

Minty's experience with women had left him with little doubt of their ability to look after themselves. The women who drifted in and out of biker gang life were hammered steel. They weren't looking for anything beyond security and affection. Some had a drug habit they were supporting, and others had grown up in the culture. They had a strength that meant they could take more punishment and put up with shit that would make men cry.

One time, years ago, during a two-day orgy of drugs and booze, Minty had stumbled across a Locust whose fists were splattered red with blood. A naked woman lay at his feet, her face pulped, eyes swollen shut. Minty felt the shock of it sobering him. He thought the woman might be dead until she choked and coughed up blood. Rolling onto her side, she spat and said, "I'm going to gut you, motherfucker."

The biker had laughed and slapped Minty on the shoulder with a bloodstained hand. "You gotta respect women," he said with a drunken slur. "Anything that bleeds that much and doesn't fuckin' die deserves your respect."

The biker walked off, leaving Minty to try and help the battered woman. She told him to fuck off. An hour later he saw her, dressed, the worst of the blood cleaned up, and drinking vodka shots to kill the pain.

He heard a month later that a patched brother in their San Francisco chapter had been killed by some scar-faced bitch. She had gutted him from balls to sternum. No one knew why she had done it, and the senseless death was seen as a tragedy.

The Humvee stopped at an army camp in a parking lot in Albuquerque. Like every other temporary installation of its type they had encountered, this one buzzed with activity. Soldiers and vehicles came and went. People with papers in their hands barked orders and ran from place to place.

Somehow amongst all this, they got food and a clear patch of concrete to stretch out on.

"My butt is completely numb," Jessie complained.

"I'll kiss it better for you," Freak said with a grin and Jessie grinned back.

"She's not wrong. I feel like my teeth are still vibrating," Callie said.

"You get used to it," Minty replied and they sat in silence, leaning against a concrete block wall, watching the world go by.

"Why do you smoke?" Callie asked.

"What?" Minty stopped, a cigarette halfway out of the crumpled pack.

"You know it will give you cancer, heart disease, increases your risk of stroke, gangrene. It raises blood pressure, hardens your arteries, and destroys your lungs and immune system."

"Yeah, that's why I started. I really hate my immune system." Minty left the cigarette in the packet, wondering if he should smoke it in front of her or not.

"Seriously, as soon as you quit, your body starts to heal. It's hard. Harder than kicking heroin, but the benefits are important."

"Harder to kick than heroin? Shit, Doc, I never took you for a junkie."

"I wish. I barely drink."

Minty remembered the way she had accepted his offer of a drink on that first night. Then the second and third drink, and on it went till they were doing tequila shots and she passed out.

"You go hard when you do though," Minty said.

"I don't like the sense of losing control. I know what alcohol is doing to every system and cell in my body. It freaks me out. Smoking is a hundred times worse." Callie reached out and took the pack of Lucky Strikes from Minty's hand. She crushed it in her fist.

"The fuck?" Minty lashed out, seizing her wrist and extracting the packet from Callie's grip. "Do not fuck with my smokes. I turn into a big, green version of Lou Ferrigno when I don't get a smoke."

"You don't get to look like that if you are smoking a pack a day," Callie said, rubbing her wrist where Minty had grabbed it.

"You could on steroids," Minty replied, carefully inspecting the paper packet's precious cargo of tobacco.

"Maybe, but steroids have unfortunate side effects. Like shrinkage where you don't want it."

"No wonder he got mad all the time."

Callie didn't smile. "Cigarettes cause your blood vessels to contract. This can cause erectile dysfunction," she said.

"No shit?" Minty lit a kinked cigarette and blew smoke out of his nose. "Just leave my fucking smokes alone."

Dukes appeared through the foot traffic. "Did you guys eat?"

"Yes, thank you, Sergeant," Callie replied.

"Get some rest; we're leaving again in a few hours." Dukes walked off.

"Where's Freak?" Minty said, looking around.

"He was with Jessie, they were here a minute ago," Callie replied.

"Damn prospect." Minty climbed to his feet. Callie stood up more easily.

"She can take care of herself you know," she said.

"It's not Jessie I'm worried about," Minty replied.

Teenage hormones spark innovation like nothing else, and Minty gave up the search after ten minutes. Wherever Freak and Jessie were, he hoped they were using protection and she was consenting. If he heard otherwise, he would have no concern about beating the young prospect senseless.

Sleep wasn't easy on the concrete. Callie dozed against Minty and he leaned against the wall. Around them the soldiers seemed used to sleeping rough as they arranged themselves in bizarre positions and went right to sleep.

Even with a couple of blankets to keep the night's chill at bay, Minty and Callie woke up, stiff and cold, when Milquist nudged them awake.

"We're moving out," he said, crouching down in front of them. "There's infection here. A squad has been rounding up people showing symptoms, but it is spreading fast."

"Oh hell," Callie said.

"Five minutes. Get your shit together and be ready to leave." Milquist stood up and went to finish loading the Humvee.

After a cigarette for breakfast and a visit to the latrine, Minty was warming up his bike when Freak and Jessie came hurrying.

"You okay?" Minty asked Jessie. She blushed and nodded. Freak grinned like he had won the lottery.

"We need to go," Minty said to Freak. Both bikes grumbled as the V-twin engines idled. Callie slid into position behind Minty and looked at Jessie.

"Morning. Sleep well?" she asked.

"Yeah." Jessie looked brighter than she had the day before. Which Callie took as a good sign.

The Humvee pulled out into the street, the bikers following once again. An area across the street had been fenced off with barbed wire, and struggling civilians were being forced through a gate that put a few of them at a time into a mesh cage and then through a second gate into the small compound. Soldiers in full NBC suits stood guard. Even from here Minty could see that some of the civilians were in the pre-violent stages of infection.

"Nothing we can do for them now," Minty said.

"Soon though. God I hope so," Callie replied.

They fell silent as the bike picked up speed. With only army vehicles on the streets, they made good time across the city and back on to I-40. As the sun rose in a ball of orange through a haze of smoke from fires somewhere east of them, they reached the open highway and rode the miles to the Texas border without pause or incident.

At Amarillo they stopped well back from a blockade of shipping containers and trucks across the interstate. With binoculars, Dukes could see that the roadblock was well defended by men wearing a mix of camouflage pattern and khaki. Some wore baseball caps and T-shirts with patriotic slogans on them.

The men's faces were covered with bandannas, and they carried AR-15s and sidearms. A Republic of Texas flag fluttered in the dry wind.

"Are they Guard?" Milquist asked.

"Looks like a local militia."

"So we going through them or not?" Milquist asked.

"I'd rather not risk it. If they have control of this section of the highway that means the army don't. Whether that means some kind of coup has taken place here, or we just don't have the resources, I'm not willing to get into a fight unless we have to."

A pickup with three men on the back and two in the cab pulled out onto the highway in front of the barricade. It accelerated toward them.

"Garrett, on the SAW," Dukes ordered. "Everyone, stay behind the Humvee."

The pickup came to a halt, almost broadside across the highway. The guys on the back aimed their AR-15s at the group.

"This is Sergeant Kyle Dukes, US Army. Lower your weapons," Dukes shouted across the open space between the two vehicles.

The passenger door on the pickup opened and a man slid out, his massive belly straining against the white T-shirt he wore. His sleeveless army jacket was studded with patches declaring his support for Texan sovereignty.

"We do not recognize your authority here!" The man yelled back. "You are a foreign military force entering the Republic of Texas. I suggest y'all turn around and go back where you came from!"

"Sir, I appreciate what you are saying. I'm Sergeant Dukes. My men and I need to cross this bridge and be on our way!"

"I have all of them in my field of fire, Sergeant," Garrett advised from his position. "Awaiting your order to end this shit."

"At ease, Specialist. We're still talking."

Dukes stepped forward. "This is a difficult time, sir. I understand that you are doing what you must to protect your families and your homes. We are not a threat to you; we just need to get on down the road."

"We're well prepared to defend our homes and our families. We don't need you."

"Shit," Dukes muttered. Then, to the man: "Fair enough. Can you give us some directions on a safe route east? We'd be happy to leave Texas in your capable hands."

"Y'all can take the state route south around Amarillo."

"Duly noted. Thank you for your assistance."

Minty and Freak turned their bikes around while the Humvee did a U-turn and followed them. The militia on the truck whooped and hollered, excited by their victory.

The Humvee took the secondary highways around Amarillo. Working their way across the patchwork of roads, they passed scenes of desperation and terror. Abandoned cars, crashed vehicles with infected raging inside them. They passed a man standing next to a car with the hood up. He held up a cardboard sign with the word *HELP* painted in shit. A woman and two crying kids sat on the ground in front of the car. She didn't look up when the Humvee drove past.

An hour down the road a grey-haired man came charging out of an RV, waving them down as he stood in the middle of the road. The Humvee slowed and then stopped as the man moved to keep in front of the truck. He put his hands on the grill and panted for breath.

"Stay put," Dukes ordered. He got out and covered the man with his rifle.

"Sir, I need you to return to your vehicle."

"Please," The man said. He was breathing hard, as if he had just run a mile. "My wife. We came from Dallas. There's some kind of riot happening there. My wife, she was attacked. She needs medical attention. Please."

"Sir, you need to step aside."

"Please listen to me!" The man yelled, his face contorting into a savage scream. Dukes raised the rifle. The white lines of infection stood out against the man's flushed complexion. The rifle fired, a spray of blood and the man toppled backwards.

From the RV came the sound of a scream. A woman stumbled out and ran toward the sprawled figure, screaming and crying.

"Harvey! Oh, God! Harvey!?"

"Ma'am, stay away from him," Dukes ordered. "He is infected." The woman ignored him, trying to cradle the dead man against her chest.

"Sergeant, there is nothing we can do here," Stahl called from the back of the Humvee. Dukes stepped back, sliding his rifle into the cab and closing the door as he took his seat.

"Drive," he told Milquist.

CHAPTER 28

Camping off the road suited everyone that night. The soldiers distributed MREs and water. The vehicles were refueled and Dukes relented to the idea of a small fire.

"All we need now are marshmallows," Jessie said.

Freak laughed. "Yeah, anyone know any good scary stories?"

The silence that followed could have been spread on soft bread.

"Milk, Garrett, Dawes, guard duty. Standard shifts. Wake me if anyone comes within four hundred meters."

The fire was buried and people turned in.

Minty made a bedroll out of blankets next to his bike. He stomped the lumps flat, pacing up and down like a dog circling before it slept.

Callie came over as he was smoking his last cigarette of the evening. She didn't say anything, just folded her arms and stared up at the sky.

"You ever wish on a star?" she asked.

"Nope," Minty said, because it was true.

"I used to wish on shooting stars when I was a kid. I thought they were God's way of inviting me to send up a special prayer. One that he would always answer."

"How did that work out for you?" Minty crushed the cigarette butt under his boot.

"Pretty good actually. I guess you can turn anything into an answered prayer if you believe. I have seen friends and family of patients praying their hearts out for a miracle. I guess there were no shooting stars that night."

Minty sat down, loosening his boots but not sliding them off. His socks needed changing, they probably smelled as bad as the rest of him.

"Can I stay with you? Tonight I mean?" Callie asked.

"Sure." Minty made room on the bedroll. Her warm body pressed against his side and he draped the blanket over them both. Callie's head settled on his shoulder and he inhaled the scent of her hair.

Around their campsite the soldiers loosened their boots and lay down with their poncho liners as blankets and assault packs for pillows. They spooned with their weapons and slept secure in the knowledge that their buddies on watch were wide awake.

The sound of Jessie giggling, quickly muffled, came through the dark. Minty hoped that they were keeping it under covers; the night-vision gear the soldiers on guard duty had could see everything on a clear night like this.

Callie pulled Minty's arm around her. "Tell me it's going to be okay," she whispered.

"I don't know if that's true," Minty murmured.

"Tell me anyway."

"It's going to be okay," Minty said.

⚔

Dawn meant more water and a breakfast of Meal, Ready to Eat rations.

"You ever see that movie? The Australian one, about the guy who hunted alligators?" Garrett asked.

"Crocodiles. Australia's got crocodiles," Minty said.

"What the fuck ever. That line in the movie? He says, you can live on it, but it tastes like shit. That asshole, he'd never tried to live on fucking MREs."

Dukes paused between mouthfuls. "Garrett, quit your bitching. Police up your gear and make us ready to roll in five minutes."

They buried their waste and got back on the road, Jessie now wearing Freak's leather jacket with the LOCUSTS PROSPECT patch. Minty narrowed his eyes. That shit would not fly.

He waved Freak down a hundred meters along the highway. "Chick's don't wear your patch. Even if you are a snot-nosed fuckin' prospect. Not-fucking-ever," Minty warned.

Looking guilty and embarrassed, Freak stripped the patch vest off the jacket and put it on, leaving the jacket for Jessie to wear again.

"What kind of bullshit is that?" Callie said with a laugh.

Minty twisted in the saddle and stared hard at her. "It's my kind of bullshit. The kind I take seriously. The Locusts have laws. Those laws don't change just because the world is ending. They sure as fuck don't change because some maggot prospect is getting his dick wet."

Callie blinked, her mouth opening to say something. Minty didn't need to hear it. He started the bike rolling again, opening the throttle to catch up with the Humvee, the engine noise making conversation impossible.

Dukes led them east, angling northward till they came back to the interstate. Oklahoma City was the next large population center on their route, and while he didn't want to go anywhere near it, they were going to need to stock up on fuel. The Harleys had worse gas mileage than the Humvee, and their spare gas cans were running out.

The desert gave way to rolling green pastures, and along the highway they passed through more army checkpoints. The traffic lined up in both directions for several miles as civilians were checked by soldiers wearing full biohazard gear and dogs that went into a frenzy of barking when they detected infection.

The Humvee stopped at an outpost with trucks, medical tents, and a closely watched crowd of civilians trying to keep cool in the scant shade.

"Sergeant Kyle Dukes, California National Guard, ma'am." Dukes snapped a salute at the female lieutenant. She barely looked up from her clipboard.

"What can I do for you, Sergeant?"

"I have been advised I need to speak to you about continuing on through Oklahoma City, ma'am."

She looked up at that. "Why do you want to do that, Sergeant?"

"I'm on a priority mission, ma'am. We are escorting essential personnel and materials to the CDC in Atlanta."

"News to me," The lieutenant replied.

"Yes, ma'am. I understand that communications have been an issue in light of recent events."

"Sergeant, the evacuation and screening of thousands of uncooperative civilians with no clear indication of where they are to be evacuated to, or what we are to do with anyone showing symptoms of whatever the hell it is that is making them sick, that has been an issue. Your road trip and whatever orders you are operating under are somewhat less important to me in terms of priority."

"Yes, ma'am."

"Is there anything else, Sergeant?"

"We will need to refuel and resupply, ma'am."

The lieutenant stepped out into the sunlight. "That tanker there is full of diesel. That one is carrying potable water. Try not to get them confused."

"Yes, ma'am."

Dukes returned to his squad, who were fielding questions from concerned civilians about the situation west of their current position.

"Milk, take the fuel cans and get them filled at that gasoline tanker. Jackson, you and Potenski, fill our water cans. Water is in that tanker over there. Dawes, move these people back."

The soldiers went into action, following Dukes' orders without question.

"We need to stay away from population centers and groups of people," Callie said. "It's not just the infection that will kill us. There's all manner of diseases caused by poor sanitation and lack of supplies. Not to mention the violence that will come as people get more desperate."

"Jethro would say that these people are not yet worthy of anarchy," Minty said.

"That guy was a psychopath," Callie replied.

"Maybe. But he did have a grand vision. A society ordered by awareness of others and cohesion of desire. Self-sustaining peace where people worked together to achieve a greater good, without law or a ruling government."

"Nobody has yet managed to create anything even close to that. Anarchy, by its very nature, requires rules. Even if that rule is 'there are no rules,' it still has to be followed and enforced," Callie said.

Minty shrugged. "The best we can hope for is a complete collapse of the current system and for someone with the balls to enforce a better way, to come to power and get enough support."

"Realistically, if the world does fall apart, we are going to be back in the Dark Ages—no, even earlier than that. We are going to be back to hunter-gatherer communities, with life spans of maybe twenty-five years and high infant mortality rates, within two generations."

"I don't think they give a shit." Minty nodded in the direction of Freak and Jessie, who were sitting astride his Harley and making out.

"That's just hormones and lust. They are hiding from reality by focusing on the one thing they can control. Feeling good is all that matters when it's all you have."

"When you put it like that, Doc, it sounds a lot less sweet."

Dukes gave the order to mount up again, and the bikes wound their way through the crowd and vehicles.

With the route through Oklahoma City clogged with traffic, Dukes turned the Humvee off the road and the bikes followed. They zigzagged through suburban streets, spending the rest of the day working their way around the metropolitan area. Everywhere they saw a shifting sea of panic and sirens. EMT, fire, police, all racing from one emergency to the next. People clogged parking lots of stores and jammed the roads as they tried to flee. Any rumor of infection or supplies caused a flood of people to either run away from or toward the epicenter of the rumor.

Panic in all its forms spread ahead of the infection. It would only be a matter of time before it reached Oklahoma, from Texas, California, or Mexico.

Traffic density increased east of the city until the highway was clogged with cars, vans, trucks, and RVs. The afternoon echoed with the sounds of gunfire and the screams of people. Vehicles and corpses burned uncontrolled, the fires spreading from one car to the next. People fled into the fields and trees; they invaded farms and homes whose residents were armed and ready to defend themselves. The death toll climbed as the panic spread.

The Humvee made a path for itself, bearing down on anyone who didn't get out of the way fast enough. A burst of SAW fire over their heads scattered anyone who tried to block the convoy. The Harleys followed in the Humvee's wake, staying close and keeping their speed up.

Minty watched the people they passed. Any one of them would gladly tear him from the bike and take his place. It didn't matter where they were going—away from this Hell would be enough for a start.

Callie carried an AR-15 slung over her back and a pistol tucked in the jacket she wore. Minty hoped she would know when—and how—to use it.

By nightfall they had reached the bridge over the Arkansas River, where a state of war had broken out. Civilians had spilled out along the banks, camping among the trees, huddled around fires, some partying and others fighting amongst themselves.

The river was thick with corpses and the flailing bodies of the wounded who were trying to swim for shore.

All four lanes of the highway bridge were blockaded at the Oklahoma side by National Guard. Steady gunfire cracked as they exchanged fire with an unseen enemy further along the bridge.

Recreational boats were speeding up and down the river, some firing at the National Guard, others at the militia, all ignoring the cries of the floaters. Spotlights from the Guard pinpointed the attacking boats and concentrated fire destroyed the crews, sending the boats careening off into the darkness, unmanned and out of control.

Tracer fire filled the night and Dukes called a halt. Keeping low, he headed up to the barricade. He answered a challenge from a rear guard. They sent him on to speak to a Corporal Lanning.

"Corporal? Sergeant Dukes, California National Guard. Who's in charge here?"

"Shit, Sergeant, I guess it's me."

"What's your situation?"

"Our last orders were to prevent civilian traffic moving possible infection. We blocked the bridge, and yesterday, these assholes started shooting at us."

"You have any support?"

"Negative, no air support, no artillery. We don't have anything except a couple of squads and a few rounds."

"Where's your commander?"

"I have no fucking idea. The rest were ordered to head towards Dallas. I hear it's bad there. Real bad. I haven't had new orders in two days."

"Can we get across the bridge?"

Corporal Lanning shook his head. "They've killed anyone who steps out of cover."

"You have any boats?" Dukes asked.

"Not a fucking one. There are some guys who will charge you a thousand bucks per head to get across the river. Can't say what you will find on the other side."

Dukes had a fair idea what he would find on the other side: fear, panic, and civilians who would shoot first and not bother with questions.

"Do you have any kind of support weapons? SAWs? Antiarmor weapons?"

"Sergeant, we aren't authorized to—"

"Open this barricade, Corporal."

"Christ, all right. But do me a favor. When you get to wherever the fuck you are going, you find who is in charge of this fucking mess and you fucking tell them that I am fucking done."

Dukes turned on the corporal. Lanning's eyes were red-rimmed and brimming with tears.

"Get your shit together, Corporal. You're a fucking soldier in the US-fucking-Army. We don't fucking quit. Am I clear?"

"Yes, Sergeant!"

"Now get this fucking barricade opened up and get your men together with all the weapons you have. We are going to clear this bridge."

Lanning shrugged and started issuing orders to his men. It took them twenty minutes to clear the roadblock materials. They operated under fire. Dukes ordered the machine guns to concentrate their fire on the end of the bridge. The barrage was backed up by rockets. The bridge squad only had three left, and Dukes sent them all down the highway in streaks of fire and smoke. A truck parked across the far end of the bridge exploded in fire and shrapnel.

"Move!" Dukes yelled. The Humvee surged forward and the SAW on the roof blazed, cutting down the militia who stood out in stark silhouettes against the burning truck.

Five minutes later it was all over. Dukes didn't take prisoners; he took their weapons. The bodies of the dead were laid off to one side of the road.

Dukes took Lanning aside. "If anyone in authority comes through here, you tell them you were following orders. Now, you keep this bridge open. You let people cross for free. You make sure that they aren't fucking killing each other."

Lanning nodded. "Understood, Sergeant."

Dukes gathered his squad. "We are running out of time. We drive through the night. Make sure the bikes are fueled up, and everyone keep your eyes open."

They crossed the bridge and drove on into Arkansas. Behind them a stream of civilian traffic and pedestrians started trekking eastward.

Fort Smith, Little Rock, and finally over the border into Memphis. Towns and cities where the population were moving, south, north, east, west. Crowds moving in different directions collided and jammed the roads. People gave up and either camped out or turned around and tried to go back, tangling themselves even deeper in the press of bodies and traffic behind them. Movement ground to a halt until even Dukes' squad couldn't get through.

"This is unacceptable," Dr. Stahl said for the third time in ten minutes.

"We have no choice. We either walk, or we sit here," Dukes explained again. He paused for a moment, looking out at the sea of chaos around them, then said, "Fuck it. We're walking."

Dukes handed the Humvee over to two medics to use as an ambulance, after Milquist and the other soldiers stripped the vehicle of everything except the fuel.

"We are still on mission," Dukes reminded Stahl. "We will get those samples to the CDC. You too, as long as you can walk."

"No way we're leaving our bikes, right, Minty?" Freak looked to the older biker for confirmation. Minty parked his hog under a tree, leaving the keys in it.

"We've got maybe twenty miles of gas left. The roads are blocked. We won't get far going off-road. So yeah, I'm leaving my bike here and going with them."

Freak looked torn. The idea of abandoning the bikes brought him down to the same level of the pedestrians. Without a hog, he was just another asshole trudging down the highway.

"Sooner we start, the sooner we get there," Jessie said. She shouldered a backpack and fell into step behind the soldiers.

Callie and Minty started walking. Freak swore for another minute and then came hurrying after.

CHAPTER 29

On foot it was slow going. On each side of the highway suitcases, laptops, photo albums, stuffed animals, and anything not mandatory to survival was being shed. People walked in silence, staring at the ground, lost in the rhythm of the endless walk. Babies cried and children wailed. People shuffled aside as the soldiers marched through their midst. Minty found himself struggling to keep up with their ground-eating pace. Callie kept in step with him, grim faced and silent. After four miles the sun came up and the road started to fill even more with people who had rested overnight.

Stahl complained until the soldiers slowed their pace, and even Callie was silently relieved. When their marching cadence slowed to a casual stroll, the squad smoked and talked shit as they walked.

"I cannot fucking believe you left the bikes, man. Are we not fucking Locusts? Do we not live and die by our rides?"

Minty stopped in the middle of the road so suddenly Freak had to sidestep to avoid colliding with him.

"Freak," Minty said. "Listen carefully."

Freak stepped closer to hear what Minty had to say. The older man's fist came out of nowhere and hit him in the jaw like a sledgehammer. The punch lifted the younger man off his feet and sent him crashing to the asphalt.

"First, you are not a Locust; you're only a fucking prospect.

Second, that ride, it belonged to Chops. Chops is dead, you're alive. So quit your fucking bitching and keep walking."

Minty turned away and walked off. Callie hesitated a moment, then followed him. Jessie crouched down and helped Freak to his feet.

"You okay, babe?" she asked.

"Yeah . . ." Freak spat bloody mucus on the ground and grinned like a zombie clown. "For an old guy, he's fuckin' tough."

"You could take him," Jessie said.

"A fuckin' tank couldn't take him. He's Minty. They call him Jethro's Fist."

The couple started walking, keeping the soldiers in close view. "You wanna know why they call him Jethro's Fist?" Freak said.

"Sure." Jessie didn't really care, but she humored him.

"They say, back in the day, when the Locusts were carving their share of the California drugs 'n' guns and shit market, there was a narc. You know, an undercover cop? Right, so Jethro and Minty they work out who this guy is. They take him with them, on a long ride, all the way to Seattle, like in Washington. They say they're meeting a contact, in the restroom of this bus station. They get this guy in there and Minty kills him. He beats this fuckin' cop to death, with his bare hands." Freak shook his head in wonderment.

"That made the Locusts legend. Jethro would give the orders and everyone would jump right to it. They didn't want him unleashing Minty on their asses."

"Oh my God, you mean he's a murderer?" Jessie whispered.

"Minty's killed plenty of guys. He was in the fuckin' Marines, way back when they invaded Iraq, you know, the first time."

Jessie nodded, not sure what that meant.

"He's killed sand niggas and assholes. You can't ask him about it though. He doesn't like to talk about it."

"I don't need to ask him anything." Jessie took Freak's hand. "You talk enough for everyone."

"Minty and Jethro, they were in this hole, somewhere in Iraq. Minty's just a regular Marine and Jethro, he's like an officer or something. Way I heard it, Jethro saved Minty's ass and Minty's sworn to protect him for ever and ever, amen."

"Is that true?" Jessie asked.

"It's the story I heard."

In Memphis the infection was spreading as mobs of enraged rioters swept through the streets, tackling anyone who couldn't run fast enough. Some were torn to pieces and others crawled away until the infection took hold and the psychotic rage overcame their need to die.

Screaming civilians ran blindly through the streets, cars collided and buildings burned. A cop stood in the middle of an intersection, no longer trying to direct traffic. He drew his sidearm and started firing into the crowd racing past him. For each infected he killed, a fleeing civilian went down.

Dukes followed their previous tactic, circling the densely populated areas of the city and keeping the group moving east. Georgia was miles away and Atlanta miles more.

"Sergeant, there's a whole heap of trouble coming," Potenski reported.

"Shit," Dukes muttered. "We need a secure location. We can hold up until the streets are clear."

Garrett pointed up the street. "Coffee shop at eleven o'clock."

"Move it people," Dukes ordered.

When the group reached the next block, they forced their way into a barricaded coffee shop and put down a mob of infected who charged after them. They had been trying not to waste ammunition until they had to defend themselves, so each man focused on achieving single headshots to put down the attackers.

"Barricade the doors with furniture. Check this place is clear," Dukes barked.

Ten minutes later the blinds were down and tables and chairs barricaded the door. Dukes nodded; for now they were hidden from the street outside.

"Power's still on," Garrett announced.

"Get some coffee going, and food. Not from the display case; Christ knows how long that has been sitting there."

Jackson and Potenski raided the storage freezer and soon the store filled with the smell of hot food cooking.

Minty sat in a booth, groaning a little as he rested his legs on the bench seat.

The other civilians looked dead tired too. The hard pace and walking marathon had taken it out of all of them. Only the soldiers still looked fresh.

"Sergeant," Dawes called from where he maintained a watch at the front door. "We've got another wave of civilians coming through. They're coming the other way this time."

"No one comes in or goes out," Dukes reminded him. "We keep this place secure until dark and then we can move out."

"Sergeant, I'm going to try contacting the CDC," Stahl said. "If the phone lines are still working, they could send a helicopter, or a car to pick me up."

"Be my guest, Doctor. There might be a phone out the back."

Stahl limped across the floor and everyone sat in silence. A few minutes later she returned, her fury evident in her expression and the way her hands shook.

"The CDC is, and I quote, under siege. They cannot spare any resources from the local Guard units to assist us. They are, however, awaiting our arrival with great interest and anticipation."

"But not enough to send a chopper?" Dukes asked.

"Apparently not." Stahl took off her glasses and pinched the bridge of her nose. "The infection is causing severe disruptions across the south. It appears that the outbreak has not spread to the northern states yet."

"Temperature," Callie said. "If the fungus is tropical, it might not have adapted to a cooler climate. Slower growth rates, spores will find it harder to germinate."

"The spores grow inside people, Doctor Blythe. When I studied biology, human beings tended to operate at a constant temperature."

Callie's lips thinned. "Just sharing a hypothesis, Doctor Stahl."

"Are there any reports of animals being affected?" Dukes asked.

"What has that got to do with anything?" Stahl asked.

"Maybe Doctor Blythe is right. Maybe temperature is important. If animals have a different body temperature, then they might not be susceptible to infection."

"There is no evidence of a temperature requirement for successful infection," Stahl insisted.

They all jumped when something collided with the door. A woman screamed outside. Her cries were immediately swallowed by the howls of the infected.

"Supper's ready," Jackson announced.

The food came out hot, nourishing, and surprisingly well made. Jackson knew his way around a kitchen. The coffee was a bonus: hot, strong, and in large volumes.

"Get some sleep," Dukes said after the plates had been cleared. "We'll move out again in a few hours."

No one argued; instead they sacked out on the booth seats. Dawes remained on watch, peering out to the street through a gap in the barricaded door.

Minty woke up a few hours later, his sense of threat honed to razor sharpness after his years in the military and with the Locusts. He lay still, not moving, listening for any sound out of order.

A woman's voice, a familiar voice. *Stahl?* Minty lifted his head. Stahl was at the door that led to the kitchen. She appeared to be whispering to herself. Minty sat up and put his feet on the floor. For a big guy, he could move silently when he needed to.

"You have the coordinates?" Stahl whispered. "Fifteen minutes, I'll be on the roof. No, just me. Don't be late." She raised her hand and touched her ear.

Bluetooth and a cell phone, Minty thought. What is that bitch up to?

Stahl opened the kitchen door and slipped through. Minty froze in the dark until she had gone. He moved across the room until he reached the counter. A shadow rose up out of the dark and Dukes nodded at the biker.

"Did Stahl just break up with us?" Dukes whispered.

"I think she's calling a cab and getting the fuck outta Dodge," Minty replied.

Potenski appeared out of the darkness. "Sergeant?"

"It's cool, Potenski. Wake the others. Do it quietly. No noise."

Potenski nodded and vanished into the shadows again.

"We could just let her go," Minty said.

"Yes, we could. But, does that feel right to you?"

"No fucking way," Minty said.

"Me either."

The squad came together in silence. They haunted the coffee shop like mute ghosts.

"All right, listen up. Stahl is heading to the roof. Seems she has a backup plan involving her and a helicopter." Dukes waited while his men muttered and cursed.

"Yeah, you can shed tears about it later. I can say one thing in her favor, though: she's a dedicated professional."

"Minty?" Callie had woken up.

"Here, Doc."

"What's going on?"

Minty caught her up in less than a minute. Freak and Jessie emerged from a dry goods storeroom looking tousled.

"We leaving?" Freak asked.

"Yeah," Dukes replied. "Arm up. Don't fire on anyone or anything unless absolutely necessary. The less attention we get the safer we'll all be. We follow the doc, out the back and up the fire escape. That would be the quickest route to the roof. Milk, check our exit."

"Why would she leave without us?" Callie asked.

"Because she's an asshole?" Minty suggested.

"She's just trying to do her job, under extremely trying circumstances," Dukes said.

"So, why don't we just let her go?" Freak asked.

"Because it irks me, son," Dukes snapped. "I have humped my shit and the shit of my men from California to Memphis. People have died so we could deliver that fucking sample to Atlanta. We did not come this far to bon-voyage our VIP on a fucking bird."

"Fuckin' A," The squad chorused in a low murmur.

Milquist hurried in from the kitchen and closed the door. Leaning against it he announced, "Sergeant, alleyway's still clear, but we have a fuck-ton of infected on the street," Milquist reported.

"Confirmed. Go back and watch the street," Dukes replied. "Everyone ready to move?"

The group nodded. The civilians stood together and waited while the soldiers filed out of the café toward the back door. Milquist crouched behind a trashcan and signaled the others to stay low and keep quiet.

Twenty feet away the infected in the street were pacing up and down, unable to rest or find peace.

"Fire escape is behind us. Garrett, get the ladder down and do it fucking quietly, man," Milquist whispered.

Garrett nodded and with one eye on the infected he crept out into the alleyway and approached the fire escape ladder. Just how the petite Dr. Stahl had gotten up there wasn't clear to him.

Reaching up, Garrett unhooked the ladder. Rusting metal squealed and he froze. The crowd didn't respond to the sudden noise and Garrett's heart started beating again. He got the ladder down to the ground. Their target was two floors above the alleyway and he fancied he could already hear the sound of a chopper beating its way toward them through the darkness.

"Ladder's down," Garrett whispered and started climbing. He reached the first landing and went up the metal stairs to the second landing. Dukes sent the squad and civilians into the alleyway, motioning everyone to keep low and move fast.

Callie tripped in the dark, catching her foot on a trashcan and sending it flying. The metal lid clattered and bottles clanked.

"Shit," Dukes said. Everyone turned and looked toward the street. The infected crowd stared back at them as their fungus-ridden brains processed that fresh meat waited a few meters away.

"Fucking move," Dukes ordered. The spell broke and the civilians ran for the fire escape. Minty pushed Callie up the ladder and Jessie went next. The remaining soldiers spread out across the narrow alleyway and started firing at the infected charging toward them. The howls of the rioters and the crack of gunfire brought more infected to investigate.

Garrett fired from his position as Callie and then Jessie slipped past him and kept climbing toward the roof. Freak hesitated. "You first man," he said to Minty.

Minty fired his AR-15 into the chest of a man covered in blood. "Move your ass, prospect!"

Freak bolted up the ladder and Minty swung up behind him. The squad retreated toward the ladder. Minty and Freak took up firing positions on the landing above Garrett. They fired down into the seething crowd.

"Get up that fucking ladder!" Dukes roared. He fired with a steady beat, and each shot dropped one of the advancing infected.

The rest of the squad clambered up the ladder. Dukes came last, his rifle swinging on the strap as he climbed. Infected reached for him, blood spilling from their mouths as they howled. The sergeant kicked at the reaching hands. "I've come too fucking far and seen too much shit to get fucked by you motherfuckers," he growled.

A final boot to the face gave him a heartbeat to climb out of reach. On the first landing he jerked the ladder up as the infected started to swarm over it.

"Garrett, get up top. There's too many of them. We can't secure the fucking ladder."

The private nodded. Running up the metal steps, he pushed the others ahead of him. "Head to the roof!" Garrett yelled. "Secure the roof."

Dukes fired the rest of his magazine into the faces scrambling up the ladder. He ran, double-timing it up the steps, waiting for the burning touch of a fevered hand to clamp on his ankle or belt, dragging him down into the swarming crowd below.

The rest of his squad fired over the edge of the flat roof. Their shots zipped past Dukes' head and hit the infected coming behind him.

"Sergeant, move yo' fuckin' ass!" Milquist yelled. The alleyway had filled in seconds with a surging crowd of infected. They climbed over each other and onto the landing on the fire escape. The shrieking crowd clawed and tore as they climbed. The metal staircase creaked from the increased weight.

Dukes rolled onto the flat roof while his squad kept shooting.

"Where's Stahl?" he asked.

"Haven't had a chance to look for her yet," Minty replied.

"Stay back," Dukes ordered and sprang to his feet. "Doctor Stahl? Are you up here?!"

With few places to hide, the rooftop could be searched in a minute, maybe two. Dukes started his sweep; the obvious place to hide was behind the air conditioner units.

Stahl stood up when Dukes approached. "Don't shoot." She clutched the biohazard sample bag to her chest.

"What are you doing?" Dukes asked.

"I thought I heard someone breaking in. I got scared and came up here."

"Was that before or after you called in a chopper rescue from CDC?"

Stahl's mouth dropped open, "I . . ."

"You've got big shiny metal balls, Doc. We'll be joining you on your flight," Dukes said.

"My survival is imperative. The samples must reach the lab quickly."

"Sergeant, a chopper is inbound!" Milquist shouted across the roof. The noise of the incoming Blackhawk drowned out the howls of the raging infected. They were being shot, stabbed, and smashed down from the edge of the roof. Broken bodies tumbled and crashed onto the squirming mass below.

Minty pushed Callie and the others back as bloodstained hands scrabbled at the edge of the roof. The first of the infected climbed onto the roof as the raging pyramid of humanity behind them created a ladder for them to climb.

The bikers opened fire, joining the soldiers who fired and stepped back. With nowhere to go, they didn't back up far. The Blackhawk helicopter that flew overhead didn't fire on the infected. A spotlight jabbed through the darkness and then danced across the rooftop, displaying a scene of bloodshed and terror.

"Get down here!" Stahl screamed at the aircraft. The pilot lowered the helicopter in a fast dive. The tail swung around and the side door slid back as it settled in a hover.

"Come on!" a crewman yelled from the deck of the chopper.

Stahl didn't need to be told twice. She ran for the helicopter, bent nearly double as she passed under the spinning rotors.

"We have to go, now!" Callie yelled. She grabbed Jessie by the arm and ran. Freak followed, the AR-15 in his hands still hot from firing. He kept the rifle raised, covering the helicopter which floated only inches above the roof.

"Get on the chopper!" Dukes yelled. Minty thought *Fuck it* and ran. The chopper was a civilian model—getting everyone on board was going to make it a tight fit, and he wondered about the weight limit.

The squad fell back, firing at the rising mass of infected who crawled over the edge of the roof and charged after them.

"I'm out!" Potenski yelled. He turned his rifle around and smashed an infected in the face with the butt.

First Potenski, then Garrett, Dawes, Jackson, Milquist, and finally Dukes were pulled aboard the Blackhawk.

"Go! Go!" Dukes yelled from where he crouched in the door of the helicopter. His rifle hung from its point sling and he fired into the crowd with a sidearm. A shotgun fired with a deafening boom and another infected went down. Garrett pumped the slide and fired again as the chopper lifted skyward.

Infected snatched at Dukes feet. He fired his remaining pistol rounds into the upturned faces and then hung on as the helicopter tilted and gained altitude.

"Garrett, where is the perfectly good M4 rifle that the government kindly issued to you?" Dukes asked as he slid into a seat in the crowded helicopter.

"Right here, Sergeant. The shotgun was in the chopper and I figured it might be better for crowd control."

They rose above the dark city, through the smoke of myriad fires and over the raging crowed of infected, who swirled and flowed like a flooded stream through the city streets.

CHAPTER 30

"Holy shit," Callie said. She was trembling and pale. Minty had no words of comfort for her.

"Who are you people?" The helicopter crewmember demanded.

"Sergeant Dukes, US Army. These men are my squad. The civilians are consultants on a matter of national security. I sure as hell hope you are taking us to the CDC."

"You're damn lucky we were in the area. This is the last flight out, literally."

"Lucky you found us when you did," Dukes said while staring the crewman directly in the eye.

"Amen," he replied.

The flight to Atlanta was made in silence. Most of the passengers slept in a fitful doze. Dukes sat on the edge of the Blackhawk deck, his feet hanging out into space as he stared into the darkness. Down there his world was falling apart. After Atlanta, what next? How long would the chain of command last? How long until he couldn't follow orders and had to make a decision to protect himself and those who looked to him for leadership?

He had options, secure locations that he knew would be ready and prepared for the kind of collapse that seemed to be coming.

If the reports about the northern states were right, then they might beat this thing yet. As summer rolled out, nowhere south of the Arctic

Circle would be safe. South of the equator, Australia or Antarctica? Did they even have cocaine in the Southern Hemisphere? At least it was winter down there. If the temperature theory was right, then they might be safe. Either way, the US was going to be forever changed.

Dukes felt confident that if the outbreak could be brought under control the country would recover. They would bury their dead and rebuild. It had been done before, though never on such a scale. Maybe this could be a good thing, a clean slate and a chance to change society for the better.

Or, maybe it would just turn to shit and his fellow Americans would be living in caves and eating each other in twenty years.

The helicopter turned and began to descend. Dukes could see the crowds pressed up against a high fence that had been erected around the CDC campus.

A narrow-beamed spotlight swept the sky and locked on to the helicopter.

"I sure hope the pilot knows the right challenge response," Dukes said.

The helicopter settled on a helipad on the roof. Lights shone on them and armed guards wearing biohazard gear aimed weapons at the craft until the rotors wound down enough for conversation.

"Step out of the helicopter! Keep your hands up!"

The passengers climbed out onto the roof. Hands raised to shoulder height, they came forward until ordered to halt.

By now they knew what to expect, and the dogs gave them the clean bill of health.

"I am Doctor Evelyn Stahl. I need to see Milo Feldman immediately."

"Take the doctor through," one of the masked guards ordered. Stahl walked off without a glance at the men who had saved her life.

"You're fucking welcome, bitch," Garrett said to her back.

"I'm Sergeant Kyle Dukes, US Army. This is what is left of my squad. These civilians have been instrumental in delivering a sample of the infectious agent to this facility. We could use a shower, some hot food, and a little fucking gratitude."

"Private Hammond. Get these people processed."

Dukes detected a female voice under the gas mask and close-fitting hood. "Much obliged," Dukes said. He gave a casual salute, though the guards wore no rank insignia that he could see.

Dukes' squad was escorted down into the building. They followed orders, unloading their weapons and gear before stepping into plastic-lined shower cubicles. Minty and the others followed suit.

"Strip," The guards said. After a moment's hesitation they started peeling off their stinking clothes. Everything went into biohazard bags and was taken away. Minty snatched up his patched jacket.

"In the bag, asshole," a guard ordered.

"Go fuck yourself," Minty replied.

A murmured discussion took place between the guards.

"We don't have time for your bullshit," The guard said.

Minty pulled his colors back on and stood there. Naked except for his jacket, he folded his arms in defiance.

"Fuck me," The guard said, shaking his head. "Turn around."

Minty did and they were sprayed with a foul-smelling orange liquid and then hosed down. They followed it up with a harsh scrubbing. His patched vest hadn't been cleaned in years by anything other than rainwater.

When everyone was clean and dripping wet, they were handed cotton pants and tops, which Callie recognized as surgical scrubs. Slippers of similar material were provided for their feet.

"Follow Corporal Shipton," Their masked escort ordered. A woman wearing army fatigues waved through a glass window in the door. They went out into the hallway and were escorted to the elevators.

Shipton popped gum as she spoke. "You guys must be important for them to bring you in. This place has been locked up tight since the crowd started gathering outside."

"What about the infected?" Callie asked.

"Hasn't been too bad. Most of them outside, they're either screaming for a cure or demanding the scientists inside admit they released some kind of virus."

"That's bullshit," Callie said.

"Maybe. No one knows what's causing it." Shipton stepped into the elevator and swiped a security card before stepping out again. "Please wait at the floor below for everyone to arrive."

People filed in, filling the elevator. The remaining soldiers came down in the second lift, with Shipton chewing gum the whole time.

In the depths of the CDC building people bustled about as if it were just another day in a corporate office. The civilians and their military companions stood awkwardly, dripping water on the floor in their issued scrubs.

"This way," Shipton said, marching out of the elevator. They followed her into a break room.

"Take a seat, refreshments will be brought to you shortly." Shipton turned on her heel and marched out again, closing the door as she went.

"Now what do we do?" Freak asked.

"We wait," Dukes said as he leaned back against the wall and closed his eyes.

It became clear that sleeping was the only option. The room they were in was locked. Knocking on the door got an escort to the bathroom and straight back in again. Food turned up, cafeteria cooking, sodas, and bad coffee. The chairs were comfortable for the first hour; after that they got harder until they grew spikes which made sitting down a literal pain in the ass.

When the sleeping was done and the food reduced to crumbs, they sat in silence. No one had anything to say. The soldiers waited; for them this was how it always went. You waited and then you went into action. Then you waited again.

Eight hours later Minty was beyond ready to stab someone for a cigarette. Previous attempts to light up had set off a smoke alarm and armed guards had come in, making it clear that smoking was not permitted.

Now the biker paced up and down, feeling trapped and edgy. They were here now, the samples had been safely delivered. They had no reason to stay. Leaving would mean taking his chances out there in the insanity. Heading north seemed like the only viable option. Maybe all the way to Canada, or somewhere cold enough to stop the infection in its tracks. At least until summer came; then he could keep moving on to Alaska. Start a new chapter of the Locusts in Barrow, or one of those dogsled towns.

The door opened and a balding man in a suit, plain tie, and reading glasses entered, followed by two armed security guards.

"Good afternoon," he said. "I am Doctor Arthur Tomlin. I apologize for the inconvenience. However, as you are aware we are dealing with a national health crisis at the moment." Tomlin paused, peering at them over his spectacles as if awaiting questions.

"Very good," he continued. "We thank you for your support of our research. You will now have your belongings returned to you and you will be escorted off the campus."

"I should report to the local National Guard command," Dukes said.

"Quite," Tomlin agreed. "What you do after you leave here is of course no concern of mine."

"Wait," Callie replied as she stood up. "What is going on out there? Is it spreading? Are you going to be able to produce an antidote? A cure? Or a vaccine?"

"Ma'am, we are working on a range of solutions to the current outbreak. Our current guidelines suggest that all civilians should remain in their homes and await further instructions."

"Frankly, that is bullshit!" Callie snapped. "Have you seen what is happening outside your lab? Do you know what this infection is doing to people?"

Tomlin removed his glasses and regarded Callie with interest for the first time. "Oh yes. We have had an opportunity to examine the infection quite closely in the last seventy-two hours. A most remarkable fungal organism."

"And are any medications working against it?" Callie asked.

"Topical and intravenous antifungals have proved ineffective. Low temperature reduces the spread of the infection outside a living host. It appears that an environment of at least sixty-six degrees is required for the spores to germinate."

"Speaking as a clinician, Doctor Tomlin, that doesn't inspire much confidence when the homeostatic temperature of the average human being is ninety-eight point six degrees."

"Ahh, you're the medical doctor?" Tomlin nodded. "We hypothesize that the spores respond rapidly to a drop in surrounding air temperature. They take time to come out of their shells once the environment they are placed in becomes more suitable to their development."

"Summer is coming. It's just going to get hotter and that is going to help this thing spread," Callie said.

"Indeed, we expect by August, a mere three months away, we will be facing the peak of infectious range for the spores. By then of course we will have a suitable vaccine or treatment agent."

"By August, most people in the in the southern states of the continental USA are going to be dead," Dukes spoke up.

"We will do what we can to minimize casualties and infection rates. My initial advice still stands. People should remain in their homes, reduce contact with infected persons, and await further instructions."

"You're just going to let the world burn for three months while you make some kind of cure?" Minty asked. "Surely, a disaster like this means you can push things along a helluva lot faster. Shit, when Ebola broke out, you guys had a vaccine in couple of weeks."

"This is a new fungal agent. Ebola was a well-known and minutely studied virus. A vaccine was discovered years ago, but there had been no commercial demand for it. Therefore it never went beyond the laboratory."

"Well, this fungus shit certainly has a commercial value. You've got customers spreading fast across the lower states and as it gets warmer they're going to be opening new franchises right across the fucking country," Minty said.

Tomlin laughed slightly through his nose and replaced his glasses. "The situation is contained. A state of emergency has been declared. The National Guard is enforcing a blockade along the eastern border of Nevada and the southern borders of Oregon, Utah, Colorado, Kansas, Missouri, Kentucky, and Virginia. No one is allowed to travel north of those state lines."

"That line will not hold," Dukes replied. "There is no way."

"It only needs to remain secure for a month," Tomlin said with a knowing smile.

"A month?" Callie asked. "You know you won't have a viable treatment for one hundred million people in thirty days."

"Steps are being taken," Tomlin said, his voice the calm, reassuring sound of government omnipotence.

"What about Mexico, South America?" Minty asked.

"We are not concerned with the security of other nations," Tomlin said.

"Other nations? Jesus Christ!" Callie threw up her hands. "Mexico is part of the same continent. Half of California's population is Hispanic."

"We have a responsibility to protect our own citizens," Tomlin said, still smiling.

"I give up." Callie sat down, folded her arms, and closed her eyes.

"This shit started in South America. It must be bad down there, right?" Dukes asked.

"What have you heard?" Tomlin asked.

"Some," Dukes replied. "At a security station back in California, I saw some footage from a border patrol reconnaissance. DEA or INS or some shit, filmed from a helicopter. They flew over the Rio Grande, except the river isn't there any more. It's filled with bodies. The rest of them are just walking over the top. The fence is going to fall."

"There are measures being implemented to ensure the continued security of this great nation," Tomlin said. He could have been reading from a teleprompter. His smile evaporated as he turned away. "Be sure to see them escorted off the premises safely," Tomlin said to the guards as he left the room.

"Come this way," The guards ordered. The soldiers stood up first, more used to following orders, relying on their skills and training to survive in a rapidly changing situation.

"Let's go," Minty said. Callie, Jessie, and Freak filed out of the room. The guards closed the door and they were taken to the elevators.

"We will need our weapons and equipment," Dukes said.

"Your gear is waiting for you outside."

"You fucking assholes," Freak said.

"Shut up, Freak." Minty shoved the prospect into the elevator. The rest squeezed in. They rode down in silence. The doors opened and another guard waited to escort them out of the building.

In the spring sunshine, Atlanta was warm and glorious. Beyond the shining buildings of the CDC campus, the world was tearing itself apart.

"Well, fuck," Freak said, running his hands through his hair. "Now what the fuck do we do?"

Dukes took a deep breath of the surrounding air, inhaling the scent of fire and death. "We'll report to the Georgia National Guard. See what orders they have for us. You're civilians, they'll have no interest in you except for putting you in a refugee camp."

"Fuck that," Minty said and the others nodded.

"Once we get out of here, you can go where you like. Do what you want."

"Anyone have friends or family in Georgia?" Callie asked.

No one responded.

"Great. Well, we could just turn around and head back to California. I'm sure it's all under control there now." The bitter sarcasm in Callie's voice burned.

"You said your old man lived in Alabama?" Freak asked.

Callie blinked. "What? Yes, Gadsden. He's the sheriff."

"Could we get there?" Freak asked, looking to Minty for approval.

"We should head north. Canada or Alaska. Somewhere it's likely to be too cold for this thing to have much kick," Minty replied.

"You heard that asshole Tomlin, he said the Guard has the state borders closed off," Callie said.

"They have a fence across the Mexican border, and people get across there every damn day," Minty reminded her.

"That is what I'm afraid of," Callie said quietly.

Dukes put his hands on his hips. "This should just be happening here, the US, South America. Maybe Europe, the Chinese, the Brits even, they will come and save our asses."

"I wish they would hurry up," Jessie said.

Freak giggled, a sharp sound that he immediately quashed with a blush.

"You Dukes?" a National Guardsman with a specialist shield asked.

"Sergeant Dukes," he replied.

"Sign here please, Sergeant." He accepted the clipboard and pen and then made a slash mark in ink across the signature window.

"Your equipment, weapons, and personal effects," The soldier said, indicating a pile of discarded gear and stacked M4s.

"Pick it up," Dukes ordered his squad. They descended on the gear and picked up clothes, body armor, rifles, and kit.

"Where's our ammo?" Dukes asked.

The Guardsman hefted a canvas bag. "I threw a couple of extra magazines in there. We can't spare much, but shit if you're going out there, I'm not one to let you do it with your dicks in your hands."

"Much obliged," Dukes saluted.

"Where's our guns?" Freak asked.

"No orders here for civilians to be armed," The corporal replied.

"Fuck that," Minty said. "We came in here with weapons. We are leaving here with weapons."

"Corporal, do me a favor and find these good people their weapons and ammunition. It's not just us who don't need to be out there without shit for defense."

"Sergeant, I—"

Dukes stepped up to within an inch of the corporal's nose. "They came in with us. They are leaving with us and with weapons. Understood?"

"Yes, Sergeant." The corporal stepped back and shouted orders at two privates, who searched the back of a truck and handed over the canvas bag of guns and ammunition that had traveled from California to Georgia.

"Have a nice day," Dukes said.

"Hey," Minty asked the corporal. "Where can I get some cigarettes?"

"Smokes? Uhh . . ." The corporal patted himself down and handed a pack over.

"I lost my lighter in the showers," Minty said as he tore the packet open and slid a cigarette out. The corporal handed over his own lighter, allowing Minty to get his first nicotine hit all day.

"Thanks, man." Minty pocketed the lighter and walked away. The corporal opened his mouth to object, but then shut it again.

Dukes and his crew followed directions out to the recently armed and reinforced gate. Two Humvees and a support squad behind sandbags watched a crowd of chanting civilians armed with placards who stood across the street.

"Least we know there's no infection in that bunch," Dukes said.

"Where the fuck are you going?" a sergeant at the checkpoint asked.

"Sergeant Kyle Dukes, visiting from California, Sergeant," Dukes said.

"Well, fuck me," The sergeant replied. "To what do we owe the dubious fucking pleasure, beach boy?"

"We're looking for deployment," Dukes replied.

"Got any paperwork?"

"We're at the ass end of a priority operation, Sergeant. Do you normally carry documentation of your mission around with you?"

"You can stand here while I try to get the TOC on the line." The sergeant walked off. Dukes waited while the sergeant talked on the phone.

When he returned, it was with a grim face. "There is shit going down all across the south. I don't have any orders for you, except stay alive and wait for order to be restored."

"That's it?" Milquist asked. "We're cut off?"

"Stand down, Milk," Dukes snapped. "Sergeant, we appreciate your time and effort. We will move out of your area of responsibility now."

The sergeant nodded. "Sooner you are out of my sight, the sooner I can go back to dealing with real problems."

Dukes led his squad through the gate and out into the Atlanta street.

"Which way?" Callie asked

"Alabama's that way." Minty gestured westward.

"Gadsden's maybe three hours drive," Callie said.

"Well, let's go that way," Minty said.

Milquist gestured to Dukes. "A word if I may, Sergeant. Where are we going?"

"We're the National fucking Guard, Corporal. We are professional soldiers in the US Army. We will report to our command structure and receive our orders for current deployment."

"Hooah," The squad echoed.

"Sergeant? Where the fuck is our command structure?" Jackson asked.

"Blessed as I am with superior intelligence to that of a mere private, Jackson, I will lead you to the promised land. Nobody in California knows where we are, nor are we accountable to them. That means we are on our own. I am considering our options. One, we can haul ass back to California and report our mission accomplished and get reassigned—"

"Fuck yeah. Back in the game," Potenski grinned.

"Or we can complete our current mission. That means getting these civilians to a secure location and completing a recon of the doctor's family home in Gadsden, Alabama."

"And if her old man is fucked?" Dawes asked.

"We cut them loose and join up with any operational National Guard unit in the area. Questions?"

"You're just going to drop us in the middle of shitville?" Freak asked.

"We have a job to do. You are not that job," Dukes replied.

"There is only so much we can do for the US Army," Minty said. "I think they should try it on their own for a while."

"But, fuck . . ." Freak said.

"Garrett, secure a vehicle, a truck or van preferably," Dukes ordered.

"On it."

"Rest of you, start walking." Dukes shouldered his rifle and the squad moved out.

CHAPTER 31

Pickups were everywhere in Georgia. Garrett helped himself to a Ford F-150 and didn't invite questions about how he started it without the key.

"Specialist Garrett, did you gain the written permission of this vehicle's owner to take possession of it?" Dukes asked.

"Yes, Sergeant," Garrett replied.

"If I request this written permission, you will be able to provide it?"

"Yes, Sergeant. Though I do not have that written permission on my person at the present time, Sergeant."

"Drive on, Specialist."

Callie and Jessie rode in the cab, while everyone else found space in the back. Once they cleared the Atlanta city limits, the confusion and traffic thinned. People who were getting out were already gone. The ones who were staying home were turning their houses into bunkers.

Three hours later they arrived in Gadsden, a small city by most standards with around 37,000 people. The road into town was blockaded by a pair of trucks and a local militia. Dukes called a halt and after a few shouted words each way, they approached.

The truck stopped again twenty feet from the blockade. Dukes climbed out, hands clearly visible, and gave a casual wave.

"We're looking for Sheriff Blythe," Dukes called.

"Who are you again?" a voice from the blockade asked.

"Is that you, Johnny Dew?" Callie stood on the runner step of the truck and called into the darkness.

"Who the hell? Goddamn, Callie? Hey guys, it's Callie, she's back."

"Where's my daddy at, Johnny?" Callie called out.

"It's Deputy Dew now, Callie. He's in his office."

Callie climbed out of the truck and walked up to the barricade. "How about you get these trucks out of the way, before I tell the sheriff to cite you for traffic violations?"

Several boys with semiautomatic rifles hopped down from the decks of the trucks. They got the vehicles moved and the Ford drove through, stopping long enough to pick up Callie from among a grinning throng of admirers.

The city looked no different than any other Alabama town Minty had been through during his years of riding. Pickup trucks with weapon racks, everyone armed and looking for a reason to shoot, and outside every courthouse a Civil War soldier statue remembering the honored dead of the Confederacy.

Callie gave them directions to the sheriff's department. She was out of the truck before it had stopped out front, running up the ramp and heading inside.

By the time Minty and the others had gotten to the front door, Callie came back out, her arm wrapped around a gentleman with grey hair and the body of an athlete.

"Daddy, this is Minty, Francis, Jessie, Sergeant Dukes, Corporal Milquist, Privates Jackson, Potenski, Dawes, and Specialist Garrett."

"Much obliged y'all found time to see my little girl safely home," Sheriff Blythe said.

"Sir," Dukes said, "I'd like to talk to you about any military activity around this area."

"Sure thing, Sergeant, come on inside. Rest of y'all make yourselves comfortable. Callie, get some coffee for these boys."

"Whaddya reckon, Milk? All set?" Jackson asked.

"Looks legit alright. Soon as the sergeant gives the word, we can find the nearest Guard outfit and go back to doing what we are paid for."

"We could stay here," Freak said. "The doc's home. The people seem okay. We have a good in with the local sheriff."

"You planning on settling down and getting a real job, prospect?" Minty said.

"Fuck that," Freak laughed and shot a look at Jessie, who acted like she hadn't heard him.

"Roots make it harder to leave," Minty replied. "Gets to the point where you forget who you were meant to be and why you ride."

"I'll come with you," Jessie said. "I can't go home. I ran away from my foster family with Todd."

"What about your mom?" Minty asked.

Jessie shrugged. "I have no idea who she is or where she is. She might be a superstar or she might be a meth head."

"There are worse ways to go," Minty suggested.

"Yeah," Freak spoke up. "You could get infected with this mutant mushroom shit and go crazy."

"Why don't the infected people die?" Jessie asked. "They get shot and bit and hurt so bad. They just don't die."

"Maybe it makes you numb to pain?" Freak suggested.

"I'd like that." Jessie nodded to herself and stared off into the night.

Callie and Dukes emerged from the sheriff's office and Callie came over to Minty and the other civilians. Dukes went to bring his squad up to date.

"We can stay at my dad's house," Callie said. "He has room for guests."

"How long would we stay there for?" Minty asked.

"I don't know. A few days I guess."

Minty frowned. "Thanks, but I'd like to keep moving."

Callie's expression hardened. "You're leaving?"

"This isn't my place. I need to find any surviving Locusts."

"You'd rather go off in search of a biker gang than stay here, where it is safe?" Callie folded her arms.

"Your family is here, Callie. This is where you belong. The Locusts are mine. I belong with them. Freak and Jessie, they can make their own decision."

Minty walked over to the truck. He took an assault pack off the back and started loading it with MREs and some bottled water.

"What are you going to do?" Jessie asked Freak.

"Shit," Freak replied. "I have no fucking idea."

"I'm going to stay here, sleep for a week, and then think about what to do next," Jessie said.

"I'd stay with you. If you want." Freak blushed and grinned.

"You want me to tell you to stay with me? I will if that is what you need."

"What's that supposed to mean?" Freak asked.

"I'm telling you to do what you want. You're not tied to me. I don't need you."

"What the fuck?" Freak said, his expression confused.

"Don't you get it? There are no promises anymore. I thought all I wanted was to run away to Vegas with Todd. Get married in one of those Elvis chapels and live happily ever after. Now I understand that surviving is all there is. That doesn't leave room for other people. It's all about taking care of myself."

"I can take care of you," Freak replied.

"Sure. But if we get too close, you get sick. Then what? I have to shoot you or abandon you? What if one of us screws up and we both get killed? Better we just go our ways and have nice memories."

Freak grinned. "You, uhh, wanna find a quiet spot and make some more memories?"

"You'd better go. Minty is leaving and you should go with him. He can take you to the others in your gang. He's right. It's where you both belong."

Jessie kept staring out into the darkness the whole time. Freak stood for a moment, then sighed in defeat and left her alone.

Dukes waited until his squad had gathered around. "Alabama Guard's all over the shit. Our best bet is to go back to Atlanta. Standing bodies who can take orders are going to be in demand. Sheriff Blythe made contact with the Atlanta brigade and we have their authorization to hump it back there and be under their command."

"Are things going to shit, Sergeant?" Potenski asked.

"Faster than anyone would like to admit," Dukes replied. "Asses on that truck, we are leaving in five minutes. I wanna be back in Atlanta before midnight."

"Why midnight?" Dawes asked as they gathered their gear and climbed on the truck.

"Sergeant turns into a pumpkin if he's not in his cot by oh-dark-thirty," Milquist said.

"Minty, we'll give you a ride. If you are planning on going back to Atlanta," Dukes said.

"It's a start. I'll head north from there, find the Locusts chapters in Ohio or Indiana."

"Your people are all over the place, huh?"

"Only a few states. But we make our mark."

Freak came shambling over and climbed onto the back of the truck. "Jessie coming?" Minty asked.

"Nah, she's going to stay here. Safer I guess."

"And you're not staying?"

Freak looked Minty right in the eye for the first time ever. "I may only be a fucking prospect, but my place is with my Locust brothers." Freak raised a fist in salute.

Minty regarded him for a moment, his face unreadable. Then he raised his fist and they knocked together, knuckle to knuckle.

"Give me your patch," Minty said as the truck started up. Freak shrugged out of his vest and handed it over. Minty drew a knife out of the sheath on his belt. With a few quick cuts he stripped the PROSPECT tag off the back and tossed it out of the moving vehicle.

"You know what it means to be part of the Locusts," he said with no trace of question.

Freak nodded and Minty handed him the leather. "Welcome to the family, brother."

⚑

Atlanta burned on the horizon, and the glow lit the fleeing citizens in a flickering silhouette.

The Ford F-150 slowed to a crawl for the last mile. Most of the people were on foot, having abandoned their cars in the gridlock of panic deeper in the city.

"Wish we still had our bikes," Freak said.

"There will be others," Minty replied.

The truck slowed to a halt and the occupants dismounted. Forming up into a group, they started walking, watching for signs of infection among the flood of people coming the other way.

"Atlanta got fucked up today," Garrett said.

"It was just a matter of time," Milquist replied.

"We keep moving," Dukes ordered. "The local Guard units are going to need our help more than ever."

"We're gonna fuckin' die in there," Jackson muttered.

⚑

The burning wreckage of a light aircraft had plowed into the CDC's main building. The campus was a crawling hell of screaming infected and savaged corpses. The soldiers were gone. All that remained of the tactical operations center were some smoldering vehicles, scraps of tent, and at least a dozen dead and nearly dead infected.

Dukes surveyed the carnage from a safe distance and then returned to his team.

"Now what the fuck do we do?" Potenski asked.

"We secure a position, sit tight, wait till daylight, and then we find where the hell they moved the TOC to."

"Hey," Freak said with sudden excitement, "I hear bikes!" He stepped out into the street, listening with keen attention, turning slowly to isolate the direction of the noise.

Minty listened to, a cold feeling building in his gut. If the riders were a rival gang, or even just some bunch of motorbike enthusiasts, shit could go down.

A strange parade came down the street, a fleet of Harley-Davidsons followed by two military Humvees, escorting a mix of civilian cars, pickups, and vans. The riders fired on the infected that surged toward the new noise.

"Locusts!" Freak yelled in delight. "Fuckin' A!"

The bikes roared and filled the street outside the burning CDC campus. The Humvees were spray-painted with symbols and words. The stink of blood and death hung over the entire crowd like a fog.

"The fuck is this shit?" Dukes asked.

Minty squinted through the flickering light. The riders wore Locust patches, and he started to pick familiar faces out of the crowd. "We need to go," he said to Dukes. "We need to go right-fucking-now."

Dukes nodded. The chaos of the new arrivals concerned him. They shrieked and did burnouts on their bikes. Guns fired into the air and at anything that moved toward them.

A ragged figure climbed out onto the hood of one of the Humvees. He raised both arms. One ended in a bloody and bandaged stump at the wrist.

"Jethro . . ." Minty whispered. "Shit."

CHAPTER 32

"Freak! Get the fuck back here!" Minty yelled over the noise. The other biker didn't hear him, too excited by the arrival of friends.

"Hey, you motherfuckers!" Freak yelled, stepping out of cover and waving his hands. "It's Freak!"

The first bikers to notice Freak almost shot him. Bullets zipped past his head and Freak ducked. "Fuck off!" he yelled, still waving frantically. "I'm a fucking Locust!"

Someone heard him. Two bikers dismounted and came forward. They checked his colors and then playfully punched him in the head, laughing at how close they came to killing one of their own.

"You going to join your friends?" Dukes asked.

"Nope," Minty scowled. He had run out on Jethro. Abandoned his brothers and left them for dead in LA. Jethro did not forgive and did not forget. If he stepped out, Minty knew he would die. Maybe not tonight, but sometime soon. It would be a slow and painful death. An example to others of why Jethro was not to be fucked with.

Freak was dumb enough to be forgiven, at least allowed to slip back in among the curs and lower members. When Jethro ordered Minty's execution, he knew Freak would be baying for his blood along with the others.

"Who are these assholes?" Milquist asked.

"The Locusts, mother chapter. Back when all this started they shot up an army gunship and your guys didn't take too kindly to that. They hit our place pretty hard with some air-to-ground shit. We were already under siege by rioters so I got out. I thought they were all dead."

"They look plenty alive to me," Garrett said.

"The guy on the Humvee, that's Jethro. He's the leader. He's batshit-fucking crazy. He wanted to create a new world of anarchy out of the chaos."

"Some kinda paradise for long-haired assholes?" Garrett asked.

They watched as Freak was taken to Jethro. They couldn't hear the conversation, but it seemed clear that Freak was filling Jethro in on the details of their adventures. Jethro nodded and smiled. He jumped down from the hood of the Humvee and said something to the two goons. They grabbed Freak and kicked his legs out, pushing him down on to his knees.

"Minty!" Jethro yelled into the sky. "Show your stinking face, you cunt!"

Minty didn't move. Jethro pulled a gun from his belt with his remaining hand and pressed the muzzle to the back of Freak's head.

"Minty! Come out! Or your bitch dies!"

The Locusts went silent and started looking around, sensing something important was going on.

"Squad," Dukes ordered. "Be ready to fire on my command."

"I'm gonna have to go out there," Minty said.

"Make sure you don't block our line of fire. He shoots the kid, or you, and we will drop the sonovabitch."

Minty stepped out into the street. Walking through the drifting trash and smoke, he kept his hands out to the sides, casual and unarmed.

"Hey, Jethro!" he called out. The Locusts turned and watched him approach.

"Minty, you export-grade asshole. Where the fuck have you been?" Jethro's voice grinned, but his face was a mask of cold fury.

"I thought you were dead. I got the hell out before the army killed me too."

"Locusts are not rats, Minty. We do not run away from a fight. We rise up and destroy those who oppress us."

"Freak isn't oppressing you, Jethro. Let him go."

"This prospect? He's just a tool. A pawn in their game."

"No one is playing, Jethro. Freak's a Locust now. He proved himself on the road. He's a patched brother. You should show him respect."

Jethro laughed. "Where was your respect, Minty? Where were you when they rained fire and death down upon us? The seed of chaos germinates in fire. In rage and smoke the walls were cast down and we rose triumphant!"

"I'm sorry about your hand," Minty said.

"They bit the hand that feeds. I cut it off. I have clarity of vision now, Minty. I have touched the soul of the beast. The purity of the anger of the infection fills me. I alone can control it!"

Jethro kicked Freak facedown in the street and raised his bandaged stump to his mouth, tearing the bandage off with his teeth. Minty blinked as white tendrils unfolded from the wound. They waved, searching and probing in the flickering darkness.

"You're infected, man," Minty said.

"I am enlightened, motherfucker."

"Freak," Minty said. "Get the hell away from him."

Freak scrambled on his hands and knees, scuttling away like the beaten mongrel dog that could have been his totem animal.

"You're over, Jethro. The anarchy you crave, it's an illusion. There is no purity in this chaos. There is just suffering and death."

"You are not worthy of this gift. Those who have transcended the shackles of humanity understand the primal core of what it is to be alive."

Dukes' squad moved silently, keeping to the shadows, their faces blackened with dirt and oil. They spread out, covering the bikers who were for the most part bunched up.

The sight of Jethro with his missing hand and the white strings probing for new life confirmed what Dukes already feared. The biker was infected—which meant he needed to be put down.

"Select your targets," he murmured into the comms unit. "Wait for my command. Milk, be ready to take out the guy with one hand. When he is down, the rest of you hit your targets, copy?"

"*Roger, Sergeant.*"

"Fire," Dukes said.

M4 shots cracked in the night. Jethro leapt aside, vanishing behind one of the Humvees.

"*Missed,*" Milquist reported. The rest of the squad had better luck, and the bikers ran for cover, returning fire blindly into the night as they were gunned down.

Minty dived for the ground, keeping low as bullets whizzed overhead. Garrett ran past, weapon ready to fire as he checked both sides of the Humvee.

"Look out," Minty shouted. Garrett spun around and Jethro shot him in the chest. Garrett staggered backwards and fell down. Jethro bolted into the darkness and a moment later the Humvees roared into life and the surviving Locusts bailed out on their Harleys and support vehicles.

"Fuck," Minty said. "Dukes! Garrett is hit." He crawled over to where Garrett was pulling at his body armor.

"That fucking asshole. That complete fucking asshole," Garrett said.

"Are you okay, man?" Minty asked.

Garrett pushed a hand under the armored vest and plucked out a thick wad of bills.

"He tried to shoot the money. That motherfucker . . ."

"They are paying you way too much," Minty said. The rest of the squad closed in on their position. Garrett was confirmed unharmed and Dukes raised an eyebrow at the thousands of dollars the private had stuffed in his clothes.

"We should get out of here," Milquist advised. "We have a shit load of Tangos inbound."

"Everyone off the street," Dukes ordered.

The squad ran, firing into the infection-twisted faces of the rioters as they went. The Ford truck waited where they had left it. Dukes took the wheel and the rest of his men piled into the back.

"Where are the fucking hippies?" Milquist asked.

In response the roar of bike engines closed in. Minty and Freak pulled up, each astride a Harley with the Locust emblem on the gas tank.

"Where to?" Minty asked Dukes.

"Fort Benning, Columbus, Georgia." Dukes said. "It's the Ranger and Infantry schools. It's better equipped than anywhere else to make a stand for a long time."

"There's also Fort Stewart, in Georgia," Milquist said.

"They still have the Third Infantry Division?" Dukes asked. "More military than civilians in Georgia."

"Sergeant, there's those two Ranger battalions, the First at Hunter Army Airfield near Savannah and the Third plus Ranger Brigade HQ at Fort Benning," Potenski said.

"Safer than in your momma's arms," Dukes said.

"We have to go to Georgia via Alabama," Minty said. "I'm not leaving Callie and I reckon Freak's gonna pine if we don't get his girl as well."

"A doctor could be useful," Dukes agreed.

"You know where we are heading?"

"I can find it," Minty replied.

"All right. You get your collective asses to Benning. If Benning is compromised, we will head towards Eglin Air Force Base, near Valparaiso. That's in Florida."

"Valparaiso, Florida. Got it. Stay safe, man," Minty said.

"If you aren't caught up with us in a week, we'll assume you're dead."

"Dead, or we had a better offer," Minty replied.

"Time to go!" Freak yelled. The crowd had caught up with them and they shrieked with ravenous fury.

The Ford pulled away, the bikes followed and then peeled off after two blocks, each on their own mission now.

CHAPTER 33

The humid air felt free of the scent of death for the first time in three days. Minty led a ragtag convoy of civilian vehicles as they drove south, toward Fort Benning. The city of Columbus, Georgia, was a scene from Dante's *Inferno*. Bodies lay rotting in the streets, and the infected howled in the night as they suffered their own agonies.

They rolled down US-27's Victory Drive and stopped short of the overpass at Central Avenue where the highway had been sealed off by a tank blockade.

"I hope they're still here," Callie said from her position behind Minty.

"I hope someone is still here. Things are falling apart so fast, I'm not sure this place can hold out like Dukes hoped."

Minty put the kickstand down on the bike and slid off. Long hours in the saddle made his legs stiff, and it felt good to walk on the hot road. He wore a sidearm, and an AR-15 hung on a strap from his shoulder. He hoped the sentries would understand.

The sweltering air shifted and the smell of rot wafted over him. Minty stopped, eyes scanning the surroundings. It could be a mass grave, or body dump for anyone who came to close.

"Anyone there?" he called out.

There was no response. With his balls crawling up into his kidneys, Minty started walking again. Insects buzzed, and other than the well-kept grass, nothing moved.

A dark smear of blood had sprayed up the side of the tank. Minty crouched down and peered underneath it. A corpse wearing a tank crew Nomex flame-retardant jumpsuit lay facedown at the back of the tank, skin already darkening with decay. The network of white fungal spores had spread as far as the blood. It looked like a close-up picture of a snowflake on a dark background.

He found more bodies around the other vehicles. Most had gone down fighting, though the smears of blood on the ground suggested others had walked or crawled away.

"How's it looking?" Freak asked, scaring Minty half to death.

"Shit. I think we're too late."

Freak looked around. The heat rose off the roadway in a pulsing wave. The buildings and cars along the road were silent and empty looking.

"We go around, see if we can get a view into the camp," Minty said. "Go tell the others."

Freak went back to give the convoy an update. Minty wondered again where would ever be safe. Callie had discussed the idea that the fungus would eventually spread into the water supply, the food supply, or even release spores into the air. It would be a matter of time before the entire country was infected. Every living thing would die.

They shot the few dogs they saw. Most of them were foaming like they were rabid, the fungal strings tangling through their fur.

Cracker Dan, former leader of the Georgia chapter of the Locusts, had been a nomad for the last two years. He had an extended family of free-ranger bikers. They were more like gypsies than hard-core hell-raisers now. Dan's people rode with Minty, curious to see what was happening and pleased to be able to demonstrate their loyalty to the club.

No one had seen Jethro or his followers, which made Minty nervous. While Jethro was out there the madness of the infected seemed like a secondary concern. You could count on the afflicted to attack with an insane fury. Jethro was never that predictable. Infected or not.

Minty went back to his bike. The engines started up and the convoy rolled around the blockade. People started emerging from the trees, ragged, bloodstained, with the white veins of infection standing out on their skin.

Florida seemed like it might be their only choice now. That meant heading south into wild country where the infection would be spreading. All of Minty's instincts told him to go north, but he had to know if Dukes and his crew had made it.

Thousands of dull-eyed people came out onto the road as they drove. The infected would soon outnumber the survivors. *Would they survive the next winter?* Minty wondered. Would humanity re-create a society based on living with a parasite fungus spreading through your blood and into your brain?

The convoy followed the highway past Fort Benning, and all they saw was death and madness. Infected charged at them, civilians and military personnel. They saw no sign of resistance, no holdouts waiting for rescue, and no sign of Dukes or his squad.

Minty waved and they turned away. Georgia was lost. They drove into Florida without looking back.

CHAPTER 34

Over the next week Minty's convoy swelled and faded. People joined and left or they died. Infected were shot at the first sign of the fungus manifesting in their skin.

Callie took a lot of notes, and she confided in Minty that most of the infected they saw should be dead by now. After three days in the summer heat dehydration alone would have killed them. For many, their injuries should have killed them even faster. None of the infected showed signs of sepsis in their wounds. The fungus seemed to protect its host against all other invaders.

"What happens when they do die?" Minty asked. "Are they gonna get up again?"

"I don't think so. There is only so much the fungus can do. This isn't something that is turning people into zombies. It's just a natural disaster, not science fiction."

Minty nodded. He hadn't read much science fiction since he was a kid. Their current circumstances seemed like a living nightmare, not the creation of some hack writer. He appreciated Callie coming with them. She could have stayed, cared for her father and been safe in Gadsden. Instead, when they came back for her and Jessie, the two women were packed and ready to leave within the hour.

"Daddy's placing his faith in God and the law," Callie said. "I don't want to be trapped here when the infected come. I don't want to see him die."

Jessie simply warned Freak not to leave her again.

⚓

They were camped in the middle of the highway and preparing to move on at dawn when the aircraft flew over. All eyes turned to the sky and Minty wondered if it might be in trouble as white smoke started to pour out of the underbelly.

"They're spraying!" Callie said. "Everyone, get under cover!"

People ran for their vehicles or scuttled back into their tents. The white mist fell and covered everything with a harsh-smelling dust that had the consistency of flour.

"The fuck is this?" Cracker Dan demanded.

"It could be an antifungal? Maybe some kind of pesticide? Try not to breathe it in," Callie called across the camp.

People emerged, some with gas masks and others with cloth tied around their heads.

"We should get moving," Callie said. "Get away from this stuff."

They saw the plane again as it flew a grid across the area, spraying until it was empty and then heading south, the same direction they were going.

Driving down the highway they saw the now familiar scattering of dead bodies. The white dust had settled on everything, coating the corpses like radioactive fallout.

During their travels the convoy had stopped trying to communicate with survivors in small towns. People tended to shoot or run away when approached. The infection hadn't spread outside the larger population centers yet. Callie predicted it was coming. Staying in their homes and shooting strangers would simply delay the inevitable.

Following Interstate 10 instead of Route 285 kept them out of Valparaiso. According to the map, turning south onto Route 85 would take them to Eglin without bringing them too close to people.

Aircraft continued to pass overhead, nothing close enough to make out specific markings, and the flights seemed focused on spreading the white powder.

They saw streams of cars, trucks, and RVs going in all directions. Anywhere that people were fleeing from, other people were racing toward. They heard constant rumors and shouted warnings about outbreaks, or gangs of looters. Miami was a free-fire zone. Tallahassee was overrun with infection. Orlando was a refuge with the army in control, but the next group they met was fleeing Orlando for their lives.

Minty didn't tell any of the refugees they encountered of their planned destination. He had no way of knowing if Eglin Air Force Base would be safe or already lost like Fort Benning.

The Northwest Florida Regional Airport chilled them all. Only a few aircraft remained on the ground. Smoke drifted from the terminal building and luggage had been strewn across the ground outside. The parking lot was a scrap metal yard of crashed vehicles. Cars were abandoned from a mile up the road, and someone had driven through the fence.

The infected were here in vast numbers, thousands of people, screaming and charging toward the convoy. They only fired when necessary, as they didn't have nearly enough ammunition to kill every person with the fungus crawling through their veins.

The mob followed them the last few miles to Eglin. Aircraft flew in low, spraying white powder in thick layers like crop dusters being paid by the gallon. The infected slowed as the white powder kicked up and settled again on their skin. Minty looked back and saw they were stumbling, losing their forward momentum, and finally collapsing.

The road ahead was a crush of fallen bodies. A few infected still crawled toward them, their skin peeling off in thick strips of ash-grey flesh.

"Seriously," Callie shouted through her bandanna. "Do not breathe that dust."

Eglin AFB seemed free of infected. Soldiers in NBC suits came out to meet them in two Humvees. The SAWs mounted on the trucks were kept trained on the ragged group.

"We're looking for Sergeant Kyle Dukes, California National Guard. He asked us to meet him here!" Minty yelled across the open space between the two groups.

"Are you infected?" a voice on a megaphone called back.

"We are not infected," Minty yelled back.

"Leave your vehicles and any weapons. Come forward, slowly," The megaphone voice ordered.

The convoy was exhausted after a week of running, fighting, and struggling to survive in the collapse of all they knew. This new world was harsh and unforgiving. They shuffled forward and instead of dogs, the soldiers examined them.

"Finger," one said. Minty blinked, wondering if he wanted him to flip him the bird.

"Hold your finger out," The soldier repeated from behind his gas mask.

Minty extended a finger and it got jabbed with a needle like a blood-sugar test.

Everyone went through this process and the soldiers made no comment, but they moved two of the civilians away from the others.

"*Stabsgefreiter Schmidt, nehmen diese menschen in für die dekontamination,*" The soldier holding the megaphone said.

"Germans?" Minty asked. "Are we being invaded or something?"

"Not at all. We are here as part of a NATO exercise. Your domestic situation has required all available hands to lend their support."

"Is there a Sergeant Dukes here? He's from California," Callie said.

"*Ja*, he has been here for several days now. Quite a story he tells. You can see him after you have been cleaned."

"I hope that is German for shower," Callie said.

The German soldiers escorted the larger group of civilians through the gate. Minty glanced back. "What about Jim and Sarah?"

"They showed blood signs. Further tests will be needed," Corporal Schmidt replied.

Eglin AFB buzzed with activity. Soldiers in different uniforms marched and ran. Aircraft landed, refueled, and took off again in a steady cycle.

In a tent complex, they were showered with more of the orange spray and hot water hoses. All the runoff was pumped into tanks and they were issued fresh army fatigues to wear.

"What are the aircraft spraying?" Callie asked the German corporal when they emerged from the tent.

"Some poison for fungus," Schmidt replied. "We have no infected pushing down our fences because they die before they get too close."

"What about noninfected people?" Callie asked.

Schmidt shrugged. "You should be fine now."

They ate in a mess tent, surrounded by German and US soldiers. They were all business, eating and leaving the mess again as soon as possible.

"There is something weird going on here," Minty muttered. "Did you see some of those aircraft? They aren't spraying chemicals. Those really big ones, they're bringing in troops, equipment, and probably weapons."

"Well, we could use all the help we can get," Callie said and grimaced at the taste of the coffee she was drinking.

A US private snapped to attention and saluted. "Doctor Blythe?"

"Yes?" Callie looked surprised.

"Sergeant Dukes sent me. He requests your presence."

"Okay." Callie slid out from the table. Minty, Freak, and Jessie stood up as well.

"Sorry," Callie said. "These people go where I go. It saves me having to repeat everything when I get back."

The private nodded and marched out of the mess. Dukes and his squad were in a tent that smelled of gun oil and sweaty socks.

"Dukes," Minty said. "How are you, man?"

Dukes grinned. "Minty, Doc, Freak, Jessie. Glad you guys made it."

Callie looked around. "Garrett, Milquist. Where are the others?"

Dukes' face went blank. "Fort Benning was overrun. They didn't make it out."

"Shit, sorry to hear that, man," Minty said.

"I've been hearing reports about your friend, Jethro," Dukes said. "He's got a lot of people believing he has a cure. Getting quite the following. Currently they're moving around too much to be confronted, and we have bigger issues with infected."

"This aerial spraying?" Callie asked, "It seems effective."

"It's a new mix the CDC cooked up before Atlanta was hit. They have some kind of vaccine in testing too. Just no cure yet. Seems once the fungus has advanced into your brain, the damage is permanent."

"If it's a fungus, you can't vaccinate against a fungus," Callie said.

"CDC reckons you can do something to prevent it. They are engineering an immune response to the spores. They think it will destroy it before it takes hold and grows in the tissues."

"Does it work?" Minty asked.

"How the fuck would I know?" Dukes asked. "They play their cards close. They've been testing it on animals."

"The infection has crossed the species barrier," Callie said. "We saw dogs with full-blown symptoms."

"Yep. They have started eating infected corpses. Seems to be infecting them."

"What the hell is happening here?" Minty asked, changing the subject to something they could talk about.

"NATO. Seems there was some exercise planned, about a hundred German soldiers. They've only been here a week. There are a couple of ships offshore too."

"Does that seem normal to you?" Minty asked. "For an exercise?"

"Christ, nothing is normal anymore."

"Who are you reporting to now?" Minty asked.

"That's where things get complicated. Technically we are reporting to the National Guard. Realistically, we are working with the Germans. All US National Guard units stationed here have been shipped north to the quarantine line. We kinda fell through the cracks so we are officially assigned to support and sentry duty."

"The Germans seem to be in charge," Jessie said.

"Sure. They have the resources, the supplies, the men."

"Are they invading us, the Germans I mean?" Jessie asked.

"That's some crazy bullshit," Garrett laughed.

Dukes rubbed his jaw and stared out at the troops walking up the loading ramp of a Hercules cargo plane.

"This is still America, right?" Milquist asked.

"Yeah . . ." Dukes said.

"The CDC, they came up with the antifungal powder for aerial spraying?" Callie asked.

"That's what we were told."

"You think the German troops brought it in?" Callie asked.

"They seem well prepared for a spraying operation," Minty said.

"You're just fucking paranoid," Dukes said.

"You guys are staying here?" Freak asked.

"Sure, we're still part of this nation's armed forces. That means we are on active duty until told otherwise."

"It's safe," Callie reminded Minty. "The spraying is keeping the infected back."

"We should stay here, man," Freak added his agreement.

Minty scowled. "For now, I guess."

CHAPTER 35

Minty spent a few days catching up on his sleep. When he was awake he dedicated himself to the all-consuming search for cigarettes. Callie had been offered a volunteer position in a clinic that was treating the civilian casualties, which meant anyone who had been cleared of infection and had some other medical issue. She seemed happy, and with Freak and Jessie only having eyes for each other, Minty felt restless as a dog with two dicks.

They lived in tents and had access to all the mod cons. There was even satellite TV. News was sporadic, with footage from low-level flyovers and endless hours of men in suits talking about what was happening.

Dukes and his men spent their days patrolling, guarding the fence, and exercising.

Each morning the few aircraft left would take off and fly on spraying or reconnaissance missions. Minty walked the base until German soldiers ordered him at gunpoint to turn around and go back to *die ziviles gebiet*, which seemed to mean the area of the base where the civilians were being housed. Instead, he went to find Dukes.

"Where is everyone?" Minty asked.

"Most of the base have been relocated up north," Dukes replied.

"There should be more US soldiers. You should have a commanding officer telling you what to do."

"You thinking of reenlisting?" Dukes said with a half smile.

"Fuck that." Minty lit a cigarette, the last in the pack. The idea of being without a smoke did not improve his mood.

"This is a large military base in the midst of a serious national crisis, Minty. You said you have done time overseas. You know how it looks. Resources go where they are most needed. We are in enemy territory. We have a defensive force and we are providing critical support and recon assets."

"That defense force just about shot me for walking too close to one of their restricted zones. There's some shit going on around here. I want to talk to a US officer in charge." Minty exhaled smoke into the stifling air.

"What is going on here, old man, is that you have way too much time to think."

"You need a fuckin' hobby," Milquist said from his cot.

"I should be on the road. The guys are getting itchy feet."

Dukes stared at the biker. "Where the fuck are you going to go?"

"North. This is just going to get worse."

Dukes waved Minty's concerns away. "Yeah, summer is coming and the northern states are going to be in shit just as much as we are."

"Doc still says when summer really hits the shit is going to hit. You've seen what they are saying on TV."

"They are containing the situation. The southern states are under a state of martial law and we are quarantined."

"Sergeant!" Garrett came running. He ducked into the tent, his eyes wide.

Dukes and Milquist stood up, ready to go to war.

"Mexico. They fucking nuked Mexico," Garrett said.

"The fuck? Who did? Where exactly?"

Garrett held up a hand. "No serious intel. Word on the wire is that some general in Texas took things into his own hands and they fired some tactical ordnance into the infected coming across the Texas border."

"That's impossible," Dukes said.

"Shit, Sergeant, a month ago I would have said that crazy people tearing the country apart would have been fuckin' impossible."

"Christ, what's the response from DC?" Dukes looked grim.

"Fuck if I know, Sergeant. You think they tell me anything?" Garrett replied.

"Did it work?" Milquist asked.

"What the fuck?" Garrett asked, a sour laugh squeezing out of him.

Milquist rolled off his cot and marched over. "Did it work? Did the nukes stop the infected coming out of Mexico and fucking every last one of us?"

"They . . . well yeah, the army's holding the border now. But when this gets out, people are going to shit," Garrett replied.

"Okay, Garrett. Get back out there and find out what is happening. Stay alert for new orders. Milk, head over to the TOC, find out what they are doing about this development. Fuckin' move."

Minty waited until the two soldiers had left the tent. "Did Garrett just say we nuked another country?"

"Tactical nuclear weapons were used against an enemy force," Dukes replied.

"I know what tactical means. Do you really think just because it wasn't a fucking ICBM that flattened an entire city, the world is suddenly not going to give a flying fuck?"

"Probably not. Hopefully, all the shit going on will keep this out of the news."

"We fucking nuked Mexico," Minty said again.

"Hooah," Dukes replied.

⚜

The mainstream media held out like a kid needing the bathroom for nearly twenty-four hours. By then the amateur footage and civilian reports were all over the Internet. The networks threw their hands up in a *what can we do?* gesture and started broadcasting news of the attack on the Texas border. The key messages were carefully massaged to distance the US government from the officer in charge. He had acted outside his authority and the matter was being treated as serious crime.

No one would officially comment on the effectiveness of the strikes, which turned out to be two field warheads of less than twenty kilotons. Fuel-air explosive ordnance was still the official response, delivered by air strikes.

Russia, China, and North Korea led the international outrage against what they called an unprovoked act of war against a sovereign nation. Russia dropped all pretense of diplomacy and sent armored columns across the border into Belarus. Compared to the crisis in the US, the rapid annexation of the former Soviet state back into the newly expanding Russia barely rated a mention in international media.

⚔

"Can I ask you something?" Callie's voice came as soft as a lover's touch in the dark of their shared cot.

Minty gave a grunt in reply.

"Jessie said you once beat a man to death. An undercover police officer? Is that true?"

Minty lay still for so long that Callie wondered if he had gone to sleep. "That's the story. The story isn't the truth though. There was a narc, an undercover cop. He'd worked his way into our ranks and I don't know how he found out, but Jethro had him marked. He told me that it was going to be taken care of. Told me that this was the point in history where the Locusts would become something or die. We took the narc on a run up to Seattle, fed him a bullshit story about meeting some high-time drug dealers. Kid was nearly drooling at the bust he thought was coming.

"In a bus station bathroom, I kicked that kid's ass. He would have lived when I finished with him. Sure he'd be eating through a straw for a few weeks, but he would have gone skulking back to his agency and they would know that the Locusts were not to be fucked with."

Callie wriggled back against the warmth of Minty's body pressed against hers.

"Jethro wasn't done though. He wasn't satisfied. He stepped in when I was done and started hitting that kid. He had a rage on him like nothing I have ever seen. Cold and silent. He punched that kid until the narc's face was mush and his eyeballs popped out."

"Oh my God . . ." Callie whispered.

"God turned away that day. We cleaned up and walked out of there. Leaving the dead narc in the bathroom stall. Jethro told everyone that I'd taken care of the narc. When the news broke, the word was that I'd beat him to death. Jethro wanted the Locusts to love him. He needed me to be his dark lieutenant. The one that everyone would fear. The sword to balance his calm wisdom."

"So it was all a lie?"

"Not the first time I followed Jethro through bullshit, not the last either."

Minty slipped out of bed and pulled on his jeans. Callie murmured something and rolled over, the smooth skin of her naked back gleaming in the dim light.

The biker lit a cigarette outside the tent. The runway for the recon flights in and out was far enough across the base to be slept through. Callie scolded him about his smoking, but in a world where so many things could kill him, he figured cigarettes were an acceptable vice.

The late night air felt as thick as sauna steam. Walking gave the illusion of a breeze, and Minty strolled toward the roadside fence without any purpose in mind.

Sentries glanced at him, then went back to watching the empty ground beyond the fence. Spotlights swept the night, but so far the white powder that lay in a thick firebreak hundreds of yards across had kept the infected at bay.

A sound came through the night air, no louder than the crickets and other insects that chorused in the dark. Minty stopped as a weird flapping sound, like a stunned bird falling out of the sky, reached him.

A moment later he yelped and leapt backwards as a body landed with a wet crunch a few feet away from where he stood. The woman was naked, her skin a network of fungal infection. The white lines stood out on her face like the vessels in a skeletonized leaf.

"Fuck!" Minty yelled. Boots pounded on the concrete and soldiers came running. The woman crawled, her face smashed and oozing blood. The white tendrils of the fungus wriggled out of her wounds until they waved like hair floating in water.

Another body landed, hitting the concrete headfirst, and the sound of the man's neck breaking echoed across the compound.

The soldiers fired, shooting both of the infected in the head. Further away an alarm started to howl, voices yelled, and vehicles started up.

"Where the fuck are they coming from?" Minty asked the nearest soldier. He shrugged and moved on.

A van rolled up and four men in biohazard gear clambered out. They unpacked body bags and buckets of white powder. The bodies were sealed in bags, and the men sprinkled white powder liberally over the still forms. Minty backed away as a flamethrower poured burning oil on the bloodstains.

A moment later the reinforced gate erupted in an explosion of fire and concrete shrapnel. Minty threw himself flat, landing hard and rolling in the smoke and sharp debris.

The biker crawled into cover as more bodies fell from the sky. The infected that didn't land on concrete got to their feet and started advancing into the military base.

An M923 truck painted in army green came thundering toward the shattered gate. It smashed through, sending metal and wire spinning away into the darkness. The truck ground to a halt inside the fence.

The back of the vehicle fell open and bodies tumbled out. The infected were packed inside tighter than desperate Mexican immigrants being smuggled across the border.

Without a weapon Minty knew he could either hide or run. He got to his feet and bolted. The civilian area remained out of reach of the advancing invaders for now.

People clambered out of their tents, gathering children and personal items as they went.

A commanding voice echoed from speakers on poles in a calm and reasoned tone over a background of sporadic gunfire that echoed across the base. "*All civilians are to remain in their quarters. All military personnel report to your assigned positions.*"

Freak and Jesse appeared, the boy still belting his jeans. "Minty, what the fuck is going on?" Freak asked.

"Are we being attacked?" Jessie asked.

"Infected, someone is throwing infected people over the fence. Get armed and get ready to get the fuck out," Minty called as he ran past.

The biker stumbled into the tent he shared with Callie. She had dressed and was stuffing clothes into an assault pack.

"You read my fucking mind," Minty said.

"Are the infected breaking through?" Callie asked.

"No, they are being flown in," Minty replied.

Callie stopped what she was doing and stared at him.

"That is I think they are being tossed over the fence."

"Infected corpses?" Callie asked.

"No, well, they are alive before they land. Some of them are still alive afterwards."

"We should stay here. Let the soldiers take care of things." Callie stopped shoving clothes into the bag. "Here is safe."

"Callie." Minty put his hands on her arms and turned her to look at him. "Nowhere is safe. We stay here and we are going to be under siege. When they break through we will be trapped inside these fences. Just like what happened back at Lucky's."

Callie blinked. "What did you say?"

"Nowhere is safe? We're going to get trapped if we stay here?"

"No, no, siege. You said we are under siege."

"Yeah, we are going to be under siege until they break through," Minty replied.

"Medieval castles. Attacking armies would use trebuchets to throw massive rocks at the walls. Sometimes they would throw corpses of plague victims, or just dead people, over the walls to spread disease and weaken the defenders."

"Which is why they call it the good old days," Minty shrugged.

"You and Jethro, you were in the army together, right?"

"Marines," Minty corrected.

"What department?" Callie demanded.

"What?"

"What did you do in the Marines?" Callie said through gritted teeth.

"I was a fucking grunt. Jethro was an engineer, built bridges and shit."

"You think maybe a guy who quotes seventeenth-century French poets and was a trained engineer might have a few fucking clues about making medieval-style siege weapons?" Callie snapped.

"Fuck me," Minty laughed. "Fucking Jethro."

"So we can safely assume that Jethro and whatever posse he has gathered behind him are attacking the air force base. Throwing infected at us as basic biological warfare."

Minty picked up the assault pack. "Inside there are at least a hundred troops. Guns, aircraft, highly trained professional soldiers. Outside there are millions of infected, and now Jethro-fucking-Williams, and how ever many crazy-assed motherfuckers he has picked up along the way."

"He has a particularly fucked-up personality type," Callie agreed.

"We can't stay here. I don't care how many soldiers we have. Jethro will survive and he will fuck us."

Callie's nose wrinkled. "I really hope you mean that figuratively."

"If we are lucky, sure."

"So we get out and go north?" Callie asked.

"My plans haven't changed. We get out, we head for Canada or Alaska."

"Finland, Norway, Iceland. Those are options too."

"Except Alaska is still the USA. We don't need passports to go there."

"You don't need a passport to drive into Cana—" Callie stopped as Minty gestured her to be still.

From outside the tent a moaning sound came through the distant chatter of small arms fire.

Minty crept to the flap of the tent. It was darker in the tent than out and he could see an infected man limping past.

The man's head snapped around and he bared his teeth, snarling as he stared at Minty, who froze and held his breath.

A moment later the infected man launched himself at the tent. Minty snatched up the edge of the tent flap and the infected man charged into it. The biker stepped around him, wrapping the freak up in the khaki canvas.

"Callie, fucking move!" Minty held the thrashing bundle against his chest. Callie raced out of the tent and Minty let go. Grabbing the doctor by the arm, he started running. If they were lucky they might get out of sight before the infected man got untangled.

They headed toward the barracks where Dukes and his squad were housed. Around them people ran in all directions, some shooting, some screaming. Some were screaming and shooting.

Minty skidded to a halt outside the barracks. "Dukes!" he yelled over the sounds of gunfire and snarling.

There was no response and Minty tried the door. It was locked.

"Minty, we can't stay here!" Callie called. He glanced back and, seeing the way was clear, went back to peering through the dark window set in the door.

The howls of the infected grew louder and Minty muttered a full breath of curses as he stepped back. "We'll find a car, truck, or something. Time to get the fuck out of Dodge."

Callie just nodded, her face white with terror. "What about Jessie and Freak?"

Minty hurried away from the barracks and down a line of tents, Callie on his heels. "Freak? If they survive, then that's fucking great. We can celebrate later. Right now, we get the fuck out of here."

Callie was in mind to agree; survival always came down to the individual. Only when she and Minty were safe could they worry about others.

The biker stopped at the end of the tent row and looked both ways, peering into the darkness. A tent across the avenue shuddered as someone collided with the back wall from inside. The two of them froze and then glanced at each other. Callie nodded and they turned left, hurrying through the space between tents as a canvas shelter behind them collapsed in a growling heap.

At the end of the row an empty expanse of grass bordered the wide desert of concrete that marked the edge of the maze of runways. "There were a dozen fuckin' trucks here yesterday." Minty threw up his hands in disgust. Callie looked around and started walking along the grass edge. Minty followed her; standing still would help no one.

"We should head towards the soldiers," Minty suggested.

"Why would we do that?" Callie called back over her shoulder. "We can only find the soldiers by the gunfire. If they are shooting, then they are facing infected and that's the last place we want to be."

"Good point," Minty agreed.

"Truck," Callie announced and started running. Ahead of them an army Humvee appeared out of the darkness. Callie waved her arms and yelled. The vehicle drove straight at her. She leapt aside at the last moment and the truck vanished into the night.

"Assholes!" Callie yelled at the rear of the vehicle.

Minty ran past and scooped her up. "Zombies are coming," he explained. He set her down behind a tent. They crouched there, waiting until the roving infected had passed by.

"Technically, zombies are dead people," Callie whispered.

"Whatever."

Callie kept looking for more infected who might be coming up on them.

"I need a weapon. Not even a gun, just something." Minty felt naked without something to defend them with.

"We could try the armory?"

"Maybe, but if it isn't already stripped, it'll be locked up tighter than a nun's bunghole."

"Nun's anus," Callie corrected and then stifled a giggle.

"Christ, we did not come this far to fucking die in Florida." Minty peered around the edge of a tent. The way seemed clear for now.

"The barracks will be safer than the tents," Callie said. "We can break in and secure ourselves."

Minty nodded. "It's this way." He stepped forward and Callie caught his arm.

"Barracks are this way," she said and slipped out into the dark.

CHAPTER 36

"Francis," Jessie whispered.

He looked up from the lock he was trying to pick. "Yeah?"

"Someone's coming."

Freak left the door and joined Jessie behind a stack of crates. The storage building had a curved roof of corrugated iron and a concrete foundation. There were at least two rooms inside, and an aluminum interior door had stopped them.

"Did you lock the outside door?" Freak whispered.

"I . . . shit, I don't know," Jessie replied.

The door at the front of the building rattled. They heard the snarling howls of infected. The people outside snapped their teeth and fought to get closer to whatever it was they could sense behind the door.

"Stay behind me," Freak whispered as the outer door shuddered. Looking around, he pulled a fire extinguisher off the wall. It was a powder-charged type; at the very least it would give them a few seconds of distraction and cover.

The door handle twisted and the door sprang open. The first of the infected tumbled onto the floor. Their broken nails clawed at the concrete as the others trod them underfoot.

Freak and Jessie backed into the corner as the narrow spaces between the stacked crates of supplies filled with a stinking crowd of infected.

"Hold your breath," Freak whispered and Jessie squeezed his hand. He straightened, swinging the fire extinguisher up to shoulder height and squeezing the trigger in the face of the nearest infected. A dense white cloud roared out of the funnel and everything disappeared in a choking fog of ammonium phosphate.

Using the extinguisher as a club, Freak smashed their way through the bodies. Hands clawed at them, blinded and disorientated by the choking powder. It took the full extent of a captured breath to reach the open door. Jessie and Freak stumbled out into the dark, coughing and choking as the last of the extinguisher's contents spewed out around their feet like dry ice fog.

"Not dead yet," Freak managed to grin.

"Run," Jessie gasped. They took off, ducking around the side of the supply building and out of sight, Freak cradling the fire extinguisher in his arms.

"I knew they would leave us behind," Jessie said.

Freak wasn't phased. "Minty wouldn't abandon us. We're brothers. We just have to find the army guys and stay with them."

Jessie turned slowly. "Then we should head that way; there's a lot of shooting going on over there."

Freak started walking, his hand reaching out and taking Jessie's in its warm grip. It felt right when he held her, safe, certain, and like she always imagined love would be.

The noise of small arms fire grew louder as they crossed the base. The sky lit up with the flash of tracer fire and the occasional boom of explosive detonation.

"Hang on," Jessie said as she darted aside and snatched up a dangling tent rope. She twisted the heavy plastic stake from the end and brandished it like a knife.

"Cool," Freak said, grinning.

Moving as fast as they dared through the dark, they edged around the tents and buildings. "Wait," Jessie ordered. Ahead of them an infected woman stumbled into view. She snorted like a pig and sniffed the air. Jessie waited until she turned away and then dashed forward and stabbed the woman in the back with the tent peg. The woman howled and spun around; Jessie ducked under her wild swing. Freak smashed her face in with the bottom of the fire extinguisher. The infected fell onto her back and he kept hitting until her skull was a pulped mess on the ground.

"She's dead, Francis." Jessie put a hand on his shoulder and Freak almost swung the extinguisher at her.

"Oh, shit. You okay?"

"Yeah," she said, her expression calculating.

Freak looked relieved. "Keep moving."

They moved on through the base, dodging wandering groups of infected. Jessie stabbed a naked man in the throat when he charged at them from the darkness. As she pulled the stake out of his neck the tendrils of infection reached out of the wound and curled around the plastic blade.

Jessie hissed in disgust and jerked her hand back. Freak smashed the extinguisher into the man's face. "Back off, asshole," Freak said and struck again. The man's head snapped back and more strands of the fungus crawled out of the fresh wounds on his face.

Freak swung the extinguisher like a club and the blow twisted the infected man's head so far his neck cracked.

"Francis!" Jessie screamed. Freak danced back, moving his feet like a prizefighter.

Jessie screamed again as two more infected dragged her down. Freak lashed out with the gore-stained metal of the extinguisher, knocking the two howling people aside. Jessie clutched her arm against her chest and blood oozed out between her clenched fingers.

"Run for fuck's sake," Freak shouted. He dragged Jessie to her feet and they bolted. The infected behind them howled and scrambled in pursuit. Freak ran out into the open ground beyond the tents and buildings. A machine gun post of sandbags and crates had been set up and they ran toward it; it would be a place to hide.

The first burst of machine gun fire tore up the concrete in a line to Freak's right. He dodged left, dragging Jessie with him. The infected behind them ran straight into the next burst. The rounds tore them open and sent the snarling creatures tumbling across the concrete. M4 rifle fire shattered their skulls as they stood up again, dropping them for the final time.

"Francis," Jessie said as they stopped running. "Wait . . ."

Freak looked back. Jessie stumbled and he hurried to where she stood, sinking to the ground. Her arm still cradled against her chest.

"They bit me," she said, her eyes brimming with tears.

"Where?" Freak asked. He lifted her arm, peeling her bloodstained hand away from the wound. A crescent of purple bruising, and seeping blood, stood out above her wrist.

"You're going to be okay," Freak said. "They didn't get you."

"Are you sure?" Jessie searched his face. Freak forced an easy grin. He would kill her himself, he thought, but only if she really went crazy.

Freak looked around and snatched up a flat shard of concrete. "Hold real still." He seized Jessie's arm and scraped at it with the concrete. She gritted her teeth, a whimper slipping through her pale lips. The wound opened up and bled freely, but the teeth marks were torn away.

"Yeah, you're good." He pulled her up.

"Freeze!" a German-accented voice ordered. Freak raised his hands.

"Identify yourselves!"

"Fre— Francis and Jessie. We're civilians. Been here for a week."

"Do not move!" Boots ran across the concrete and a flashlight blinded them.

"Are you bitten?" a second accented voice asked.

"No," Freak replied immediately. "Just a few cuts and bruises."

"Move, that way. *Schnell!*" They followed the soldier past the machine gun post, where other troops opened fire a moment later as more infected came charging out of the rows of tents.

Two flatbed trucks waited on the edge of a runway. People working under the glow of flashlights attempted to staunch the flow of blood from the dozen wounded that lay writhing and screaming on the ground.

German soldiers stood nearby, watching the injured, their weapons ready to fire. One of the bodies on the ground sat up, howling and thrashing.

"*Zurückschieben!*" a German yelled. The two medics fell back as the troops opened fire. The infected man shuddered with the impact and finally collapsed as his head came apart in a shower of brain and bone shards.

"We need to isolate these people," one of the medical team said.

"Where the fuck do you suggest we put them?" an American soldier asked.

"Kill them. *Töten sie alle*," a German sergeant ordered. The soldiers pushed the protesting medics aside and opened fire.

The wounded shuddered under the impact of gunfire. Men, women, and children screamed and tried to crawl away. Jessie and Freak stood apart, watching in stunned silence as the wounded civilians were slaughtered.

A soldier turned his weapon on Jessie and Freak. "What about them?" The others turned to face them, weapons ready, fingers creaking on triggers.

"We are not infected!" Freak yelled as he stepped in front of Jessie, his hands up.

"Only one way to be sure," one of the Americans said, his M4 snapping to a ready-to-fire position.

"No, no, no," Freak replied.

"Stand down!" a familiar voice barked. The soldiers glanced aside. Dukes came jogging up.

"I'm Sergeant Dukes. Exactly what the fuck is going on here?" Dukes demanded.

"Isolating infected, Sergeant," a Hispanic sergeant replied.

"Those two are not infected," Dukes said, pointing at Jessie and Freak. "So are you planning on murdering them?"

"No, Sergeant."

"Get up to the machine gun post, secure these trucks against actual infected. Move!" The soldiers scattered, leaving Dukes, Jessie, and Freak with the medical team and a steaming pile of fresh corpses.

"We should clean this mess up," a medic in blood-splattered gloves said.

"No, you should get the keys for that truck and drive as far away from here as you can," Dukes replied.

"But these people—"

"These people are dead. If you don't want to be dead, get out of here."

The medical team moved slowly at first and then with increasing confidence. They threw their gear into the back of the truck and piled onboard. Within a minute they drove off into the darkness.

Jessie found her voice. "Where are the others?"

"They are safe. Come on, we need to go. There's no point in staying here."

"Minty and the doc?" Freak asked.

"We've got them. Keep up or die." Dukes double-timed it away from the scene, Jessie and Freak on his heels.

CHAPTER 37

"There's more of them coming from that way." Callie jerked a hand to their right.

"We can hide over there." Minty didn't look where Callie pointed. Better to face the terrible things coming at you than the terrible things behind you.

They reached one of the prefabricated buildings. Minty ran the last fifty feet, shoulder charging the door and smashing it inward. He regained his balance and heaved the door back into place after Callie slipped through the gap.

"Is there anyone here?" The doctor whispered into the dark storeroom where shelves were stacked with catering-sized cans of food.

"We knocked," Minty muttered. The door latch hung out of the lock plate, as useless as a broken arm. He left the door wedged closed as best he could.

Callie called him from a commercial-sized kitchen. Ovens, giant pots and pans, and industrial equipment gleamed with polished chrome and enamel in the faint moonlight.

"Now we're talking." Minty passed his hands over a selection of cleavers, butcher knives, and boning knives. He took a long-handled cleaver; it had a good, solid weight in his hand. "Can I get you something?" he asked Callie.

"I'm good, thanks." Callie hefted a steel bar that she had unscrewed from one of the machines.

"Now we just need a ride." They moved through the kitchen, checking the corners for hidden threats. A short corridor at the end led to a door marked LOADING BAY.

"Delivery truck?" Callie asked. "Stop me if you've heard this one."

Minty grunted. "It worked last time, didn't it?"

"Last time we were lucky," Callie reminded him. They opened the door, revealing an empty space between where they stood and the garage roller door that led outside.

"Fuck," Minty swore.

"Ouch," Callie said. "What is your plan B?"

"I don't have a fucking plan B."

Something collided with the garage door, rattling it and silencing them both for a long moment.

"Back," Minty whispered. "We'll find another way out."

They closed the loading bay door and crept down the corridor to the kitchen until a snarling sound froze them in their tracks.

"Raccoons in the kitchen used to be a real pain in the butt back home," Callie whispered

"Fuckin' big raccoons," Minty replied.

They stopped at the kitchen door and listened. From the snarls and grunts of infected, Minty counted three beyond the door.

"Stay behind me," Minty whispered. He pushed the door open and ducked down under the prep bench. Callie went around the other side. The nearest infected, a woman who barely looked college age, had caught a reflection in the gleaming chrome face of the walk-in refrigerator. She swayed, teeth bared as she snarled at it.

Minty stood up behind her; she turned as she caught sight of his silhouette in the shining steel. He struck, and the cleaver amputated her arm and left a dent in the refrigerator door. The girl howled, swinging her stump at Minty's face. He dodged back, avoiding the spray and swinging the cleaver at the woman's other arm.

The cleaver buried itself between the woman's fingers, splitting her hand down to the wrist. She jerked back, her hand spreading impossibly wide.

Minty struck again, the familiar terror of staring death in the face driving him to hit her again. This time he buried the cleaver's heavy blade in the woman's skull. She sank to her knees with a sigh, dragging the blade down with her. Minty stood on her chest and jerked the cleaver free. Straightening up, he saw Callie stabbing at a man, also of around college age, with the end of the metal bar she carried.

"Fuckin' hit him," Minty hissed.

Callie didn't take her eyes off the man lunging toward her. She lifted the steel bar and jammed it into his eye. His forward momentum drove it through the thin bone at the back of his eye socket and deep into his brain. Callie stirred it for good measure, feeling the metal grind against the bone shell of the dying man's skull.

The bar came out with a wet, sucking sound and the body slumped to the floor.

"Wait, I'm sure there was another one," Minty said.

"There's no sign of him now," Callie panted.

"Let's get the fuck out of here." Minty headed toward the end of the kitchen. The storeroom lay beyond it, and the dining hall was on their left. The first grey light of dawn was coming through the windows of the mess hall. Outside, torn and bloodied figures stumbled past the building.

"We need to work out where we are going," Callie said.

"Motor pool?" Minty suggested.

"Is there anything left?" Callie asked. Minty wasn't sure. The soldiers shipping north weren't quite reduced to riding bicycles, but they were damn close.

"You think Dukes and his squad made it?"

Minty nodded. "That guy is tough and resourceful. He knows his shit."

"He says the same about you." Callie gave Minty a warm smile.

The old biker raised an eyebrow. "Just trying to survive."

"Minty," Callie hesitated. "If we don't make it, I just wanted you to know. I'm glad I ended up seeing the end of the world with you."

"Damn, Doc, you going soft on me?" Minty grinned at her.

Callie blushed. "Way to ruin a perfectly sweet moment, asshole."

"Thanks, I'm glad you're here too," Minty said and they didn't look at each other for a moment. "Let's get the hell out of here," he added.

"Yeah." Callie looked outside; more infected were coming toward them. Driven by rage or madness, they came loping toward the mess hall like half-human beasts. Monsters with an insatiable hunger for blood and destruction.

Minty didn't speak, he ran, Callie beside him, as they dashed across the open ground. The acres of concrete and painted lines that guided taxiing air traffic lay before them in a clear desert of exposure. They would run out of energy before the pursuing horde did. Then they would die.

The biker came to a halt, his chest tight with a gripping band. His breath wheezed out of his lungs and he doubled over, wracked by a fit of coughing.

"I keep telling you smoking is going to kill you," Callie said.

"Don—don't wait. Go. Run, for fuck's sake."

Callie stood her ground, the metal pole in her hands raised like a spear against the mob bearing down on them.

"You going to die on your knees, old man?" she asked.

"Fuck . . . no." Minty straightened up, the cleaver ready to strike.

"God, if you're still there, forgive us and take us up into your loving embrace." Callie hadn't prayed since she was a child. Her years of studying medicine had pushed her childhood beliefs aside. Now, facing certain death, her faith renewed itself. She was comforted in the reassurance of the ultimate protector and the sudden certainty that if death was coming, then what lay beyond would be perfect and she would be reunited with her mom.

The sudden chatter of an M249 SAW belt-fed machine gun drowned out the howls of the approaching infected. A Humvee roared toward them, the weapon mounted in the roof scything through the approaching freaks with a deadly efficiency.

The truck lights flicked on and the vehicle rolled forward, bathing them in a blinding wash of light.

"Hey ladies, need a ride?" Garrett leaned out of the driver's side window and grinned at them.

The passenger door opened and they tumbled inside. Milquist and another soldier dragged them into the truck and slammed the door.

"Let's go, Garrett," Dukes ordered.

"Freak, Jessie," Callie managed.

"They are fine," Dukes replied. "Already on their way out of the camp."

"Good to hear," Minty said.

"Hang on, motherfuckers," Garrett said and the Humvee's engine roared as it smashed through the infected still standing. Everything inside bounced and Callie came down hard, the wind knocked out of her.

"Move over," Minty said, pulling himself up into a sitting position. He dragged Callie out from the forest of feet and sat her on his lap.

Dukes navigated while Garrett drove as fast as he dared between rows of tents. "Right, then follow the road, there should be a gate five hundred yards further on."

The Humvee's lights illuminated a scene of carnage. Civilians and infected had crashed together in an explosion of blood and terror. Bodies squirmed as teeth tore flesh from bones. Women and children were dismembered, their limbs ripped away and tossed aside as the infected spent their rage against the soft bodies.

"Do not stop," Dukes ordered. Garrett pushed his foot down and a second later blood sprayed across the windshield of the Humvee. The tires bit deep into the uneven surface, grinding the meat to mush under the treads.

The truck rocked and the engine roared as the heavy vehicle crashed through the crowd. The gate ahead had been hit by one of the rocket-propelled grenades that had nearly killed Minty earlier.

"Hit that," Dukes ordered. "Hang on back there." The passengers grabbed on to anything they could as the Humvee picked up speed and ripped through the weakened gate. Mesh and steel frame squealed against the paintwork and they drove out into a cloud of white powder being kicked up by the fast-moving truck.

CHAPTER 38

The speeding Humvee swerved across the road. The vehicles abandoned by recent arrivals had been pushed on to the shoulder and the way ahead was clear. Only the tire tracks left by military trucks marked the toxic white powder that formed a fire break around the former air force base.

"We heading north?" Minty asked.

"Affirmative," Dukes replied. "We are going to the quarantine line. From there you'll be processed into whatever refugee camp system they have set up."

"Cuz that worked so fucking well last time," Minty said.

"At ease that shit." Dukes turned in his seat and glared at Minty. "We could have just as easily left you to die with everyone else."

"We appreciate you coming back for us," Callie said. "Where did Francis and Jessie go?"

Milquist spoke up. "They're on a truck with a medical crew. Heading the same way we are. Maybe five minutes ahead of us."

"Slow down, Garrett, we don't want to hit anything," Dukes warned. The Humvee slowed from over sixty miles per hour to a less hair-raising forty.

A mile down the road they came to a halt. Less than a hundred yards ahead the road was blockaded. Armed figures covered the road from behind a barricade of trucks, and they even had an Abrams M1A2 tank as the centerpiece of the display. Several vehicles from the air force base were parked off the road already and the Humvee pulled up next to them.

"The fuck is this shit?" Milquist muttered.

"Everybody stay where you are." Dukes opened the door and slid out to stand on the road.

"I'm Sergeant Dukes. You need to clear the road!"

"Well a fine howdy-do, Sergeant Dukes!"

Minty's balls crawled cold and clammy up into his gut at the sound of Jethro's voice.

Dukes remained behind the cover of the Humvee's thick armored door. In the light of the rising sun, he could see that Jethro had gathered quite a force. Bikers and gangsters, the desperate, and the terrified. The Locusts leader had an animal magnetism and the charisma of a politician. Now he was seriously armed and if he had brought his band of misfits all the way to Florida, it suggested they were looking for revenge. Dukes scanned his gaze over the mismatched range of vehicles in the barricade. Jethro's voice sounded amplified, but he remained out of sight.

The soldiers and few civilians in the trucks that had preceded them were hunkered down in their vehicles.

"Jethro!" Minty had climbed out and now called out across the open space between the two lines.

"Minty, I have been waiting for you. I need to know, why have you forsaken me, Judas?"

"Let these people go, Jethro. It's me you want. They aren't important."

"If they aren't important, then you won't mind if we kill the men and fuck the women," Jethro called back.

"It's not gonna happen, Jethro." Minty stepped away from the Humvee. He raised his hands, showing he was unarmed.

"After all I have given you. After my sacrifice and dedication. I gave you everything and this is how you repay me?"

Minty wasn't moved. Jethro loved to lay the theatrics on when he had an audience. Pumping up a crowd, like he was a southern preacher running a tent revival.

"I thought you were dead," Minty replied. "I made a choice to get out before I ended up dead too."

"We have faced death together in the past, Minty. You know the best option is to trust in me when the reaper rasps his fetid breath in your face. Instead you succumbed to cowardice. You ran. I faced death and I conquered it!"

The last proclamation brought a cheer from the armed men and women visible over the top of the blockade.

"You are infected with the same fungus that is killing people all over the south, Jethro. Just how fucking long do you think you have?"

"I have conquered death!" Jethro yelled. "I have mastered the invader. Made it my own! It has whispered its secrets to me! Shared the knowledge of destiny! I am the future! I am e-fuckin'-volving right now!"

Minty had no reply to that. He wished he had a rifle, or an A10 on air strike standby. Even one of those tactical nukes the Texan general had used on the rampaging Mexicans would be acceptable right now.

"Good for you, man," Minty said. He was tired. Tired of fighting, tired of running, and mostly, tired of Jethro's bullshit rhetoric. "You don't need us to evolve. You just go on and do your thing. We're leaving. Heading far away. You can make that perfect anarchist state you always dreamed of. The slate has been wiped clean, man. You can create whatever you want."

"I can and I will," Jethro's voice floated back, an eerie calmness to his tone. "However, there are those who have been loyal to me, Minty. Those who did not doubt me or show fear when the change came upon the world. It is for them that I seek justice. They demand retribution and they will be paid in blood!"

"Jessie?" A figure clambered over the hood of a school bus and dropped down in front of the barricade.

Minty squinted into the early morning light. Todd? That fucking lame-assed kid had hooked up with Jethro?

"Todd?" Jessie's voice came from the back of one of the trucks. There were protests and muffled curses. She climbed out and jumped onto the road.

"Jessie!" Todd ran forward. He wrapped his arms around the girl and lifted her off the ground in a hug. Jessie remained stiff and unresponsive.

"I've been looking everywhere for you," Todd explained.

Jessie squirmed free, barely glancing at Todd's smiling face. "Well, you found me," she said.

Freak jumped down from the back of the truck and stared hard at Todd. Jessie glanced at him and gave a slight shake of her head.

"Come on, you're safe now. You can come with us." Todd seized Jessie's arm and tried to drag her toward the barricade. She resisted, pulling away from his grip.

"Todd, no."

Todd turned back, his face going cold. "What do you mean, no?"

"She means, fuck off you fucking loser," Freak said and stepped closer.

"Oh look, it's the fucking prospect," Todd said.

Freak grinned, his whole body swinging as he walked, a loose and gangly, disjointed swagger. "That's where you're wrong, bitch. I'm a full brother now. You, you are just a fucking civilian."

Todd pushed Jessie aside to get to Freak. The young biker's grin could have been mistaken for a snarl. The two young men came together, Todd swinging his fist in a wild punch that Freak easily swayed under. Freak's answering blow was a fistful of carbon-black steel sharpened to a razor edge. His swing was an uppercut that slammed the blade through Todd's lower jaw and up into his head.

Jessie screamed as Todd sagged, his eyes wide and unblinking in the last moment of his life.

"They killed Todd!" someone yelled from the barricade. Minty dove for cover as a hail of fire erupted from the skirmish line. Freak scrambled back, covering Jessie as they tumbled behind the truck. The soldiers exited the vehicle and rolled into the shallow drainage ditch beside the road, from there they returned fire. Shooting with well-practiced control and professional accuracy, they took out fifteen of Jethro's people in less than thirty seconds.

Garrett opened up with the M249 SAW. The windows on the blockade vehicles exploded in a shower of safety glass. Bullets spanged off the tank's turret and punched holes through the panels of the unarmored vehicles. A moment later the air filled with smoke and fire as a fuel tank exploded with a dull *whumph* behind the blockade.

"Squad, fire semiauto and make your shots count!" Dukes ordered. The air filled with the crack and pop of rifle fire. The Locusts with Jethro fell back, leaving their dead and wounded strewn among the burning cars and trucks of the blockade.

"Good thing they didn't have any shells for that tank," Minty said from where he was pressing himself into the roadside gravel.

"Allah is truly merciful," Dukes replied drily. The Abrams M1A2 belched smoke from its exhaust and jerked on its heavy tracks. The turret twisted across an arc of ten degrees before the barrel focused on the Humvee.

"Oh, shit . . . Clear the Humvee! Now!" Dukes screamed into his comms.

Garrett swung himself out of the roof hatch and hit the ground running. The Abrams 120mm gun roared like a dragon spitting smoke and fire.

The Humvee disintegrated in a ball of flame and red-hot shrapnel. Minty felt the debris raining down around him, hissing as it hit the ground. He tried to breathe and found the air had been sucked away in the explosion.

Dukes was yelling. He sounded like he was speaking through a mouthful of glue. Minty blinked at his blackened face, too stunned to understand.

"Move your ass, old man!" Dukes roared. He stood up, grabbing Minty by the back of his jacket and dragging him to his feet. They ran forward, closing the distance between them and the tank. They arrived against the flank of the giant metal beast, too close for any of the weapons it carried to be effective.

"Callie?" Minty mumbled. He tasted blood, and his ears were filled with a static howl.

The tank ground forward. Minty and Dukes darted out of the way, ducking into the cover of a nearby truck.

"Callie?" Minty called again. Louder this time, the roaring in his ears becoming a secondary concern to the doctor's location.

Behind the tank several dog chains ran out up to twenty feet. At the far end, infected people wearing heavy leather leashes howled and strained, their skin black and peeling from the tank's searing exhaust. Dukes fired, putting them down as he almost gagged on the stench of cooking flesh.

Jethro's voice boomed from speakers on the Abrams tank. "Regard your soldiers as your children, and they will follow you into the deepest valleys; look on them as your own beloved sons, and they will stand by you even unto death."

The tank started to roll backwards, the tracks clanking on the concrete road. What the driver lacked in experience, he made up for in confidence. Dukes pushed Minty into the cover of the abandoned school bus as the tank twisted in a slow three-point turn and drove up the highway, following the fleeing Locusts and the rest of Jethro's army.

"Callie?" Minty called.

Milquist carefully stood up on the roadside and waved at them. "She's over here, man." Minty and Dukes jogged out of cover and joined the group gathering beyond the burning remnants of the Humvee.

Callie lay with her head in Jessie's lap. Two medics were applying a dressing to the woman's face. Minty couldn't see any blood through the flash burns, but she wasn't moving either.

He pushed the others aside and sank down next to Callie, who lay so very still.

"You okay, Doc?"

"She got hit when the Humvee went up," Garrett said.

Jessie wiped her nose with the back of a hand, tears trickling down her face. "She's still alive. She's going to be okay, right?" Jessie asked the medic.

"I'm not sure. She needs hospital care. Burns, and shrapnel damage to her eye. She might lose sight on the left side."

"Fuck me. Can she travel? Can we get her to the quarantine line? Get her to a hospital up north?"

"Sure, we can try," The medic nodded.

Minty stood up and turned to Dukes. "Take the trucks, drive north. I'll catch up."

Dukes regarded Minty with a steady eye. "Where the fuck are you going, man?"

"I'm going to do what I should have done years ago and kill that motherfucker, Jethro Williams."

"We'll take the interstate when we can and stop at nightfall. Catch up with us, that's an order."

Minty nodded and walked to the barricade, now breached with the gap where the Abrams M1A2 tank had been parked. He walked through and looked around before gathering up a selection of weapons from the dead.

"Locusts never leave a brother behind," Freak said. Minty turned with a start.

"Christ, you almost got shot."

"Locusts don't ride alone."

"This time, this one does," Minty replied.

"Minty, the Locusts are all I have. Now that the world is gone to shit, the Locusts aren't what they were. If you're going to cut the head off the snake, then I need to be there."

Minty stared at him for a long moment. "Got any cigarettes?"

Freak grinned and pulled a pack of Lucky Strikes from his jacket pocket. Minty lit up and savored the nicotine hit.

"Jessie okay?" Minty asked.

Freak shrugged, his usual grin rising to half-mast. "I killed the guy who tried to hurt her. She's scared shitless, but she told me to come back when this is done."

"Alright then, let's find a ride."

They found two hogs, painted with the LMC logo and abandoned at the back of the roadblock. A minute later Minty and Freak were riding north along the highway. Harley-Davidsons and a shitload of weapons, in true badass, outlaw biker style.

CHAPTER 39

Minty and Freak stopped their bikes after thirty minutes of hard riding. The tank could be seen half a mile up the road, gleefully crushing the abandoned cars and infected people that littered the highway. The surviving convoy of vehicles that carried the Locust army was somewhere ahead.

"When are we going to kill him?" Freak asked.

"We aren't doing shit. You stay the hell out of it. Am I clear?" Minty replied. "We keep following him. When he stops and gets out of that tin can, then I fuck him up."

"Hooah," Freak said.

They kept their distance for another twenty miles. Jethro seemed to have a destination in mind as the tank rolled on at a steady pace, following the main route north. Minty felt a nagging concern that when it stopped they would have arrived at a fortified position with more of Jethro's followers and heavy armament. Jethro knew how to lead and fight and organize.

It was moments like this that Minty wished he had been a Marine sniper rather than just a grunt.

"You think they know we are following them?" Freak called over the rumble of the bike engines.

"Nah, not a lot of windows in a tank, and there's no sign of anyone coming up top and having a look-see."

They continued north along Route 85, passing road signs advising they were approaching Crestview, Florida. The tank rolled on to the northbound lane of the bridge over Pearl Creek.

Movement on the southbound bridge caught Minty's attention as a figure stood up, a rocket launcher resting on its shoulder. A moment later the weapon fired and the rocket hit the tank skirt just behind the turret and flames erupted from the engine compartment as the turbine was destroyed by the high-explosive antitank round.

Freak and Minty skidded to a halt. The tank twisted on its tracks and crashed into the concrete barrier. The force of the impact almost sent the tank over the low wall where it would plunge into the creek below.

The Abrams engine shuddered and went quiet. A hatch popped open, but the rocketeer had ducked out of sight again. Minty waved Freak into cover and dismounted himself.

"Fuck me," Freak said.

"Stay here," Minty replied. Stooping low he ran to the bridge, one eye on the southbound bridge and the other on the crippled tank.

Jethro crawled out of the tank hatch and rolled down the chassis. Minty went down on one knee, feeling his joints creak in protest. Aiming down the M4 sight, he squeezed the trigger. The gun kicked and the shot ricocheted of the tank's armor. Jethro sprang up like he had been stung, diving out of view on the other side of the tank.

"Jethro!" Minty yelled. "Come out and face me, you piece of shit!"

"Minty? You're still busting my balls? Well shit, why didn't you just say so?"

"I'm calling you out, you murdering fuck!" Minty swept the rifle from side to side, waiting for Jethro to show his face.

"Come on now, Minty! You see where things are going! You know what is needed now. Strong leadership. We must prepare the world for the new age!"

"You are not going to live to see it!" Minty shouted back.

"I am not destined to die by your hand, brother!"

"I'm fine with shooting your sorry ass!" Minty replied.

Jethro's response was a laugh that sounded like it might tip over into insane giggles.

After watching Minty advance toward the tank, Freak crossed the grassy divide between the two bridges. Keeping low, he peered around the end of the concrete wall on the southbound side and looked along the length of the bridge.

It took him a moment to see the shapes in the bundle of people that were crouched halfway along. There were two heads, one with long dark hair and pink sneakers on her feet. The other wore his hair short under a blue baseball cap.

"Samuel, let's go home," The girl said. Samuel ignored her; he was working on wrestling an AR-15 away from the tangled straps of the knapsack that lay between them.

"Keep quiet, Tara. They aren't all dead yet."

Neither of them looked or sounded older than kids to Freak.

Tara turned around and sat against the concrete wall, her arms folding in a gesture of sulking defiance.

"Hey," Freak hissed. Tara squealed and scrambled to her feet. Freak ran forward, knocking the young girl into the boy and pinning them both down. The M4 Freak carried kicked him in the balls; he grunted and tried to blink away the sudden flaring pain.

"Get the hell off me!" Tara insisted.

"Stay down," Freak insisted. "I'm not going to hurt you."

Both kids crawled out from under Freak and scooted backwards on their butts.

Freak risked a look over the concrete wall. The other lane with its bridge was at least twenty feet away. The massive hulk of the Abrams tank had mounted the wall barrier and the turret now pointed toward the sky at a forty-five-degree angle. He heard Minty calling out to Jethro and then Jethro's response.

"Dad is going to kill you," Tara said. Freak couldn't tell if she was talking to Samuel or him.

"What the hell are you kids doing out here?" Freak asked.

"We're not kids," Samuel replied, his voice cracking.

"Okay, what the hell are you people doing out here?"

"Dad is going to kill you," Tara warned again.

"Tara, shut up," Samuel snapped. "We heard Dad saying that there were bad people coming this way. The other guys had left guns behind, so we stole one."

Freak grinned in disbelief. "You stole a rocket launcher and blew up a fucking tank, man."

Samuel frowned and then grinned back. "Holy shit," he said. "We are in so much trouble."

"Keep your heads down, okay?" Freak glanced over the wall again.

A second Locust crawled out of the driver's hatch. A big guy, bleeding from a gash across his forehead.

Minty ignored the new arrival, his focus on where Jethro might show his face.

Freak rested his M4 on top of the concrete wall and trained it on the biker crawling away from the driver's hatch down the chassis toward the back of the tank.

"You're gonna have to walk out sometime, Jethro," Minty called. He watched the Locust drop to the ground.

"Minty? Is that you, man?" The big guy called out. He straightened up, shading his eyes and squinting, his vision blurred by the blood streaming from the gash just below his hairline.

"Fish? Move away from there!"

"Hey Minty?" Fish waved.

"Get the fuck out of the way!" Minty called. Fish looked around, as if wondering what he could possibly be in the way of. He shrugged and shuffled forward, walking toward Minty, hitching up his jeans as he came.

"Fuck it," Minty swore. Fish's impressive bulk was blocking his view and it just got worse as he came closer.

Freak breathed in slowly and then held it. The flicker of movement on his left was all he needed. He squeezed the M4's trigger, hitting Fish in the side of his chest and making the big man grunt and stagger.

Minty stood up, moving away from the concrete wall that sheltered him.

Fish sagged and dropped to his knees. Jethro came into view behind him. Minty fired as he sidestepped. Three shots in quick succession, the first one missed, the second hit Jethro in the chest, and the third took him in the shoulder.

"Minty? You okay, man?" Freak yelled. He couldn't tell who was hit and who was just keeping low.

The old biker ran forward, passing Fish who lay on his back gasping like his namesake. Jethro hadn't gone down even after being shot twice. Jethro raised the stump of his arm and Minty saw how it had changed since Atlanta. The white feathery strings of probing fungus had thickened and solidified into grey and gnarled tree root–like fingers that flexed and clenched.

"Check it out, Minty, I'm just like a real boy now!" Jethro crowed with a manic grin. The grey-knotted fist swung at Minty's head as he came charging and struck him with the force of a sledgehammer. The biker stumbled, seeing stars and staggering.

"C'mon boy, show me what you've got!" Jethro danced around, ignoring the spreading blood on his shirt from the gunshot wounds. "You think you can kill me? I am fuckin' immortal!" Jethro taunted.

Minty twisted his grip on the M4. He lifted the butt and smashed it into Jethro's face, just like the Marines taught him in bayonet training. Jethro twisted aside and the stock hit him in his good arm but didn't shake him. Jethro grabbed the weapon and wrenched it from Minty's grasp. Minty let the rifle go and drew a knife.

Jethro welcomed the charging Minty with open arms, which at the last moment slammed together to form a double fist that caught the biker in the midsection. The blow knocked the air out of his lungs and drove Minty to his knees.

"Coulda made you one of us, brother," Jethro said. "Coulda shown you such fucking wonders. Made you a part of the truth and the future."

"You always said I live too much in the past," Minty wheezed as he regained his feet. "My problem is, I remember too much. What you did at Khafji. Good men died because you're a fucking coward, Jethro. Always have been."

Jethro's face went pale, the rictus grin on his face setting like a concrete mask. Minty didn't wait; he lunged forward, the knife coming up from below. He stabbed Jethro under the ribs, driving the knife upward and deep into his heart. The way he had been taught. The way he had killed men before in the name of freedom on foreign sands.

Jethro grunted, his gnarled, grey fist slamming into the side of Minty's head hard enough to stun him. Minty stabbed again, feeling the elastic resistance of flesh and the rocklike scrape of bone against the blade. Jethro's fists and the heavy knife drew the two men together in a morbid embrace. Minty was bigger, but Jethro had the immunity of the infection's legacy in his veins.

Minty struggled against the tightening grip of Jethro's arms. He worked the blade free and slashed across the other man's front. Jethro's shirt peeled open, his guts sagging out of the wide gash in his belly. Minty nearly choked at the stink of it, then he saw the white feelers of fungal infection reaching out of the cavity. Minty slashed again, higher this time, slicing through Jethro's throat. His blood didn't spray, it oozed, but he let go and Minty kicked him away.

"I told you, man," Jethro's voice rasped like a file on flesh. "I am fucking immortal." Jethro's good hand, the one that still had flesh and bone instead of warped mushroom fibers for fingers, reached out and closed around the blade of Minty's knife. With a slow and deliberate movement he turned the steel until the point aimed away from his chest. Minty resisted, the tendons on his arms straining as he pushed back against the unstoppable force of Jethro's strength.

The crack of a rifle echoed and at the same instant Jethro's head jerked back, skull shards and blood bulged in a net of infection that strained to hold his head together in the wake of the bullet's passing.

Minty seized the moment and jerked the knife free from Jethro's grasp. He slashed and stabbed, driving the knife deep into Jethro's neck. The blade twisted, grating against bone until, with a final push, Jethro's head toppled back off his shoulders.

Strings of the infection rose from the stump of Jethro's neck and waved in a desperate farewell to his skull, now barely connected to his body by a narrow strip of flesh.

Minty let Jethro fall. Then he walked away, the familiar aftermath of adrenaline threatening to explode out of his gut and puke on his boots.

"Minty?!" Freak yelled.

"I'm okay," Minty replied. Then louder, his voice reaching across the distance. "I'm okay!"

"Did I get that fucker!?" Freak yelled.

"Yeah. Yeah you sure did, Freak. Right in the head."

Freak whooped and Minty thought he heard the voices of children.

Minty dug though Fish's pockets until he found a pack of cigarettes. He lit one up and intoned, "The king is dead. Long live the king."

CHAPTER 40

Callie whimpered a low, soft murmur of pain. The army medic tapped a needle and slowly injected a fresh dose of morphine into the doctor's arm.

"Is there anything else we can do?" Minty asked.

"Nope," The medic replied. "She's going to be in pain for a long while yet. If we can keep her wounds free of infection, she'll be okay."

"Fungus or regular?" Minty asked.

"Regular infection. From what we have seen, if she was infected with the fungal agent, she would be up and around already." The medic paused. "Talk to her. Let her know she's not alone."

Minty frowned as the medic walked away. It felt weird to be talking to the still form on the camp bed. Half her face was bandaged, and the dope kept her knocked out.

"Uhh . . . Hey Doc, it's me, Minty." He hesitated. "Jethro's dead. If you were awake, you could probably tell me why he was infected but still walking around, acting like an asshole."

Callie didn't respond, so Minty took a breath and kept talking. "We were in the Marines, not together, but at the same time and in the same shit. There's a town in Saudi Arabia, on the coast of the Persian Gulf, called Khafji. You've probably never heard of it, but in the first Gulf War, the Marines kicked some Iraqi ass there. See, in January of ninety-one, Saddam sent his army into Saudi territory. We knew they were coming. The Coalition had observation posts set up along the border and the highway to Khafji. The Iraqis actually took the town for a couple of days. Me and some other guys were providing support to a couple of engineers. Their job was to organize ditches, wire barricades, minefields, shit like that.

"So late one night, the Iraqi Army come rolling in and we were standing there with our dicks in our hands. Being Marines, we engaged, though it didn't do much against their tanks and shit. So we got the order to pull back. In all the shit, me and Jethro ended up in a hole with Iraqis driving over us and bullets flying and no way to get back to our side.

"Two fucking days, in the desert heat with no idea if we were behind Iraqi lines or in no-man's-land or just AWOL for no good reason. I'm shitting myself, itching to fight, but not wanting to die. Jethro, he's sitting there, frosty as a cold beer. And the whole time, he's talking. Saying shit that I cannot begin to understand. He's preaching at me, not about God or Jesus, but about man's inherent destiny. How we hold the power to determine our own fate. Then after two days, the Coalition got down to business and tore the ragheads a new one. We were in the middle of the shit again, except now the Iraqi Army was retreating over us instead of advancing.

"Jethro stands up in the middle of the biggest shitstorm of weapons fire I have ever seen. He reaches down, takes my hand, and says, 'Let's go home.' We climbed out and started walking. I've been out of water for over twelve hours, so I'm sure as hell not thinking straight. We're walking through small arms and rocket fire. Bullets are zipping past us like grit in a sandstorm. Then there's artillery fire, and right behind us, the hole we had been in for two days took a direct hit. Jethro just shrugged and said he felt it coming. We humped it back to the Coalition forces without a scratch.

"If Jethro hadn't been there, I'd have died in that hole. But you know what the real fuckin' kicker is? The entire time we were there, Jethro had a working radio. He could have been giving sit rep updates to our forces. He could have arranged for us to be extracted and had us back with our unit in an hour. He chose to sit out the battle and kept me there until he knew we had to move or get fucked over by friendly artillery. I've never told anyone before. Carried that with me for over twenty years. Good men died because of him. Jethro's a fucking coward."

Minty fell silent, Callie was breathing easier now that the pain relief had worked its magic. He stood up, found a pack of cigarettes, and put one in his mouth before stepping out into the baking heat of the Florida day. Lighting up, he looked around at the small camp. Civilians and soldiers worked together, distributing food and keeping watch for approaching threats.

Dukes had sent men out on supply-gathering missions and had warned when they returned that the entire group would be moving north. The Quarantine Line, now an official designation and the federally defended front of this new war, was their destination.

Minty didn't like it. Anything that took them toward population centers could only mean trouble. Staying in Florida wasn't an option either. The entire southern USA was fighting and dying as the infection spread in the summer heat.

He wished Callie could be moved, he wished that they had never ended up on the wrong side of the developing apocalypse, though mostly he wished he was back in Los Angeles, sitting in the Locust clubhouse, drinking cold beer, and watching some hot chick do a slow striptease.

The world had changed and it would never be the same again. A disaster on this scale would destroy the infrastructure of the United States. Whatever the status of the government in the north, the country that Minty had been born to and had fought to protect had been shattered.

People in the group talked constantly about when things would be back under control. When life returned to normal. Minty couldn't see it happening. Even if the fungal plague was stopped at the Line, so much of the country's wealth was produced by the affected states. Minty felt sure that California, Texas, and even the vast retirement village of Florida were some of the most important economic areas of the country.

There had been radio chatter suggesting that Texas had seceded from the Union. The general who used battlefield nuclear weapons against the Mexican infected was said to be in control.

Maybe he had a point. Right now that kind of response made sense. Minty felt a pang of regret, wondering what Jethro would say about the way things were going. In spite of his bullshit vision of an anarchist utopia, Jethro had always been the smartest man Minty ever knew.

The biker finished his cigarette and watched the people preparing to move out as soon as the order was given. His attention fell on a young Latino couple, the woman with long hair and flashing white teeth, holding a tiny bundle that wriggled and fussed in the heat. A muscled and unshaven man who could have been her husband, boyfriend, or brother, Minty couldn't tell, stood over them, protective and hovering, ready to step in and help.

"Christ," Minty muttered. "What kind of world are we bringing children into?"

Dukes seemed certain that because they were uninfected, the people in their group would be allowed to pass through the Line. No one had any ideas on what to do if they were turned away.

Minty opposed going north, at least through official channels. Crossing a quarantine line that stretched across so many states should be easy. There were places up there, in Canada or even west into Alaska, where he could disappear with a few people and survive until . . .

Until what? The crisis was resolved? The world returned to normal? Or maybe until generations passed and a new tribe of people emerged. Savage, wild folk with limited technology, living a hunter-gatherer existence. Jethro would have loved that; the ultimate stripping back of all mankind's unnecessary burdens. He often said, feasting and fucking were the true drivers behind everything people did.

Minty ground out the smoldering butt of his cigarette. People were moving to the edge of the campsite, and he could see sunlight reflecting off the windshields of approaching trucks.

Everyone kept a weapon within reach at all times; you couldn't trust anyone these days. The passenger door on the first of the trucks opened and Milquist stepped out onto the running board and waved. Dukes' salvage team had returned, and brought more survivors with them.

By the time the trucks had been parked, along with two new RVs and several smaller SUVs, Minty had joined the crowd watching the new excitement.

"Minty, come over here," Dukes ordered after a quick conversation with his corporal. The biker wandered over; he was in no rush. But he followed Dukes' orders because what he said usually made sense.

"Milk says they crossed that bridge, saw the Abrams tank," Dukes said.

"Alright," Minty replied, not sure what this had to do with him.

"Your friend, Jethro? He wasn't there," Milquist reported.

"So? Maybe animals ate him or freaks dragged him away?" Minty suggested.

"The fat guy, the one you called Fish? His body was there. The tank had been stripped and Jethro's body was gone." Milquist spoke like he was being debriefed.

"You think I'm lying?" Minty asked, his eyes going cold. "I cut that fucker's head off."

"Not saying you didn't," Milquist replied. "Just reporting that he wasn't there when we drove through."

"It's only been twenty-four hours. Seems weird that he would have been carried off," Dukes said.

"Or maybe he got up and walked away?" Milquist asked.

"Fuck that," Minty snapped. "There's no fucking way that sonovabitch got up and walked away. His fucking head was cut off."

"We've seen what this fungus can do. The way it reaches out to try and reconnect parts. Close wounds and shit," Milquist said. "Maybe it screwed his head back on."

"Maybe you need your head screwed back on," Minty snarled.

"Stand down," Dukes ordered. He waited for a few moments while the two men glared at each other.

"We don't know what happened. We may never know. Milk, right now I want to talk to the civilians you brought back."

Minty recognized two of them, the kids that Freak had been hanging with while on sniper duty. They were clutching knapsacks and the girl looked like she had been crying.

Minty walked away from Milquist and approached the pair. "Hey, Tammy, isn't it?" he asked the girl.

"T-Tara," she said, shying away from the big, bearded man.

"I'm Minty, remember? You and your brother were on the bridge, with the tank?"

Tara nodded and Samuel watched Minty closely. "Where's Freak?" The boy asked.

"He's around. Where's your folks?" Minty asked.

Tara looked like she might cry again; Samuel's jaw clenched. "They're dead," he managed to say. His voice cracking only a little.

"Shit," Minty muttered. "I'm sorry to hear that. What happened? Was it infection?"

Samuel shook his head. "It was guys like you," he said and then looked at the ground.

"Bikers?" Minty asked, a feeling of dread settling over him.

Tara nodded. "They had that same jacket."

Minty slipped his patched rag off his back. "You mean this leather vest? With the same words and everything?"

Tara nodded again. "Dad told us to hide, but they went through every house and said those who wanted to come with them could. Some did. They only let white people join them though."

Samuel shivered. "The Fergusons and Mister Chu, they made them stand together in front of our house. They shot them. I saw them fall down. They didn't get up again."

"Dad and some others, they had their guns, so they started shooting the men in leather." Tara paused. "Daddy didn't come back inside. We hid in the attic until the army showed up."

"You did the right thing," Minty said. "You're safe now. No one is going to hurt you or let those people hurt you."

"I want to kill them," Samuel said with a sudden fierceness. "I'm going to find them and I'm going to kill every last one of them."

"You and me both, kid," Minty agreed.

Minty straightened up as Dukes walked over.

"Seems the town got taken by the Locust convoy," The sergeant said. "They report there was a guy in charge. No one heard him talking, but he had a weird hand. Like it was made of grey rope or something." Dukes swept a grimy hand through his short hair. "There is something seriously wrong when cutting off a freak's head doesn't kill it."

"I should have made sure," Minty said.

"Too late now. We have to get ready to move out. I want to be well on our way towards the line when your friends get their shit together enough to start looking for us."

The biker opened his mouth to reply that the Locusts were not his friends, but Dukes had marched away, shouting orders to his troops and the civilians. Everyone responded quickly to his commands.

Minty lit another cigarette with shaking hands and walked away to the edge of the camp. The sun beat down as he stared out at the smoke from a thousand uncontrolled fires staining the horizon.

It was going to be a long, hot summer.

ABOUT THE AUTHORS

Paul Mannering is an award-winning writer living in Wellington, New Zealand, where he lives with his wife Damaris and their two cats.

Bill Ball is a retired Sergeant First Class who served in the 82nd Airborne Division and the Michigan Army National Guard. A veteran of Airborne, Air Assault, Light, Mechanized Infantry and the Field Artillery (self-propelled) who is now and engineer for a major hand tool manufacturer. He lives in a very small town in rural Michigan with his wife Jonelle who is the local librarian.

Visit Bill's website at www.deadvsalive.com

14

Peter Clines

"A riveting apocalyptic mystery in the style of LOST."
—Craig DiLouie, author of The Infection

Padlocked doors.
Strange light fixtures. Mutant
cockroaches.

There are some odd things about
Nate's new apartment. Every
room in this old brownstone has
a mystery. Mysteries that stretch
back over a hundred years.
Some of them are in plain sight.
Some are behind locked doors.
And all together these mysteries
could mean the end of Nate and
his friends.

Or the end of everything...

PERMUTED
PRESS

THE BREADWINNER | Stevie Kopas

The end of the world is not glamorous. In a matter of days the human race was reduced to nothing more than vicious, flesh hungry creatures. There are no heroes here. Only survivors. The trilogy continues with Book Two: *Haven* and Book Three: *All Good Things*.

THE BECOMING | Jessica Meigs

As society rapidly crumbles under the hordes of infected, three people—Ethan Bennett, a Memphis police officer; Cade Alton, his best friend and former IDF sharpshooter; and Brandt Evans, a lieutenant in the US Marines—band together against the oncoming crush of death and terror sweeping across the world. The story continues with Book Two: *Ground Zero*.

THE INFECTION WAR | Craig DiLouie

As the undead awake, a small group of survivors must accept a dangerous mission into the very heart of infection. This edition features two books: *The Infection* and *The Killing Floor*.

OBJECTS OF WRATH | Sean T. Smith

The border between good and evil has always been bloody... Is humanity doomed? After the bombs rain down, the entire world is an open wound; it is in those bleeding years that William Fox becomes a man. After The Fall, nothing is certain. *Objects of Wrath* is the first book in a saga spanning four generations.

PERMUTED
PRESS